Pirates

of

Ashlen

Published by Nick Leja

ISBN 978-0-615-33080-8

Printed in the United States of America

I would like to specially thank Kileean, Scott, Herman, Lisa, Greg, Noah, Laura, Angela, Deana, and Lee for reading and providing editorial feedback for my rough manuscript. Without their praise, support, and comments, Pirates of Ashlen would never have made it to the printer.

And most importantly, I would like to thank you, the reader, for venturing into the world of Lassar. You are the magical energy that brings all these characters to life.

Thank you.

Dear Reader,

I hope you enjoy the story and the characters! Thank you for reading!

Contents

Prologue

The front door creaked open.

Jay Perry lifted his head from his pillow, blinked several times, and scanned the room. Everything appeared normal. Then his gaze fell on the square window. Someone was staring at him from outside. A male. Silhouetted by the pale moonlight.

Jay's heart leapt and pounded against his chest. He rubbed the sleep from his eyes, and then the shadow was gone.

He shrugged, attributing the shadow to his imagination, and snuggled back under his thin cotton bed sheets. He closed his eyes, trying to occupy his mind with something that would lull him to sleep, but he still saw that dark shadow outlined on the backs of his eyelids.

He tossed and turned, but felt even more awake than before. He *knew* he had not been imagining the shadow; it was too real. But who would be out this late? Everyone in Morad was asleep; no one would be lurking in the streets. Even *if* someone was in the streets, why would he stop to stare at him through the window? A thief, perhaps?

Jay had to check it out, for his curiosity would not let him sleep. He swung his legs over the side of the bed, slipped his bare feet into his icy slippers, and walked out of his room and to the front door.

Once outside, he looked right, looked left, and there, up ahead maybe fifty yards, he saw the shadow drifting soundlessly past a giant tree poking up from the pebbled street. Goosebumps enveloped his skin as a chilly summer breeze blew over the village; he heard the waves from the ocean crashing on the nearby sandy shore, the ocean's misty spray humidifying the air.

Jay decided to pursue the shadow. At fourteen years old, his slender form allowed him to move swiftly and silently in the figure's wake. The bottoms of his worn slippers dampened as they rubbed against the cold, stone streets, but he hardly noticed. His full attention was on the mysterious man, whose blackened figure looked only a couple years older than he. He smudged a clump of sleepiness from his eye down his cheek and brushed it off his face.

The wooden signs hanging from nearby stores creaked under the wind, masking the sound of Jay's footfalls across the pebbles. If he could just get a few paces closer, he may be able to make out the man's face under the moonlight. Swallowing a sea of anxiety, he hastened his step. Rhythmically, his feet carried him closer and closer to the blackened man. The edge of the man's face faintly came into view. Only a few paces more until he could—

The stone beneath Jay's foot cracked, making a little noise that sounded like a gun blast. The man ahead whirled around. Jay froze. Like a general leading an army of thousands, his mind barked commands to every muscle in his body. But the frozen soldiers refused to move. He was a statue.

To his dismay, the man crept towards him. Jay's muscles twisted, started throbbing, and refused to move. Every part of his body tensed—the hair on the back of his neck sharpened like needles, his chest compressed, his thighs pulsed.

Nearer and nearer the man came. Jay knew he would soon be discovered. His eyes darted from side to side, searching for an object to hide behind. Nothing. His face tightened.

The man stopped—Jay was sure his secrecy was shattered, but then the man turned back around, his dark cloak riding a gust of wind.

Splashed with relief, Jay's body relaxed; his legs felt like rubber, causing him to nearly collapse. Too close. He needed to take more precaution.

The path bent to the right as he neared the end of the rows of stone houses, then straightened as it led to the governor's mansion, a square brick building with giant arched windows lining the upper levels.

As he neared the building, Jay's lungs burned from inhaling the cold air. Still, he darted across the stone path faster and faster. The clouds rolled off the pale moon; its blue light splashed against the soil brighter than before.

Finally, as Jay reached the mansion, moonlight poured over the man. If the man turned around, Jay would be able to see his face illuminated by the recent surge of moonlight.

Then it happened. Just before passing through the opening in the wrought iron gate leading to the mansion, the figure again turned around. Jay dove behind some dense shrubs to the side and peered over them. He recognized the man at once: Thyran Vilkus, his stepbrother. Jay rubbed his eyes and gave a double take; fear and confusion swirled inside his head.

A few seconds passed. Thyran turned around and continued along his path to the mansion. Scanning his surroundings to ensure no one was around, Jay emerged from the shrubs and crept several yards behind his stepbrother.

Thyran did not enter the front door as Jay expected, but rather vanished around the corner of the house. Jay scurried up to the mansion and skirted around the side, allowing only the balls of his feet to skim the ground.

A dense pack of clouds captured the moon, leaving Jay staring into blackness. Unsure of his stepbrother's whereabouts, he frantically searched the area, but all he saw were the faint outlines of bushes, the iron fence, and the brick wall of the mansion.

Hearing a scratching noise nearby, he looked up to see Thyran's feet, outlined by the dim moonlight, slip into a window three stories above. Running his fingers over the wall, Jay felt a pattern of alternating bricks protruding from the wall. Wiping the sweat from his palms on his pant leg, he grabbed onto the exposed side of a brick and clambered up to the window.

By the time he reached the window, his lungs throbbed with exhaustion. He paused a moment to gather his breath and then slowly lifted his head until his eyes broke the plane of the windowsill.

He was staring into the governor's room. Several wooden bookshelves, filled with ancient books glazed with a thin veil of dust, stretched along one of the walls, leaving only a small opening in the corner near the window. A bright red book on one of the shelves seemed liberated from the prison of dust trapping its neighbors, indicating it had been examined recently.

Opposite the bookshelf, the governor lay asleep, rolled on his side, sheathed in an extravagant bed padded with superfluous layers of cushioning. The dense comforter reached to his neck, revealing only the mat of greased, dark hair on the back of his head.

Thyran, however, was missing. Jay lightly pressed against the clear window, which swung open effortlessly—Thyran must have forgotten to lock it. But that wasn't like Thyran; he never forgot anything.

As soon as Jay's feet hit the ground, the doorknob squeaked and turned. Leaving the window ajar, Jay dashed for the small crevice in the corner between the bookshelf and the wall. He heard footsteps enter the room, but the bookshelf obstructed his view of the door. He could only see the governor sleeping quietly, unaware of the two intruders in his bedroom.

Jay held his breath. After a short pause, he heard the door slowly close; the *click* as the door locked echoed off the walls. He noticed a shadow covering part of the bed. He adjusted his head, giving him a wider range of sight, allowing him to see Thyran's narrow face concentrated on the governor. Thyran's right hand held a rolled up piece of aged parchment. Jay watched him tuck it in a stout black tube fastened to his back.

After securing the parchment behind his back, Thyran reached his right hand across to the left side of his waist and wrapped his fingers around something as he approached the governor's bed. A breeze swept in the room. Thyran looked up to the window.

Jay's eyes watered with fear as Thyran examined the room. Did Thyran know he was there? Thyran must have seen him earlier in the street, even under the dismal lighting. His stepbrother was the most cunning man he knew; he would have remembered shutting the window.

Running a hand through his fiery brown hair, Thyran again focused on the governor. Briefly, he studied the governor's face before throwing his hand in the air. Jay saw a flash of moonlight reflected off the fine blade now visible in his hand. Horrified, he surrendered his cover and leapt away from the wall.

"No!" was all Jay managed to scream before Thyran's hand swung down and stabbed the knife into the back of the sleeping governor. His heart pierced by Thyran's blade, the governor rolled over on his stomach.

Thyran's head jerked up at him. "Jay. Good to see you."

"What did you just..." Jay said, backing up to the window as Thyran advanced to him.

"Ashlen waits for me. Her death will not go unnoticed."

"Who's death?" Jay felt his back brushing against the wall.

Loud footsteps thundered up the stairs near the door. Thyran's dark eyes gleamed with triumph. "Looks like the governor's guards heard your scream. Please do not take this personally, brother. This needs to be done."

"What are you talking about?"

Confusion masked the fear inside Jay—just earlier that day they had been playfully dueling each other with wooden swords in a field, and now his stepbrother had just murdered the governor of Morad. He could not fathom what pushed Thyran to commit such an evil act.

Jay jumped as men pounded against the locked door of the governor's bedroom. Thyran seemed undisturbed by the din.

"My men are waiting for me. I fear this will be the last time we shall see each other. Don't worry, my cousin will watch over you."

Before Jay had time to respond, Thyran kicked him in the shin and shoved him into the wall near the bookshelf, allowing the knife to leave his hand as he did so—Jay fell to the floor beside the bloody knife.

"Good-bye, Jay." Thyran said as he swung over the windowsill and dropped out into the night.

"Ugh..." Jay moaned as he raised himself up, one of his hands pressing the knife that lay on the ground. Subconsciously, Jay picked it up as he stood, ready to defend himself should Thyran reappear. Once he got to his feet, the lock snapped and door swung open.

Four muscular men, each with their steel swords drawn, stormed into the room, the lead man bearing a flaming torch. In sync, the men looked at Jay, then down to the bloody knife in his hand, and then to the dead body of the governor on the bed. A pool of dark blood soaked the back of the governor's blue-striped shirt.

"Governor Almsy...he's dead!" the man with the torch shouted. Instantly, his gaze shifted from the governor to Jay. Shaking in rage, the man pointed at him and bellowed, "Arrest him!"

His hand trembling, Jay tossed the stained knife to the floor, threw himself out the window, snatched two bricks poking out from the wall, and began descending to the ground. Two-thirds down, his shaky palms caused him to slip and plummet down the wall. Landing on his feet, he bent his knees to absorb the impact. Glancing up to the window, he saw the man with the torch staring down at him, a look of hatred plastered on his red face. He could hear the man giving instructions, but his mind was racing too fast to make sense of them.

Jay's feet hurled his body away from the mansion. Soon, he was through the iron fence that enclosed the governor's property. His eyes adjusted to the dark, murky air—

Up ahead, Thyran approached the row of houses. The only place for him to go was the surrounding forest or the ocean.

Jay heard the rustling of men behind him in the distance. Without looking back, he scurried faster, forcing himself to accept this was real, not some sort of nightmare.

Racing through the village, Jay could see Thyran speeding towards the beach. All the windows of the houses were black; the entire village was asleep except for him, Thyran, and the crowd of guards pursuing them.

Cascades of icy tears dripped down Jay's cheeks as he pushed his body beyond its physical limits. His feet dug into the soft sand of the beach, his loose hair waved in the wind. He bolted after Thyran, a hundred paces away from the restless ocean, faster and faster. Thyran had nowhere to go.

Then, when Jay arrived at the edge of the beach, Thyran continued forward, sloshing through the water. Where was he going?

When Jay reached the ocean, he saw his stepbrother climb aboard a small boat in which another man waited. Instantly, they began paddling farther into the ocean, away from Morad.

Thyran was getting away.

Jay plunged in the water after him but realized it was useless; Thyran and his companion paddled faster than he could swim.

"Thyran!" Jay screamed, thrashing his arms in the air. Tears rolled down his burning cheeks. "Thyran! Come back! You...murderer!"

"There he is!" a man yelled behind him.

Jay paid them no attention.

"You won't get away with this!" Jay's heart sank deep in his chest, shattered by sadness. His knees dropped into the wet soil under the water. "Ahh!" he cried, pounding his fists into the defenseless ocean.

"Don't move!" a man ordered, grabbing Jay's shoulder.

Enraged, Jay squirmed out of the man's grip and dashed farther into the water, determined to catch Thyran before it was too late. As he further trailed into the ocean, the massive water pushed against him. No longer able to walk, he tried to dive into the stinging cold water, but one of the governor's guards slammed the edge of the torch on his head.

Streams of water rushed along his face as his head dropped below the water's surface. Several men grabbed his arms and dragged him back to the shore. His face drenched, he opened his eyes.

Thyran stood proudly at the edge of the boat. A look of satisfaction filled his face. His conniving smile rent Jay's insides asunder. A gangly man with a crooked nose approached him and whispered something into his ear. Thyran turned towards his rear and examined the outline of a massive ship in the distance. Facing Jay again, he nodded his head, and then his boat faded into the night.

1

Four Years Later

Wind blowing in his face, Jay gazed across the open ocean. As he leaned against the wooden rail, his blue linen shirt fluttered in the breeze. The bright sunlight rode the choppy waves. In the sky, the scattered white clouds appeared to unveil an avenue for travel as the ship skimmed the calm water.

He heard a man approach from behind.

"Hey, Lil' Blue."

Jay's eyes remained transfixed on the rumpling water. "Time for some more training, Hector?"

"Hah, 'fraid not."

Hector jabbed Jay's shoulder, then he leaned against the rail beside Jay and bit into a green apple; its juices shot down his scruffy brown beard.

Jay smirked. "What's wrong? Still exhausted from yesterday?"

Hector raised his eyebrows. "Ye referring to our little match? Ha! I wouldn't get too overjoyed. That was a one-time thing, mate. Didn't want to crush yer pride is all."

Lunging himself off the rail, Jay unsheathed his curved cutlass and brandished it in the air. "Don't do me the honor this time," he challenged, fighting back a smirk.

Coolly, Hector sunk his teeth into the juicy apple and ripped out another wedge.

"Jay...how could I live with meself if I injured ye on a day as beautiful as this?"

Jay's muscles tightened, his feet gripped the wooden deck; he stood ready to attack. "Draw your sword. I'm ready."

Hector wiped the flecks of apple off his beard but dropped the fruit in the process.

Without thought, Jay glanced at the falling green apple. In that split-second, Hector's blade slammed against his, the two swords rattled violently, and Jay gasped as his own blade jerked free of his grip and fell to the floor. He bent down to recover his sword but stopped when the tip of Hector's blade pricked his tender neck.

Licking the apple juice from his lips, Hector held his blade aloft. "What was that? I missed what ye said."

Letting out a sigh, Jay leaned back up with a small hint of humiliation flowing through his veins. Laughing, Hector sheathed his sword and swung his arm around Jay's shoulders.

"Come on, the cap'n wants us gathered down below."

Together, they walked along the wooden deck. As they neared the stairs, Jay said, "I'll get you one of these days."

"I'm sure you will, once ye learn to block out distractions."

Three adjacent staircases huddled together at the stern of the ship. The two outer staircases led up to the bridge; the center staircase led below deck. As Jay approached the bridge, he saw Gideon at the wheel. Gideon's thin gray hair caked his head and stretched along his cheeks and across his mouth. His face resembled one who had spent ages sailing the seas and had loved every minute of it: he held his head up high, smiling into the wind as he steered the ship. Before Jay descended the stairs, he waved at Gideon, who pleasantly returned the greeting.

Jay entered a narrow corridor. Straight ahead resided the dining room, the alcove that would host the captain's meeting. He heard the chatter of the crew up ahead. He treaded across the creaky floorboards and entered the room.

A long, timbered table occupied the center of the room. Crevices and dents saturated the aged table. Numerous pirates sat in the uncomfortable wooden chairs lined along the table's longer sides; a more luxuries and polished chair headed the table at the far end for the captain. Noticing a vacant chair, Jay moved towards it.

Next to his seat sat Lynk and Blynk. The two brothers were cleanly shaven and slender. They were engrossed in a thrilling tale as Lynk's hands wavered over several tarnished coins, all neatly stacked in towers on the table.

"But," Lynk said, "as they traveled through Storm Isle, the beast rose from the sea and the crew vanished!" With a flick of his fingers and a wave of his hand, the towering coins disappeared.

"Impossible!" Soleus, a short, plump pirate opposite the table, exclaimed, slamming his bulky fist into the table, creating a small indentation. He jumped up in a flash, his red-tainted cheeks bouncing gently. "They're in yer lap!"

Lynk's face at once turned scarlet and sweaty. "N-No they're not Soleus...they've vanished."

Grinning, Soleus shook his fist with glee. "Yes they are! Finally! I have figured out yer tricks!"

Blynk peered up at his brother worriedly. Lynk looked at Soleus and said, "I think you sho—"

"No! Stand up now and let's see those coins!"

Shrugging his slender shoulders, the pale-faced Lynk stood up. The sound of coins clashing against the floor never arrived—Soleus's gleeful face twisted with confusion. "Where be the coins?"

Lynk looked down at his brother and spoke with his usual acting voice. "My dear brother, where do you think those soldiers vanished to?"

Blynk scratched his chin. "Hmm...I guess we'll never know."

A dark-haired woman sitting next to Soleus scoffed. "Well big boy, looks like you out-did yourself once again." Jay shuddered at the tinge of venom in her voice.

Shaking with rage, Soleus once again pounded the table with his knuckles. "I saw the coins fall into his—"

A cluster of coins just like the ones Lynk had made disappear flowed down his green sleeves, clanging together as they formed a messy pile on the table. Soleus stared, speechless. All the pirates, except for the dark-haired woman, whose face was concealed behind her silky black hair, erupted with laughter as Lynk and Blynk stood and took a bow.

"Up to your old tricks again, eh?" Jay asked as he sat down next to the brothers.

"Aye mate!" Lynk said, winking at Jay.

Interrupting their commotion, the door creaked open, and Captain Gaden entered. A long, frizzled brown beard and scruffy mustache adorned his face. As he walked, his muscular arms swayed back and forth as if he was grabbing the rail of a staircase to propel himself forward with each step. His greasy brown hair covered his head and hung down the side of his face to his shoulders. Some strands of hair were braided together to prevent them from obstructing his vision.

Silence washed the room as the captain approached the head of the table. When he reached his chair, Jay noticed a drawing suspended on the wall just behind the captain: the large, white paper, yellowed with age, containing sketches of the floor plans of the Eulia Castle. Various x-marks were scattered on the map with arrows indicating their designated paths. Everyone sat in silence, waiting for the captain to speak.

"Ehem..." the captain cleared his throat as he stood in front of the drawing. He held a long, sturdy, black pointer in his right hand. "Me crew, lend me yer ears. I'll make this short an' quick. This be a perilous mission we be takin', but the rewards are as precious as a lady's heart."

Some of the crew chuckled quietly.

"As ye all are aware, this weekend, Eulia be hosting the annual Gorgrim Tournament. And the prize be a diamond locket, far more precious than anything I set me eyes on during me life."

The ship rocked to the side, causing some of the rope dangling from the ceiling to sway. Captain Gaden's eyes, hidden under his bushy eyebrows, gazed at his crew.

Ankin, an elder pirate, stood up. His frail hands hung by his side. "Surely such a locket will be cleverly hidden."

The captain's massive form shifted as he turned to Ankin; the numerous gold and silver treasures hanging from his brown jacket clanged together like a wind chime. He said, "Until its presentation to the victor, the locket be kept hidden in the king's bedroom locked away in some sort of device."

"Is this information Karen sent you?" Hector asked from the back of the room.

"Aye," the captain said. "She's been gatherin' information 'bout this treasure for the best of a month now." He slapped the pointer to a square room drawn in black ink on the yellow-tinted paper. "We will steal the locket tomorrow night from King Emory's chambers." He flicked his pointer into his open palm. "Cain will lead the charge."

Jay glanced back at Cain, who had slithered in silently and leaned in the shadows near the door. His black linen sleeves fell past his fingertips. A midnight blue bandana wrapped his black hair to his head. His hand-carved, willow walking-staff was propped up against the wall by his side.

"Ehem..." the captain cleared his throat again to get everyone's attention. "The rest of ye will follow Cain's instructions to get Jenkins into that room."

Across the table, Jay saw Jenkins, skinny as a stick, leaning back in his chair twirling his twig-like lock pick between his fingers. "I'll pick whatever lock ol' Emory has in store for us. This baby has never failed." Jenkins flicked the white lock-pick in the air, caught it, and kissed its coarse teeth.

"Don't worry Jenky. We'll help get ya there." Lynk tilted back in his chair and flipped a coin in the air.

Jenkins scowled at Lynk. "Jenky? I don't believe anyone named Jenky is on board."

"Don't fret Jenky. We'll get ya there," Lynk repeated with extra emphasis this time. Jay could not suppress a smile.

"Ehem!" the captain blurted. "Do I have a crew of pirates or babblin' children?" The pirates shuffled in their seats, immediately giving the captain their undivided attention.

"Arg...ye make me feel like a mother sometimes." Shaking his round head, the captain again slapped the slim pointer on the wall. "Ye all will enter here—"

"That's the front entrance!" Soleus blurted out.

Gritting his teeth, the captain said, "I know that's the front entrance. Do I look like a—"

"We'll be identified immediately!" Soleus said.

The captain's face reddened. In a calm voice, Ankin

said, "Easy Soleus, I'm sure the captain knows that."

Hector scratched his beard as he looked at Ankin. "The entrance will be heavily guarded due to the Gorgrim Tournament. Ye sure we can get through?"

Ankin scrunched his eyebrows, considering the question. "Well, we could—"

"E-HEM!" the captain shouted. "One more outburst from the lot of you and ye will be yappin' with the sharks, ye hear?" He glared at Soleus, who nodded and slumped back in his chair. "Good." He turned to address the entire room again.

"As I was saying, ye will enter here. I had Karen find a way in through the washing room. Ye all will meet her at the Wicker Pub in Eulia, where she will tell ye how to get past the guards. Delcato..." the dark-haired woman sitting next to Soleus perked her head, "...I have a feeling she'll be needing you for this part."

"Aye." She nodded behind her veil of black hair.

"Hmph, very well," the captain mumbled to himself. "Cain'll be giving ye all instructions on what to do from there. I want no bloodshed—we must enter and leave with the kingdom of Eulia unawares. Lynk, ye and yer brother will devise the best way to go about this."

Lynk sat proudly. "We'll sneak in and vanish without a trace, just like the coins," he smirked at Soleus, watching anger bubble over the pirate's chubby face.

"Err...very well then," the captain said. "Just don't screw up." The captain's bulky structure weaved to the other side of the board. "As I was sayin' before, the locket will be in this room. After ye secure the—"

"But guards will be swarming the castle, especially the king's chamber! How are we—"

"SOLEUS!" the captain bellowed, snapping his pointer in half. "SILENCE!" he threw the two halves to the ground. The ship rocked to the side, causing the snake-like ropes dangling from the ceiling to shake and the floorboards to creak. "Blynk! Fetch me another stick!"

"Yes cap'n, aye cap'n!" Blynk stuttered as he flew from his chair out the door in under half-a-second.

"Urgh..." the captain mumbled as he massaged his temples with his meaty fingers.

Delcato shook her head beside Soleus, who scooted down in his chair so low he nearly slid off. "Sorry cap'n, I was just—"

The captain lifted his hand. "Silence, Soleus...silence."

No one dared make a sound until Blynk returned, hoisting the new pointer in the air and giving it to the captain. Snatching the pointer from him, the captain returned to his board. Stabbing the parchment so hard that the pointer punctured a hole in the white paper, he said, "We will not enter through the door." He paused for a moment, as if anticipating another outburst from Soleus. Hearing nothing, he exhaled a breath of relief and continued.

General Arthur McClevin assembled his men on the grand beach of Eulia. His shiny armor rattled as he strutted around in the warm sand. Although not very muscular, his form reflected strength and poise. He adjusted his brass-trimmed, steel helmet to fit more comfortably on his head. "Alright everyone, this is it, hoist those banners high!"

McClevin watched as his motley crew, clad in uniforms splashed with emerald and blue, colors of Eulia, assembled in a rectangle. The four men stationed at the corners gallantly held up a stick with a long tawdry banner swinging loosely; the banners contained an embroidered bird in flight with a trail of bright red letters spelling 'EULIA.'

"Good, good!" McClevin said. "The king'll love it!"

He darted down alongside the men, throwing his hands in the air. "Now bring out the trumpets and drums!" Sunlight glistened off the golden trumpets as several men along the perimeter lifted their instruments in the air.

"Ugh...the blasted thing has sand in it," a shorter man said as he examined his trumpet.

"Lord love a duck!" McClevin rushed to the man and snatched his instrument. "Better keep it off the sand then, don'tcha think Duc?"

Duc threw his blotched headpiece to the ground. "This is stupid! We are going to look like a bunch of misfit clowns waltzing into a funeral procession." Everyone began mumbling to one another in agreement, examining each other's oddly-colored wardrobes.

"Yeah, why do I have to wear this?" a tall man asked in the middle of their formation. He wore bright orange pantaloons and a flashy purple shirt.

"This is stupid," another objected.

"Enough!" McClevin bellowed, growing redder. The vein along the side of his head began pulsing. "This'll be the best cavalcade the king has ever seen! This is a major time for Eulia, and we have to show our guests all we can be!"

"A bunch of goofy buffoons?" Duc asked.

McClevin shoved the instrument back in his hands—Duc stumbled back under such force.

"It's all clean, now hold it up!" McClevin retreated several steps to observe the formation. "Good, good. Now, raise the stool!"

Several men in the center grabbed an edge of a skinny platform with a stool centered on top and lifted it in the air. Four other men climbed on the platform and knelt down, each grabbing a leg of the circular stool. The man in orange pantaloons sighed and reluctantly jumped on the platform and climbed on the stool, which was only wide enough for one of his feet to fit. He folded the other across his knee.

"Up, get it in the air!" McClevin said, waving his hands upward.

The four men gathered their breaths and then hoisted the red-faced, orange-pantaloon wearing, one-legged man in the air. He wobbled slightly, but found his center of gravity.

"Okay, now let's get the other stool." McClevin motioned towards an identical stool lying in the sand.

"Uhh...is this really a good idea?" Duc asked.

"Of course it is, right Chip?" McClevin said.

Chip struggled to maintain his balance on the stool. "Yeah, sure boss."

McClevin clasped his hands, excitement flooding his body. "Great! Now get the other stool up!" His helmet's blue horsehair crest shook as he skirted around the men. His white face filled with glee as the men held their formation. "The king will reward all of us greatly for this! Now come on, quickly!"

The men grumbled as they handed the stool to Chip. He skillfully flipped the stool upside down so the round ends from both stools were snug against one another. He then balanced himself on the wooden support beams that stretched between the stool's posts. Standing erect, he reached inside his purple shirt and removed five dark-colored balls. After securing his balance, he threw the balls in the air and juggled them.

"Perfect!" McClevin rushed towards the front of the men. "Okay, now, just like we practiced! Any questions?"

"Do we have to do this?" someone asked from the rear.

"Of course we do! This is for our great King Emory!

Don't screw it up...any blunder will make us look like fools."

"We don't need a blunder to accomplish that," someone muttered.

Ignoring him, McClevin said, "Let's show everyone what the Kingdom of Eulia is made of!" He whirled around, unsheathed his shiny steel sword, and swung it in the air nobly. The trumpets sounded. The men faced forward. "Ready...march!" McClevin shouted from the front.

The wobbly cavalcade marched in sync. The four men holding the stool high in the air locked their arms and tried to subdue their trembling. The drummers and trumpeters blasted their instruments. A rush of excitement and bliss consumed McClevin, who proudly led his men off the beach and down the main street of Eulia towards the castle.

People stopped momentarily to watch the passing parade. Most of the kids giggled and pointed at Chip as he juggled. "Look at the goofy man in purple, mama!" one shouted. Chip sighed dejectedly as he continued his performance.

The low-budget, precarious parade continued down the street. Up ahead, kids danced around with a ball, playing some sport. "Steady men..." McClevin said as he noticed the potential danger. Beads of sweat dripped down his round cheeks when they neared the kids who appeared not to notice his magnificent parade.

"Welcome, welcome to Eulia!" he shouted to the crowd, partially to greet the many merchants, partially to warn the kids.

"Get out of the road!" an angry woman yelled at the kids; turning their heads to the incoming parade, the kids scattered to make way for McClevin and his men.

Relieved at the extinguished threat, McClevin lifted his chin high with glory and pressed on.

From the corner of his eye, McClevin noticed a ball shoot out from the crowd towards his men. He hesitated a second but then continued onward. They were soldiers. They could handle it.

"Whoa...watch your step!" someone yelled from behind.

Maybe not.

"Keep moving!" McClevin yelled, afraid to look back. But when the instruments began to blare out of tune, he glanced back and saw the soldiers stumbling over the ball. Unbelievable.

"Keep playing!" McClevin shouted, facing forward.

One of the men holding the platform planted his foot directly on the ball, causing it to sweep his feet from underneath him. He crashed to the ground, causing the platform to tilt. The four men holding the stool quickly lost their balance and slid down the platform. The stools that supported Chip jerked forward as the rear of the platform flung high in the air.

When McClevin finally turned to look back, Chip toppled over the men in the front, making them all crumble to the ground. The final instrument died out as the few men standing looked at the mess before them. The kids roared in laughter as their parents tried to hush them, but McClevin caught a few parents in the corner of his eye struggle to stifle their own laughter.

His parade was compromised. By a ball.

"This is a disaster!" McClevin cried. He rushed around trying to help his soldiers. A crowd gathered around them as the soldiers stumbled to their feet. "H-Hold on everyone, we'll get this back in order soon," McClevin said, sensing the enormous frustration from his men.

"Ugh..." Chip moaned. "I think I'm done for the day."

He rubbed his bruised back.

Seeing no one badly injured, McClevin let out a breath of relief. "No, we can still pull this together, the king will—"

"Sir!" A scrawny knight interrupted, standing firm next to McClevin.

Shaking with rage, red-faced with embarrassment, McClevin turned to face him. "What is it?"

"We need you in the palace at once. It concerns...." His eyes wandered the crowd. He leaned forward and whispered, "...it concerns *it.*"

"Grr...alright. Men, clean this up. We'll call it a day I suppose. Lord love a duck...."

He followed the soldier up the grassy hill towards the luxurious castle. Once inside, they climbed the stone staircases to the top floor where the royal family slept. In the hallway, many guards chatted quietly as the two entered the king's bedroom. "I'll leave you alone," the skinny soldier said as he waited outside the room.

Inside, a slender, young lady waited by the window. Her long, green satin gown glimmered from the sunlight pouring through the window. Her skin glowed with a scent of purity, and her straight, snowy hair rested against her shoulders. "Thank you for seeing me, McClevin."

At once, he dropped to a knee and bowed his head. "Princess Alexandra!"

She turned around and smiled. "You know there's no need for formality around me."

Raising his head, he stood up. Her innocent eyes looked at him worriedly. "Is something wrong?" he asked.

She remained silent for a few seconds, and then she walked over to the bed where a sturdy chest lay open. Following her lead, he approached the bed. He gasped.

"Is that it?"

She nodded.

Inside the chest was a circular, diamond locket, shinier and smoother than anything he had seen; its majestic nature made it appear to have a phosphorescent glow in the dark chest.

"That is amazing," he said, mystified. "I bet the fisherman who found this made a fortune."

"Indeed, but that's what concerns me," she said.

He looked up at her. "What do you mean?"

Her eyes sunk lower as she stared at the locket. "King Cornelius knows we hold a very valuable treasure. He agreed to let Eulia host this year's Gorgrim Tournament in exchange for our promise to bestow upon the winner this locket. He obviously feels confident someone from his kingdom will win."

"What makes him so sure?"

"A man named Lasheer has supposedly captured Kreios, the most vicious of all the gorgrim, known in the ring as the King of the Gorgrim. I've heard tales of it...it's a vicious monster." She sighed, rubbing her hand against her shoulder. "My father agreed to Cornelius's bargain since the economy of Eulia will be greatly aided by the influx of wealthy merchants gambling on the tournament."

"So, why are you upset?" he asked.

She looked at him. "Nothing can happen to this locket. If it goes missing or someone steals it, Cornelius will take it as a direct insult to his kingdom. He's a heartless man and would accuse us of backstabbing him for economic gain. The militant fool may even go so far as to disturb the peace between our kingdoms that so many men and women died for."

McClevin's heart sank as he noticed her emerald eyes

watering.

"I don't know why," she said. "But I am afraid something will happen to it. I can't allow that...not for my people. They can bear no more suffering." Her sadness flowed into her voice. "Promise me, McClevin, that you won't let anything happen to this locket."

Overcome with a valiant feeling, he said firmly, "I promise you. Nothing will happen to the locket. I will post my troops all around this castle, securing it so that no one will get in."

She wiped her dripping eyes. "I don't know why I'm so upset...I just know how greedy people are, and I couldn't bear another war with Valkadia."

"I understand. I won't let anything happen to it," he assured.

"Thank you. I must leave now." She rested her soft palm on his armored shoulder briefly. "You've never failed me before, McClevin. I know you'll keep it safe."

She walked out of the room, leaving the general alone with the diamond locket safely tucked away in the chest.

The crew members resting along the mast immediately jumped to their feet and rushed back to their tasks as Jay and the other members of the ground team resurfaced on deck. The young pirate ascended the stairs to the bridge. "How ya feelin' kid?" Gideon asked.

Jay's face felt cold. "Fine..." he lied.

"You sure? You're looking awfully pale for a youngster like yourself to be 'fine.'"

Wiping his face, trying to scrub away his nervous expression, Jay turned and looked away. "No, I'm fine. Just feeling a little ill." He treaded towards the edge of the ship and flapped his arms over the rail.

Off in the distance, inches above the water, several winged birds known as azura flew freely alongside one another. Their long wings were splashed with blue feathers on top and white feathers underneath: their cyan bodies appeared thin when matched with such massive wings. Their sharp, stubby, green beaks curved delicately to allow them to snatch prey from the sea. The azura chased one another above the clear blue water. They frolicked in the sky, soaring over one another like children rolling on the grass. He could almost hear their laughter. The sky was theirs; they could do as they pleased without worry.

Jay envied these beautiful creatures—they lived such a carefree life and never seemed to experience conflict or sadness. Watching them made him relax inside. His stomach loosened, his face cooled. For a moment, he was one with the azura; he was free. He closed his eyes and let himself escape into the endless sky. The wind in his face, he glided only inches above the sea as drops of water flecked his face. An azura flew beside him on the left, and a second soon accompanied him on the right. Together, the three raced over the gentle sea.

Jay smiled as he imagined himself in flight with the azura. Wave after wave passed beneath them while cloud after cloud passed above. In perfect harmony, together they turned and dipped down even closer to the water. His winged friends began twirling in the air as they flew. They soared above him and danced together as they played. The two azura spread their wings above him to form a brilliant pattern of blue and white. Jay felt protected; he felt secure.

Suddenly, the sea warped from blue to black as clouds of darkness captured the sun. Startled, he removed his head from the water as his winged friends abandoned him and flew away in fright. Up ahead was a pirate ship, black as death. The sky crackled with menacing thunder. Looking around for his friends, Jay felt lost and alone. His vision again shifted towards the ship ahead as he saw a figure approaching the stern. Straining his eyes, Jay realized it was his stepbrother, Thyran. It had been four years since he last saw him, but he could still see the devious grin on his face from when he left Jay alone on the beach of Morad. Shortly after another slam of thunder, Thyran turned his back to Jay, and he felt a hand press against his shoulder.

Startled, Jay jumped away from the rail and looked behind him. When he saw Captain Gaden looking back at him, he snapped back to reality.

Rescinding his hand, the captain asked, "What be troublin' ye?"

"I...nothing. I just came up for some fresh air."

Captain Gaden smiled underneath his fluffy beard. Jay knew he didn't believe him. "Me first time stealin' something this great was a nerve-wrecking time, to say the least. But ye have a talented crew behind yer back, although they acted like deaf seahorses in a trilling contest a moment ago."

"Hmm..." Jay stared off into the blue horizon. Four years ago, the thought of stealing never crossed his mind. He lived an honest life.

The captain grabbed his hips and straightened his back. "Ye are free to stay on board should ye like."

True, but if he did, what would the rest of the crew think of him? A coward? One too weak to be a member of the crew?

"No," Jay objected, looking at the captain. "I have nowhere else to go. I need to do this to survive." He nodded firmly, mentally justifying the act of stealing.

The captain coughed, clearing his throat. "Very well then. I'll be here if ye need anything." Jay said nothing, just stared blankly toward the ocean. Captain Gaden wrapped his massive arm around Jay's shoulders. "Yeh'll do fine lad. I won't let anything happen to you. That's a promise, and ye know I'd sooner die than fall back on one of me promises."

The captain's words mitigated some of his anxiety. "Thank you cap'n. I appreciate all you have done for me."

"Ha!" the captain laughed. "Couldn't afford not to bring you on board, the swift scoundrel ye are! I've been meaning to thank Hector for finding such a clever kid for me crew."

The two laughed, and then the captain turned and walked over to Gideon, whistling as he did so. "Get some rest, boy. We should be at Eulia tomorrow morning."

"Aye cap'n."

Jay gazed out again at the azura. Most of them had gone, leaving only the vast sea separating them from the Kingdom of Eulia.

2

Wicker Pub

The next morning, Jay's sense of justification vanished like smoke. He dug his nails into the wooden oar he used to paddle the rowboat closer to the docks of Eulia. Up ahead, he saw swarms of people rushing around the streets. During such a busy time, the king would no doubt have increased the level of security, which greatly increased the danger of their mission. But Cain would be leading them, which was good—Cain always had a knack for choosing the best course of action. That was the only silver lining Jay saw, which helped keep him calm.

When the crew reached the dock, Jay lobbed up the ends of two thin ropes and waited as men on the docks wrapped them around the wooden pilings. By the time Jay's boat was secured, he saw Captain Gaden, wearing a long, gray fleece coat, exit his boat.

A man, much smaller than the captain, in bright green shorts and a blue shirt bustled down the deck with a beaming smile on his face. When he reached the captain, he said,

"Allow me to be the first to welcome you to Eulia! My name's Jack Porter." He lifted up a small black book and flipped it open to a page marked with a pen resting along the binding. "May I have your name, sir?"

"Me name's Jim Dallas," Captain Gaden said.

"Ahh..." Jack scribbled something in his little book. "'Tis a pleasure, Mr. Dallas. How long do you plan on visiting Eulia?"

"Three days."

"Two nights then? Alright, the cost for using the extended docks for a night is twelve drags. So, twenty-four drags."

The captain dug in his pockets and removed a handful of coins similar to the ones Lynk made vanish the previous night. Standing beside the captain, Jay admired the intricate dragons inscribed on each coin.

Shuffling through the dragon-faced coins, the captain removed two red coins and four blue coins, each color with a different dragon, and handed them to Jack. Cain stood leaning against his walking staff behind the captain and waited.

"Take the men into Eulia," the captain said as Jack took the coins and scribbled something in his booklet. "I will meet you there."

"Aye," Cain said. He turned towards the rest of the crew who were still making their way out of the boats and motioned with his hand for them to follow. Turning away from the glistening ocean, Cain led the crew down the long, narrow dock into Eulia.

As soon as their feet hit the dock, Lynk and Blynk zipped past the captain and Cain. "See ya guys there!" they shouted without looking back as they flew on ahead. Cain shook his head and pressed onward.

Soleus waddled up next to Jay and walked alongside him. "Wow..." Jay said, awed by the magnificence of Eulia; it was quite an improvement from the village of Morad.

Straight ahead, he saw the marketplace, where vendors were eagerly selling useless trinkets to the visiting merchants. At the center of the marketplace stood an elegant stone fountain, but Jay was still too far away to make out the details. In the far left, beyond the marketplace, a large, grassy hill overlooked the ocean; on top of the hill stood the glorious castle, radiating strength and nobility. After admiring the elegance of the castle, Jay turned his head and noticed a roofless cylindrical building on the opposite side of the city that stood out from the encompassing forest.

"What's that?" Jay asked.

"Huh?" said Soleus.

Jay lifted his hand to point at the cylindrical building.

"That building over there."

Soleus gazed in the direction of Jay's finger. "Oh, that one! That's where the Gorgrim Tournament is being held. Nasty creatures them Gorgrim be—wouldn't want to cross one of them on a bad day, if ye know what I mean. It's a good thing we aren't breaking into the Gorgrim Stables tonight, or else I'd be hidin' back on the ship!"

"I see..." Jay said, his eyes transfixed on the building. "When does the tournament start?"

Soleus scratched his chin and looked up at the sky as if the fluffy white clouds held the answer. "I believe it started a few days ago. Tomorrow is the last—"

Neither of them noticed Cain had stopped, and Soleus, his head still facing the sky, bumped into Cain. After a violent shove from Cain's wooden staff, he stumbled back.

"Whoa! Why'd you stop? You lost or somethin'?" Soleus said and began laughing, but stopped instantly under the heat of Cain's scorching glare.

"Fool, are you trying to attract attention to us?" Cain said in a quiet, yet stern, voice.

"I—"

"Quiet! Do not speak of the plan until the proper time. Now, let's pick up the pace. We are meeting Karen shortly." Cain spun around and continued walking down the dock.

Soleus leaned down to whisper in Jay's ear. "Who

shoved the stick up his—"

"Move it Soleus!" Cain grumbled. Jay grinned as Soleus snapped his mouth shut and straightened his back like a soldier disciplined by a superior officer.

Hearing footsteps behind him, Jay turned to see Hector, Delcato, Jenkins, and Ankin catching up. They all reached the end of the dock and stepped on the stone path that guided them into the marketplace. People scurried everywhere, visiting the various huts and purchasing their little trinkets. There was everything: weapon smiths, clothing shops, food tents, and myriad other vendors. Most of the stores in the area consisted of a tan, canvas tent with several shelves inside that held merchandise.

"Out of the way!" Jay heard someone shout. He dove aside just in time to avoid collision with a horse-drawn cart trundling down the stone street; a few apples dropped over the edge as the driver jerked the horses to the right to avoid hitting him.

"Watch where you're walking next time!" he shouted back.

"Watch where yer goin' grumpy!" Soleus said, shaking his fist at the driver. "He's the one who should keep his eye on the street. I oughta teach him a thing or two about—"

"Obedience?" Cain suggested in a harsh tone.

Soleus opened his mouth to defend himself, but Jay patted him on the back. "Come on, you know what he's like when he gets angry. Let's just keep up."

As they neared the fountain at the center of Eulia, the crew was swarmed with people selling assorted crafts. To the side, Jay saw a skinny, aged man wearing an unusually heavy coat for such a warm day. Catching Jay's attention, the man rushed towards him and swung open his dark coat; several beaded necklaces hung from his wrists and dangled from inside his coat. They were all made from different shells and artifacts of animals washed up on the beach.

"Lucky necklaces sir!" said the man in a cracked voice. "When wearing one of these, no harm can touch you! See this, this one here!" the elderly man pointed to a bright green gem centered on one of the necklaces. "This gem was blessed by the Empress Icis herself!"

Inspecting the necklace, Jay noticed an emerald sea of liquid swirling around inside the gem. Occasionally, specks of red would mystically appear in certain areas like small fiery explosions, and then the liquid increased its speed, swirling faster and faster, until it changed sky blue and its swirling ceased. After a few seconds, fiery explosions again filled the gem, and the liquid returned emerald.

"Give this to any woman and melt her heart! This could be your lucky night! What say you?"

Jay hesitated. He had never seen anything like it. What kind of material changed colors like that? Was it magical? No...despite what Lynk and Blynk liked to argue, there was no such thing as magic. Perhaps they would know what would cause such an unusual behavior of a gem.

"Sorry sir, we have no money on us," Hector said, approaching Jay's side.

"These necklaces go for one hundred drags," the man continued, ignoring Hector's response, "but I'll make you a deal: this necklace can be yours for only thirty drags! What a bargain! Come on, what d'ya say?"

"I say no thanks." Hector put his arm around Jay's shoulders and walked away. Jay heard the man grumble to himself and retreat back to his post, waiting for the next victim to walk by.

After they were a safe distance from the necklace vendor, Jay said, "Thanks Hector."

"No problem, mate! Always here to help." Hector smiled as he slapped Jay on the back, causing the young pirate to stumble forward to maintain his balance. "Err...sorry Jay—guess I don't know me own strength."

Jay laughed. "Ha, you're just trying to get revenge from the other day. I see how you are."

"You better watch it Lil' Blue. I wasn't the one who let his guard down to admire an apple."

Jay shook his head. "You guys may call me 'Little Blue' thinking I'm all innocent and such, but I won't be so innocent during our next sparring match, I promise you that."

Hector chortled. "We'll see, we'll see...."

After a few minutes, they were in the heart of the marketplace, and Jay now noticed the magnificence of the stone fountain. A circular, stone bench surrounded the pool of clear water at its base. Just above the water, several dolphins were carved into the stone with water gently arcing out of their mouths. As the vase-like structure grew, it narrowed with swirling curves coursing along its structure. Somewhat blinded by the sun, Jay saw a beautiful azura, carved in a shiny metal, perched on top of the thirty-foot fountain. That sight, along with the peaceful sound of water splashing into the pool, soothed his concerns for the mission, temporarily.

While Jay and Soleus admired the fountain, Cain stood with his back to it, waiting for the others to catch up. "Where are Blynk and Lynk?"

"Those two?" Ankin said when he reached the fountain. "They're probably already at the Wicker Pub with Karen waiting for us."

Cain rolled his eyes. Soleus whirled around to face the crew. "Come on ye lazy bunch! Let's not keep them waiting." He looked over at Delcato. "Come on Del, I'll save ya a seat!" With a beaming smile, Soleus left and darted ahead to the pub.

Jay shook his head and grinned at Soleus's feeble attempts to impress Delcato. She sighed and mumbled, "Can't wait...."

As they followed Soleus, Jay glanced back at the necklace-seller. He had managed to lure a young girl wearing a very clean, light blue dress. Her curly hair bounced against her dress as she leaned forward, allowing the man to hang a necklace around her neck. Jay realized that it was the same necklace with the mysterious gem the man tried to sell him.

With the necklace around her neck, the girl began twirling around with excitement. An older lady, though still young, with long auburn hair and a plain green bodice extended a hand containing several coins to the man. As if she assumed the vendor to be hard of hearing, she spoke in a loud and clear voice. "Thank you, sir. Her grandma in Selia will be very happy!"

The lady bowed to the man, took her daughter's hand, and began walking down the street towards the cylindrical dome. Jay turned back to the crew and followed them to the Wicker Pub.

Kyros Raven paused a moment to watch something peculiar in the ocean.

In the water, a sailboat was heading towards the Eulian docks. The velvet blue skies offered a welcoming breeze that blew inland, propelling the boat, its sail convexly bent towards land.

Then, as the boat drew closer, something strange happened. The serene water began creating resistance. Waves formed around the boat that pushed it farther from the dock. Despite the strong breeze, the boat rocked and moved against the wind. On board, the baffled sailors scampered around in confusion.

Kyros tilted his head, perplexed. On the beach, he saw a young woman who watched the sailboat intently. She wore a loose pair of dark blue cotton pants tight around her waist but baggy down her legs. Her shirt consisted of two straps that scaled her shoulders and cerulean cloth that dropped down inches past her bosom, revealing her dark-brown stomach. Two hairpins—one resembling a unique purple flower exploding with delicate light blue petals and another resembling a slender tendril of green sea-weed—gathered patches of her long, sapphire hair.

By her feet was a kitten, dark blue with light stripes, chasing something around in the sand.

As the men aboard the sailboat struggled to change their ship's direction, she leaned back and laughed hysterically. Her bare feet sinking in the sand, she danced around on the beach, flinging her arms through the air. Whenever she stopped dancing and concentrated on the sailboat, it would rock and flow backwards even faster.

She flung her head back, looked up at the bright, yellow sun, and twirled in the sand with her arms extended like a ballerina.

Kyros stood a moment, taking in the scene, wondering if she somehow played a part in the ship's moving against the wind. But then he cursed himself for thinking such nonsense. He shook his head as the woman whirled in the sand like a little child. "How annoying..." he muttered.

Ceasing her dancing and laughter, she spun around. Her eyes met his. Damn. She must have heard him.

Scowling, she stomped through the sand towards him. Behind her, the sailboat in the distance started moving with the wind again as the water around the boat calmed.

He pretended not to notice and quickly continued walking along the beach with his black leather bag in his right hand. His thin black shirt grew hot under the sun.

He heard the young woman skipping after him, humming some childish melody. He closed his eyes, praying she would leave, but then he heard her yell,

"Annoyance! Is that what you called me?"

"Don't bother me lady," he grumbled and continued walking without looking back.

"Lady!" she exclaimed. In a noble and proper voice, she said, "You shall not refer to me as naught save for Miss Alcina!"

Kyros stopped and turned around, nearly causing the lady to bump into him. His eyes fixed on her face, which he actually found quite attractive, he said, "I shall not refer to you as nothing except for Alcina? So, then I can refer to you as anything excluding Alcina, which means I'm right on track by calling you an annoyance, am I not?" Without waiting for her to answer, he left her with his play on words and continued along his path.

After pausing a moment to digest his last remark, Alcina continued trailing him. "Do not jest at my diction," she objected.

"It is not your diction to which I make jest," he said. "Rather it is the origin of that diction of whom I made a quip."

Alcina gritted her teeth and clenched her fists. "What is your name, mister?"

"My name is one sound I desire not hear from any *annoyances*."

No longer on the beach, they strolled on the compact dirt behind the vending shops. The vast amount of trees with wide canopies shaded them as they walked. He slowed his pace and concentrated on the backsides of nearby stores.

"What are you carrying?" she asked after a few seconds of silence.

"A bag."

Alcina clicked her tongue. "Well, you don't say! I'm not as stupid as I look, mister."

"I had assumed as much when I learned you could comprehend the national language."

"You would shut your mouth if you knew what was good for you!"

"Likewise, miss." He continued examining the buildings, never casting her a glance.

He noticed the arm of her shadow lift a few inches above her head, then she launched it forward—he felt a cold ball of water explode over his spiked hair.

Jumping from the shock of the icy water against his head, he whirled around. The chilly water dampened his crimson hair and trickled down his face. Seeing her hand extended towards him, he said, "Have you nothing better to do with your life than going around bugging people?"

Bringing her sleek finger to her lips, she nibbled on her fingernail, blushing, admiring his angry face. "Ohh...I'm sorry, did someone get a lil' wet?" The nobility of her voice vanished.

"I'm warning you," he said, clenching his fist, "you are trying my patience. Hit me again, and you'll pay." He turned around and hurried farther down the back of the marketplace.

She wasted no time catching up to him and then waddled by his side with her hands crossed behind her back. "So, what put you in this foul mood today?"

"I wonder." He nudged his wet face against his black

sleeve, trying to dry himself.

"Only water, my dear, I promise."

"I am not your dear."

She giggled and peered up at his face. "Whatever you say, my dear."

Quietly grumbling, he ignored her and continued.

They walked a few paces before Alcina spoke again. "Whatcha looking for?"

"Peace...peace and quiet."

She smiled and gazed ahead. The grassy ground dipped to form a small valley. She bit her bottom lip, and he thought he saw her celestial blue eyes glow for a brief second. He nearly said something but thought it best not to indulge her.

As he neared the valley, Alcina let out a tiny, suppressed chuckle. He shot her a menacing glare and opened his mouth to say something when his right foot plopped into a puddle and sunk in up to his knee. "Ahh! What the?" The cool water soaked his tan pants. He leapt out of the puddle onto the other side of the valley and narrowed his eyes at Alcina.

Biting her lower lip to refrain from laughing, she batted her almond-shaped eyes innocently and asked, "What is it dear? I didn't say a word."

Realizing she couldn't possibly be responsible for the puddle, he spun around and muttered, "Nothing...."

A few paces later, he stopped behind an elegant building, constructed of granite rather than skin or cloth like the others. He paused, knelt to the ground, and dropped his bag of supplies in front of him.

"What are you doing?" Alcina asked, stopping beside him. She glanced over his shoulder, trying to identify the contents inside his supply bag.

He said nothing.

After a minute, she spoke in a harsh voice through clenched teeth. "You have some nerve, mister!"

Alerted by her loud tone, he finally looked into her eyes. For once, he felt more concerned than angry. He considered stabbing her heart, for she was a risk to his operation: if she told anyone of his presence here, his plans would be ruined. But the woman, she seemed so...aloof. He doubted she even realized what he was doing let alone cared enough to alert the knights. Killing her would be riskier than simply letting her stay.

"Quiet!" he said. "I'm trying to concentrate."

"Then tell me your name," Alcina said.

"My name is Kyros. Please, Miss Alcina, be silent as I concentrate." He turned back to his supplies.

When he said her name, she hopped on the balls of her feet and smiled down at her blue kitten that had been following them since the beach. So childish.

Kyros removed some red, cylindrical rods with a thin, black filament on one end. A firm, coarse rope bounded the rods like prisoners bound to the mast of a ship. After removing the fire sticks from the bag, he retrieved his pocket knife. Alcina jumped back as its shiny blade ripped through the fresh air.

"What's that blade for?" she asked.

"Quiet!" he whispered.

She scowled at him then stepped back a few paces. Seconds later, another water grenade splashed against his back, drenching his dark shirt.

Jumping to his feet with his pocket-blade gripped in one hand, Kyros glowered at her. "I've had enough of this nonsense." He rushed towards her.

Laughing, the woman retreated back. Her eyes suddenly began glowing bright blue. Puzzled, Kyros squinted and tilted his head, unwilling to accept the mysterious glow as being real.

Her hands waved in the air, and then he was struck on the side of the face with another blast of cold water.

"Wha—" he muttered, turning around to see who threw the water from behind. Seeing nothing but scattered trees and low building walls, he began to turn back when two more spheres of water slammed into his chest and face, knocking him back.

Blinded by the water, overcome by his anger, he dashed towards her, swinging his knife through the air. She effortlessly sidestepped him, and he plunged forward into another deep puddle. His feet slipped across the slick grass, sending him crashing to the moist ground. Catapulting himself into the air, he whirled around to face her as three more balls of water bombarded him. His entire body awash, he raised his hand.

"Stop," he panted, wiping his face again with his drenched sleeve. What she did was impossible, but he could no longer deny it. "What is this magic you perform?"

Glee appeared to fill her heart as he finally showed interest in her. "What magic, my dear?"

Kyros shook his head and ran his fingers through his hair, pulling it back to its spiked form. "It's as if you control water. I've never seen any sort of power before."

She laughed and again bit her bottom lip as she drifted towards him. He focused on her smooth palm as she displayed it in front of his face. His face warmed as the water droplets detached from his skin and glided towards her palm. When his face was dry, he felt his previously-damp clothes hang loosely from his body as Alcina sucked out the water. Completely dry, he watched the water in front of her palm fall back to the soil. She crossed her hands behind her back and wagged her hips. "Pretty neat, huh?"

Kyros stood bewildered. "What's your name?"

"I told you, my name is Alcina Venclin."

"*Venclin?*" he repeated.

She smiled and knelt down, running her nails over her kitten's forehead. "Hear that Miuji?" she said to her kitten. "He finds me interesting now, doesn't he?" She looked up at him and batted her eyes.

"Interesting, very interesting indeed. Thyran will be most pleased. Come with me, Alcina." For the first time since he met her, he smiled. Kyros guided her back to the building where his supplies lie scattered across the grass.

Jay treaded alongside Hector and admired the luxurious kingdom. As they walked down the street, the stores grew more stylish. Rather than the deerskin tents that frequented the marketplace, these buildings were made of brick or stone.

Up ahead, Jay could see the giant hill with a shiny, limestone path leading up to the enormous castle at the top. People strolled up the noble walkway, most appearing to be traveling in groups of three or more carrying a small chest or light bag suspended by a string.

"Gifts for the king," Hector mentioned, noticing Jay's watchful eye.

Jay constantly leaped aside to avoid collisions with the countless people in the streets. Men wearing light, navy blue wardrobes with the emblem of Eulia—an azura in flight, resembling the one atop the fountain— sprinkled the crowd. They held long poles with a sky-blue flag with emblem of Eulia encompassed by a golden circle.

As they neared the pub, he smelled a hint of charcoal

in the air, followed by a wave of freshly cooked meat lathered in foreign spices and seared to perfection. He saw chefs outside the pub grilling various meats, including pork, steak, chicken, and gorgrim (massive, ferocious animals full of tender meat). The chefs chanted cheerful songs and danced around their grills as they flipped their food in the air, creating an impressive show for the visiting merchants and nobles.

Hector stopped behind Cain and said, "We're here."

Looking up above the swinging, wooden doors, Jay saw a sign: Painted into the auburn wood were skeleton-like green letters that spelled:

WICKER PUB

Cain looked at Hector, his tapered black beard resting on his chest. "Well, we won't get very far admiring the door, will we?"

Led by Cain, the crew entered the Wicker Pub. Their ears rattled due to the thundering noise radiating inside. At every circular, willow table, men slammed their molded cups and roared with laughter. Sunlight poured through the tainted windows, giving off a drab yellow light. In the tiny areas between tables, ladies danced around, occasionally leaning against a drunken man and slipping coins out from his unguarded pocket.

"So...many of them. All...so pretty," Soleus said, his eyes nearly popping out of his head.

Delcato clicked her tongue in disgust. Ankin stepped forward and whispered in his ear. "They'll be plenty of time for that later."

"There's Karen," Cain said and began weaving through the labyrinth of tables.

Karen sat at a table with someone in the dimly lit corner. Her acorn hair dropped to her shoulders alongside her face. Clad in a forest green kirtle that fell to her ankles, she ran her thin finger along the rim of her drink. When Cain reached her table, he whispered her name.

Startled, she jumped in her chair and spun around, her silky hair swinging across her pale face. "I...you're early, Cain."

The man seated across from her rose to his feet. "Well, it appears you have company, so I'd best make my leave." He spoke in a deep voice. His black, silk bandana covered his thick black hair, leaving only a few strands falling in front of his privy eyes. His dark leather coat fell from his shoulders down to his shins and met his black boots.

Cain eyed the man suspiciously. "Who is this?"

Karen looked at the man. "Thank you, Cyril. It was nice meeting you."

"Cyril?" Cain interrupted. "How do you know each other?"

Cyril smiled. "You too, Karen." Ignoring Cain, he rose from his seat and left the pub.

Karen took a long sip of her drink. "I see your people skills are as good as ever."

"You shouldn't be too friendly here...we do not want to attract any unwanted attention." Cain leaned against wall, allowing the rest of the crew to sit around the table.

"I've been here for over a month! How do you expect me to do my job without socializing?" She shook her head as everyone took a seat. Her round eyes scanned the table. "Where are Blynk and Lynk?"

Hector adjusted himself in his seat. "We assumed they were already here with you."

Delcato sighed. "Apparently, the two are exploring

the town, unaware of their responsibilities."

Soleus leaned back, extending his arms to puff his chest. "We can go look for them if ye want. You an' me!"

Jay saw Soleus's beaming smile; the pirate was fully concentrating on Delcato. He felt bad for Soleus. Delcato was indeed very pretty, but all of Soleus's attempts to impress her only pushed her further away. If only he would use a little more tact and be less blunt all the time, he might soften her up.

"You can embark on that journey tonight, after we leave," she said.

"Oh come on, ye know y—"

His chair wobbled off balance and sent him crashing backwards. The deflated pirate threw the chair back up and slithered back on it, hoping no one noticed his debacle. Jay felt his face burning with embarrassment for Soleus.

Ankin placed his elbows on the uneven table. "They'll be here shortly. Let's begin anyways. We have a lot to do before nightfall."

"Alright," Karen said. "This is going to be slightly more complicated than we anticipated."

"Has something come up?" Hector asked.

"Yes, the king has doubled the guards stationed in the castle today."

"Why is that?"

She sighed. "I'm not sure. The knights have all been acting frantic this morning."

Setting his walking staff against the wall beside him, Cain said in a gruff voice, "Maybe all of your *socializing* caught a breeze up to the king."

She shot him a cold glare and drummed her nails on the table. "Or maybe the thousands of guests prompted the king to increase security."

"Hmph," he mumbled, sinking back into the shadows.

"Alright, now let me explain how to get into the castle." She caught glimpse of Soleus yawning. "Geeze!" she flung her back against the chair. "Have you lazy bunch been baking in the sun all these days or what?"

"Except for lunch and dinner," Soleus said.

Karen put her hand against her forehead and sighed. "You'll need this." She lifted a glass vile containing a clear liquid inside—so clear it was undetectable except for the refracting light rays passing through it. She set the vile on the center of the table.

"What is it?" Jay asked.

"Vorún Blood," she said, pushing up her glasses. "This acid was taken directly from the stem of the vorún plant, the most acidic in Lassar. A small amount of this acid eats away at nearly any type of rock or stone. However, judging by the thickness of the castle walls, it will take several days to eat through, so one of you must place this soon."

Jumping out of his seat, Soleus slammed his hand on the table and said, "I'll do it!" Jay noticed him subtly glance down at Delcato.

"Shut up!" Jenkins said, dropping his white lock-pick so it bounced back against his chest. "You might as well stand on the table and announce our plan to the whole bloody pub!"

"We cannot afford to screw this up," Cain said. "I am familiar with the inside of the castle, so I will take care of this."

"Mmph." Soleus plopped back into his chair.

Cain kicked off the wall and scooped up the vile. "Where does this go?"

"In the washing room along the southeast corner. But,

before you go, let me explain what you need to do once inside the castle. It is going to be quite difficult to enter the king's bedroom unnoticed, especially with you in there Soleus."

Hearing the creaking of the pub door swinging open, Jay looked towards the entrance to see the two slender brothers storm in.

"Did you see the look on their face?" Lynk asked loudly.

"Ha! She had no idea where her ring went!" Blynk said, spotting them in the corner.

Lynk shook with laughter as he neared the table. "I know! She woulda killed us if we hadn't made it reappear."

"We made out pretty good in tips!" Blynk held a small pouch in the air, jiggling it, causing the coins to clatter.

"I know! Those people don't know what hit 'em."

Admiring the bag, Blynk said, "This'll help mum out, don'tcha think?"

"Yeah, definitely."

"Punctual as always I see," Karen said as they drew closer.

Lynk looked away from his brother. "Karen! Good to see ya!"

Smiling, Karen nodded. "You too."

"You guys get lost?" Soleus asked.

"Nah... just stretchin' our legs," Lynk said, scooping up a mug from a nearby table as its owner focused on one of the dancing ladies. He took a long drink and smacked his lips. "Hmm...delicious."

"There will be time for plenty of that tonight, boys." Delcato said.

"So, what's the plan mates?" Lynk asked, kneeling down beside the table.

In a hushed voice, Karen explained the plan in detail. The thunderous chatter and smell of salty meat swirled in the air while she spoke. An hour later, when she finished, the pirates all polished off their drinks and left the pub.

Cain gathered everyone in a circle outside the Wicker Pub. "You all have your instructions," he said. "I'll place the Vorún Blood in the washing room. You three," he motioned to Jay, Soleus, and Delcato, "find something on board to do as Karen mentioned. Hector, Ankin, you two know what you need to do. Be back at the ship before sunset. Jenkins, come with me and Karen."

Gripping his walking staff, Cain and Karen headed towards the castle riding atop the hill with Hector, Ankin, and Jenkins trailing close behind.

After hearing the plan fleshed out, Jay felt even more concerned than earlier. Karen's plan left many openings for things to go awry; one mistake would capsize their entire mission. He gazed up at the mighty castle. Herds of guards patrolled the entrance, wolves protecting their cave. His gaze climbed the stone castle towards the roof where several windows lined the wall. The king's bedroom had to be inside one of those; Jay's head ached and throbbed the more he thought about the mission.

Massaging his sweaty palms with his thumbs, Jay heard a sound like damp sandals sloshing in the moist sand. Behind him, Soleus was devouring a slab of ribs lathered with dark sauce that dripped down his round face. Jay forced a weak smile and said, "Easy now, your food's not going anywhere."

Soleus paused for a second to glance up at him, his lips pasted in the reddish-black sauce. "It's so 'ood" he mumbled, gulping a large chunk of meat.

Delcato shook her head and walked back towards the

fountain. Seeing her on the move, Soleus polished off the remaining meat hanging from the bone and tossed it in a stone garbage bin lined with a thin film of navy blue paper.

"Whoa! That gorgrim is huge!" Soleus said, pointing in the distance.

Secured by several ropes, an immense creature stomped down the path ahead as frantic people leapt out of the way. Its extended, snakelike tail stuck high in the air, motionless, with a hooked stinger thick as a cobra and long as a scimitar at its tip. Squinting, Jay noticed three ropes tied around it held by guards on the path to prevent it from escaping.

The ground shaking with the creature's every step, Jay perched on top of a barrel outside one of the vendor's tents to get a better view. The creature's ash gray fur wavered as it walked with its head buried in the crowd.

A cracking sound filled the air as a whip lashed down upon the beast. Roaring, the gorgrim battled its restraints and raised its head above the crowd. A short, stout horn protruded from the center of its forehead. The massive gorilla-like creature thrashed against the ropes as it towered two stories in the air. The sound of children crying and people gasping in front accompanied its angry roar. Numerous men yanked on the ropes, forcing the creature back down to the ground.

Jay watched in awe. "That's a gorgrim? I've never seen one before."

"Yes." Delcato said. "The wealthy hire trainers to capture and train those monsters. Then, in these tournaments, they are pitted against one another. They fight until one is knocked out or killed."

As the escorts passed the fountain, Jay noticed a woman in front wearing an elegant, white dress. She wore a coronet on top of her long, snowy hair. "Is she the gorgrim's owner?"

Delcato shook her head. "That's Princess Catherine Alexandra, daughter of King Emory. The last thing she would do is participate in such a brutal tournament. Women have decency."

"Waddya mean?" asked Soleus. "Women are always brutal towards men."

"Soleus, just because *you* are unable to charm any woman does not mean that we are inherently evil," she said.

He nudged his shoulder against her. "C'mon darling. I'm just sayin' you have to lighten up."

"I'm not your *darling*. I am—"

Soleus leaned towards Jay and whispered in his ear. "See what I mean? Vicious, vicious creatures they are!"

"Unbelievable! Your skull is so thick!" she said and stormed towards the fountain in the center of the marketplace.

"Well, if you're not so vicious," Soleus said, stumbling after her, "give me a chance. One drink, after the mission. Waddya say?"

"Not a day goes by without you nagging me!" Delcato said without looking back.

"Ah! I've got it!" said Soleus.

Delcato turned around, a stony expression plastered on her narrow face. "What now?"

"If I don't bug yeh for the rest of this mission, then yeh'll have a drink with me. If not, we'll forget it."

He smiled wide, revealing his pearly teeth. She glanced at Jay and pondered a moment. Rolling her eyes, she said, "If you bug me once, then it's over."

Clenching his fists and shaking them with victory, Soleus said, "Alright! I won't let yeh down!"

"Please do..." she mumbled under her breath as they continued towards the ship. She gazed over the ocean and noticed the sun falling to the horizon. "We'd best be heading for the ship to get those supplies ready."

"Right," Jay said.

Squeezing through the crowd, the three moved back towards the dock. Jay caught one final glimpse of the castle. In three days, when the sun set and the crowds cleared, their mission would begin.

3

The Mission

The days and hours ticked by, slowly torturing Jay, who paced back and forth across the deck for the better part of the evening on the third day. The pirates readied their weapons: arming themselves with small axes, daggers, swords, and gullies. They studied detailed maps and reviewed the plan over and over until they had it memorized.

"What is that?" Delcato asked during the evening, pointing to the bottles Lynk and Blynk were strapping to their belts.

"Why, some rum," Lynk said. Blynk nodded in agreement.

"Geeze you two...you can't even go one night without it, can you?"

Lynk shrugged his shoulders after fastening the small bottle to his waist next to a leather pouch. "I'm telling you, you never know when rum could come in handy."

Jay smiled as Delcato rolled her eyes and glanced back at the parchment with their plans scribbled over it. They all continued with their preparations for the mission.

Under the late evening sky splashed with fading crimson rays from the dying sun, Jay gripped his cutlass and swung the blade through the air, practicing his form to relieve his anxiety as Thyran taught him when they were younger. The very thought of Thyran spiraled him into an abyss of mysteries. For four years, he wished to find Thyran and confront him about Governor Almsy's murder.

"Ashlen waits for me. Her death will not go unnoticed."

What did Thyran mean by that? If he could figure that out, he may have a clue where his stepbrother could be hiding. Jay continued thinking of Thyran and that cold night in Morad throughout the rest of the evening as he swung his cutlass through the air.

After the sun set, he heard the captain summon him from the edge of the ship where they were loading the boats. Sheathing his sword, he walked to the boats and, after catching the captain's friendly nod of encouragement that meant more to him than any words could have, he boarded the boat. He closed his eyes as the boat descended to the rocky sea.

The waves quietly chattering in the night, Cain led the boats to the beach. Everyone rowed in silence. Even Lynk and Blynk dared not disturb the noiseless air. The streets and shops were empty except for the large crowds gathered in the pubs and taverns.

When they reached the beach, they heard the trickle of water from the fountain in the distance. Sliding the boats up onto the sand, the furtive pirates treaded across the beach behind the buildings. "Be quiet. Do not to attract any attention," Cain whispered.

Silently, the crew followed him through the sand on the backside of the buildings. Through the openings between the shops and houses, they saw guards patrolling the streets. Fortunately, the sand and grass cushioned their footfalls, and the loud din of laughing and cheering flowed out of the Wicker Pub as they walked by, further concealing their presence.

"Keep your weapons hidden," Cain whispered. His leather jacket concealed his sharp daggers and gullies; Jay and Delcato slid their blades in sheathes attached to their hips; Soleus stretched his gorgrim-skinned gloves over his meaty hands; the rest ensured their weapons were properly fastened and hidden.

As they neared the base of the round hill supporting the castle, Cain motioned towards a group of trees halfway up the hill. "Hector, Ankin, set up there. Jenkins, go with them."

"Aye," Hector said as the three of them, ducking close to the tall waving grass, slyly approached the trees.

"Alright," Cain said as he turned to the rest of the crew. "You two," he pointed to Lynk and Blynk, "after we get in, wait until we are in the washing room before meeting up with the others."

"Right," they both nodded in agreement.

"Ready for this, kid?" Cain said, facing Jay.

Looking at the castle, Jay felt his face turn pale. One wrong move, his life would be over; he would be returned to Morad and executed. Cain's determined face lifted his heart slightly and eased his headache. Fidgeting with his hands, he said,

"Yeah."

"Haha, alright Lil' Blue, let's do this." Soleus smiled and pounded his fists together.

"Follow my lead." Cain said, and, aided by his wooden walking staff, he began limping up the hill.

At the castle's entrance, several guards paced the perimeter with their spears and shields ready to attack should danger present itself. Cain huddled the pirates behind a thick bush near the top of the hill. When the guards passed the castle's entrance, they left it temporarily unguarded. "Now. You two, go in." Cain said, ushering Lynk and Blynk towards the castle.

In silence, they grabbed the bottles of rum strapped to

their belts and took a heavy drink. "See you soon," Lynk said with a smirk on his face.

Each holding their bottle of rum, they toddled towards the castle while the guards continued walking away. Glancing around, the two reached for the handle of the giant castle door.

"Hold it right there," came a coarse voice. Two guards wearing their blue Eulian uniforms slid out of the darkness near the castle and hurried towards the two brothers, their spears pointing menacingly.

"Run guys. Get out of there..." Jay mumbled, trembling feverously.

"Shh!" Cain said, peering over the bush. "Quiet!"

"Hey!" Lynk shouted, throwing his hand in the air. "Wanna drink?" he held out the bottle of rum towards the guards.

"What are you two doing here?" one of the guards asked as they advanced towards them.

Slowly retreating from the guards, Lynk said, "Whoa there fellas. We're jes tryin' to find the pub." He examined his surroundings and leaned towards Blynk. "Ya know bro, I don't think this is the pub. There aren't any women!"

"I know!" Blynk said. "What's up with that?"

"You are not allowed near the castle at this hour. What are your names?"

"Maybe they're in here!" Lynk yelled as he pushed the castle door open and stormed in along with his younger brother. The guards charged after them, dashing into the castle and leaving the door slightly ajar.

After a few seconds, Cain said, "Let's move." The four pirates rushed towards the castle. Peering inside the cracked open doors, Jay saw Lynk and Blynk making a ruckus down the hall with several guards chasing after them.

"Where's the drinks?" Lynk shouted in a drunken voice as the guards grabbed him.

"Forget the drinks, where are the female dancers?" Blynk yelled.

"If you drunks don't get out of here this instant, you'll be thrown in the dungeons," a guard said as he secured Blynk. "Let's escort these clowns out of here," he said to the other guards.

Lynk glanced down the hallway and saw the crew had not yet entered the washing room. He grabbed onto the guard's shirt. "Now you listen here! We are going nowhere until we get some d's and g's!"

"That's right, drinks and girls!" Blynk said.

"It'll be the dungeons and gallows you'll get if you keep this up."

"Wait a tick, bro," Lynk said, acting lost in thought. "I don't think this is the pub."

All of the guards' backs were towards the entrance. Cain glanced to his immediate right and motioned to the door Jay assumed was the washing room. "Quickly!" Cain whispered.

Silently, they entered the castle, crept towards the door, and slid into the washing room.

The hollow room had a circular pool of clear water in the center with several towels and buckets lining its circumference. Tall, thin mirrors with golden fringes hung along the walls.

Cain hurried towards the corner of the room, removing three daggers from his coat. "Lynk and Blynk should be here any second. We have no time to waste."

Kneeling down next to the wall, he ran his coarse fingers along the stone. Finding a small crevice where the

Vorún Blood had seeped through, he jabbed the three daggers into the wall along the crevice. "Help me budge the wall."

Soleus and Jay knelt beside Cain; each grabbed the handle of a dagger and pushed inwards and upwards until a chunk of wall popped out. "Wow, that acid stuff is strong," said Soleus as he heaved the slab of stone no thicker than a large tree trunk out of the wall.

"Follow me," Cain said as he crawled into the short tunnel. Crouching down and looking over Cain's shoulder, Jay saw a wooden wall up ahead blocking the other side of the tunnel. Cain snatched one of his sharp gullies and began cutting at the wood, creating a hole they could climb through.

"Uhh...Cain...the guards are coming back," Soleus said, still standing out in the washing room.

"Then you'd best watch your loud mouth." Cain chided as he worked his gully through the wood. "There, got it. Soleus, lean the slab of stone back up against the wall when you enter so no one will notice unless they get close."

Soleus did as Cain requested, and the four followed Cain through the tight tunnel into a room lined with wood, resembling a cabin hidden away in the middle of a forest. An aroma from the polished wood engulfed the air; various hunting implements and game hung on the logged walls. Soleus coughed as they crawled in the room. "Man! That's a strong smell."

When the four of them were all in the room, Cain looked at Delcato. "Did you bring the keeton juice?"

"Yes. It should only be five minutes until the fruit's juice takes effect."

"Alright. Hurry up. The guards should be expecting their drinks soon." Cain stepped aside from the door leading to the hallway.

"Let's go, Del" said Soleus. Jay sensed his strong effort not to be his usual blunt self in trying to impress her.

Nodding, Delcato moved towards the door, cracked it open, and glanced left and right. "Okay, it's clear."

Jay followed Delcato and Soleus out of the cabin-like room; Cain softly closed the door behind them.

In silence, they treaded across the stone-tiled floor down the hall of the castle. Jay examined the numerous portraits lining the walls: waterfalls crashed on jagged rocks in one portrait while colorful birds warbled on a tree branch in another. The ceiling stretched high above them with silver chandeliers emitting a bright white glow.

Reaching an oak door, they spun around and slammed their backs against the wall. "You ready?" Delcato asked, slipping a black, silk bandana over her mouth.

Tying black bandanas over their mouths, Jay and Soleus nodded.

"One...two..." Delcato counted, gripping her blade, "...now!"

Thrusting the door open, Delcato led Soleus and Jay into the room and quickly slammed the door behind them. Pots and pans dangled from the shelves, clanging together as the maids prolifically cleaned and stored them away. They shuffled cold, raw meat around, storing it in coolers for the next day's feast. No one noticed them until Delcato whipped her scimitar in the air.

"Nobody move!" she yelled, gripping a nearby maid by the neck. Delcato held her deadly blade against the unfortunate maid's tender skin; the short, young maid turned white with fright, her eyes watered instantly.

All of the workers froze. Water droplets crashed on the floor from the dripping kitchen supplies they held. Inhaling a breath of soap-scented air, Delcato said, "All of you, on the floor now."

Jay caught a glimpse of one of the male workers dressed in a dark green smock slyly grasp a butcher's knife and hold it behind his back. While everyone glanced around uneasily, he slithered towards Delcato.

"On the floor!" she screamed. She yanked on her hostage's brown hair, revealing more of her vulnerable neck. "Do as I say or I'll slit her throat!"

"You'll kill us anyways!" the man in the green smock said. Suddenly, he whipped the knife high in the air and charged towards her. Jay dived in the way, gripping his wrist and twisting it sharply, causing the knife to drop—sweeping the man's feet with his leg, Jay forced him to the ground.

Jay's heart pounded from the action; his shaky palms grew sweaty.

"No one will die if you all cooperate," Delcato said, looking back up to the rest of the maids. One by one, the whimpering maids all dropped to the ground. "Good. Hold her." She tossed her hostage to Soleus, who grabbed a nearby butcher's knife and held it to her throat.

Delcato skimmed into the kitchen and scanned all the maids on the floor. Spotting one with dark hair like herself and relatively the same frame, she pointed and said, "You, stand up and give me your uniform."

Reluctantly, the dark-haired woman stood up and removed her forest green smock, leaving her clad in white cotton shirt and knickers. She handed the smock to Delcato, who threw it over her shoulders. "Where are the drinks for the guards?"

Looking surprised, the quivering maid pointed to a metal tray filled with goblets. Delcato reached inside her pocket and removed the small, purple bottle of keeton juice. She walked over to the tray and poured the purple juice into each goblet.

"Hold them here," she said as she lifted the tray and walked towards the door. "I'll be back in a few minutes."

"Be careful," Soleus said.

She nodded and left the kitchen.

In the hallway outside the king's bedroom, McClevin was deep in conversation with three of his knights. "Good, now make sure—"

"General!" a stout knight with an oversized helmet drooping down his face shouted as he flew up the stairs.

"Yes Winston, what is it?" McClevin asked.

Stopping short of McClevin, he said, "You requested to be informed of any disturbances."

At once, McClevin's face tightened. "What happened?"

"Well..." the guard stammered, "nothing major. It's just, a couple of drunks barged in apparently thinking this was the pub."

"Where are they now?"

"Our guards escorted them out...I just thought you should know."

"Hmm..." McClevin scratched his chin. "Very well. Thank you Winston. We'll keep a sharp eye for any danger. Let me know immediately if anything else comes up."

By the time Delcato returned to the kitchen, Jay and Soleus had bound all the maids' hands and feet and tied cloth over their mouths. Upon barging in, Delcato said,

"We need to go. The juice will take effect soon." Then she looked at the maids and spoke in a gentle tone. "If you all remain silent, no one will be harmed.

The three exited the kitchen and hurried down the hall to the cabin-like room where Cain waited.

"Any problems?" Cain asked as they entered the room.

"No," Delcato said as she removed her costume. "But we need to go now."

This was it. Time to act. Taking a quick breath, Jay wiped the sweat off his palms, and the four of them left the room. Carefully eschewing the guards, they ascended the grand staircase up to the second floor and lingered in the shadows for a moment, watching the guards pace around.

A minute passed.

"Ughh..." one of the guards moaned as he grabbed his rumbling stomach. "I need to use the water closet," he said as he hurried off down a narrow corridor to the side.

"Ooww...me too," another said and soon, every other guard fled to the water closet as the keeton juice tore through their digestive system—the second floor lobby was temporarily unguarded. Jay was surprised the keeton juice acted as reliably as it did.

"The tower is this way," Cain said as he led the pirates into the lobby and down one of the torch-lit corridors. Only the flickering flames and pale moonlight pouring from the segmented windows gave light to this floor, making it much darker than the lower level. Their faces faded in and out of the moonlight as they passed the symmetric windows.

They came to a sturdy metal door. Someone had etched the letters 'WEST TOWER' in stone near the top of the door.

"Quickly, get in," Cain said, holding the door open.

Jay and the others hurried into the tower. The damp stone floor chilled Jay's feet; he felt the spray of water vapor from the thin mist in the air. A gentle breeze whistled against the windows that lined the winding tower walls. As they dashed up the narrow, stone staircase that spiraled up the tower, they were careful not to bump against the jagged rocks protruding from the tower wall.

"Here's the rope," Soleus said as they came to a coil of rope resting like a snake beneath a window.

Eying the rope, Cain said, "This must be the rope Karen left us. Open the window."

While Soleus opened the window, Cain retrieved a match and a slim candlestick from a pouch about his waist. Drying the windowsill and scraping a match against it, he lit the candle and set it next to the open window, which let short, crisp gusts of wind blow into the tower causing the pirates to shiver; fortunately, the flame withstood the wind.

Looking out through the window, Jay waited in silence, and then, a few seconds later, he saw the tiniest speck of yellow glimmering in the distance from the trees where Hector and the others had taken cover.

"They're ready," Cain said. "Lower the rope."

Jay tied the rope around a hooked stone pointing to the ground and tossed the rest over the windowsill. Seconds later, the only sounds were the rustling of his shipmates climbing the wall and the warbling of the crickets prancing in the grass.

When Jenkins reached the windowsill, Jay and Soleus pulled him into the tower. Once inside, he knelt down and dipped his rope-burned hands into a shallow puddle of water on the uneven ground.

As Jenkins stood up, Lynk and Blynk hopped through the window. They held up their palms towards Jenkins. A large leaf covered each palm. "Never go rope-climbing without 'em, Jenky," Lynk said to Jenkins with a smirk.

"Yeah yeah..." Jenkins muttered as the brothers pocketed their leaves and pulled up the rope.

Cain pushed through them. "Let's keep moving." After Lynk coiled the rope and tossed it over his shoulder, they
followed Cain to the top of the dark tower.

"What are you lazy slugs doing?" McClevin yelled as
the guards trickled out of the water closet. "We are under
high security and you *all* felt it necessary to take a beauty
break together? The little girl's room is over there!" He
pointed to the corridor on the opposite end of the lobby.

"Ughh...sorry general. That drink tore through our
systems." The guard held his stomach and nauseously waddled back to his station.

Another guard followed closely behind. "That lady
was suppose to come back...." His head hung low in disap-
pointment.

"What lady?" McClevin asked, stepping in front of
the guard.

"The one who brought us drinks. I've never seen her
before, but man, was she somethin' else."

Enraged, McClevin grabbed the guard's shoulders
and shook him furiously. "You let an unknown lady give
you drinks and didn't report an intruder?"

"I don't know all the maids. I'm sure I've seen her before...she just looked...so pretty under the moonlight." The
guard smiled and drifted into a daydream.

McClevin released his grip on the guard. "Lord love a
duck! I'm going down to the kitchen to investigate. Man
your posts!"

Approaching the final window at the top of the tower,
several feet above the roof, Cain whispered, "You'll descend

from here to the roof. I'll wait here for your return."

Jay's heart dropped at the thought of leaving Cain behind, but he realized that descending the rope would be difficult with a limp leg. At least he could rest assured Cain would be there for them when they returned. Shaking his head and trying to shed his concerns, Jay rubbed his hands against his pants.

Lynk wrapped the rope around a vacant, metal torch-holder. Everyone but Cain climbed down the rope and landed on the angled roof of the castle. Cain tossed the rope down to them before they took off across the roof.

Nearly ten stories above the ground, Jay gazed out and saw the pallid moonlight spread over the vast city. Lights flickered from the pubs down below, but the rest was dark and silent. The surrounding forest wrapped around Eulia, stretching from the castle to the gorgrim coliseum.

Jay's cheeks flushed as blood rushed to his face. He crouched down to balance himself on the slanted roof. A mixture of coolness and anxiety caused his body to quiver as he followed the others. He could not back out now; if anything happened, if there was any minor flaw in their plan, their capture was inevitable. Chewing on his anxiety, he followed the others to the edge of the roof.

"We're here," Delcato said. "Now, we just need to find some place to tie the rope." Delcato hunted for a rock or protrusion of some sort, but the roof was smooth.

"Leave it to us," Lynk said as he and his brother unstrapped their leather pouches around their waists and knelt down. Lynk removed a small, metal pyramid with holes shooting through the center. Blynk held a chisel and hammer while Lynk poured a silver liquid on the roof which made a faint hissing sound. Blynk chiseled four holes in the roof, and the liquid poured into the holes. Lynk quickly pushed the four corners of the pyramid base into the roof. Blynk then dripped a green potion over the silver acid and watched it cool and harden to a dark gray color.

"Was this Karen's idea?" Jay asked.

"Aye," Lynk said. "She's a real genius when it comes to chemicals, isn't she?"

Blynk pulled on the pyramid, tested its durability—it didn't move. "Alright," he said. "It's ready."

"You guys never cease to amaze me," Soleus said.

"You sure it'll hold?" Jay asked, eying the flimsy structure.

"Sure it will," Lynk assured.

"Come on," Jenkins said. "Let's get going and get out of here."

"Alright." Lynk threaded the rope through the pyramid and tied a knot. "Blynk and I will go first and open the window for you two."

Jenkins and Jay nodded as he re-fastened his pouch around his waist.

"See you in the royal bedroom!" Lynk said as he slid down the side of the castle towards a window nearly twenty feet below. When he reached the window, he used his tools from his leather pouch to pry the window open and spring into the king's bedroom.

Blynk and Jenkins quickly followed Lynk and descended to the room. Jay shook his hands, trying to wave them dry.

"Alright Jay, you're next." Delcato said.

Jay swallowed. "Okay." Trembling, he walked to the edge of the roof. The flat wall seemed to drop into an endless pit of darkness. Wiping his sweaty hands against his cotton pants, he lifted the rope and turned with his back towards the roof's edge. He looked at Delcato. She nodded approvingly. Here goes.... He clenched the rope and leaned back over the edge of the roof, hundreds of feet off the ground.

Gravity yanked his body downward; he gripped onto the rope tightly to support his weight. Step by step, he inched his way down the flat, stone castle wall. The rope burned through his hands as he tightened his grip. Inhaling deep, controlled breaths, he tried to calm his racing heart which thundered inside his chest. Soleus and Delcato peered over the roof.

"You're almost halfway there Lil' Blue!" Soleus called down.

Whew, Jay thought. Almost there. Only a few more steps and he would—

His foot slipped on a wet stone, sending his feet swinging off the wall and towards the ground. His body crashed against the solid wall; a sharp wedge of stone slashed across his stomach and cut through his shirt and skin. He cried out in pain as he felt the wind knocked out of him and a stinging sensation in his side where the rock cut him.

"Hang on, mate!" Soleus cried from above.

"Ugh..." Jay moaned as he lifted his knees and attempted to replant his feet against the wall. Pain soared into his stomach like someone stabbed him with a knife—his hands grew sweaty, making holding onto the rope more and more challenging. He could feel himself slipping—

Almost there. He brought his knees to his chest. When he kicked his feet into the wall, trying to regain his stable position, his slippery hands couldn't support his body, and he fell—

Jay closed his eyes—

Focusing all his strength in his arms, he clenched his hands around the rope. He managed to slow his speed, but he was unable to stop his plummet. His body scraped and banged against the wall—

He screamed in pain as the rope ripped through his palms. The rope burned hotter and hotter. It was too much. He could not hold on any longer. Physically unable to grab onto the rope, his hands let go, leaving him to a freefall inches above the window—

"We gotcha Jay!" Lynk yelled as he and Jenkins reached out the window and snatched Jay's arms; his body crashed against the wall beneath the windowsill with a painful thud. Holding tightly, the two pirates pulled Jay up over the windowsill and safely into the room.

Panting, Jay lay on the floor to catch his breath. It took him a few seconds to acknowledge that he was indeed still alive.

"Man, you descend rope with style!" Lynk said, laughing quietly.

His body scraped with an ugly gash in his side, Jay winced in pain and rolled on his side. "Thanks for catching me." He glanced at the bed, which was empty. "Where's the king?"

Lynk shrugged. "Not here. Lucky for us! Now, let's get this treasure and get outta here!" The four of them began delving the room for the diamond locket.

Gold and silver trim weaved along the walls of the luxurious bedroom. Enormous dressers and fine furniture created an uncomfortable sense of elegance for Jay. A flash of his shabby house in Morad surfaced to his thoughts momentarily.

Jay stumbled to his feet and walked over the velvet carpet covering the sleek wooden floor. He saw Lynk nearly knock over an hourglass-shaped lamp as he examined the desk.

"Here it is!" Blynk whispered with excitement a few minutes later as he lifted the heavy chest the size of a ten-liter fish tank from a secret compartment beneath the king's robes inside the closet. He heaved the massive, black chest in the air, leaning back to support its weight, toddled towards the bed, and plopped it on the thick mattress.

"Give me a minute to unlock it," said Jenkins as he knelt down before the chest and lifted the string necklace that held his white lock pick around his neck. He inserted the skinny pick into the lock and began prodding around, trying to release the lock.

"Why don't we just carry it out?" Jay asked as he eyed the door.

"Too heavy..." Blynk said.

"We'd be caught on the way out," Lynk said.

"Quiet!" Jenkins snapped. "I'm trying to bloody concentrate here."

They waited in silence as Jenkins tried to open the chest that hopefully contained the diamond locket.

Winston's short legs scrambled to keep up with McClevin as they stormed through the halls. "So you want the entire squad to search the first floor?"

McClevin's heavy feet slammed against the stone floor. "Yes. Have them thoroughly search the first floor. I have another squad backing up the guards on the second floor. Lord love a duck, why can't my guards be more attentive? The king will not be pleased."

Winston pushed his helmet up as it fell in front of his eyes. "Alright, I'll inform them immediately."

"Hold on," McClevin said. "I want to make sure all is well in the kitchen." They stopped in front of the thick oak door. McClevin grabbed the handle and flung it open.

He stared in shock. His teeth clattered as he bit down in fury. The maids all remained still, bound and gagged, lined up against the wall. He bent down to pick up a butcher's knife lying on the floor and then sliced open the gag of the nearest maid.

Coughing for air, the teary-eyed maid said, "Intruders.... There were three of them...."

McClevin's vision blurred with rage. "Where did they go?"

"They took the drinks," she said. "Two men and a woman. They had bandanas over their mouths."

McClevin's jaw dropped. How had three people infiltrated the castle with his guards patrolling every entrance? Whoever it was had to be skillfully trained—he needed to find them before the king learned of the breech.

"Winston! Alert the guards at once. Heighten security around the castle. No one enters or exits. It's no doubt the Valkadians trying to steal the locket. I'll head upstairs to the king's bedroom to get the locket. Move!"

"Y-Yes sir!" Winston stammered as he fled the kitchen.

"Almost...there..." Jenkins said as his lock pick rattled inside the chest.

The next sound they heard was not the satisfying click of the lock releasing. Footfalls thundered down the hallway outside the door. They all stared in dead silence at the slit of yellow light flowing underneath the door. No one moved. The footsteps grew louder, and the light underneath the door blackened. The curved handle wiggled briskly. Then, they heard a key slide in and unlock the door.

Jay's eyes watered as the door flew open: they had been caught.

A shadowy, cloaked figure outlined with the bright hallway light snuck into the room and closed the door. Under the moonlight, her golden hair glimmered. She locked the door and spun around, stepping back with a surprised expression. Her black cloak draped over her round shoulders with its hem a foot off the ground. She defensively swirled her wooden staff which contained sharp arrowheads on each end.

Lynk and Blynk instantly drew their swords and held them at ready. "Don't make a sound, or it'll be the last thing you do!" Lynk whispered.

"Who are you?" she asked, stepping towards them. "The king's guards do not wear such filth."

"Quiet I said!" Lynk and Blynk moved between her and the chest. Jay had never seen them look so serious. "Hurry up with the chest," he said to Jenkins.

"Give me one bloody minute."

The woman sidled away from the door. "Hmm...petty thieves." His hands trembling, Jay drew his cutlass. "Give me the chest," she said.

Lynk laughed. "You seem to be at a disadvantage. There's only one of you and four of us."

"I don't have time for this." Her stern face focused on the chest while she held her bow with one hand. She moved in short, silent steps that made her appear as if she was slowly gliding across the floorboards.

Lynk stepped towards her. "Drop the bow, now."
Click!

"Got it!" Jenkins said as he flipped open the top of the chest.

Lynk glanced back to the chest, but he only caught a glimpse of it before the woman's bow came crashing against his skull. Seeing his brother fall to the ground, Blynk gripped his blade and swung it madly at her. She expertly deflected his attacks with the bow and whipped her weapon against his side, knocking the breath out of him and sending him to the ground.

"Give me the locket!" she yelled, briskly walking towards Jenkins, who had grabbed the locket and clutched it firmly in his hand. The locket glimmered and gave off a faint pale light.

"Stop her!" Jenkins said as he tucked the locket in a brown pouch about his waist.

Jay charged at her from the side. She swung her bow in his direction, flinging one of the pointed ends towards his stomach. Instinct kicked in, and he leapt to the side, using his blade to avoid her attack. Remembering his training with Thyran, he slashed his blade towards her exposed side, but she leapt back and again flung her bow at him. The two parried back and forth. She was swift, but Thyran had been even quicker, so his reaction time allowed him to evade her numerous attacks.

Blynk and Lynk regained their composure and stumbled to their feet. Noticing Jenkins edging towards the window, the woman swung her bow against Jay's blade, kicked him in his exposed ribs, and shoved him off his feet. Before they could stop her, she bolted towards Jenkins and flicked her bow's arrowhead against the tan strap tied to his belt. Flinging her bow back, the arrowhead sliced the string, and the pouch fell to the floor. She dove towards the pouch and snatched it amid a summersault towards the window. Standing on the windowsill, she faced the four pirates while holding the pouch with the locket.

"You have nowhere to go!" Jenkins said as the pirates gathered around the window. "Hand us back the treasure."

"You thieves underestimate the value of this treasure," she said, glancing up the rope towards the roof where Soleus and Delcato waited. Her gaze then focused on the door; they could hear guards thundering down the hall. Jay's pounding heart echoed inside his head; his body tingled as he struggled to maintain his grip on his cutlass and ignore the pain in his side.

Lynk spoke in a calm voice. "Listen. You can't get out of here alive. We'll help you escape, and we'll give you a portion of whatever that is worth. Alright?"

"Fools. The value of this locket far surpasses that of silver or gold. This is the key to something far greater." She tucked the pouch inside her drab cloak.

"Get her!" Jenkins yelled, and they all dashed towards the window.

To Jay's disbelief, she spun around and dove off the windowsill. Jay leaned over the edge and watched her flapping cloak sink into darkness. He remained there, shocked, until Jenkins said, "Lock the door. Guards are coming!"

Lynk and Blynk locked the door and pushed one of the king's massive dressers over it. The guards slammed against the door, causing the dresser to shake.

"Alright, we can't get out the door as planned," said Jenkins. "We'll have to go with our backup plan. Quickly, let's get back up to the roof. Jay, you first." Jenkins held the rope for Jay to grab.

Sheathing his blade, Jay brushed his bruised hands together and wiped them on his pant. There was no time for mistakes this time. He grabbed the rope from Jenkins and started climbing back up to the roof. Perhaps from determination, perhaps from fear, he gathered enough strength to ascend the rope without slipping. Soleus and Delcato helped him on the roof when he was close enough.

"What happened?" Delcato asked.

"Someone..." Jay coughed. "Someone broke in the room and took it. The guards are outside the room now."

Delcato's face flashed white, the same ghostly complexion she had after waking from one of her frequent horrific nightmares. They all were speechless.

When Lynk, the last one to leave the bedroom, was halfway up the rope, Jay heard the guards plow open the door and knock the dresser to the ground. Lynk hustled to the roof and pulled up the rope.

"Back to the tower!" Delcato said as they sprinted across the slanted roof atop the castle of Eulia.

Anger swelled inside McClevin as he inspected the opened chest. "Damn them!" He threw the empty chest onto the floor. "They've stolen the locket!"

"Sir!" a tall guard with short, curly black hair called from the open window. "I just saw someone pulling up rope from the roof."

McClevin poked his head out the window and stared up to the roof. "They're on the roof," he said. "Send extra guards to secure the castle's perimeter. We cannot let these thieves escape! They are most likely working under King Cornelius's command, so consider them very dangerous. Move!"

"Shall I alert the king?" the tall guard asked as the rest scattered out of the room.

"No, Kileean, we have little time to waste. We'll notify him after we capture those criminals and return the locket to its rightful place. He's in the hospital wing comforting the queen; he doesn't need any additional stress."

"Yes, sir!" Kileean bowed and left the room.

McClevin closed his eyes and envisioned his conversation with Princess Alexandra the day before. "I will uphold my promise, Princess," he said aloud, kneeling before the bed and bowing his head. "I won't let you down."

"Well, where is it?" Cain demanded as they returned to the tower.

Jenkins pulled up the rope and untied it from the torch holder. "We ran into trouble."

"Trouble? What happened?" Cain asked as Jenkins wrapped the rope in a coil.

"This woman, she barged in the room and stole the locket."

"A woman?"

Lynk looked back over the roof to ensure they were not being followed. "She was very skilled. She caught us off-guard."

Frustration building in his voice, Cain asked, "And where is this lady now?"

"She jumped," Lynk said. "Jumped out the window of the king's bedroom."

Jay stood in front of Cain. "We must hurry. Guards are on the way."

"Guards! What guards?"

"They stormed in the room after we left. I don't know how they found us."

Without further discussion, the pirates dashed down the spiraling staircase to the base of the tower. Through the windows, Jay saw guards swarming outside the perimeter of the castle, though the remainder of the kingdom rested silently as the crowds had left the pubs and returned to their dwellings for the night.

When they arrived at the window where Jenkins, Lynk, and Blynk climbed up, they stopped. Jenkins fastened the rope around the hooked rock and tossed it over the windowsill. Without a sound, Jay and the others slid down the rope to the grassy ground.

Cain tossed his hand-carved staff down out the window before swinging over the windowsill and, with some difficulty, reached the ground, where Jay handed him his staff.

Jay's heart froze when torchlight suddenly illuminated the grass around their feet. "Over there by the tower!" someone shouted.

Before they could move, guards rushed towards them, forming a semi-circle and trapping them against the wall. Light flickered from the torches they bore. Their glistening shields, swords, and spears pointed towards them.

As the guards surrounded them, Jay and the others huddled together with their backs against one another and weapons drawn. "No one move," Cain instructed. Sweat dripped from Jay's brow, his lungs burned.

"Well, well." A shudder traveled down Jay's spine as he heard a threatening voice from behind the other guards. "Thought you could break into the king's bedroom, take the locket, and escape unharmed, eh?"

The guards shuffled to create a spot for him in their line. His plated armor and cerulean-crested helmet differed from the navy blue uniforms the rest of the guards wore. His powerful hands grabbed his sword as he brandished it at them. "Give me the locket."

Fear pulled on Jay's chest like a leaden weight; guards surrounded them in every direction, each pointing their weapons at them. Blood rushed to his head as he held his sword at ready. He continuously glanced at Cain, awaiting further instruction.

Cain said nothing.

"Give me the locket!" the silver-armored guard repeated.

Again, silence.

"Fine! Then I'll pry it from your dead—"

"The only prying that'll be going on here will be me prying me crew from your care, good knight."

Behind the guards, Captain Gaden firmly held a long-barreled pistol pointed towards the silver-armored guard. Relief washed over Jay's face when he saw his burly captain, stern and confident, coming to their aid.

"Ahh, another thief for the dungeons," the guard growled.

"Since I'm feeling a tad generous, I'll give ye 'til the count of three to release me crew afore I blast away your face." His hand remained still, pointing the deadly barrel at the guard's chest.

"Ha! Don't you dare threaten me you—"

"One."

"Drop the gun immediately or you'll be hung by dawn!"

"Two."

"You filthy, conniving, rotten—"

"Three."

"Wait!" the guard pleaded.

The captain laughed. "I dunno how long me finger can wait. It's awfully temptin' you know...."

The guard glared at them. "Release the prisoners."

"A wise decision," Captain Gaden said.

The guards hesitantly created an opening. Jay and the others quickly took refuge behind the captain, where he saw Ankin waiting in the distance. Where was Hector?

"Should anyone dare follow us," the captain said, "I'll do them the honor of introducing them to me pistol." Stepping backwards, the captain began descending the hill.

"Where's Hector?" Cain asked Ankin as they moved.

"I don't know. He said he had to check something. I hope he's safe."

"By King Emory's name, justice will be served!" the silver-armored guard shouted, waving his sword menacingly at the pirates.

When they were about a hundred yards away, the captain raised his pistol above the guards' heads. "To the boats!" he shouted as he fired his pistol. The loud bang surprised the guards; they all ducked while Jay and the others rushed down the hill.

"After them!" the guard yelled behind them.

A few minutes later, the pirates, led by Captain Gaden, reached the bottom of the hill and dashed through the town with the Eulian soldiers close on their tail. Houses and stores zipped passed as they sprinted for the beach. The smell of the fresh ocean surrounded the air as they got closer and closer to their ship—the crew could almost taste their escape. Jay glanced at his right as they ran. He recognized one of the more elegant jewelry stores he had noticed on the way to the Wicker Pub earlier that day.

"Hector!" the captain said.

Up ahead, Jay saw two people, one with a bow, the other with a sword, each facing each other about to engage in combat.

"You!" Lynk said. "You're still alive?"

The woman began backing up, the look of a cornered animal emblazoned her face as the crew of pirates approached. She glanced up at the stampede of guards only fifty yards behind them—within a few seconds, they would ambush the pirates and her.

"Eee-aaa!" she yelled as she swung her bow at Hector, who stood between her and the beach. Hector remained still.

Before she could strike, a loud bang shattered the air—the jewelry store behind them exploded. The blast threw Jay off his feet and sent him sprawling to the ground. When he looked up, he saw pieces of stone and rock soaring through the air. The debris rained down atop the Eulian soldiers, slowing them down during their pursuit.

The explosion had thrown all of Jay's crewmates to the ground, except for Hector. The woman's head smashed into the hard stone path, knocking her out cold.

Jay and the others stumbled to their feet.

"What the hell was that?" Lynk asked.

Jay listened to the unfortunate guards cry in pain from the pouring debris.

"I don't know," Hector said, "but now's our chance. Let's keep moving!"

"Captain," Jay said. "She has the locket."

"What? I thought you had the—well, we don't have time. Bring her with us!"

"Aye, cap'n." Hector sheathed his sword, scooped her up in his large arms, and flung her over his shoulder.

The pirates continued toward the beach. Several hundred yards back, the guards examined their wounds and burns.

"Get a medic here at once," McClevin ordered one of his men. "And request reinforcements immediately!"

The blast killed no one, though the debris injured all his men. Thoughts bombarded McClevin's head. The pirates were escaping. He could not let this happen. He had made a promise. "Stay here and wait for medical attention. Send in the reinforcements when they get here!"

"General, you can't go alone," a soldier groaned as he

held his burnt leg. "You'll be killed. I'll go with you."

"You're in no condition to fight. I'll be fine. Stay here, that's an order." Slightly burned and battered, McClevin collected every ounce of energy he had and pursued the pirates to the beach.

Captain Gaden's feet were first hitting the sand. "Quick, get into the boats."

The captain assisted Hector in carrying the woman into one of the empty boats. Jay glanced back to see Cain struggling with his walking staff to run through the sand. Behind him, the guard with silver armor chased after him.

"Get in the boat, Jay!" Captain Gaden ordered.

"But Cain..." Jay began.

"I'll get him. Hurry!"

Jay obeyed the captain and hurried into the boat.

The captain pushed off the boat with him, Hector, Ankin, and their female captive. Lynk, Blynk, Soleus, and Delcato filled another boat leaving one more for the captain and Cain.

Jay gasped when he saw the guard only feet behind Cain. Before the guard could attack, the captain rushed back up the beach and confronted him. Jay watched with awe as Captain Gaden raised his thick sword in the air and swung it at the guard, who lifted up his shield to block the attack. The guard then clashed his blade into the captain's and charged his shield into the captain's shoulder, causing him to stumble back.

Again and again, the guard used his shield to bash the captain, nearly trapping him against the ocean front. The captain gave a forceful, deep-throated yell as he slammed his sword with all his might against the guard's shield, causing it to shake uncontrollably. Smashing it again with his sword, the captain dislodged the shield from the guard's grip; the shield fell onto the sand.

"Now the playing field is even," Jay heard the captain say.

"It'll be life in the dungeons for you and your despicable crew!"

Without a shield, the guard swung his blade fiercely at the captain. Captain Gaden's meaty hands grabbed the guard's wrist before he could strike and jabbed the hilt of his sword into the guard's unprotected head—the guard fell to the sand.

With Cain safely in the boat, the captain left the guard on the beach, climbed on the boat, and, with Cain's help, rowed out into the ocean.

Jay, sitting in the boat, safely rowing towards their ship, watched the guard wobble in the sand trying to focus. The guard snatched his sword and raised it up towards the crew. But by the time he regained his senses, the pirates were too far for him to reach.

Jay felt relieved with their distance from land when he saw dozens more Eulian soldiers pouring onto the beach. His adrenaline pumped through his veins with such ferocity he could hardly focus.

Hector nudged his shoulder. "Well lad, we did it."

Jay smiled feebly. And in a tone of neither satisfaction or joy, he said "Yeah, we did."

4

The Diamond Locket

Jay tossed and turned all night; many things occupied his mind—the surprise appearance of the woman and her survival after such a long plummet, the mysterious explosion of the jewelry store that saved them from capture, and the lady's remark, *This is the key to something far greater*. What did it mean? And on top of that, now the authorities had a legitimate reason to hunt him down; breaking into the royal bedroom and stealing something of such value was surely a offense warranting death.

As if anticipating Jay's worries, Hector woke him early the next morning for a training session. Jay's eyes stung from lack of sleep, but he dragged himself out of his bed, got dressed, and grabbed his cutlass from his sheath resting against the bedpost.

Once outside, the blue ocean glistened under the morning sun in the cloudless sky. On deck, Jay limbered and then began training with Hector.

"Good!" Hector said as Jay smartly evaded his attack. "Now remember, keep your guard up!"

Hector charged at Jay, flicking his blade this way and that. Deep in focus, Jay blocked each attack. Then, Hector attempted to deal a massive blow, but Jay caught his blade in the air with his and held firm. With their blades locked together, Hector faked a kick towards Jay's side, causing him to flinch—

Hector whipped his blade against Jay's neck but

stopped just short of his skin. "What did I tell ya, mate? You gotta focus. You need to tune out distractions."

"Arg..." Jay grumbled as he knocked Hector's blade from his neck. He continued training with Hector for nearly an hour; time after time, Hector outsmarted him and stopped his blade just short of delivering a fatal blow.

"One more," Jay said after Hector swept his feet and flicked his blade against his chest.

"As you wish, Lil' Blue." Hector extended his hands and gave a short bow.

Again they clashed, wildly swinging their blades at one another. A few of their shipmates stopped for a moment to watch them as they expertly parried each other's offenses.

Jay concentrated more than ever. He knew he could win this—if he would just concentrate and not give in to any distractions. His blood pumped faster as he advanced towards Hector, causing him to move back towards the rail. This was the first time Jay had taken such an aggressive offensive; however, he tried to keep his eagerness low and concentrate on the battle.

Behind Hector, Jay saw a bucket of water used for mopping the deck. Seizing the opportunity, he slashed his blade into Hector's, whirled alongside him, scooped up the bucket with the tip of his cutlass, and sent the bucket of water splashing in Hector's face. Doused with water, Hector leaned away, trying to dry his eyes.

Now that he finally had the upper edge, Jay's blood pumped faster; he could not subdue his eagerness any longer. He flung his blade towards Hector's exposed neck.

Hector's agility surpassed Jay's, and he snapped up his sword in defense just in time to smash Jay's cutlass away from his grip. "Yer getting better," he said as he held the point of his sword at Jay's heart. "Got a little overanxious though, didn't ya?"

Gritting his teeth, Jay picked up and sheathed his sword without answering.

"Don't fret, Little Blue," Lynk said as he sauntered towards them. "You can hold your own against any pirate on board save for Hector and the cap'n."

"Yeah," Soleus said, walking behind Lynk. "Yer a fearsome fighter at such a young age, if I do say so meself."

Jay smiled, then he heard the captain thundering across the deck towards them.

"Well done, mates!" the captain said. "Our lady prisoner did indeed have the locket, which is safely in our hands. She seems to be claimin' we be blunderin' idiots for not understandin' the value of the locket or somethin'."

"Yeah, she said that before she stole it from us," Jay said.

"Hrmph..." the captain stroked his frizzled beard. "Well, perhaps there is some legacy of this treasure we be unaware of. It is odd...we can't seem to get the blasted thing open. So, it may behoove us to find out whatever knowledge she may have. Jay, perhaps yeh'd best have a chat with her. See what you can find out."

"You sure cap'n? Perhaps Hector or Soleus—"

"There'll be no second guessin' me today, Jay. We all know yer the best dealin' with people...ye have that charm about yeh, mate. I think yeh'd best have a talkin' to with miss...err...still don't know her name. But ye best be gettin' down there afore long. I need to decide what to do with her."

Jay hesitated a moment, but decided there was no use arguing with the captain; perhaps he would be able to pry some information from her. "Aye cap'n," he said and moved towards the stairs, but stopped after a few paces and turned back. "Oh, and cap'n...thanks for helping us back in Eulia."

"Bah! Me word is me word. I promised yeh'd be safe. Now get goin'!" His eyes flicked from side to side at the other pirates, who were all watching and listening intently. "What are the rest of ye scurvy lot doin'? Back to work!"

Jay headed towards the stairs leading below deck. Dozens of his crewmates bustled across the deck, some on watch, some cleaning, some guiding the sails, some off-shift drinking rum. Some giggled as he walked by, encouraging him to take full advantage of his interrogation with the female prisoner. Jay looked away in disgust and traveled below deck towards the bottom level. As he descended the stairs, he heard noises of some of the crew in the cellar celebrating their victory.

On the lower level, the dark hallway stretched the length of the ship. As the ship rocked, doors on the left wall swung open and closed, creaking with every movement. He heard the swishing of water as it rubbed along the ship's exterior. A few torches hung from holsters along the wall opposite the rooms; the silent flames radiated a flickering orange light that illuminated parts of the hallway, leaving several blotches of darkness. Walking in and out of the light, he neared the end of the hallway where the prisoner waited.

When he reached the room, he grabbed a box of matches next to a candlestick on a tiny round table outside the door. Setting a match ablaze, he lit the candle and grabbed it, along with the keychain from a hook in the wall, unlocked the door with the key, and stepped inside the room.

Aside from the flickering flame on candlestick, blackness engulfed the room. A musky smell of rotting wood in the air, Jay moved the candlestick to illuminate the vertical metal bars of the cell. As the candlelight illuminated the bare wooden floorboards, he noticed a few black rats scurry to avoid the light.

A stool resting in front of the steel cage materialized out of the darkness as he approached. The captive woman was leaning against the damp wall at the back of the cell, her head tilted towards the ground with her dirty hair dangling in front of her face—she appeared to be sleeping.

Back in Eulia, his head had been pounding too fiercely to make out her appearance. Though now, with his nerves settled, he could see her clearly. Her smooth skin and young face indicated she was probably in her early twenties, or maybe even late teens. Though she appeared slender, he remembered how she handled her bow in swift, crisp movements back in the castle, indicating she was not as fragile as her appearance. Her dirty golden hair dangled before her face, blocking her eyes and nose. He watched her smooth hair move gently with her every breath.

He set the candlestick on the stool, approached the bars, and opened his mouth to say something, but she spoke first.

"What do you want with me?"

He closed his mouth as he shuffled through his thoughts, trying to locate the right words. One wrong word, and she would close off to him.

"I have a few questions."

"I do not talk to scum," she snapped as she looked up at him; her green eyes glimmered in the candlelight.

"Err...well..." he said, delving for something intelligent to say.

A moment passed, and then her head sunk back to the ground. "Just kill me or leave me for dead. I have nothing to say to you."

He set the candle on the ground and sat on the wooden stool. "We are not going to kill y—"

"Then what do you want with me?" she said without looking up.

"Err... Are you thirsty or anything?" Jay asked, hoping kindness might soften her up.

She seemed surprised by his abrupt change of questioning. After a pause, she said, "No."

"Are you hungry...or cold? Maybe I can get you a blanket or something?" He realized the captain would have taken a much more direct route in prying information from her, but he would find something that she wanted.

"A blanket? Am I at an inn or something?" She looked up and narrowed her eyes at him. "Just tell me what you want from me."

"Alright then. I want to know why you were after the locket."

She hesitated. "You wouldn't understand."

"Then explain it to me."

She sat in silence.

"Please," he said, but still, she remained quiet. Listening to the light tapping of water dripping from the ceiling to the floor, Jay sat in silence for a couple of minutes. He glanced out at her ripped cloak and her bow resting against a wall outside of her cell. It was such an odd weapon for a woman, the bow, but she had apparently mastered its technique.

"Well, can you at least tell me your name?" he asked at last.

Still, she stubbornly said nothing.

Realizing he was getting nowhere, he sighed and walked out of the room, leaving the candle to illuminate the darkness. A few minutes later, he returned with a glass of fruit juice and a plate with some food.

"I figured you might be hungry. Here's some pineapple juice and bread." He set the plate in front of her cell. "It should be fresh. We stocked up in Eulia last week."

She eyed him suspiciously as if expecting some sort of trickery, but after a few seconds, she crawled towards the front of the cell and examined the food. Her green eyes staring into his, she grabbed a slice of the bread and took a bite.

Watching her eat, Jay sat on the stool massaging his palm with his thumb. After a few minutes, his eyes traveled around the room, which was rather bare: just some empty barrels, fragments of rope, and breadcrumbs the rats had horded. How depressing it would be to live down here.

"Lyssa," she said, after swallowing some of the juice.

Jay looked at her.

"My name is Lyssa," she said, licking her lips.

Smiling, he said softly, "My name is Jay Perry." He thought he caught a surprised look on her face, but he ignored it. "Please know, Lyssa, that I do not mean you any harm. The cap'n will release you when we next arrive on land, but he is curious what you meant when you mentioned the unique value of the locket."

"You're all just a bunch of thieving pirates," she said "All you understand is gold. And if that's your definition of value, then the locket is worthless to you."

She watched a black rat snatch a crumb of bread with its tiny claws and nibble on it. "Please, give me back the locket. I'll pay whatever you want, just...let me have it."

But Jay felt determined to get more information.

"You said it was the key to something far greater...what did you mean by that?"

"You and your limited intelligence would prevent you from understanding," she said, scooting back to the wall and leaning against it.

"Try me," Jay said as he leaned forward.

Pressing her head against the wooden wall, she tilted her head upward. "I was told it is a map to a greater treasure, one hidden and protected by Ashlen."

"But that's a myth," Jay said. "For centuries, men have sought that treasure, but no one has ever found it."

"Well, if it's a myth, then it's worth nothing to you, is it?"

"Okay, well, what is this supposed treasure Ashlen hid?"

She looked at him and raised her eyebrows. "Are you not familiar with the legend?"

Jay shook his head. "I've heard stories of Ashlen, the wizard who supposedly created this world, but I've always been under the impression that they were just fairy tales."

"Ha! Fairy tales. I wish! Haven't you ever considered the design of this planet? Two kingdoms, one standing for freedom, the other, oppression. The planet's only one thousand years old. Do you think civilization advanced this far in that short of time?"

"Well then what does the legend say to explain that?"

Lyssa's eyes fell as she rehashed her recollections. "When Ashlen created this world, he only created a single kingdom: Eulia, as a symbol for freedom. He created this world to escape from the tyranny in his own. A powerful warlock named Mystro created a ravenous army of the most foul races on that world, and they called themselves the Dark Tide. Shortly after Ashlen created Lassar, he battled Mystro while all of Ashlen's men fled to our planet through a portal. Unfortunately, several of Mystro's men also managed to make it through the portal, too many for Ashlen's army to stop. Thankfully, Ashlen stopped Mystro before he himself could reach Lassar.

"The hundreds of the Dark Tide who made it to Lassar created the Kingdom of Valkadia. They hope to somehow revive the portal and return to their master."

Jay blinked several times, digesting her story. "So, will this hidden treasure somehow reopen that portal?"

Her eyes shifted to the candlelight flickering off the bare ceiling. "I am not entirely sure, but it was something very precious to Ashlen. Something, at least some believe, that will bestow upon the finder a special power. Maybe it's a secret weapon or a magical artifact? I really don't know."

A tone of disbelief in his voice, Jay said, "So this locket is really a map to that treasure?"

She nodded.

"But it looks just like an ordinary locket, well, except for the fact it's made out of pure diamond."

"But you haven't been able to open it, have you?"

Jay's eyes widened. "How did you know that?"

"That's what he told me...that the locket is sealed shut until it's taken to Ashlen's Tomb, deep in the Dryfus Mines."

"Who's *he*?"

He sensed her tense up at this question; she squeezed her eyes shut and shook slightly, like she was having a horrible nightmare.

"Lyssa?"

"I...he was just another pirate, like you."

"If all pirates are idiots, why believe this one?"

"Does it matter?"

"It might. The cap'n will want to know where you are getting this information from, and I just—"

"Enough!" She threw her rumpled hair out of her face and glared at him. "I've told you everything I know about the locket. You promised you would let me go."

Jay withered under her frightful stare. He knew he

was getting nowhere with those questions. Speaking softly, he said, "How do we open the locket?"

"I told you. Go to Ashlen's Tomb."

"But what do we do when we get there?"

Lyssa looked at him, folding her arms over her bent, dirt-covered knees. "I don't know."

Jay could tell by her tone she was being honest. Lifting himself from the wobbling stool, he said, "I need to tell the cap'n and see what he wishes. You will be released though, I promise."

Her face turned away from him in silence. Grabbing the plate, glass, and candle, he exited the room, leaving her alone once again to a pitch black cell as he walked upstairs to the captain's cabin and explained what he learned.

"Ehem," the captain cleared his throat after listening to Jay. Walking over the red carpet in his cabin, the captain strode to the wide window lined with fine strips of shiny metal on the outside. "A map, eh?"

"Yes cap'n."

"And we need to go to the Dryfus mines, eh?"

"Yes cap'n."

"Funny," he said, scratching his beard, "Hector suggested we go there too."

He rubbed his hand along the tapestry—an embroidered map of Lassar with numerous pins stabbed in various locations where they had plundered treasure—that hung next to the window.

"Yer sure she's not tellin' ye fairy tales? I'm not one for sending me crew to chase make-believe riches."

"I think...she seemed to be telling the truth."

"Hmm." The captain hulked over to his table and grabbed a gray bottle. Leaning back exposing a section of his round, hairy stomach, he took an appreciative drink. Wiping his lips with his sleeve, he said, "Those blasted mines have been deserted for years anyways, and we're only a day's travel away. We shouldn't have too much trouble. Let Gideon know our destination."

He grabbed a pin with a red, flat head and stabbed it into the tapestry beneath a mound-shaped symbol with the label 'Dryfus Mines.'

Warm day turned to cool night as their ship sailed closer to the Dryfus Mines. Jay joined the crew in the cellar that night to further celebrate the success of their mission; he watched some assemble around round wooden tables sharing drinks and tales of their exaggerated triumphs, but he noticed many gathered around a square table where Cain and Jenkins were enthralled in a game of Elementum. Stacks of dragones were strewn across the table as the spectators gambled on the victor. Jay shuffled closer to watch.

Cain resolutely moved his black dragon game-piece over a mountaintop near Jenkins's wizard piece. Deep in thought, Jenkins leaned forward with his chin resting on his hand.

"Lil' Blue!" Soleus shouted as he entered the cellar and moved towards the table.

Jay smiled. "How's it going?"

"It's going good, I was just about to—oh!" his eyes shifted to the checkered game board. "Cain's playing and no one told me! Who's winning?"

"Soleus, quiet!" Jenkins snapped.

"I'm guessing Cain," Soleus whispered to Jay.

When Jenkins finally moved his wizard piece, Cain instantly pushed another dragon piece across the board to a square next to Jenkins's wizard and, with a flick of his wrist, smashed the bottom of his dragon against Jenkins's wizard, knocking it on its side.

"Nice try," Cain said as he scooped up a small bag of coins from the table and stood up. Most the crowd cheered as they collected their winnings from those who bet against Jenkins, who stared at the board, replaying his final moves in his head.

"Hmph," Cain said. He glanced at Jay under his hooded eyes for a second before limping out of the cellar.

"Enough of this!" Lynk yelled, pushing his way through the crowd. "Blynk! Get over here!" Lynk jumped up and stood on a chair as his brother hurried to his side. "Now that the grouch is gone, let's begin the celebration!"

The crew shouted in agreement as Hector carried in a huge barrel of rum and slammed it on the table where Lynk was standing. Lynk readied his wooden fiddle while his younger brother raised a green harmonica to his lips. They tapped their feet once, twice, thrice, and the music rang through the air as the pirates filled their mugs with the pungent beverage.

Jay backed away from the stampede of pirates eager for their well-earned drink. He watched Soleus fill two gray mugs to the top and weave through the crowd over to Delcato, who appeared oblivious to his advance.

"Gotcha a drink Del!" Soleus blurted in her ear.

She jumped from the sudden loud noise in her ear and looked over her shoulder to see a beaming smile etched on his round face. "Go bug Karen." She dismissed him with a wave of her hand.

But Soleus ignored her and sat down on a short barrel right next to her. "But we had a deal. I didn't bug ya during the mission, did I?"

She thought a moment; then, rolling her eyes, she said, "Alright, one drink, but that's it." She brushed her black hair out of her face so she could drink.

"Yes!" Soleus bounced with joy. Shaking with excitement, he adjusted himself in his seat and swung the mug towards her; he failed to see her lean forward and dropped his jaw with horror when the mug rammed into her chest and the liquid splashed all over her lap. Frantically, he grabbed a tattered rag from a nearby table and wiped her lap with it. "Sorry Del!"

"Soleus!" she yelled, slapping his vagrant hand away. She inhaled a large breath of air, clamped down tightly on her jaw. "Just...give me the drink," she said between her gritted teeth.

"I just—"

"Let's just have a drink, okay?" Taking her now half-empty mug from him, she sank into her seat and began sipping the drink.

Shaking his head at the poor pirate, Jay leaned back against the wall. He watched Karen and Hector, their elbows locked, prance around the floor, kicking their feet to the melody from Lynk and Blynk, who danced alongside the others. Soon, more and more pirates joined in, and the ground rattled as their feet slammed against it in sync. Arms flung through the air, pirates spun around each other, rum spilled over half-drank mugs thrashing hither and thither, and the roaring laughter echoed off the cellar walls.

Nodding his head along with the music, Jay thought about his talk with Lyssa. Her story seemed farfetched at best, but she did seem sincere. She was aware they couldn't open the locket—but who was the pirate she was talking about? And why wasn't he with her when she tried to steal it? He forgot to ask her how she survived such a fall from the window. Maybe it had something to do with the locket. Maybe it had some mystical powers.

No...it couldn't. The idea was ridiculous. The whole

thought of magic was absurd, a childish fantasy.

Karen's silky hair whipped across Jay's face and disturbed his thoughts. "Come on, dance with us!" she said, grabbing his wrists and pulled him off the wall.

"No really, I'm fine, I was just—"

But she was not listening. She guided him to an open spot in the floor, spun around to face him, clasped his hands, and swung her hips along with the rhythm. She placed one of his hands on her velvet corset as she spun around. Concentrating on his feet and hands, Jay followed her lead.

Lynk tossed shreds of tawdry silk fabric they used for magic tricks into the air, creating a jubilant atmosphere in the typically dark, musky cellar. The room and all its commotion—the stomping feet, shouting people, blasting instruments, falling fabric—whirled around as Jay danced on the rumbling floor. He had completely forgotten about Soleus and Delcato until he heard Soleus's booming voice right behind him.

"So...yer hair looks nice and straight..." Soleus said.

Jay thought he heard Delcato click her tongue in disgust.

"Yer eyes make me think of—"

*Please stop...*Jay thought. *You're only making this worse on yourself.*

"Soleus, enough," she pleaded. "I've finished my drink like we agreed. I'm going to go now."

"Come on you two!" Lynk said. "Quit being such a grouch Del! Get up an' dance!"

"No, I'm going to bed." She stood up. "I already had my drink with you like we agreed."

"Please Del, just one dance," Soleus said.

"Yeah," Jenkins said, holding a bottle of rum in his left hand as he leaned back at a table with his feet propped on an adjacent chair. "Just one dance for the man. Don't be such a bloody grouch. You're turning into Cain."

Sighing heavily, she said, "Fine. One dance, then I'm leaving."

Jay could practically feel Soleus leaping out of his skin with joy. Soleus flung her off the barrel and dragged her on the floor. Before they began dancing, Jay caught Lynk deviously wink at his brother. The fast-paced music suddenly slowed into a peaceful, romantic melody. Lynk's head shook with dreamy drama as he played his fiddle beside his brother.

Soleus stumbled closer to Delcato and slid his hands down to her waist. Casting a venomous glare at Lynk and Blynk, she moved along with him. As the song progressed, Lynk moved closer and played the music even louder and more dramatic right beside them. Peering over the two while they danced, Lynk played his heart out; he reminded Jay of a music conductor who had just found the sweet spot in a song and was relishing every second of it.

Then, in a daring move, Soleus took her hand and lifted it in the air for a spin, but he clumsily stepped on her shoe and stumbled. In a frenzy not to make a scene, the hefty pirate attempted to regain his balance; in doing so, he brushed Delcato with his massive shoulder and knocked her to the ground.

The music came to a sudden halt, the crew roared with laughter. Her face a bright shade of scarlet, Delcato stormed to her feet and dashed out of the cellar without a word.

Lynk walked over to Soleus and patted his back. "It's okay mate, at least you had a dance with her."

Even though Soleus shrugged and slapped on his usual wide smile, Jay sensed his sadness. Jay glanced at Karen, who smiled and nodded, and he invited Soleus to finish the dance with her.

Lynk and Blynk continued playing their instruments while the crew celebrated through the quiet night. Free from fear or anxiety, the crew drifted into a night of bliss. With the precious locket tucked safely away in the captain's drawer, their ship, *Isabella*, glided along the calm ocean, away from Eulia and towards Ashlen's Tomb.

5

Dark Clouds

Inside the Eulian castle, General McClevin hurried in King Emory's wake as he stormed across the stone-tiled floor. McClevin was careful to avoid the king's sky-blue robe billowing out behind him.

"Who was with him?" the king asked in a demanding tone.

"A band of pirates," McClevin said running to the king's side.

"And all of them managed to escape?"

"Yes my king; they fled by ship."

The two rounded a corner and ascended a wide stair-case.

"Their destination?"

"Unknown."

"Damn them!" The king's gray hair thrashed as he ran up the stairs.

McClevin darted up ahead to open a hulking metal door, which led to the king's throne room; the king entered briskly.

Upon the king's entrance, twenty assorted knights and elders rose and faced the king; their murmuring dwindled as the king swiftly advanced towards his stone throne at the far side of round, granite table. McClevin hurried after the king and stood by his side as the king threw himself down in his throne.

"What's our status, Orrin?" he asked.

Orrin, an elder man with a tapered, white beard and dirt-speckled gray hair, remained standing while the rest seated themselves. Pushing up his round glasses, he said, "The thieves have eschewed our forces."

The mighty king pounded his fist on the hard table; Orrin took his seat.

Marcus, a man clad in a white uniform with a golden shield embroidered across the chest, stood. "My king, we have managed to identify one of the rats: Jay Perry."

"The man wanted for the murder of Governor Almsy," one of the knights added.

"Indeed," McClevin said. "And he was traveling with a horde of pirates."

"Pirates!" the king repeated, throwing his hands in the air. "How did such an inane group of imbeciles penetrate my castle unnoticed, break into *my* room without difficulty, and escape with my most precious treasure unscathed?"

Orrin leaned forward. "Begging your pardon, but they were very wise; they knew perfectly well what they were doing. We were able to retrace their route successfully, but one thing mystifies me still. The knights found a flimsy, miniature parachute dangling from a tree branch beneath your bedroom window, but McClevin saw them climbing down from the western tower. It appears one of them leapt out of the window and separated from the others."

"And what does that mean?" the king asked.

Orrin stroked his beard, staring at the center of the table, lost in thought.

"I am not sure, Your Highness."

The room went silent. The king held out his sinewy hand and rotated his precious, black diamond ring his wife gave him.

"My anger rests not within the loss of the locket, but

rather with the consequences this will have on the integrity of the peace between our nation and Valkadia."

"You think the peace will be compromised?" Orrin asked.

"Surely they can't hold us accountable for an act of pirates!" said McClevin. "That's absurd!"

"I wouldn't put it past the old coward," said Marcus.

"We had an agreement," the king explained, "that Eulia could host the Gorgrim Tournament, but in exchange, we had to give up our diamond locket to the winner. Cornelius will no doubt blame us for reneging on our agreement. The extent of his reaction...I'm not sure."

A thin woman slithered out of her chair; strands of black and gray hair fell from her head concealing all of her face except parts of her dark eyes.

"Perhaps it is wise to out-maneuver that worm Cornelius and assemble our soldiers," she hissed. Her black, tight robes complimented her dark hair and eyes.

"Your haste for hostile action concerns me, Agatha," said Orrin.

"Your persistence for peace weakens the defenses of this kingdom," she shot venomously.

"Watch your tongue, Agatha," said McClevin. "You're in the presence of the king."

"Always a pet, aren't you McClevin?" She curled her black lips, baring her white teeth. "Whether it be today, tomorrow, or years from now, Cornelius will eventually destroy the peace treaty between our kingdoms, and if we remain so saturated with the dream of peace, our army will weaken and we will succumb to the Valkadian Empire. My King, we *must* be proactive."

"And be proactive we shall, Agatha," the king said. "However, be reckless we shall not."

"Well if you hadn't prohibited the use of firearms, even from our own soldiers, they wouldn't have escaped, now would they?"

"Silent!" McClevin yelled. "You know what happened to the queen!"

"But that's no reason to—"

The king motioned with his hand for her to sit. "Enough, Agatha. Enough."

McClevin was sure he saw her mumbling as she bowed and slumped back to her seat; her scrutinous eyes glared around the room.

Orrin again rose to his feet. "Shall we postpone the tournament until we have recovered the locket? I am confident we can formulate a logical reason for the delay."

King Emory took a moment to think before responding. "Cornelius cannot receive word of what happened here last night. We will grant his kingdom permission to host the final matches of the Gorgrim Tournament as a gesture of kindness. Hopefully, the flock of merchants to his kingdom will deter him from questioning our motives."

"And when he finds out we don't have the locket?" Agatha asked.

Again, silence swept the room. All eyes gazed at the king, awaiting his decision. McClevin remained still, wearing his plated armor, his sword by his side, his helmet riding his head, his entire body waiting for the king's command.

Quiet murmurs filled the room, and when the king stood, everyone followed his lead and got to their feet. When the ambient murmuring ceased, the king announced his decision.

"Dark clouds approach our shores once again. We must work together to ensure the safety and prosperity of our people. The order I am about to issue, if unsuccessful, will no doubt sever the trust between Eulia and Valkadia, which will send us spiraling down the path of eventual warfare once again. It is therefore vital that we do everything in our power to ensure that does not happen."

His commanding eyes shifted across the room.

"Marcus!" he yelled.

"Yes, my king?"

"Send word notifying King Cornelius that Valkadia can host the remainder of the tournament. Inform him that he may use any of our resources for preparing the event."

"It will be done."

"General!"

The king turned towards McClevin, who snapped to attention, his armor clanking as he did so.

"I bestow upon you the most important task. Assemble the Knights of Voorus. You must capture those pirates and recover the locket before the tournament. Take the *Liberáte*"

McClevin felt nauseous, his hands grew clammy. The *Liberáte* was the most powerful Eulian warship. His heart raced as he swallowed the importance of his mission. "Your Highness, the pirates are heavily armed with guns. May we—"

"Yes, you have my permission to man the soldiers with firearms. Just...I don't want a re-occurrence of what happened with my wife."

"Yes, my king."

King Emory again addressed everyone around the table.

"I implore you all to offer your assistance. Much of the lives of our people depend on the secrecy of last night's events and the return of the locket. Do what you can to help. Orrin, meet me in my chambers after everyone departs. You all are dismissed."

McClevin began his stride for the door, but King Emory grabbed his arm. McClevin looked over and saw the king's uneasiness in his wide blue eyes.

"I fear we may only have ten to fifteen days until Valkadia will complete their preparations to continue the tournament. You will have that long to find and return the locket."

McClevin raised his chin nobly. "I will not fail you, my king."

"Good." A faint smile spread across the king's narrow, wrinkled face.

When the king loosened his grip, McClevin shuffled passed the crowd of people and exited the room to find Winston waiting for him outside. "Gather the Knights of Voorus and have them ready by the dock," McClevin said. "We leave in an hour."

"Yes, general," said Winston, pushing his oversized helmet above his eyes. He scurried down the corridor.

McClevin heard a venomous voice from behind.

"A little tense, general?"

McClevin clenched his fist. "Agatha," he scowled without looking.

"I would be too...after letting such a clumsy band of pirates break into the royal bedroom and escape without a scratch."

"I will not answer to the likes of you." He moved to walk forward, but she jumped in front of him, blocking his path. "Out of my way!"

She lowered her head and glanced up into his eyes; McClevin cringed at the sight of her: her narrow, venomous eyes; sharp, pointed white teeth; chilling dark skin and blackened lips. Her appearance screamed she was nothing more than evil, conniving, and manipulative.

"Just know, my brave general, that while you are sailing the seas on your wild goose chase, I shall prepare the soldiers for combat."

"You're despicable!"

He pushed her aside and approached the stairs.

"Do you have a heading, wise general?" she asked, and when he glanced over his shoulder, he saw her black lips melt into a devious grin.

"I have never failed my king; I will find those pirates. I promise you that.

She tilted her head back and laughed. "You don't even know where to begin. You'll be a pathetic dog chasing his own tail. The king is unwise entertaining such an optimistic attitude of your success. When Cornelius—"

"Silence! Or I'll have you arrested for—"

"For what, general?"

His face burned. She was testing his patience. "You are unwise questioning the king, Agatha."

She grinned. "Ahh, we shall see in due time. Run along now, brave soldier. Take a good look at the kingdom before you set sail. It may be the last time you see it in all its glory."

Quivering with anger, McClevin whirled around, stormed down the staircase, and left the castle. Blinking as his eyes adjusted to the bright sun, he descended the grassy hill towards the city. Halfway down, he looked to the side and saw a woman wearing a sandy brown kirtle with her knees folded against the green grass. Her two daughters, they must have been only four or five years old, scuttled nearby collecting flowers. "Daddy'll love this one mama!" one of them called out.

"No! He'll like this one better!" the other challenged.

"Oh come on you two, daddy'll love them the same." She smiled and shook her head at the two.

"I'm gonna get the most!" said the older one.

"No you're—"

The younger girl stumbled on a rock poking out of the ground. Like a small explosion, the flowers shot up in the air and rained down upon the girl as she landed flat on her face in the grass, which was moist from the morning dew.

The older one at once broke into a chant. "You lost your flowers...you lost your flowers..."

Tears flowing down her cheeks, the girl lifted her head from the grass. "Mama...that's not fair!"

The mother crawled on her hands and knees towards her daughter and lifted her to her feet. "Oh come on now," she spoke in a babied tone. "I guess you'll have to work twice as hard to beat your sister." She leaned and whispered something into the daughter's ear, and then the daughter sprang back into action, full of newfound excitement, and began her own chant.

"Mama said I can beat you...Mama said I can beat you!"

The mother glanced over at McClevin and shook her head again, a wide smile on her pale face. He returned her smile, remembering briefly some of his childhood, the joys of having not a care in the world, just having a blast playing with friends. He needed to protect his kingdom so every child could live as carefree and have as much fun as he had.

Within an hour, he gathered the necessary supplies for travel: weapons, food, drink, sailing implements, and whatever else struck him as being useful. After making his final trip across the dock to the ship, he took a moment to examine the city and admire the serenity: the laughter in the streets, the baking sun, and splash of cool ocean water on the beach. He closed his eyes and engraved that snapshot into memory; that image was what he swore his life to protect and preserve.

"Beautiful day to be sailing," Jack Porter said, stepping beside McClevin.

"Hmm...yeah."

"You know, in all the years I've known you, you have never spoken in such a dreary tone. Something wrong?"

Forcing a chuckle, McClevin said, "Ha, not at all! Just a little tired. Late night last night, guarding the castle and all."

"Hmm...that be the truth, eh?"

McClevin swallowed.

"Anyways, I've done as you asked. All the sailors and supplies are on board. The Liberáte's ready to set sail when you are."

McClevin nodded and flicked open his eyes. Resting a hand on Jack's shoulder, he said, "Thank you, Jack."

As he ascended the rickety ramp to the ship, his men assembled on deck and awaited orders while the sailors prepared the ship for departure. "Alright men," he said when he reached the deck. "Winston should have briefed you of our mission." He scanned his specialized soldiers, the Knights of Voorus, who, wearing blue uniforms with a light azura embroidered on the front encompassed by a golden circle, stood at attention. "Now, to your stations! We leave immediately!"

While Kileean and Winston handed out instructions to the men, McClevin walked to the ramp and bent down to heave it in, but he stopped when he heard a thumping noise running up the ramp. It was a woman in a jade skirt that hung loosely over her white bodice; she held a dark green hood over her snowy hair. When he recognized her face, he gasped, dropped to a knee, and bowed his head.

"Princess Alexandra!"

"There's no need for formality," she said softly.

He rose from his knee. "Why are you here?"

"I am coming with you."

"Lord love a duck! Your father would not want you voyaging on such a perilous quest."

"He can say what he will. I am not going to sit comfortably in the luxuries of my room and do nothing while my people face danger."

He shook his head without any thought. "I cannot let you to come with us. Does your father know you are here?"

"No. I told him I was going to Delphina to visit Marcie. I told him I would be accompanied by some of your men."

"That's absurd! It would take several days to travel that far."

"Which is why he'll never know I'm missing." She tried to weave around him, but he stopped her.

"If something were to happen to you, I would be held responsible."

"But you need my help to find those pirates."

"I—what? What do you mean?"

"What experience do have you navigating the seas?"

"I, uhh—"

"Exactly! During the war, I was forced into hiding and traveled from village to village across the ocean. My familiarity with these waters will assist you in finding those pirates."

He felt like a kid stealing a bowl of ice cream before dinner—he wanted her help, but the king would be furious if he ever found out. His chest felt hollow. Time was running out. He needed to make a decision.

Grinning as if she sensed his mental conflict, the princess pushed him aside and boarded the ship.

6

Ashlen's Tomb

The image of the silver-armored guard's stern face burned in Jay's mind through the night, robbing him of what few hours of sleep he had hoped to get. His stomach churned—the guards had seen him. Eulian soldiers would be swarming around Lassar, hunting him down. And this time, he would have nothing to say in his defense; he had committed a crime.

Jay sat on the stairs leading to the bridge. Up ahead, he saw the Dryfus Mines. Under the overcast sky, the mine rose up from the dark misty sea like a giant turtle's back, a mossy green color on top fading to a light gray near the splashing waves. The entire mound was drab and weathered with age. On the far left side, barely in view, was a narrow, cave-like mouth where a thin stream of water flowed inside.

A steady thumping of Captain Gaden treading across the quarterdeck caught his attention. "Alright me crew, close yer lips and open yer ears. We be nearin' the mines an' we've no time to waste. Hector! Secure the sails. Jenkins! Drop anchor. Soleus! Fetch me my blade. Jay! Bring up the prisoner."

"Aye cap'n," Jay said as the captain continued barking orders to the remainder of the crew. He descended below deck, snatching a short coil of rope on the way, where Lyssa was waiting. He lit the candle and entered the holding room; her dark violet blouse was rumpled and dirty from being crammed in the damp cell.

"Time to go ashore." He placed the fiery lamp on a wooden barrel. Its light glimmered around the room.

Her eyes widened at the sight of the rope. "I shall not be bound."

"Then you will remain in here."

"But you promised I would be released once we arrived on land."

"The captain wants to make sure what you said was true. We are at the Dryfus Mines now."

It was hard to tell under the dim lighting, but he thought he saw her leg jerk subtly at his mention of the mines.

"I.... The Dryf...."

"Please place your hands through the bars."

"Do not talk to me like I'm an animal!"

"I'm sorry, I cannot let you out without binding."

She slammed her hands against the metal bars of her cage. "Oh and where am I going to go? I would be stranded on an island if I fled."

"The captain was very strict with his orders." She seemed honest, and he doubted she would do them any harm if he trusted her. But what would the rest of the crew say if she did somehow put them in peril?

She rescinded her hands. "I will not go with you treated as a slave. Find Ashlen's Tomb on your own."

This was harder than he anticipated; he thought she would have been overjoyed to be finally let out of her cell.

"Lyssa, I trust you, and I know you wouldn't backstab us. Please understand I really have no choice. If I let you up there without any bindings, the crew will restrain you at once. I give you my word, as soon as you show us the way to Ashlen's Tomb, we'll release you."

She stepped to the front of her cage; her smooth face

was now fully illuminated by the flickering candlelight. "If you don't, I will find some way to break free and show you no mercy when I do."

Jay nodded. "I understand. Now, please, put your hands between those two bars."

"One more thing, when this is over, I want my bow back."

Jay glanced to her bow propped against the wall.

"Alright. Is it worth a lot or something?"

She clicked her tongue and rolled her eyes. "Always thinking in terms of money, aren't you?" When he did not respond, she said, "It's very sentimental to me, and I want it back."

"I'll give it back as soon as you help us find Ashlen's Tomb."

A moment later, he guided Lyssa, whose wrists were bound by rope, up on deck. The ship had stopped moving, save for the swaying with the wind and ocean currents. Those pirates not involved in the Eulian mission sneered at the captive woman, whom they had never seen; Jay kept a watchful eye on them.

"That'll be quite enough," the captain said to the sneering crewmates. "Man the ship while the rest of us go ashore."

"Cap'n!" Gideon shouted, standing beside the main-mast.

"What be troubling ya?"

"The entrance is on the other side. Wouldn't it be easier if we—"

"Harr harr...that be unnecessary. We wouldn't want unexpected company spotting our ship, now would we?"

"Ahh okay. We'll keep a weather eye for trouble cap'n! For the crew."

"For the crew, Gideon." The captain walked over and patted him on the back. "The rest of ye...to the boats!"

Jay held onto the dry rope and pulled Lyssa to the edge of the ship where three boats awaited. Jenkins boarded one of the boats with a brown pouch attached at his waist. Jay motioned to the boat.

"Get in first."

Delcato and Soleus, who was carrying a handful of iron torches, entered the boat after them. Hector and Ankin lowered their boat when they had all seated; on their way down, Jay caught a glimpse of Cain on deck dropping a round grenade into his black jacket's inner-pocket and then limping to the captain's boat. Only the members of the ground team who had infiltrated the Eulian castle entered the boats, leaving the rest to man the ship.

When their boat landed in the calm water, Soleus and Jay each manned an oar and began rowing for the mines. They paddled in stoic silence for several minutes.

"Such a marvelous locket..." Jenkins thought aloud, staring up into the cloudy sky. "And to think, it could be worth even more than we thought."

"Must be worth a fine bunch of drags," said Soleus. "I can buy Del here a mighty fine coronet."

"If you act like you did in Eulia, you'll be in prison and won't have to worry about that," she said.

"Don't worry, I wouldn't do that to ya. Wouldn't want yeh to venture this world without the warmth of a caring man like meself beside ya."

She rolled her eyes.

"Besides, Jenkins here could get me out."

Still gazing up at the sky, Jenkins said, "Oh no...I've had my fair share of prison. Eight years is plenty enough for me."

Jay's eyebrows scrunched together. "You were imprisoned for eight years?"

"Ahh, the cap'n never told you, eh?"

Jay shook his head.

"Hmph. Yes, eight years in the glorious Valkadia dungeons. Let me tell you, I would consider myself lucky if I had spent those eight years tied to a bloody mast and whipped like a dog. The murky cells...the sadistic guards...the scanty provisions..." Jenkins shuddered. "Enough to make any man go mad."

"Were you caught stealing or something?" Jay asked, glad he was not aware of this prior to the night they stole the locket.

"I guess you could say that."

"What were you stealing—"

"I'd rather not talk about it." Jenkins appeared deeply troubled by the topic.

Jay's legs weakened as he paddled. Surely if he was ever caught, he would be thrown in the worst of dungeons, left to rot until his inevitable hanging, and probably tortured relentlessly until that day. His chest felt empty, his throat clogged. He should have stayed asleep, safe and secure in his little house in Morad.

"Look!" Soleus pointed up ahead. "There's Cain's bird-thing again."

All of them looked ahead and saw a small, black animal the size of a ferret perched on Cain's right arm; he was stroking its back with his left hand. Long, gentle strokes.

"What...is that?" Lyssa asked, leaning forward to get a better view.

"It's a mynx," Jay said. The animal craned its head, clearly enjoying Cain's affection.

"A mynx?" she repeated. "What's that?"

"We don't know," Jenkins said. "That's the only one we've ever seen. For whatever reason, it has taken a liking to Cain, but it won't let any of us near; besides, Cain always goes maniac when anyone gets too close, so even if the little rodent didn't snarl at us every time we walked by, none of us would dare lay a finger on it."

They watched Cain pet the mynx as their boat bobbed up and down in the water; it was now burrowing its little head between Cain's arm and chest. Cain continued petting it, and Jay couldn't help but admire the strange relationship between the two.

"It's the only thing he seems to care about," Jenkins said. "He seems indifferent to everything else in the world."

"Alright, stow yer yappin' and remove the shutters from yer ears!" the Captain bellowed from the same boat as Cain. Lyssa gasped when the mynx, apparently startled, rushed up along Cain's arm to his shoulder, spread its concealed fur-covered wings, revealing its dark brown underbelly, and took off in the sky, flying as free as an azura.

"I didn't know it could fly," she said, watching it soar over the water and disappear into the misty haze over the horizon.

"It's a strange creature," Jenkins said. "We've seen nothing like it."

"Ehem!" the captain cleared his throat loudly, and when his crew fell silent again, he continued. "We be nearin' the entrance. It's narrow, so fall in line and follow me lead. Veer off on yer own, and yeh'll be makin' friends with the deathly rocks below."

When Jay saw the entrance, he was surprised at the small size of the opening considering its massive height. Rocks shaped like jagged fangs hung from the roof, green moss colonized their tips. When they entered the cave, Jay noticed streams of clear water mellifluously flowing down the arched walls on either side; he heard the steady echoes of water dropping from the ceiling and plopping into the stream through which their boats skimmed.

"Whoa! Look at the—" Soleus began, gazing at the shimmering sections of rock strewn across the jagged walls.

"Quiet!" the captain snapped.

In silence, they drifted deeper into the mines. The light soon dwindled, and Delcato lifted up the torches and, using some flint, set them ablaze, which cast an orange glow over their surroundings.

"Del!" Soleus said after taking a torch. "Look there."

Jay followed his finger to the bank lining the stream, and he saw an immense skeleton, its mouth lolled open lifelessly, lying on the ground, partly buried in the dark crumbs of rock.

"A gorgrim," Jenkins said.

Jay related its shape—massive body, a long, curled tail with a scorpion-like barb at the tip—to the one he saw in Eulia. This one, although huge compared to them, was much smaller than the other gorgrim. He watched as a myriad of critters were chewing on the scraps of meat still hanging from the bones; it must have died recently.

"There's the end," Jenkins said.

The two banks rounded up ahead to close off the stream. Their boat shook as it collided with the pebbled beach.

"Outta the boats!" the captain said.

All the pirates leapt out of their boats, pulled them ashore, and began walking deeper into the mine when Jay said, "Cap'n?"

"What is it, lad?"

"Shouldn't we put the boats over there to keep them

hidden?" Jay pointed to a series of boulders off to the side; they looked big enough to properly conceal the boats.

"Of course. Good idea lad. See to it."

The crew dragged the boats behind the boulders and re-gathered around the captain, who said, "Jay, you be leading the way. We will follow. And you, m'lady," he said, addressing Lyssa, "ye try any tricks to harm me or me crew and I'll—"

"There's no need to threaten me. I'll fulfill my end of the bargain, and you better fulfill yours." Before he could respond, she treaded across the rocks down into the throat of the cavern. Before he followed her, Jay caught a glimpse of Delcato smiling at Lyssa's retort.

The walls of the passageway narrowed as they traveled farther into the depths of the mine. Metal picks, wooden crates, and other mining implements were scattered over the ground. Jay still heard the occasional dripping, and the moist air smelled of damp iron, the distasteful odor of unclean well water.

Jay stepped behind Lyssa in silence. Every time she approached a junction, he noticed her close her eyes and mumble something under her breath, like she was reciting something in her mind before choosing a path. After a few minutes, Jay realized he would never be able to navigate himself out alone. He was trying to make a mental note of his surroundings so he could retrace his steps if necessary when Lyssa's voice interrupted his thoughts.

"Why are you here?"

"Because you said this is where Ashlen's Tomb is."

"No, I meant why are you blindly following the Captain? Doing everything he says without question?"

"Oh. Well, he saved my life. I was stealing some fish in Delphina, and one of the guards spotted me. I was nearly captured when Hector helped me escape and the captain welcomed me in his crew. I've been with them ever since."

"Why were you stealing?" There was an accusatory tone in her voice, like a mother scolding a child.

Jay looked at her. "If I remember right, you were trying to steal something just a couple days ago."

"I'm not talking about that, I'm talking about—"

"I was hungry, okay?"

"But...you don't seem like the typical pirate. I don't understand why you would—"

"I had no money, no food, no family. Anywhere I went, I was hunted. What choice did I have?"

Although his eyes were focused on the mottled ground, he sensed her gaze.

"No family? What happened to your parents?"

Jay closed his eyes for a second. He had not thought of his parents since joining the crew; it was easier to ignore than try to understand.

"They were arrested when I was five. And I don't know why." They arrived at another fork in the path. "Which way?"

She thought for a moment and then continued along the left path. "So you've been without a family ever since?"

Jay shook his head. "No. My mom's friend, Matilda, let me stay with her and her son."

"And what happened to her?"

"I don't know."

"Then why aren't you still with them?"

Jay hesitated and stared off blankly down the endless tunnel. He was in no mood to retell what happened that night in Morad. "I have a new family now, a family that treats me better than the others."

"But they're pirates."

"Apparently you've had little trouble trusting pirates in the past."

She jerked her head from him, her golden hair covered her face. He had clearly upset her. He considered apologizing, but he welcomed the silence.

Neither of them spoke until they arrived at a wide, circular room in the mines. The others sped up to them and examined the room, their flickering orange torchlight barely reaching the edges of the clearing, illuminating a shallow stream of water that circled the perimeter. There were many carts filled with chisels and rocks, worn and crumbling after years of isolation.

"Very welcoming," Lynk said, staring at an intricate spider web plastered over the rail of one of the mine carts.

Lyssa halted and regarded the three passages in the blackened wall up ahead. Cain brushed against her and limped farther into the room. Curious, Jay followed him.

With the aid of his walking staff, Cain neared a stone basin with a narrow pillar supporting it. Carved in the basin was a robed man, like a young wizard, with his arm raised, his hand gripping a blazing hatchet. His other hand, dropped beside his robes, extended a slender finger that pointed at the ground where, in the background, an apple was about to land. Above the apple was a grand tree, with a thick trunk and stringy hair, and beside the tree was a small cottage with a straw roof and a narrow chimney blowing slivers of smoke into the sky.

When he and Cain drew closer, Jay saw a pool of clear water resting inside the basin.

"That seems so...out of place," Jay said, rubbing his hand along the carving. "And what's this?" He lifted his hand and moved it to the clear water—

"Don't touch that!" Cain slapped his hand aside.

"Can't you smell it?" He knelt down and picked up a mining hatchet lying on the ground. He dipped its wooden shaft in the liquid. The wood hissed and the liquid bubbled.

"Ugh! That smell is horrid!" Soleus complained.

Cain lifted the hatchet; the wood had completely disintegrated. "That could have been your hand."

Jay massaged his healthy hands. "What is that?"

"Some sort of acid," said Cain. "Jenkins, toss me your pouch."

"Why—"

"Now!"

Jenkins removed his gorgrim-skin pouch and tossed it to Cain, who looped its strings around the blade of the hatchet and, holding the shortened shaft, dipped the pouch into the pool. The liquid filled it instantly, though the thick, impenetrable gorgrim-hide withstood the potent acid. When it was full, he set the pouch down on the ground and tied it shut, careful not to let his fingers touch the acid-covered fabric. He set the hatchet down, and, holding the pouch by its slender strings, he carried it to the surrounding stream and dipped it in the water.

"What are you doing?" Soleus asked.

Another faint hissing sound, like a slab of meat being slapped onto a heated grill, filled the air as the stream washed away any remaining acid on the exterior of the pouch.

"What be the meaning of this holdup?" the captain asked, striding through the room to Cain and Jay.

"Nothing," said Cain, tying the pouch to his waist. "Let's keep moving."

"Arg..." the captain said. "At this rate, we'll be here all day."

Jay could not ignore his curiosity any longer. He

leaned toward Cain and whispered, "Why are you taking that?"

"I want Karen to identify this. It may prove useful to us," Cain said without much thought.

When Lyssa finally chose the middle path, they all followed her out of the room, but Jay stole one final glimpse of the basin and the unusual illustration, where he thought he saw the wizard's eyes glance at him as he left with the others.

The air thickened and water ceased dripping. Ancient stone cracked and crumbled underneath their feet as they walked. They found little evidence of miners down this path.

"I'm going to need you to untie me," Lyssa said.

"Not until we get to the tomb," said Jay.

"I need to use my hands to get us there."

For what? Jay looked puzzled, but realized she would not be able to flee anywhere. After glancing at the captain, who nodded his head in approval, he untied the rope around her wrists.

Lyssa rubbed her wrists where the rope had been scraping her skin. She then placed her hands against the wall and let them slide over the bumps and crevices in the ancient stone. Jay and the others followed her as she slowly stepped along the wall, sliding her hands up and down as she did so.

"Here," she said and came to a stop.

The crew gathered around and examined the wall.

"If a wall is all ye think ye need for freedom, yeh'd be wishful thinkin'" the captain said.

Ignoring him, she looked at Jay. "Put your hand here." When his right hand replaced hers, she continued walking along the wall.

He felt slivers of stone protruding from the wall.

Peering between his fingers under the flickering orange light, he faintly made out what appeared to be an emblem of three objects rotating counterclockwise: a drop of liquid, a burst of flame, and a tree.

"Okay," she said, several yards away, her hands firmly plastered against the wall. "Push inward until you hear two clicks."

Confused, Jay pressed on the stone, but it didn't budge. "Push!" she yelled.

Taking a breath, Jay heaved with all his strength and pushed on the emblem. To his satisfaction, a circular segment of rock containing the three symbols slid into the wall until it firmly stopped with a smashing sound on the other side, which, he assumed, was the sound she meant when she said 'click.'

"One more!" Again, he pushed in the emblem until it slid even farther in with another thunderous click.

"Okay, now release it," she said. It resurfaced swiftly. "Now, push it again. Four clicks."

"Is this some sort of combination?" Jenkins asked, naturally intrigued by the idea of such a unique security system that his white lock pick would never penetrate.

"Y-Yes," she stammered using all her force to push in the emblem.

The clicking sounds rattled the walls; small stones dropped from the ceiling. One...two...three...four. Jay's arms throbbed from exerting such a strong force to push the circular slab of stone inward.

"Now hold it there...*do not let go!*"

"What do you mean—" Jay jumped as freezing water splashed against his hand inside the wall. The tips of his fingers at once turned numb; he could no longer feel the emblem. Water engulfed his entire hand and wrist. His veins constricted and his blood slowed under the unbearably cold temperature.

"Do—not—let—go!" she repeated.

"What the hell?" Captain Gaden said. "What's going on in there?"

Jay's hand began tingling in agonizing pain. He could feel his hand freeze as tears streamed down his cheeks. The rushing water thundered against the inside of the walls, causing the mines to rumble as if the ocean was about to blast through.

"Tell me what's happening!" Captain Gaden demanded, grasping his cutlass.

Jay pounded his head against the wall, unable to withstand the freezing water stabbing his hand, but then the water grew warmer. Jay panted with relief as he regained sensation in his hand—he could feel his fingers rubbing against the emblem, the three objects engraved in it. His muscles loosened as the water heated and massaged his hand like a hot spring cleansing his skin. The water, as well as the emblem, started getting hotter and hotter. Jay clawed at the blazing emblem as the water turned to steam. His fingers blistered pressing against the steaming stone.

Jay screamed in agony. It felt like the emblem came alit with a flame and burned his skin. Both he and Lyssa shook uncontrollably; the scorching flames consumed Jay's hand, causing excruciating pain.

"I...can't...it's...ahh!" Jay yelled. The wall turned a crimson color and a blanket of smoke oozed out of it.

"This is madness!" Captain Gaden shouted. "Remove yer hand at once!"

"No!" Lyssa shouted, thrashing against the hot wall. "A little bit longer!"

Water streamed down his cheeks as Jay struggled

with all his might to hold his hand steady, pressed against the flaming stone, and then, the burning wall swallowed the smoke and faded to the drab, mottled gray color it was previously. The emblem cooled to its normal temperature. Jay nearly collapsed with fatigue.

"Is it over?" he asked, fearful of the answer.

She said nothing. A small pebble fell on his hand inside the wall. A crease formed between his eyebrows as he leaned his ear against the wall, listening for what was happening. Several more pebbles fell; his hand stung as the pebbles plopped onto his throbbing burns. To his dismay, he heard a loud din of clattering, but before he could react, an avalanche of pebbles rained down on his hand with increasing speed. He pounded his head against the wall—every pebble felt like a sharp dagger puncturing his burnt skin. The din grew louder, and it sounded as if the entire ceiling would collapse as the rocks stormed down from above.

Enraged, Captain Gaden grabbed Jay's shoulders.

"Wait!" Lyssa yelled. "It's almost over!"

"I'm tired of this nonsense! I will not have me crew be harmed for one of yer fairy tales. I'm ending this—"

Then rocks stopped falling, and a large gust of wind blasted Jay, Lyssa, and the captain across the passageway. Their backs slammed into the opposite wall. They all cried in pain and collapsed to the ground.

Jay shook his right hand and examined it. Ugly reddish-pink blisters covered his fingers and palm; blood trickled out of the cuts in the back of his hand from the stones.

"You fiend!" the captain yelled. He jumped to his feet, drew his cutlass, and advanced toward Lyssa, who still lay on the ground recovering.

Before he reached her, a roaring clicking sound filled

the narrow, dark hallway. Jay and the others frantically scanned the walls and ceiling, searching for the origin of the sound. Suddenly, the wall between the two emblems he and Lyssa had pressed began lifting up into the ceiling, shedding bits of stone along its sides and top. As the wall slowly crawled up into the ceiling, Jay noticed a small, hidden room that the wall had been guarding.

Soleus crouched down, bringing his torch near the ground to shed light into the room. With the aid of the glimmering orange torchlight, Jay could see a large tomb in the center of the room.

"I present you," Lyssa said, using the wall for support to stand, "Ashlen's Tomb."

The crew peered inside the room, which was bare except for the elevated sandstone tomb, dulled with age, resting on its stone platform. Jay struggled to his feet and followed the others inside. When they brought the flaming torches in the room, he noticed faint markings covered with a layer of dust on the side of the coffin. He studied the markings a few seconds, trying to decipher them, but the layer of dust blurred the markings together. He brushed his uninjured hand over the sandstone to clear the dust clouding the markings. A chill coursed down Jay's arms as the markings became clear:

ASHLEN VENCLIN

Jay's eyes traveled to the top of the coffin where he saw an illustration of a man, the same man carved in the stone basin, lying on his back, his form rising above the rest of the sandstone. His hands rested by his sides, his loose robes fell over his body. On his forehead was an indentation, small and circular.

Lyssa stepped next to him, and her fingers slid into the indentation. After feeling around, she said, "Here. Place the locket face-up."

Captain Gaden lifted the diamond locket out of his pocket by its silver chain. He glanced from the dangling locket to the tomb, contemplating whether or not to trust her.

After a few seconds, Cain stepped forward, snatched the locket from the captain's grip, and limped to the tomb. He paused for a moment, his pointed black beard hovering over the wizard's face, his hooded eyes gazing into the brown crevice in the wizard's forehead.

"Well..." Soleus asked. "Are you going to put it in or what?"

With care, he pressed the locket into the indentation: it was a perfect fit.

Nothing happened.

Cain pounded on the locket with the heel of his palm, trying to force it in farther.

Nothing happened.

"Well that worked well," Captain Gaden said dryly. "I've had enough games for one day. Lyssa, yer goin' back to the brig. Jay, give me the locket. We're leaving. Now."

Jay sighed. "Aye, cap'n." As soon as his slender fingers rubbed against the smooth locket, a screeching sound echoed off the walls and a bright, white beam of light blasted down from the ceiling to the locket, still resting in the wizard's forehead. As fast as it appeared, the light vanished and the screeching ceased. All was still.

Jay and the others glanced around the room, surprised at the sudden surge of light and sound. What caused that? Something had to have shined the light and created the noise, but the room appeared empty.

When Jay glanced down at the locket, his bottom jaw dropped slightly. "It's...open."

The pirates stared at the diamond locket, which had sprung open and was emitting a green, glowing light from inside. When looking directly over the locket, Jay noticed a green arrow, glowing magically and pointing due south.

Breathing heavily, Lyssa said, "There it is. The compass that leads to Ashlen's sacred treasure."

"Thank you," Jay heard a scornful, dreadfully familiar voice come from the entrance of the room. Jay jerked his head to the side.

Draped in a deep red jacket with a dark sash wrapped around his waist, a man leaned against the entrance of the tomb with his head tilted down. His reddish-brown hair fell before his eyes, concealing his face.

"Arr!" Captain Gaden growled as the crew stood alert. "Identify yerself!"

"Hmph," the man sneered. "I am rather surprised, Captain Gaden, it took you this long."

The voice, it couldn't be....

The captain staggered when the man mentioned his name. "Identify yerself, or face the blades of me crew!" The crew held their weapons at ready, shaking them in the air.

"Names are rather superfluous I believe, given the circumstance." The man held out his hand, apparently studying his palm under the orange torchlight.

"Enough of this nonsense. Men, restrain him!"

"Ah, ah, you may want to reconsider your request," the man taunted as several more men appeared at the entrance, completely blocking it off. Jay felt his fingers pulsing as he stepped near the captain, whose eyes flickered across the room, searching for another exit.

"No," the man said. "I fear there are no other exits.

You are indeed trapped."

The captain toddled backwards, bumping into the sandstone coffin.

The man lunged himself off the wall, his burnt brown hair falling to his shoulders. As he advanced towards the crew, his face became visible under the flickering torches. His narrow face smirked at them; his green, ravenous eyes focused on the locket resting in the sandstone.

Jay recognized him at once. His eyes widened. "You're alive!"

"You know this scoundrel?" the captain asked.

"Oh yes, we know each other. Very well actually. It's been four years, has it not?" He stepped closer, his eyes now focused on Jay.

Jay's cutlass seemed to double in weight in his hands. "I've waited so long." A slew of words came to his mouth but he had trouble speaking. "You left me to die. Why?"

"Ahh yes," the man smiled. "Indeed I did. And you survived. I must admit, Jay, I had pegged you for dead. Hmph, shows even a petty kid can catch some luck. Though, I am grateful for your escape, or else that locket you idiots stole would still remained locked."

"Thyran! You rotted piece of scum!" Lyssa yelled. "I'll pierce my bow through your heart before my time is up!"

"Lyssa..." Thyran said, his smile never wavering. "You played your part as well. Without you, these lowly pirates never would have found Ashlen's Tomb. I thank you."

"Why did you murder the governor?" Jay asked.

Thyran proudly looked toward the ceiling and ran his fingers through his flowing hair. Jay saw he had two blades criss-crossed in sheaths behind his back. "I put that imbecile where he deserves to be."

"What? Why?"

Two of the men behind Thyran entered the room. On his left was a tall, burly man, bald with numerous earrings and nose-rings, his enormous ovular head was shaped like a swelled sandbag with a round top. To his right was a much less muscular man with reddish spiked hair.

"He, as well as the cowardly kingdoms of Eulia and Valkadia, share the blame for the death of an innocent life, so young and pure," Thyran said. "Now, hand over the locket, Jay, and I'll make your death swift and painless."

"Get the locket!" Captain Gaden yelled. Lyssa ripped the locket out of its socket and clutched it firmly. Delcato moved towards her, brandishing her sword at Thyran and his followers.

Thyran took a step towards Lyssa, but the massive captain slapped his cutlass in Thyran's path. Thyran's silky hair floated as he stopped. His dark green eyes raced along the captain's blade. "So quick to draw your sword I see. Your fall will be equally as quick."

"I've had enough of this nonsense!" the captain yelled. His massive arm swung in the air; his cutlass came down towards Thyran's head. Fluidly, Thyran slid back, evading the sword.

"If you insist, my good captain." Thyran bowed, gripped one of his gold-trimmed hilts behind his back, and unsheathed his razor-sharp scimitar. Holding his weapon at ready, Thyran grinned.

Without hesitation, the mighty captain thrashed and hacked at Thyran. Thyran countered each offensive with a spry maneuver of his blade. Attack after attack, Thyran remained on the defensive, apparently exerting little energy. His wily grin haunted the room. Jay's entire body locked with tension and anxiety; he knew Thyran's fighting was full of tricks and misdirection. With every step Thyran took, Jay feared for the captain's life.

Jay stepped forward to aid his captain, but Thyran's men mirrored his movement. Unsure how many of Thyran's men waited outside the room, he froze.

"Herrah!" the captain screamed stabbing his cutlass into Thyran's heart. No, it wasn't his heart—Thyran sidestepped and the blade skimmed his black jacket. Thyran whirled around and slashed the captain's unprotected knee.

"Arrgghh!" the captain yelled as blood gushed down along his leg. Wincing in pain, he stumbled back a few paces.

"What's the matter? Giving up so soon?" Thyran said.

The lion-like captain regained composure. Jay knew his large form was slowing him down and making him weary. He needed to end this soon, or fatigue would take its toll—

Captain Gaden lunged himself towards Thyran with more ferocity than Jay had ever witnessed. Their blades clashed. Sweat poured down the captain's head, but Thyran still appeared to barely exert any effort. Every move, every jab, every attack the captain made, Thyran avoided like it was rehearsed.

Then, the captain aimed a strike at his feet, which Thyran glided over and then slithered around the captain. Captain Gaden quickly spun around and charged at Thyran, gripping his blade high in the air, preparing to deliver a blow only someone of his might could defend—

Thyran arched his knees to cushion the impact and held his blade in the air with his right hand. The captain's strike came crushing down with the fury of chain lighting—

When their blades clashed, Thyran squeezed his fingers around the sword's hilt and further bent his knees to absorb the attack, and, with his free hand, clasped the hilt of his other scimitar, unsheathed it, and charged it through the fatigued captain's chest, ripping through his heart.

Jay opened his lips to scream, but nothing came out.

"Ompf..." the captain grunted. Frozen in time, the two stared at one another. The grin on Thyran's lips deepened as his dark green eyes pierced through the captain's until Captain Gaden plopped lifelessly to the ground.

7

Thyran's Keepsake

Jay felt cold. Seconds, though it seemed like hours, passed before he forced himself to swallow reality: Captain Gaden was dead, killed at the hands of his villainous step-brother, just like the governor. Now the captain lay there, his bulky form covered in his thick brown jacket, limp and help-less. Thyran irreverently wiped his dripping scimitar against the captain's jacket to cleanse it.

"Lyssa," Thyran said in a calm voice as if they were having an evening chat by fire. "The locket." He sheathed his scimitars and held out his right hand, palm up.

Jay drew his cutlass and brandished the curved blade at Thyran. His eyes narrowed as rage mounted inside him. "I'll kill you Thyran...I swear it!"

The brawny, bald man beside Thyran chuckled, though Thyran remained placid. "Brother, I'm hurt...."

Suddenly, Cain snatched the locket from Lyssa and seized his round grenade from his pouch. After catching Cain's signal, Jenkins lobbed his torch to him, who held it menacingly near the grenade.

"Clear the entrance or I'll blow your precious locket to pieces," Cain said.

"And kill yourselves in the process," Thyran said.

"You have three seconds to move before I light this."

The orange flame flickered near the grenade in his hand and illuminated his black beard, giving him a fearsome appearance.

Before Cain counted off the first number, Thyran slowly stepped back towards the entrance of the dusty tomb. Jay and the crew followed, Lyssa glaring at Thyran, Jenkins fidgeting with his necklace, Blynk huddled close to Lynk for protection, Soleus standing between Thyran and Delcato. When he passed over the captain, Jay glanced down, tears swelled in his throat, his hand trembled, his stomach sunk.

"Don't look so sad, Jay," Thyran said. "He was only a pirate."

Jay glared at his stepbrother. "You're nothing but a murderer."

"Soon enough, you'll understand."

Jay wanted to say something hurtful, something to wipe that cool-headed expression off Thyran's face, but he could muster no such words. When he was outside the tomb, Thyran turned the corner and backed into the narrow hallway, his calm face flashing in and out of the orange, flickering light.

Jay noticed a spark in the corner of his eye, then he saw the wick of the grenade burning in Cain's hand. Jay and the others shuffled away from Cain as he held the grenade in the air.

"Your journey ends here!" he said, and he flung the grenade through the air—

The two groups dove in opposite directions. A flash of white light and a thunderous roar—

When the grenade blew, the ground shook and the walls shed stone and rock. The force of the explosion rattled Jay, but he was not injured. Lying on his back, he coughed up a mouthful of dirt. He gazed into the fog of dust, and he made out a wall of boulders completely blocking off the path where the grenade had exploded. Was that it? Was Thyran dead?

Using his walking staff to get to his feet, Cain said, "Let's move!"

Brushing off rocks and stones strewn on them from the explosion, the crew gathered to their feet. Jay gave everyone a quick glance; no one had sustained any major injuries. They darted down the corridors of the Dryfus Mines; Lyssa seemed to remember the way out, for in a few minutes, they arrived at the stream through which they had rowed. There was a small boat dragged up on the pebbled ground.

"That must be his," Jay said.

Pointing with his staff towards the large boulders near the wall, Cain said, "Fetch our boats. We'll take theirs as well."

While the others scurried to the boulders, Jay approached Cain. "Do you think they're still alive?"

Cain glimpsed back into the throat of the mines, then back to Jay. "No, but it's best to assume the worse."

They rowed out of the mines and back to the ship. Ankin and Hector pulled the boats up and helped them aboard. "Where's the captain?" Hector asked.

Climbing aboard the ship, Cain tossed the locket to Hector. "See to it that Gideon gets this. That's our heading."

Hector stared at the locket with a look of confusion. "What's this?"

"We have no time to waste!" Cain pushed passed him. "All hands on deck! We leave, now!"

"Where's the captain?" Hector repeated.

"Dead." Jenkins said, lifting himself out of the boat after Jay. "We were ambushed."

Hector and Ankin stood silent while those crewmates nearby stopped to listen. "We...we didn't see any other ship," Ankin said.

Jay craned his neck to look around: there was no sight of Thyran's ship.

Grumbling something under his breath, Cain snatched the locket from Hector. "If you all love the view so much, feel free to swim ashore and watch it. Those who want to get out of here, prepare the sails and hoist the anchor. I want this ship in motion, now!"

Jay looked at Lyssa. Her face was white and her eyes were cold. She appeared to be quivering, with fear or hatred Jay could not tell, but after Cain barked out more commands, he decided he would save any questions for later.

"Bruce, a little light over here," Kyros said.

Wheezing, the bald, bulky man stumbled to his feet, lifted the torch, and toddled over to Kyros, who was fixing fire sticks to the wall of rocks forged from the explosion.

"All set," Kyros said as he lit the fire sticks against the rubble. Settling a safe distance away, they watched the fire sticks blast through the mound of rocks, sending fragments of stone soaring in every direction.

"Clever little pirates," Thyran said as they walked through the debris. Thyran and his crewmates strode into Ashlen's Tomb where the pirate captain lay sprawled on the ground. "Salvage what you can."

Kyros and Bruce searched the captain, helping themselves to any weapons and treasures the captain bore. Thyran dipped his finger into the crevice in the wizard's forehead on the tomb. The stone felt warm, like it had been baking in the sun for days.

"It was good seeing you again, Jay," Thyran said. Kyros and Bruce glanced up at Thyran for a brief moment before continuing to rummage through the captain's possessions. "We'll see each other again soon."

"Captain," Kyros said, sliding a dagger into his boot-strap. "Shouldn't we be following Jay and the others before they escape?"

"There's no need for that. The sorceress is all we need."

"Can we trust her?" Kyros asked.

"I have ways of making people see my way of things," Thyran said, grinning.

"Whoa," Bruce lifted a small hatchet from the dead captain. "This here ax will go good in my collection." He spoke with the bewilderment of a child who just found a new toy.

Thyran ignored him. Finally, after years of waiting, Ashlen's Locket was unlocked. It had taken longer than he had anticipated to lure Jay into doing his bidding, but it was, at last, finished. All he had to do now was catch his step-brother and take back the locket, then it would only be a few days....

"That's everything," Kyros said, slapping his black pant leg over his boot.

Thyran withdrew his hand from the coffin. "Good. Let's head out."

When they arrived at the entrance, Bruce stared at the pebbled beach. "Our boat be missin', cap'n."

"I see your vision is as keen as ever," Thyran said. His eyes flicked over the stream, which rippled under the tor-chlight. "Cyril!"

Wearing black boots and a dark leather coat, Cyril re-vealed himself from behind a boulder, his thick black hair covering all his face save for his hooked nose. He dragged another small boat a few feet before dropping it and striding over to Thyran and the others.

"They left five or ten minutes ago."

"Bruce, bring the boat over here," Thyran said, and the shirtless, muscular man carried his collection of weapons over to the boat and plopped them inside before dragging it back to Thyran.

"I wasn't sure what to do, captain," Cyril said. "I was expecting to see you, but instead I—"

"It's fine."

Thyran's eyes followed the path in the ground created by several boats being dragged from behind a series of boulders to the water. Very clever, though it would not make any difference in the end.

"They have the locket?" Cyril asked.

Thyran nodded and grinned. "Yes, but everything went as planned. I even killed their captain in the process."

Cyril looked from Kyros back to Thyran, his eyes darting back and forth nervously. "I do not see how this is a good thing. We were suppose to be walking away with the locket, I th—"

"Are you questioning my tactics?" Thyran said coldly.

"No, of course not, capt—"

"Good, because I'll maroon you on this island without hesitation."

Thyran watched as Bruce pushed the boat into the water where Kyros crouched down to dip his hands in the stream. "Time to go," Thyran said, and they all settled in the boat. Bruce and Kyros rowed down the stream and then skirted around the island where their ship, the *Venator*, awaited, floating idly in the sea. The ship's dark brown coating contrasted with the clear blue water. Perched on the bow overlooking the sea was the sculpture of a wolf's head, its glaring crystal eyes glistening under the sunlight.

When their boat ran alongside the *Venator*, the boat

gave a sudden jerk. Looking over the edge, Thyran saw a mound of water materialize from the sea and lift their boat in the air. Cyril shifted around uncomfortably in his seat, but Thyran grinned and closed his eyes, welcoming the rush of cool air against his face and through his silky hair.

Soon, their boat lined up with the rail of the ship, and several pirates fastened rope to the boat while Thyran and the others boarded the ship. When the boat was secure, the sorceress, standing at the rail, threw her arms down, her eyes faded from bright blue, and the water plummeted back down to the sea. The ship rocked from the effecting wave.

"Did you see that?" one of the pirates asked another.

"How do you think she does it?" asked another.

Alcina giggled as she twirled her blue hair between her fingers.

While his crew gathered around, awaiting instructions, Thyran walked over to her. "Alcina, what direction did they head?"

"Hmm?" she said, gazing off to the sky, blatantly ignoring him.

"What direction did they head?" he asked again.

She continued examining the gray clouds enveloping the sky.

Thyran stretched his arm behind his back and latched his fingers around one of his scimitar hilts, but Kyros raised his hand for him to pause. "One second, captain." Relaxing his fingers, Thyran stepped back.

The sorceress appeared oblivious to Kyros approaching; her back was turned, head tilted up, and she was humming a sweet melody, swaying her head back and forth with the rhythm. Kyros stepped beside her.

"Alcina, please, answer the captain."

She bit her bottom lip. Thyran thought he saw her lips

curl to a grin, but she still paid him no attention.

Kyros rolled his eyes and squeezed his hands with detest. "Please, *Miss* Alcina, answer the captain."

She giggled and closed her eyes. She held her hand out to the sea. Flicking her finger towards the south, she sliced a path through water: small waves rippled apart from a line forged in the water as if an invisible boat had just skimmed through in the direction of her finger.

Thyran nodded to Kyros and then turned to address the crew, who all stood in line waiting for his command. "They have unlocked the locket." The pirates cheered, some throwing their fists in the air. "They are cunning...more so than I originally anticipated. They escaped with the locket." Some of the crew gasped and cowered back slightly, hoping to avoid blame. "We will catch up with them, seize the locket, and continue as planned." The pirates relaxed, let their shoulders droop, and breathed a sigh of relief. "Now, let's set sail. Follow Alcina's path through the water; that will lead us directly to them."

Thyran noticed Bruce waddle over to the mast and drop his newfound weapons into a pile and then pick up each one individually and carefully examine its structure and durability; weapons too weak to justify keeping were discarded in one pile while the rest were gathered in another

"Must you make so much noise?" Kyros asked when Bruce swung down the hatchet into the blade of a long dagger, which snapped in two and was consequentially discarded.

"I gotta test the weaponry. That's me job, the cap'n said so himself." Bruce prepared to swing again, now at a piece of leg armor.

"Just clean up after yourself this time." Kyros turned from Bruce and removed fire sticks, grenades, and other explosives from numerous pouches spangled over his wardrobe and set them on the deck, organizing them in groups. So absorbed with his tools, he did not notice the sorceress slithering up from behind, her blue kitten chasing her loose pant leg.

Cyril moved closer to Thyran and opened his mouth to speak, but Thyran interrupted. "Shh...one minute." From a distance, he watched Kyros and Alcina.

"Did you see it? The locket?" she asked, clutching her hands by her waist and bouncing on her heels.

"Yes," Kyros said, his voice void of any emotion.

"What did it look like?"

"I don't have time for this right now."

Raising a hand and nibbling on her nail, the sorceress summoned a ball of water out of the ocean and watched it hover over his spiky hair. "What was that, dear?"

After glancing skyward, Kyros spun around. "Drop that on me and it'll be the last thing you do."

"Oh really?" she challenged.

He rolled his eyes. "What do you want?"

She stepped closer to him, eyeing the ground innocently. "Show me that explosive stuff again."

"Fire sticks?"

She smiled cutely and nodded her head. Her hair waved in the wind.

"Later, I'm busy." He turned and continued sorting his explosives.

Quivering with anger, she clenched her hands; the water at once became choppy, and the ship started to sway, more and more, until Kyros yelled,

"Stop!"

She kneeled beside him and tugged on his sleeve. "I want to see the fire stick stuff again."

"You listen here," he made to grab her shoulder; the sphere of water hovering over his head dropped like a rock and splashed over his hair.

"Alright!" he said, his hair matted, water pouring down his face. "One moment." Alcina smiled and plopped down beside him. She scooped her kitten in her lap and rubbed behind its ears as she inspected the piles of explosives in front of Kyros.

Thyran shook his head. "Come with me." He and Cyril walked down the deck, away from Alcina and Kyros, and into Thyran's cabin. Thyran walked across the red carpet to a polished wooden desk, where several hand-carved glasses and an ornate bottle of dark wine rested. "The girl concerns me," he said, lifting the bottle and pouring two glasses.

Cyril paced back and forth over the floor. "Yes, she is unpredictable. She only seems to respond to Kyros."

"Indeed." Thyran handed Cyril a drink. They both took a sip. "We'll need to keep a sharp eye on her. Any sign of her disloyalty, and I'll run my blade through her neck."

His glass to his lips, Cyril nodded.

"I trust you'll inform me of any suspicions?" Thyran asked, walking to a corner of the room where a black cylinder was propped against the wall.

"Of course, cap'n."

"Good." Thyran grabbed the cylinder, popped off the top, and pulled out the rolled up piece of parchment he stole from Governor Almsy four years ago. Cyril watched as he unrolled it on the wooden desk and set his glass down on the edge to prevent the map from curling. Half the parchment contained a map of tunnels with the label "Dryfus Mines" above, and the other half contained cursive writings.

Thyran pointed to a room in the Dryfus Mines that represented Ashlen's Tomb; there was a symbol just below with the picture of a flame, water drop, and tree, whirling in a circular motion. A single beam of light shot up from the coffin with a note scribbled in black ink to the side: *The Light Shines only for the Virtuous.*

"This is complete," Thyran said. His finger slid to the other half of the map as he mumbled the words aloud under his breath. "The locket...unlock...enter the combination...withstand the elements...ahh yes, here. *The arrow guides through the storm to the Diamond Blade, one of the two artifacts for breaking the seal.*"

Thyran examined the image drawn below of a man smashing a weapon resembling a hatchet into a basin, and rays of lights blasting in every direction. He was so close....

"Do you think they will follow the locket?" Cyril asked.

"Knowing my brother, definitely. He won't be able to subdue his curiosity."

"What about Eulia and Valkadia?"

Thyran looked up. "What about them?"

"Don't you think they'll send their forces to stop us when they find out we are—"

"*If* they find out. When Cornelius discovers the locket is missing, they will be too absorbed in their own conflict to acknowledge our existence. By the time they realize what we are up to, it will be too late."

Cyril hesitated. "I think you are being unwise. Too many obstacles could present themselves. What if Jay outmaneuvers you and claims the blade before we do. Or what if Eulia—"

Thyran snapped one of his scimitars out of its sheath and whipped it against Cyril's neck. Cyril had dropped his glass to grab his long knife to block the attack, but he was too slow.

"Do not question me again, Cyril. I will not tolerate disobedience." Thyran glared at him.

Cyril's black hair fell before his eyes as he stared back at Thyran, but then he slipped his dagger back inside his jacket. "Forgive me, cap'n. I shall rely on your judgment." Cyril walked for the door and exited the room.

Alone in his cabin, Thyran rolled up the map and stuffed it back in its container. Stepping behind his desk, he opened a drawer and removed a heart-shaped object made of bright seashells strung together by strands of brown hair with thick, blue azura feathers holding its shape. Held by a string, the seashells rattled together as Thyran lifted the object in the air. He clutched it near his heart and bowed his head. He closed his eyes and felt the aura of the seashells grip his heart, making it beat harder, as if he was not hugging the seashells, but as if he was hugging her. "We are close, so very close, Alexia. Your death will soon be avenged, and your agony will be shared by all of Lassar."

8

The Legend of Dragons' End

The horizon had begun dragging down the sun as the *Liberáte* anchored outside the village of Morad. The Knights of Voorus assembled on deck with Chip in his shiny purple vest standing in front. Holding large, white drums against their chests, three men lined each side of the troupe. McClevin held out an overstuffed blue cushion with a stone ball resting on top.

"Okay! Let's try this again." McClevin hurried back and waved his arms to guide his knights.

Reluctantly, the knights slammed their drums while Chip balanced the cushion on his skinny head. They marched forward in sync with the beat of the drums. Then, as the rhythm sped up, Chip jerked his head in the air, throwing the cushion up to the sky. He attempted a forward flip, but landed improperly and watched in horror as the stone ball plummeted to his naked foot. He jumped and yelled in agony.

"Ugh...not again," one of the knights complained.

"What are we?" Duc asked. "Knights or dancers? We've been at this for hours. The king'll be happy just to get back the locket...he doesn't need to see a bunch of clowns waltzing up to his palace."

"Quiet!" McClevin snapped. "This locket is very important to King Emory. We must demonstrate our compassion!"

Hopping on one leg, Chip rubbed his swelling foot.

"I...I need a break." The rest of the knights nodded in agreement.

McClevin grumbled and removed his crested helmet. "Lord love a duck. Fine, take the rest of the night off. I'm going ashore to see what information I can find out about Jay Perry."

"I'm coming too." The princess stepped beside McClevin.

Scratching his head, McClevin examined her. Her hooded brownish-green tunic served as an admirable disguise; no one would suspect she was the princess of Eulia.

"Well, I guess there's no danger in Morad. Just stay close behind."

McClevin changed into a commoner's outfit (a loose tan shirt and dark brown breeches) then rowed with the princess to the shore of Morad.

The village was quiet in the late evening. The orange rays of sunlight shined down on the primitive stone houses that lined the paths through the village. A woman and two boys, most likely her sons, carried buckets of water from a well back towards their home. She eyed McClevin and the princess as they neared her.

"Excuse me," McClevin said. She looked at him with a blank expression. "Sorry to disturb you, but I need to know where Jay Perry used to live. Do you know?"

Her eyes widened. "We do not speak of him," she whispered.

"I am sorry for your troubles, ma'am," the princess said, pulling back her hood, allowing her snowy hair to drape over her shoulders. "We are merely historians from Eulia trying to conduct research on notorious criminals to help our king catch them. We wish to speak with his family."

The woman closed her eyes and thought a moment. She seemed deeply troubled by the subject. "He used to live in that house over there." She pointed to a small, square house down the street. "His parents still live there. Perhaps they can assist you." Without giving them a chance to say any more, she took her children and the water and continued down the dirt path.

McClevin looked in the direction of the square house. Most of the other houses had round roofs. "Well, let's see if they can help," he said, and the two walked in silence down the path.

The carrot-colored sunlight warmed their skin; the only sound they heard was the wind whistling through the grass. McClevin felt cool raindrops leak from the clouds and drip onto his head. By the time they arrived at the house, a gentle rain was sprinkling down in Morad. To the right of the door was a sign with the word "Vilkus" carved into the wood. McClevin knocked.

He heard footsteps approaching from opposite the door, and when it creaked open, a tall, emaciated man with a narrow, drooping face stood in the doorway and looked at them through sunken eyes. His dark greasy hair appeared as if he had just rummaged his hands through it. He spoke in a raspy voice. "Can I help you?"

"Err...yes," McClevin said. "We have a few questions about your son, Jay. Do you have a minute?"

The man studied them a moment; the rain pattered harder against the soil. He moved to close the door, but then the princess stepped forward.

"Please, sir, we only request a few minutes of your time."

"Ever since he murdered the governor, he's no longer our son."

Again, he tried to close the door, but the princess spoke first. "Please, we're historians from Eulia. We're just trying to help."

The man glowered at her, thinking of some rebuttal, but after a few seconds, he exhaled and stepped aside.

"Thank you," McClevin said as they walked into the house. He jumped as the man slammed the door behind them.

"In here," the man said as he guided them through a door-less opening leading to a room with a raggedy couch and two rocking chairs with black cushions. The man seated himself on a rocking chair and, with his hand, beckoned for them to sit on the couch. Carefully avoiding the nails protruding out of the gray couch, they sat down.

They all sat in silence for several minutes. The man rocked back and forth in a slow, steady motion; the creaking from the chair blended in with the rain beating down on the roof and walls. Many times, McClevin parted his lips to speak, but felt intimidated by the man's decaying appearance: his eyes sunk into their sockets, his lips drooped into a lifelss frown, his skin sagged from his face like it was falling off. Finally, to McClevin's relief, the princess spoke.

"You have a nice view here." She gazed at an arched window overlooking the beach.

The man's eyes flicked to the window briefly. "I doubt you traveled all this way to admire our beach."

"You're right," McClevin said, realizing this man was clearly not happy with their arrival. "We came here to talk about Jay. Are you his father?"

The man nodded. McClevin noticed his blackened hands and dirty apron. A blacksmith.

"So," McClevin said, "Mr. Perry, when was the last—"

"Vilkus," the man said harshly.

"Beg your pardon?"

"My name is Timothy Vilkus."

"Oh, but isn't Jay's last name—"

"We adopted Jay when he was five, after his parents were arrested."

"I see." McClevin leaned forward, resting his elbows on his knees.

"And to answer your next question," Timothy continued, "we haven't seen him or our son since Jay murdered Governor Almsy."

"Your son?"

"Thyran. They both went missing the same night. We assume Jay kidnapped or killed him."

"I am sorry for your loss," the princess said.

He seemed to ignore her; he continued rocking in his chair with his hands folded in his lap. Then a short, plump woman dressed in a flowered shirt trundled in the room. She stopped abruptly when she noticed McClevin and the princess. Obviously, she was first to the dinner table in this house, McClevin thought.

"I didn't know we had company!" she said, rummaging her hands through her hair, trying to look nicer for her guests. "Did you offer them any drinks, Tim? They must be parched!"

"No Matilda." Tim looked outside the window; the rain lashed violently against the glass. "Why don't you fix them some tea?"

"I'll do just that!" she said, sounding aggravated.

When Matilda retreated to the kitchen, McClevin said, "Do you have any idea why Jay would murder the governor? Any suspicious behavior prior to the incident?"

Timothy's sunken eyes never left the window. "He acted like any orphaned fourteen-year-old."

"Did he have any disagreements with the governor?"

"Disagreements?" Timothy looked at McClevin and leaned back in his chair, causing another eerie creaking sound.

"Yes, something the governor did, perhaps, that caused him grief?"

"No, nothing we noticed."

Matilda bounced back in the room and plopped down on the other rocking chair. "Tea will be ready in just a minute! Say, I don't believe I've met you two before. My name's Matilda." They introduced themselves as Martin and Kate, historians from Eulia. "Pleasure to meet you both, Kate and Markin."

"It's Martin."

"Oh dearie! I'm sorry hun. Martin, is that right?" He nodded. "Good! So, what brings you two to our humble home?"

"Matilda..." the skeletal man mumbled.

"Sush! Someone here still knows how to show some hospitality!"

"We're gathering information regarding Jay Perry," McClevin said. "He stole something from Eulia recently, something of immeasurable value. So, King Emory sent us to uncover anything that will help Eulia track him down."

"I'm so sorry," she said, shaking her head. "That boy troubled me so.... We tried to raise him the best we could."

"Do you remember any unusual behavior prior to the night of the governor's death?" the princess asked.

Matilda rested her hands on her round stomach and began rocking her wooden chair. "Hmm, no, nothing comes to mind. Poor Jay...he always seemed to struggle with acceptance. His classmates were the bullying type, you know. Jay, being so light, so skinny, he was a target for the stronger kids." She smiled slightly. "Our son would stand up for him though, and even the meanest of the bullies were afraid of Thyran. He taught Jay to fight so he could defend himself. For hours, those two would go at it in the yard...Thyran taught him everything from fighting with arms and legs to fighting with weapons. The two trained to become noble knights to guard and protect us. I used to sit out on the porch and take to my knitting while they dueled. So cute they were. I used to call them my little defenders."

The princess gave her a comforting smile. "I can picture it."

McClevin watched Matilda stare at the wall like she could see her two sons now, young and innocent, playing in the yard.

"Did the governor have a son?" the princess asked.

Matilda shook her head. "Heavens no. He was not one for children." She raised an eyebrow at them. "Oh, I see where you are going dearie. No, I don't think Jay was bullied by anyone related to the governor. He was fourteen at the time. Thanks to Thyran, he had become quite the little fighter, so most of the bullies let him be."

"Hmm," the princess said. "So, he must have been pretty close to Thyran."

"Yes, very much so."

Suddenly, the bag of bones scowled and then stood up and hurried out of the room. McClevin wondered what they had said to upset him. Matilda shook her head and threw her hands down on the armrests. "How rude! Please, I apologize for my husband. He doesn't take too kindly to guests, and he is not well."

"It's fine," the princess said.

McClevin focused on the vacant chair rocking in the corner. "Can you think of any reason the governor would want to harm Thyran?"

She began to shake her head, but then stopped suddenly. "Actually, Thyran mentioned something during dinner one day about a week before the governor's death. He seemed rather troubled by the *Night of Endless Screams.*"

"The tragedy in Selia?" McClevin asked.

Matilda nodded. "Yes. Apparently, the governor refused to send any soldiers because he was concerned another war would break out with Valkadia and Eulia. The...villagers in Selia knew that the vulpins were closing in on them, but they had no defenses. Those nasty creatures tore into the village and killed everyone, including Thyran's lady friend, Alexia."

Matilda dabbed her eye with the edge of her sleeve. "I think he held a grudge against the governor for not sending any help to Selia. The poor child...I don't blame him."

McClevin heard the teapot whistle from the other room.

"Oh!" Matilda jumped up off the chair. "Tea is ready! Let me get you a cup." She hurried out of the room to tend to the tea.

McClevin looked down at the floor, rubbing his fingers together as he thought. That had to be it; Jay loved his older brother. Thyran had helped him when no one else would—helped him protect himself against bullies, helped him restore his self-confidence. Then Thyran's girlfriend died, and he blamed the governor. "Jay must have killed the governor on behalf of his brother," McClevin speculated aloud.

"No, that does not seem to fit," the princess said immediately, as if she was thinking along the same path. "If Thyran's life was in danger, Jay would have done anything to protect him. But, given what they said about Jay, he seems far too innocent to commit murder."

Matilda reentered the room carrying two blue cups, steam rising from the top. She handed one to each of them. "Here, this will warm you on this rainy night."

Too deeply lost in thought to heed the temperature of the tea, McClevin gulped down the liquid and instantly spat it out as it seared his throat. He quickly raised the cup to his lips again and pretended to take a sip, hoping no one had noticed his brief moment of idiocy.

"Mmm...very good," the princess said. "Thank you."

They drank in silence for a few minutes until the skeleton returned and stepped in front of his wife. "It's time for you to leave. We have no more information that can help you." Matilda shot him a cold glance, but said nothing.

McClevin set his tea down upon his lap. "But I just want to—"

"Leave." Timothy said coldly.

Peering into the man's dark eyes, McClevin sighed and rose to his feet. "Come on Catherine, let's go." After a second of silence, they walked for the door.

"One more thing," Matilda said, hurrying after them. "Jay stole something from the governor. A map of some sort. Perhaps you can go to the late governor's house and seek more information there. McKeachie still lives there. He was Governor Almsy's aid. He may know something."

"Thank you, ma'am," the princess said, bowing her head.

They set their nearly-full cups of tea on a wooden stool next to the door and stepped outside. Timothy promptly slammed the door shut behind them; they heard Matilda chiding him from inside the house. "Timothy Vilkus! Have some manners!"

"Quite the charmer," McClevin said as they stood on

the porch of the Vilkus residence.

The princess pulled her hood over her head to shield herself from the beating rain. "He is probably distraught at the thought of his son committing another crime. They have had a rough time over the years, explaining their son's actions to their neighbors and authorities. Although...something bothers me."

McClevin pointed at the governor's mansion in the distance and set off across the path, his bulky feet sloshing through muddy puddles. "What?"

Her thin frame arched forward to prevent rain from splashing her face. "I still do not understand why Jay would kill the governor over something like that. Thyran's life would have to be severely threatened for someone like Jay to even consider such a crime."

McClevin shrugged. What did it matter? Jay had the diamond locket, and he needed to recover it and return it to the king. That was his duty. "I'm sure this McKeachie character will have more information for us."

The din of rain intensified as McClevin and the princess treaded towards the mansion. Battered with fat raindrops, the foliage of nearby trees continuously drooped down and then snapped up, flicking water droplets down on them as they passed underneath.

Drenched, they arrived at the front door of the governor's mansion. The building was bigger than any others in Morad. Shortly after McClevin knocked on the door, an elderly man with gray, receding hair opened the door and welcomed them inside.

"Come! Come! Get out of the rain." He closed the door behind them. "You two are drenched. Let me fetch you a towel." He scurried across the tiled floor and returned a few seconds later with two large, white towels for them.

"Dry off now before you catch a cold."

The princess bundled herself in the towel. "Thank you, Mr....?"

"McKeachie. Duane McKeachie." He pushed his thick square spectacles up on his nose. "What are you doing running around like that in the rain? It's freezing out. Mark my word, one day, you'll catch a nasty cold and will be sick for weeks. And I won't feel sorry for you, not a bit."

McKeachie stepped along the floor, leading them inside. Confused, McClevin followed. "Uhh...Mr. McKeachie. My name is Markin—*Martin*, and this is Kate. We are historians from Eulia gathering information regarding Jay Perry. We were wondering if you could help us."

"Me?" McKeachie whirled around on his heel.

"Err...yes," McClevin said.

The scholarly man waved them into a room. "Come to my study then. Let's talk about it over a cup of tea."

"What's with these people and tea?" McClevin whispered to the princess as they followed McKeachie into his study.

McClevin admired the numerous shelves of books lining the walls in McKeachie's study. By the time they sat down into the red, overstuffed chairs, McKeachie had poured them two cups of tea and set them on a glass tray on the table in front of them.

"Mr. McKeachie—"

"Drink up! Your body needs warmth." The man, who reminded McClevin of his old writing teacher, tilted his own cup over his cracked lips and gave a satisfied breath. "Mmm...nothing in the evening like a good cup of tea."

"Indeed," McClevin said, careful not to let the scolding liquid pour over the edge onto his lap. "If you don't mind, sir, we are kind of pressed for time."

"But of course," he said, his hand, wobbly with age, setting his cup back on the tray. "How may I help you?"

"We are trying to find Jay Perry. Matilda Vilkus told us that Jay stole something the night of the murder. She said it was a map of some sort."

McKeachie again adjusted his glasses, this time with both hands. "Yes, a map was stolen. We were quite surprised when it turned up missing. The governor kept that very secret. Few people even knew it existed."

"What was on the map?" McClevin asked.

McKeachie regarded them for a moment then uprooted from his chair and closed the double door of his study, locking it securely. "Since you are historians, scholars like myself, I will divulge some information. But this conversation cannot leave this room. Agreed?"

Puzzled, the two nodded their heads.

When he sat back down, he straightened his back and pressed it against the fluffy armchair. "It was a map of a hidden treasure. Not one with the value of silver and gold, but something far greater...more than any man could comprehend."

"What kind of treasure?" McClevin asked.

McKeachie rolled the edge of his glasses between his fingers. "Even I am not entirely sure. The map was passed down the generations, eventually landing in Governor Almsy's possession. The governor's father told him that, for the preservation of Lassar, no man should ever find this treasure. The governor only allowed me to analyze it enough to ensure the artifacts required to find the treasure remained hidden."

McClevin watched him sip his tea. "So, what happened after Jay stole the map?"

"Well, the night he murdered the governor, we nearly

captured him, but he managed to wriggle free from the guards and swim out into the ocean. There's no land for miles, so I'm not sure what happened to him. We sent out boats trying to find him, but no such luck. I can only imagine he's resting at the bottom of the ocean with the map."

"He's not," McClevin said. "He stole a locket from Eulia three nights ago."

McKeachie stopped in mid-sip. "A locket?"

"Yes," McClevin said.

"What kind?"

"A diamond locket. He stole it from the king."

McKeachie's face turned a ghostly pale. "A...diamond locket? Oh dear...I wonder if...no...it can't be."

"Excuse me?" McClevin asked. As McKeachie began rambling to himself under his breath, McClevin felt his face burn with irritation. "McKeachie, if you know something, you must tell us. Our time is running low."

McKeachie's eyes shifted from the ceiling back to McClevin; his face regained some color. "The...diamond locket was one of the artifacts necessary to find the treasure. It's supposedly some sort of magical compass."

McClevin rolled his eyes. "Lord love a duck! Look, I need to find Jay and recover this locket. Do you know where I can find it or not? I don't have time to hear fairy tales of magic."

"Oh no," McKeachie said, his eyes wide, "it's no fairy tale. I fully believe it to be true."

"Whatever, do you know where Jay may head now that he has the locket?"

Grabbing his cup of half-drank tea, McKeachie stood up. "Come with me."

He led them out of the study, up a flight of stairs, and down a narrow hallway to a locked, cedar door. Fidgeting with a ring of keys, McKeachie said, "The current governor refused to stay in this room. It has been kept relatively untouched since the murder." Unsure why they were going in the room, McClevin remained silent while the elderly man twisted the key in the hole and pushed open the door. Dust swirled in the air as a gust of wind blew into the hallway.

McClevin peered inside. The bed was made, clothes put away. Everything was tidy as if it were an abandoned room in a hotel. The princess put her hand over her lips when she saw the blotch of blood stained into the bed sheets.

"We kept the room as is in case we needed to delve for clues," McKeachie said, seeing her look of shock. He strode over to the bookshelf along the wall, which was covered in dust. "We can only feel blessed he didn't steal this, or we would surely be lost." Dusting off some of the books, he removed a bright red book from the shelf and carried it over to the bed.

When he plopped it down, they all stared at the cover. Vivid, blue letters spelling "Dragons' End" stood out against the crimson background. McKeachie opened the book and flipped through the pages until he was near the back. "This is the only volume produced. Written by a man named Laneth Kukorski. Aha!" he slapped his finger down on the worn page. "Here it is."

McClevin and the princess read the passage above McKeachie's wrinkled finger.

Crystallize the head
Of the late wizard during his rest
If guided by a pure heart
The holy light brightens a path
Through raging storms
Find the burning lake of death
Which drowns the curved blade

Then shooting through the blue
Seize the pearl of vanishing crimson roses
Lost in a sea of emerald
And a sky of cerulean
In the basin the rock must rest
Disturbed only by the blade
Will the power unleash
His powers thou will absorb

"We think," McKeachie said after a moment, "that this means to unlock the compass inside the locket, one must visit Ashlen's Tomb. The location of his tomb was given on the map Jay stole as the Dryfus Mines. But, only one with a pure heart can unlock it, so, if Jay's ambitions are evil, he'll never be able to unlock the compass."

McClevin brushed off McKeachie's rambling about the magical locket. "You're sure the map pointed to the Dryfus Mines?"

"Yes, absolutely."

"Then I suppose that'll be our heading." McClevin began walking to the door when McKeachie said,

"Wait a second. There's one more thing you should know."

McClevin turned around. "Yes?"

McKeachie scratched his cheek. "Given the time that's passed since you say Jay stole the locket, if he has found a way to unlock the compass, he may already be gone from the mines and heading for the next location."

McClevin clenched his fists, growing rather annoyed with the man's stories. "And where's that?"

"Well, when analyzing the riddle, we think the line 'Through the storms' is a direction towards the next artifact. The other scholars and I concluded that the next artifact is in Storm Isle. There has always been rumor that the isle is guarded by a sea monster, and, since the legend of Dragons' End, the fall of the dragons three hundred years ago, no one who set out for Storm Isle has returned to tell the story."

"So you think Jay may already be heading towards Storm Isle?"

"That is my assumption."

McClevin pondered for a moment. He had no other ideas as to where Jay would be. And perhaps Jay was just as crazy as McKeachie. If so, he probably should check both places, just to be sure. "Do you think the governor would be good enough to lend us a ship? I'll have one of my knights, Kileean, lead a ship to the Dryfus Mines and then meet me in Storm Isle afterwards."

"Another ship? I thought you were historians?"

McClevin looked at him, though he could think of no way to salvage his identity.

McKeachie smiled. "Ahh, I see. The only ship here in Morad is the *Gemline*, a small merchant vessel. I will pay its crew to sail under your command; capturing Jay is as much a priority for Morad as it is for you. Here, take this." McKeachie handed the red book to McClevin. "It may prove useful."

"Is this the weapon he used?" the princess asked, eyeing a dagger placed on a silk handkerchief on the nightstand next to the bed.

McKeachie lifted the sharp dagger in the air. "Yes. Jay stabbed the governor in the back with this during his sleep."

She ran her finger above the blade. "It must have taken deadly precision to puncture his heart through his back."

McKeachie placed the blade down. "Yeah, I suppose so."

"Hmm..." she drifted off in thought as she followed McClevin back to the *Liberáte*, which waited for them under the gray sky.

9

Treacherous Waters

Cannons blasted along the side of the *Isabella* and crashed several hundred yards away into the ocean. The crimson sun rays burned over the horizon, a mystic fire sparked by the volley of cannons. Jay and the crew stood erect, hands by their sides, chins lifted in the air. Commanded by Hector, the pirates set off another round of cannons, forming a murky cloud of smoke that floated up through the air above the fiery glow of the sun. No one moved. No one spoke. A tear coursed down Jay's cheek.

"May you rest in peace, cap'n," Hector said, standing against the rail, his back to the crew, his face gazing out to the sea. "May no humble pirate on this ship hold any grievances against you as ye pass from this world to the next."

The crew all shouted in agreement, each bestowing their wishes to their fallen captain. Cain's black mynx flapped its feathered wings and then resettled, perched on his right shoulder. Jay saw Lyssa examining the crew, her head tilted down in respect. Sadness swept the ship with the force of a hurricane—all the crew looked somber, like a flame inside all their hearts died out, leaving behind trails of smoke.

"We will avenge your death," Hector continued. Like a warrior, he unsheathed his sword and held it gallantly in the air. "I promise ye, cap'n, Thyran will pay for yer death."

He swished his sword through the air, and another round of cannons blasted over the ocean. When the thunderous sound subsided, Hector turned to face the crew. "I know we just suffered a grave loss, but we must press on. If alive, Thyran will be on our tails in no time. We'll continue to follow the compass to get whatever treasure it reveals." He breathed slowly. "Back to your stations."

Silently, the crew shuffled back to their positions. Cain limped towards Hector, his mynx still perched on his shoulder. "What do you want done with the prisoner, captain?"

Hector eyed Lyssa, who stood still. "Jay," Hector said.

"Yes Hector. Err...cap'n?"

"See to it that she is released as promised."

"Aye cap'n."

Hector glanced at Cain. "Come with me." The two walked across the deck, and just before they disappeared down the stairs, Cain's mynx leapt off his shoulder and flew into the sky.

Lyssa wrapped her fingers around the wooden rail of the ship and stared blankly in the distance. Jay walked up to her and leaned against the rail, mimicking her stance. "You are no longer a prisoner," he said, but did not look at her; instead, he focused on the thin veil of smoke slowly diminishing under the sun's deep red rays. "We will let you go when we catch sight of land. You'll be free."

She laughed. "Free...I've never known freedom. I always get myself muddled in one mess or another."

"What do you mean?" he asked.

"Never mind." She dropped her head, allowing her golden hair to fall and mask her face.

Jay drummed his fingers on the wooden rail. The air cooled as the sun sank in the ocean, leaving only a beam of light dancing over the water. He had been meaning to ask her something since their encounter with his stepbrother in the Dryfus Mines, and he could not hold back any longer. "How do you know Thyran?"

"Hmm?" she asked.

"In the mines. He called you by your name. How did he know you?"

Her head hung even lower, she said nothing.

"Was he the pirate you spoke of earlier? The one who told you of Ashlen's Tomb?"

She nodded.

Jay swallowed. Numerous questions rushed to his lips, but he only managed to fire off one at a time. "How did you know him?"

"I...was part of his crew."

Part of his crew...was she still working for him? No, her reaction to his presence in the mines was not forced. "What happened?"

"We had a difference of opinions. I left."

He looked at her and saw only the golden strands of hair over her face. "What happened?"

"I told you," she said harshly. "We had a difference of opinions."

"Did you leave voluntarily or—"

"Enough!" She snapped up to a standing position and glowered at him; he was startled by her sudden movement. "Why are you so damn persistent?"

"I'm sorry, I was just...." But it was no use; she had already stormed across the deck and disappeared down the stairs. Jay kicked himself. Once again, he had let his curiosity get the best of him and asked too many personal questions. But it was strange, her reluctance to talk about the incident with Thyran. Something must have happened. Something very grave. He tried to dismiss those thoughts, but as he leaned against the railing, more questions sprang into his head and buzzed around like trapped bumblebees. He remained there for nearly an hour, pondering his numerous strands of questions while day gave way to night, before leaving for his appointment with Ankin.

When he reached the door to Ankin's room below deck, he heard Lynk yell from inside. "Ahh! Easy there! You're suppose to be making me better!"

"Well, if you would hold still, this would be a lot easier," came Ankin's calm voice. Jay pushed the door open and stepped inside. Ankin was leaning over Lynk's arm with a hooked surgical utensil scraping at a bloody wound just below Lynk's shoulder. "That stone is wedged in there deep. This won't hurt a bit...ahh, there we go!"

"Ahh!" Lynk jerked away from Ankin, peering down at his wound, which poured blood.

Ankin held a tooth-shaped shard of rock soaked with blood in his hand and set it down on his metal tray. "Jay, I didn't see you come in."

Jay felt his arm tingle by simply looking at Lynk, who kicked his feet back and forth over the edge of the chair. Blood streamed down his arm and dripped to the floor before Ankin took a white towel and washed his arm.

"Oh come on, Lynk," Ankin said, grabbing a bandage from his tray. "Can't you make the pain vanish just like those coins of yours?"

After Ankin secured the bandage over his wound, Lynk swung off the chair and dragged himself to the door. "Good luck," he mumbled to Jay before leaving the room.

Shaking his head, Ankin waved Jay to the chair. "Come on, Jay." When Jay sat down, he added, "That boy, he has no tolerance for pain."

"Haha, yeah, although I'm probably the same way." Jay leaned back in the chair and nervously glanced at the tray; it was littered with shiny, metal devices, none of which appeared friendly or welcoming. He took deep breaths to slow his breathing while Ankin lifted up his shirt revealing the large gash in his side just below his ribcage from tumbling down the jagged wall of the Eulia Castle.

"Hmm..." Ankin said. "It's healing nicely. I'm just going to dab it with some of this." Grabbing a fresh towel, he dipped it in a pool of clear liquid. "This won't hurt a bit."

Jay clenched his teeth, preparing for the worst despite Ankin's usual assurance. The liquid stung his side, but in a cool and refreshing way. "It must have been hard seeing your brother after so many years," Ankin said.

"He's nothing like I remember. His face was different. He looked so...dark."

"Hmm..." Ankin removed the damp towel from Jay's side.

"I should have done something. I could have helped the captain. Maybe he would be alive if only I had—"

"No, no, don't go blaming yourself now. The captain was a strong fighter, one of the best I've seen. I'm sure there was nothing you could do." Ankin taped a bandage against his gash. "This should do it. In a few days, the wound should be pretty much healed, though it may leave a mark. Is it causing you any pain?"

"No, not really."

"Good. Well, I won't keep you any longer. You're all set."

Jay threw himself off the chair and headed towards the door. "Thank you, Ankin."

"No problem Little Blue. Take it easy on yourself, alright?"

Jay nodded and left the room. That was not as bad as he anticipated. Any visit to Ankin for medical attention usually involved a great deal of pain, but this time—

He heard a scream.

Jay rushed along the corridor to the stairs, and then he heard another scream, much louder than the first. A woman. On deck. As he raced up the stairs, Soleus bolted out of a nearby room, a panicked expression on his round face. "Del? Is that you again? Where are you?"

"The sound came from up on deck," Jay said, and the two sprinted up the stairs and poured onto the deck along with the other concerned crewmates. Through the darkness of night, they hurried across the deck in the direction of the screaming—Jay recognized the screeches to be Delcato's. She was yelling something, but he could not make it out.

A dozen pirates gathered in a circle at the stern of the ship. When he got closer, Jay gasped in shock. Delcato was holding a loaded pistol aimed directly at Cain's forehead. She pinned him against the rail. Her fierce gaze tore through the night, keeping the crew at a distance.

"Delcato..." Hector pleaded from a few feet away, his hands open displaying he was unarmed. "Please, put the gun down."

"No! He killed him! I saw his tattoo! It was the same one I saw in the field."

Squeezing through the crew, Soleus navigated his way to Hector. "Del, it's me," he said. "Yer just havin' another nightmare."

"No!" She thrashed her head back, flinging her black hair in the air. Her voice deepened to a low growl, so low it sounded as if she was possessed by a demon. "He killed him. He killed my father. I know it!"

"That's Cain!" Soleus said. "He's been with us for years."

She shook her head, tears streaming down her cheeks.

"He has the tattoo on his shoulder. It's the same one, I know it."

Hector grabbed the hilt of his sword, but Soleus yelled, "Stop! She's just having a nightmare."

"I have to protect me crew!" Hector said, drawing his sword and tilting it towards her. "Delcato, put the pistol down."

The pistol rattled as her hand quivered. Holding his staff calmly, Cain said, "You need to wake up, Delcato. I have not killed your father. I have no tattoo on my—"

"Liar!" she stepped towards him. "I'll kill you now!"

Jay heard a short cry from above; he made out the blackened, bird-like form of a mynx circling in the air, its wings beating rhythmically as it watched from above.

Delcato must have glanced upward as well, for when Jay looked down, Hector had lunged forward and flicked his blade, stopping it just short of her neck. "This be me last warning," he said. "Drop the gun."

"No!" Soleus dived forward, grabbed Hector's shoulders, and threw him back to the ground, flinging the blade away from Delcato's tender neck.

It all happened instantaneously. Hector and Soleus tumbled to the ground. Delcato's pistol went off. The gun blast rattled the black sky. A scream. Delcato dropped the gun and fell to her knees, her mouth agape with horror. Jay's eyes flicked from Delcato to Cain, who stumbled, gripping his staff to maintain balance. Cain stared at Delcato through his hooded eyes for a second, maybe two, and then, slower than usual, he regained his footing and limped through the crowd without a word.

"You okay, mate?" Jenkins asked as he passed.

"I'm fine," Cain mumbled as he pushed through the circle of pirates, making his way for the stairs.

Delcato buried her head in her hands, weeping. Karen stepped up from behind her and wrapped her in a fluffy, purple blanket. "There there, dear, you're okay. Let's get you inside." She helped the trembling Delcato to her feet.

"Is she okay?" Soleus asked, his chest heaving up and down with his rapid breathing.

"She'll be fine," Karen said. "She hasn't had a nightmare this severe in a while. Something must have happened that reminded her of her father's death. Probably witnessing Captain Gaden's death triggered a memory."

Completely pale and trembling feverously, Delcato walked with Karen across the deck. "I'll see you in the morning," Soleus called after them. "I promise, Del. Yeh'll be alright!"

"As captain of this ship," Hector said, regaining his footing, "I am well within me right to give you fifteen lashes for yer actions."

Red-faced, Soleus swung his clenched fists. "Ye were gonna kill her! I was—"

"Soleus," Hector interrupted. "You will receive ten lashes for your insubordination"

"But I was—"

"Now!"

Jay wanted to cry out in Soleus's behalf, but he knew their code. Any insubordination must be punished. Discipline was a necessity on any ship. His fists clenched, his head low, Soleus followed Hector away from the group towards the main mast.

Jay, unable to bear the sight of his friend in pain, looked down to the ground. He noticed something peculiar on the floorboards: a pile of gray residue where Delcato had been. The gun had indeed fired, and from such a close range, it would be nearly impossible for her to miss. Was Cain hiding his wound from them? If he was shot, he would need medical attention immediately.

"Impossible," Jenkins said, crouched down near the rail. When Jay approached, he saw Jenkins was holding a round musket ball in his slender fingers. "If the shot missed, it should be lost in the ocean."

"It had to have hit something," Jay said.

"But what?"

Jenkins and Jay examined the rail. There was nothing. No dents, no holes, or any sign of impact.

"Did the gun go off properly?" Lynk asked, examining the musket ball.

Jenkins stood up. "Yes, from the sound of the blast, it worked fine." He scratched his head.

Jay noticed Lyssa standing near the back of the crowd. She appeared to be disinterested, looking away from the commotion, but Jay could tell she was listening intently, naturally intrigued by what happened. He was too; what would cause the musket ball to stop dead in the air like that? There was no armor Jay knew about that would deflect a shot in that manner.

Just as perplexed as he, the crew dispersed, scattering in different directions. Jay wanted to talk to Lyssa again, to apologize for being so intrusive earlier, but she had vanished in the crowd of pirates moving across the deck.

Jay remained at the front of the ship, staring off across the ocean, not wanting to return to his room in fear of running across Soleus during his discipline. He allowed his mind to roam the night sky and escape into the tranquility, not thinking about Thyran or the late captain or the myth of Ashlen or any of it. He needed some time to cleanse his mind. Some time to relax.

After maybe an hour of leaning against the wooden

rail, Jay decided to head back to his room. "Goodnight, Gideon," he said as he passed by the wheel where Gideon had resumed his post.

"G'night Little Blue. Have a peaceful sleep. See you in the morning."

Jay heard Gideon whistling a jovial tune as he descended the stairs and went below deck to his room. Soleus was already there, tucked under the cotton sheets of the lower bunk, his eyes open as he relived those ten lashes against his back. Jay climbed to the top bunk and plopped himself on his mattress, the back of his head rested on his small pillow. Silently, he stared at the bare ceiling for several minutes, replaying the scene over and over in his head, trying to understand how Cain survived.

"You okay, Soleus?" he asked after a few minutes.

"Yeah, I'm alright. I just feel bad for Del, ya know?"

"Yeah," Jay said.

"I mean, she's been having these nightmares ever since I've known her."

"How long ago was her father killed?"

Soleus thought for a moment. "When she was twenty, I think."

"She's been having nightmares for six years?"

"Yeah. She must have been really traumatized. I guess he was killed right in front of her."

"Did she ever find out why?"

"Nah. She caught a glimpse of the assassin. The only thing she remembers is a tattoo on his right arm near the shoulder and a fiery cape bearing the symbol of Valkadia on his back."

"Hmm...Thyran never had a tattoo."

"I don't think it was yer stepbrother. The killer was much older than he would have been at the time."

"Oh."

"Well, no sense fretting about it all night. I'm jus' glad she's alright. Have a good night, Lil' Blue."

"You too, Sol."

Jay felt his friend's concern for Delcato; Soleus was unusually quiet, his voice stripped of its usual clumsiness. At least everyone was alright. He could not imagine Soleus's reaction if Delcato ever injured herself or another during one of her nightmares.

He closed his eyes. Images drifted against the black of his eyelids. Lyssa, she seemed strange, mysterious. She knew more than she revealed, she had some history with Thyran. And Thyran, with that collected, devious smirk on his face, unnerved by their escape earlier. He had to still be alive and was probably chasing after them. Thyran was hunting something. But what?

Tomorrow, he needed to talk to Lyssa. She would know.

Questions rained down in his head until he drifted into a restless sleep.

Three days passed while the crew recovered from the loss of their captain. Each day, the *Isabella* skimmed closer and closer to her destination. Jay made several attempts to talk to Lyssa, but he rarely saw her, and when he did, a crowd of pirates was nearby. He preferred to talk to her alone. His frustration mounted as time passed, and they sailed onward, following a mysterious compass to an unknown destination. Something was out of place, he felt it, a feeling that stole his appetite and deprived him of sleep. He needed answers.

The fourth day was a dreary one. Gray clouds engulfed the blue sky and cast a bleak light upon Lassar. The locket had guided them to the passageway of the towering landforms of Storm Isle. Jagged cliffs dropped heavily from the land masses on either side of the ship. The crew stared amazed at the weathered rock formations, beaten and torn by furious storms.

At the front of the ship, Lyssa paced back and forth, slicing the air with her arrow-headed staff. Jay caught glimpse of her, and his heart beat against his chest. She was alone. Now was his chance. Hesitantly, he walked over to her.

"Bleak day," he said.

She stabbed her bow forward, piercing the heart of her invisible foe. "I suppose it is."

He needed to choose his words carefully; he could not be so direct this time.

"You're pretty good with that."

"Amara."

"Amara?" Jay repeated.

"That's the name of my bow." She sliced the air horizontally.

"Oh. What's that mean?"

"I named it after my mother." She spoke in a matter-of-fact tone, stripped of emotion.

"I see. Where did you learn to wield a bow so well?"

"Taught myself."

"You handle it expertly," he said. "Perhaps better than I wield my sword." He smiled and watched her, curious to see how she would react to his challenge.

"As I recall," she stopped and looked at him, and for the briefest of seconds, Jay thought he caught a glimpse of her smirking, the first instance when her lips were not plastered into a stern frown. "It was you on the ground, panting, out of breath in Eulia."

"I had nearly fallen from the roof; I was shaken up."

He drew his cutlass. "Come, let's match our skills, now that we are both good and rested."

"Oh really? I'm swifter than you think." Suddenly, she lunged for him and flung her bow at his head, but he threw up his cutlass just in time to block. She smiled. "Very good. You have quick reflexes. Still, you're too—"

They both stumbled as the ship suddenly thrashed to the side. Jay frantically scanned the water, checking to see if they bumped into a rock.

"What was that?" Hector asked, flying out of his cabin, his eyes darting around the ship. "Did we hit something?"

"I—I don't know," Jay said.

"Look! Over there!" one of the pirates shouted pointing to the right.

Jay did not need to squint to see it. Climbing up the towering rocks was a large, dark gray serpent. Its slender body slid up the cliff like a snake. The creature did not have any limbs—it appeared wrapped in a wrinkled cloak of dark slime. It sped up the wall at an alarming rate.

"What *is* that?" Lynk asked, advancing to the rail.

The crew stood baffled as they watched the snake-like form slither up the wall. Its tail ended in a wide fin, like that of a fish. A ghostly silence swallowed the atmosphere, sending a chill down Jay's spine as he tilted his head to follow the creature up the wall. When it reached the zenith, it perched up on a mound-shape rock like a vulture, overlooking the valley. Razor sharp fangs lined its long, narrow muzzle. The creature flapped open its wrinkled cloak of slime, which spread into two enormous wings, its wingspan exceeding the length of the ship. Eight squid-like tentacles protruded from the serpent's chest and thrashed viciously through the air. Pointing its muzzle upward, the creature opened its mouth and gave a high-pitched screech that shook the land, causing bits of rock to rumble down the cliff. Its numerous tentacles from its dark blue underside flailed in the air, two of them holding the creature on the rock.

When the creature looked down, a scaly mane, splashed with brilliant colors of blue, expanded from its neck and waved in the air menacingly. Thin slits above its muzzle revealed its flaming white eyes. The fearsome sight left Jay lost for words. He knew the creature saw them, and it was only waiting for the right moment to—

The creature dove off the rock and, stretching its massive wings, glided straight for the ship.

The pirates yelled and scrambled across the deck.

His muscles unwilling to budge, Jay watched the serpent swoop down, growing larger and larger as it neared the ship. Before the crew had enough time to react, the creature landed on the edge of the ship, wrapping its wet tentacles around the rails and masts to hold it up. The entire ship leaned heavily to the side; the pirates slipped down the deck and struggled to grab hold of something to halt their fall. Jay gripped the rail opposite the creature. His stomach churned when he saw the creature's purple tongue shoot out of its mouth and scoop up one of his crewmates, toss him in the air, and snap its muzzle shut over the pirate, swallowing him whole.

"To arms!" Hector yelled. "Grab the pistols. Man the cannons! Aim for its tentacles!" Hector whipped out his cutlass and dashed for one of the creature's tentacles wrapped tightly around the mast. When he tried to slice through it, the serpent flung out its tongue, slapping the captain across the deck.

"Lynk!" Cain shouted as he threw a knife at the tentacle, causing the creature to screech fiercely. "You and your brother, take some men below and fire the cannons at the creature's belly on my mark."

"Aye!" Sheathing their swords, the two brothers recruited some pirates to assist them.

The giant creature towered as high as the tallest mast. Its weight kept the ship tilted at an unstable angle. Stretching its mouth wide, it tilted its head and lunged forward. Its jaws crunched down on the main mast, snapping it in half, spraying splinters of wood over the deck. The serpent threw the mast into the ocean with a flick of its head.

Carrying a large sack of weapons, Soleus scurried on deck. "I've brought up the weapons, cap'n!"

Hector grabbed a long-barreled musket. "Everyone, grab a firearm and blast the bastard if yeh've any desire to live!"

Jay rushed to Hector and snatched a pistol. Fumbling with the musket balls and gunpowder, he struggled to prepare it for firing.

Beside him, Karen pointed her pistol at the serpent's head. "Ahh!" she yelled as she blasted a small hole through its indigo mane. Instantly, the creature shot a tentacle in her direction, knocking her off her feet and slamming her against the mast. The blow knocked her out.

"Aim for the tentacles!" Hector shouted. "The damn beast is tipping the ship over." Bracing the musket against his shoulder, Hector aimed at the tentacle wrapped around the main mast and blasted it. The creature quivered with anger and screeched, but it still held on to the mast.

Finished loading his pistol, Jay aimed for the tentacle and fired, but to no effect. Some other pirates pelted the giant serpent's wings with musket balls, but they bounced off like pebbles.

"Gideon!" Ankin shouted after firing at the creature.

"Get below deck! It's too dangerous up here!"

Jay noticed Gideon dashing for the pile of weapons. "I'm part of the crew, mate!" he said. He grabbed a long-barreled pistol with a wide muzzle and approached the thick tentacle securing the main mast. The serpent leaned back, causing the ship to turn even more severely; a few pirates fell over the rail and into the sea.

"Lynk!" Cain yelled down towards the floorboards. "Fire the cannons!"

"Aye capt'n," Lynk called out from beneath the floorboards. "We're loading them now."

"Hurry!"

The ship tilted even more, and Gideon lost his footing. Sliding towards the mast, he stretched his arm and grabbed hold of rope coiled around the mast. He pulled himself closer to the mast and pressed the tip of his pistol against the dark tentacle. "For the crew!" he shouted as he squeezed the trigger, finally blowing the tentacle off the mast. The creature flapped its blue wings as it howled with fury. The *Isabella* regained some stability, although she still remained tilted under the serpent's weight.

"Good work!" the captain said. "Now, let's blow it off the ship before we capsize."

Jay watched the fray in awe; it was surreal. The creature's tentacles flicked across the deck, knocking some pirates off the ship, and lunged its head forward, crushing many pirates with its deathly jaws. All the screams of pain and fear dug into Jay's stomach, making his heart race faster; he needed to stop this. After loading his pistol again, he shot at the serpent's head; he missed, or it had no effect against the serpent's thick scales.

"Arrrg!" Gideon shouted as he lifted his pistol. "No beast messes with—" his voice was cut short as the creature scooped him up with one of its tentacles. Raising him high in the air, the creature's gleaming white eyes glared at the dangling pirate.

"No!" Delcato shouted, motioning up to Gideon. "Everyone, aim at the tentacle holding Gideon!" Those who could hear her aimed at the tentacle and fired, careful to avoid hitting their comrade.

Jay's hands trembled. He needed to act fast, or Gideon would die. The realization ripped through his body as he loaded his pistol. He saw Gideon sway back and forth, struggling to break free. The creature's forked tongue poked out from its fanged muzzle, preparing for its attack.

"For the crew!" Gideon screamed as he gathered the last of his strength to point the gun at the creature's eyes—

Jay finished loading his pistol. He pointed it at the tentacle suspending Gideon in the air—

Gideon fired—

The creature's head jerked back slightly, and before Jay could get a clear shot, it threw Gideon in the air. A second later, Gideon vanished into the creature's mouth.

"Gideon!" Jay screamed, tears exploding from his eyes.

Lynk shouted from below, "Fire!" The cannons fired in sync, some of them piercing into the beast's stomach, others smashing into the rock wall behind it. The serpent shrieked in pain; its body severed from the ship and sunk in the water. The ship flung back upright, and the crew sprawled across the deck, weary from the fight.

Recovering to his feet, Hector snatched his gun from the ground. "All hands on deck! Fall in line!" Groaning, the pirates scrambled into a line facing Hector. Jay allowed himself to join them, but he felt shattered, the vision of Gideon disappearing into the fanged mouth burning in his mind.

"Cap'n, what was that?" Soleus asked.

"That thing was bloody huge, that's what it was!" Jenkins said.

Hector loaded his gun. "I don't know, but I doubt we killed it. We are going to have to lure it in front of the cannons so we can blast through its chest."

Cain limped forward with his staff. "That won't work. Even a dumb animal avoids actions that result in pain. It won't give us another clear shot. We need the cannons on deck."

"No, we don't have time."

"Then we don't stand a chance," Cain snapped. "I think we proved pistols and swords do very little."

Hector opened his mouth to offer a rebuttal, but then glanced to the side at Ankin. "Ankin, what do you think?"

"Aye, cap'n," Ankin said plaintively. "I agree with Cain."

Hector sighed. "Very well. You all," Hector motioned to a dozen pirates, "take some of the crew down with ye and bring up three cannons. Lynk, Blynk, Delcato: adjust the sails with the wind. We need to get to land quickly. Karen, Cain, organize the crew along the ship. We need to aim for its tentacles—those we can damage. Now, let's move, we have no time to waste!"

The crew rushed to follow Hector's orders. Jay spotted Lyssa amid the bustling pirates. He hurried over to her, noticing a wide, red scratch across her left cheek. "Lyssa! Are you okay?"

She wiped her smudged hair out of her eyes. "Yes, I'm fine. You know, I was watching it, and every time it was ready to strike, it—"

Her voice drowned when the serpent dove into the air with its scaled wings wrapped tightly around its body.

Whirling like a top, it sprayed water over the crew, who gasped in horror when it resurfaced. Twenty yards in the air, it flapped open its giant wings and hung in the air like a puppet suspended by string. It craned its neck and glowered at the crew, its thick mane shaking like a rattlesnake's tail. With long, dramatic thrusts of its wings, it remained aloft in the air.

Dumbfounded, the crew stared at the immense creature, no one daring to move, no one daring to speak. Jay scanned its body looking for a weak point, perhaps a spot they could target to penetrate its scaled armor. His skin tingled when the serpent screeched, louder than ever, a screech of revenge. Its white eyes glinted brightly, sending a flash of white light through the air. Arching its head forward, it opened its narrow muzzle, and a severe gust of wind, coming from nowhere, blasted across the deck.

The wind swept over the deck and blew the crew like leaves. Jay again searched for something to grab to hold himself steady.

"Grab something for support!" Hector said, taking cover behind the mast. "Fire at its mouth!"

"We're too far away!" Cain said, crouching behind the staircase leading to the bridge.

"What else do you suggest?" Hector said. "Fire!"

The able pirates fired their weapons, but with little effect. The serpent's head thrashed violently as it mysteriously channeled mighty gusts of wind at the ship. The sails caught the wind and bent outwardly; the ship began to drift sideways, away from the creature and closer to the nearby towering wall of rock.

"Lynk! Raise the sails!" Hector ordered.

Squeezing and pulling on the coarse rope, Lynk's body lifted in the air due to the wind. "I can't cap'n! The wind is too strong. It won't budge!"

Blynk scrambled to grab hold of the rope and bring his brother back to the deck. "Hold on, Lynk!"

Standing behind one of the masts, Jay looked behind him. They were approaching the jagged wall fast; only a few more seconds, and they would crash. Suddenly, he had an idea. "The sails!" he shouted. "Aim for the sails!"

Without questioning, those nearby spun around and fired their weapons at the canvas sail; each musket ball ripped through the tan fabric. Still, the boat raced closer to the wall. The wind blew a few pirates off the ship, and Jay watched in horror as the pirates smashed into the rocks, the same ones the *Isabella* would smash into soon.

Jay heard Hector shouting over the roaring wind. "Fire at the sails! Our crew be dyin'! Blast a hole in that sail or I be blastin' a hole in you!"

Soon, the whole crew pelted the sail relentlessly with musket balls, and finally, to Jay's relief, the entire canvas ripped open, allowing the air to blow through the fabric. The ship slowed. The whistling sound of wind echoed off the canyon walls. Then the beast snapped its mouth shut, the winds ceased, and it was again silent. The serpent whirled in the air, wrapping itself again in its winged cloak, and plunged back into the water.

"Lynk!" Blynk said as he rushed to his brother, who had dropped several feet back onto the deck.

"Ooof!" Lynk examined his hands, which were bleeding from gripping so tightly on the coarse rope. "Look at my hands. I don't know if I'll be able to be performin' any magic tricks anytime soon."

A group of crewmates emerged from below deck each holding the end of a thick net that dragged a gray cannon on deck. Two more groups followed, each carrying their own cannon, and a third group brought a brown sack of what Jay assumed to be cannon balls.

"Where'd the beast go?" Soleus asked as he ripped the net off the cannon and rolled it across the floorboards.

"Down there!" Karen yelled, pointing at the sea.

Jay rushed to the rail and peered over in the direction of Karen's finger. He could faintly make out the shape of the serpent as it swam underwater next to the ship. Suddenly, it dove out of the water, sending a thunderous scream through the air. Jay jumped back as it twirled over the ship and crashed in the sea on the other side. The resulting wave nearly capsized the ship. Again, the creature bolted out of the water and latched its tentacles around different parts of the ship. Spreading its thick wings, it flicked out its tongue, snatched a pirate, and swallowed him whole. It seemed more aggressive than before, determined to kill every remaining pirate on board.

Jay spotted one of the three cannons. "Lyssa, help me move this," he said. He stuffed his pistol around his waist and sprinted to the cannon. Lyssa ran to his aid, and, each pressing on a side, they turned it to face the serpent, which was again pulling the ship to the side.

The creature wildly thrashed its tentacles about, knocking some of the crew into the water and smashing different parts of the ship. Hector leapt off the bridge to avoid a thick tentacle slamming into the floorboards.

Jay grabbed a dagger from the deck and some flint from the bag of cannonballs while Lyssa loaded a shot into the cannon. In one quick move, he sparked the wick and blasted the cannonball into the serpent's stomach. It jerked its head towards them and flung out its tongue. Jay and Lyssa dove to the side as it snatched the cannon with its tongue and whipped it into the water. It tilted its head to the gray sky and let out a triumphant screech.

Lying on the deck, Jay watched Soleus and Jenkins aim another cannon at a tentacle wrapped around a wooden post. When it fired, the cannon blew off the tentacle. Rescinding its wounded limb, the serpent slammed a healthy tentacle against the cannon, sending it flying across the deck, smashing a pirate in its path, blasting through the rail, and falling to the sea.

"Guard the last cannon!" Cain said. Jay and Lyssa immediately pulled it back, farther from the creature.

Musket balls bouncing off its wings and body, the serpent furiously gripped the *Isabella*, leaned back, and flapped its wings relentlessly; it was trying to flip the ship.

Battling the unyielding attacks of the serpent's tentacles, the crew slashed their blades and blasted their guns, screaming with rage and fear. Crimson blood gushed out of the serpent's tiny wounds.

"Jay!" Hector said, stabbing his blade into one of the serpent's tentacles. "We're going to tip. Use the last cannon, now! It's our only chance."

Lyssa shoved another cannon ball down the barrel. "Turn it this way, Jay."

She pointed away from the creature. "But, the serpent is over there—"

"I have an idea." She sounded confident. He turned the cannon sideways without waiting for an explanation. "Now, give me your pistol." He reached for the pistol tucked by his waist and tossed it to her. "Good, now, hold the cannon steady."

The pistol in one hand and *Amara*, her bow, in the other, she dashed to the center of the deck. Planting her feet firmly on the ground and bending her knees for balance, she expertly aimed her pistol at the serpent's flaming white eyes.

Jay shouted after her. "What are you doing? You're in the open without cover. Get back!"

Ignoring him, she smirked when the creature twisted its head towards her. "Eyah!" she yelled as she squeezed the trigger. The musket ball soared through the air and penetrated the beast's muzzle just below its eye. It thrashed its head back. Before she could move, its tongue shot out, aimed for her legs to scoop her up as it had Gideon—

She waited until just before the tongue reached her; she then whirled to the side and stabbed *Amara* through its slimy, purple tongue. Hissing violently, the serpent flicked back its tongue, flipping *Amara* in the air, and lunged its head for her, baring its sharp white teeth as it spread its jaws. She tried to move, but it was too late—

Ankin had already run to her aid and extended his arms to push her aside. The beast suddenly jerked its head and sunk its lethal jaws into Ankin's arm, severing his hand instantly. "Ahh!" he screamed, throwing his head back in agony.

Leaping to her feet, Lyssa's eyes flashed wide as blood sprayed from Ankin's arm. "Now, Jay! Fire!"

He suddenly realized her plan. Adjusting the cannon, he lit the wick. The cannon ball ripped through the air and blasted through the serpent's slender neck. Its mouth swung open in agony, dropping Ankin's detached hand, and the serpent raised its head, gasping for breath. It flailed its tentacles in the air, thrashed its body madly as it struggled to breathe.

Finally, after several seconds of battling for breath, the serpent collapsed on the center of the ship. Its massive form crashed through the deck and plummeted through several subsequent floors, pushing the center of the ship below water. The stern and bow tilted high in the air; before

Jay could react, he lost his footing and slid down the deck towards the submerged center. Icy water stung Jay's body as it completely consumed him.

He was lost. He could neither see nor breathe. Eddies sucked him down, deeper and deeper into blackness as the slain serpent dragged him and the *Isabella* into the cold water.

10

The Acid Lake

The air smelled putrid, like dense smoke from burning charcoal. He coughed, but not into air, into sand. Hard sand. Icy water rushed up along his legs, gluing his pants to his skin, and then settled back by his toes. He heard nothing, not the chirruping of the azura, not the blowing of the wind, not the crashing of the waves. Silence.

Jay chanced cracking open his eyelids just enough to see. He was lying on a beach. The sand was gray like volcanic ash. Beyond the beach, the land was burnt; hard black plates of soil tiled the ground. Leafless trees topped with sprays of branches poked up in between the plates, crumbling sections of the plates as they battled for room to grow. The whole environment appeared as if it was a tropical island scorched by a vicious fire, one which took no prisoners, just annihilated everything in its path.

His strength vanished, his eyelids felt like lead. They shut, and Jay again went limp.

When he awoke again, he saw Cain bending his knees, running the tip of his staff through the murky water.

"Uhh...." Jay rubbed his head.

"Welcoming, isn't it?" Cain said without looking back.

"W-where are we?" Jay managed to rise to his feet and wobble over to him.

Cain flicked a rock from the water bed with his staff. "Storm Isle."

His legs still wobbly, Jay fell to his knees. The coarse sand felt like a colony of thorns poking and ripping into his skin. "Where's the *Isabella*?"

"Went under." Digging his staff into the sand, Cain stood up. The dark clouds swallowed the sun, leaving an even more gloomy presence in the air. Jay pressed his hand against his head, which pounded relentlessly, making it hard to think. What happened? The walls...the brown rock walls that guided them, he remembered those. But then...there was something climbing up the wall, and it came down, and then Gideon...Gideon, lost forever in the creature's jaws. He could have helped, could have fired his weapon and saved him....

Then, Lyssa, she lured the creature in, and he lit the cannon...then it was cold and black.

"The creature...where is it?"

Cain brushed some sand off his black beard. "You killed it."

Killed it?

"I did? Lyssa had brought it—wait, where is she? Where's Lyssa? Is she alright?"

Cain nodded and pointed inland. Jay looked where Cain pointed, and through his blurred vision, he counted nine pirates, Ankin in the middle surrounded by the rest near a blackened tree. He caught glimpse of golden hair and the arrow-headed bow, *Amara*; his muscles loosened. Lyssa was safe. But then his stomach knotted. There were only nine of them.

"Where are the others?"

"Dead."

Cain's voice rang out over the misty silence. Jay did not know how to respond at first. His vision was slowly recovering, but he felt queasy, dizzy, unable to move or speak.

So many of his crewmates had perished, just like the captain.

He looked up at Cain, who stood still, staring out over the sleeping sea. He appeared calm, relaxed, unmoved. The towering cliffs on either side of the water stretched as far as Jay could see, lining a corridor of travel off to the horizon.

"Are you alright?" Jay asked.

"I'm fine," Cain said softly. "Go, be with the others. Ankin is injured badly. I'll be there in a few minutes."

Whatever Cain was searching for seemed to steal all of his attention, for he never once glanced at Jay. "What are you doing?" Jay asked.

"Thinking," Cain said, again, without looking.

Jay's mournfulness overpowered his curiosity. He left Cain to himself and trudged through the sand up to the hard soil plates lining the ground and made his way to his comrades. From the middle of the group came a scream of agony.

"Hold still!" Karen said, wrapping some bandages recovered from the wreck around Ankin's stubbed arm where his left hand had been. Jay winced when he saw dark blood soaking into the white bandages.

"Ahhh!" Ankin screamed. He lay on the stiff ground with his back against the charcoaled tree.

Lyssa knelt beside him and placed her hand on his shoulder. "Thank you, Ankin. You saved my life back there."

"It's..." Karen tightened the bandage over his wound; he closed his eyes and winced. "...Okay. You saved the entire crew's." He glanced down at his bandage, now securely fastened over his left arm.

"There, all set." Karen rose to her feet and examined her hands, which were covered with blood. She slipped past the rest of the crew and made her way for the beach.

Jay scanned the pirates, seeing who survived the recent attack: Hector, Lynk, Blynk, Soleus, Jenkins, Delcato, Ankin, and Lyssa. Everyone's eyes were focused on Ankin, so no one noticed Jay approach until Ankin raised his head. His eyes met Jay's, and a smile snuck its way to his lips.

"Ahh...Little Blue!" he said, sounding out of breath. "Nice shot, mate. I would get up and thank you properly, but I'm not in the hand-shaking mood."

Ankin's praise bounced off Jay's guilt with no effect. "I'm sorry, Ankin. I should've shot sooner."

Ankin winced as he scooted up the tree. "Nonsense. I consider myself lucky you shot when you did. Any sooner, you would've missed. Any later, and the beast would've finished me."

Lynk snuck up from behind and slapped Jay's back. "No kiddin' mate! That was more magical than any of our tricks!" He bent down to scoop up a coil of rope washed ashore and tossed it over his shoulder.

"Speaking of tricks," Ankin said. "How about making my pain vanish?"

Despite their recent losses, despite the bleak atmosphere, the crew laughed. It felt good for Jay. Even though his laughter was slight, it provided some release for his imprisoned emotions.

Hector smiled next to Ankin. "Glad to see yeh've still got yer sense of humor. Ye better be able to mend our wounds even with one hand, though. Our chances of findin' another surgeon like yerself in these lands be as slim as finding a lock Jenkins can't pick." His smile broadened. "Come. Let's get ready to head off. The treasure must be on this island. I'll get the compass from Cain while ye all get ready." He walked off after Karen, who was rinsing her hands in the sea, washing away Ankin's blood.

Soleus trundled past the tree and overlooked the parched land. Everything was dead as far as they could see. "Well! This be a welcoming place for our buddy Ashlen to hide the treasure. I'd feel more welcome in the Valkadian dungeons, if ye ask me."

Jenkins shook his head. "No you bloody wouldn't. Trust me on that one."

That was the last they said while they waited for their captain and the others. Everyone, even Lynk and Blynk, were quiet; mournfulness weighed down on them all.

Something in the air caught Jay's attention—a small, black animal gliding down from above. Cain's mynx. It flew down and hovered over Cain's right shoulder before settling itself on his black jacket. The mynx licked its paws and scrubbed its face while Cain stroked its back, slow, delicate strokes. He was talking to Hector about something, but Jay could not hear.

The scenery was drab, which only thickened their sorrow. Everything had a grayish tint to it...the rocks, blackened trees, barren ground, sand the color of ash. Jay had only been conscious on Storm Isle for ten minutes, and he already could not wait to make leave this forsaken place.

Jay sat with the others, rubbing his shaky palms with his thumbs. His whole body felt weak; his muscles ached, his head felt like a block of lead propped on his neck. Maybe it was due to the sadness of nearly all the crew perishing from that vile serpent, or maybe it was exhaustion from the battle, or maybe it was Storm Isle itself weighing him down. Whatever it was, the rest of the crew seemed to share his feelings.

"Alright, let's get moving," Hector called out as he, Cain, and Karen rejoined them by the tree.

"Which way?" Delcato asked.

Cain held the locket and flipped it open before his eyes. A faint greenish glow glimmered over his face; the mynx's black eyes glistened as it focused on the locket. After snapping the locket shut and stuffing it in his pocket despite Hector's request to relinquish the locket to him, Cain pointed northwest. His mynx at once fluttered off his shoulder and flew on ahead in the direction of Cain's finger as if to scout the land for danger.

Sheathing their weapons and carrying what few rations they salvaged from the shipwreck, the eleven pirates traveled along the stiff, blackened soil under the gloomy skies. Hours passed as they traveled the dry land with little conversation. Scattered, shriveled trees peppered the land. The environment was monotonous: no hills, no valleys, no rivers. With their every step, twigs or clumps of soil crunched under their footfalls, daring to break the oppressive silence.

The skies darkened, and the sun set. Ankin dropped to his knees, wheezing, clutching his handless arm. "I can't go on. I need rest."

"Me too," Soleus complained. "I'm thirsty and starving, and me legs are givin' out on me."

"We have no time for resting," Cain snapped.

Jay agreed with Soleus and Ankin; he was exhausted. They had had no rest all day, and the dried up bread and few swills of water did little to ease hunger or quench thirst.

"Hold up, Cain." Hector kneeled beside Ankin. The bandages wrapped around his arm dripped of fresh, red blood. "They're right. We need to rest. Karen, can you change his bandages?"

Cain stopped and whirled around, narrowing his sunken eyes at Hector. "What if Thyran is still alive and is right behind us? He'll catch up and slaughter us all in our sleep."

Despite Cain's harsh tone, Hector spoke softly. "Even if Thyran is still alive, he wouldn't know where we went. We have the compass. He won't know how to find us."

Jay had not even noticed Cain's mynx approaching until it perched again on Cain's arm. Cain raised it so they were looking at each other, eye to eye. The mynx made curious sounds like the chattering of a bird, and Cain was nodding like he understood. Cain raised his eyebrows and gazed farther ahead in the distance, and, after thinking for a moment, turned back to the crew. The mynx dashed up his arm and rested on his shoulder.

"There's a canyon up ahead. Its walls should conceal us from any creatures or people wandering around. Let's make camp down there."

To this, Hector gave no rebuttal. Thankful for a chance to rest, the crew hastily followed Cain a few hundred yards, and to Jay's surprise, there it was, a deep, narrow canyon lined with steep, arched walls. Jay glanced at the mynx. How had Cain understood it?

The crew carefully climbed down the steep canyon walls, which were several stories high. Lynk and Blynk helped Ankin reach the bottom of the canyon. When they all arrived safely, Hector led them to an alcove in the canyon wall where they could settle relatively hidden and shielded from any rain.

"We'll rest here a few hours," Hector said. "But we mustn't stay too long."

Some leaned up against the wall, others sprawled on the ground, thankful for rest. They shuffled about, turning this way and that, trying to make themselves comfortable, difficult given their unyielding hunger and the cold, hard ground.

Outside the alcove, Jay spotted Lyssa leaning against the canyon wall, clutching *Amara* in her left hand, staring out into the night, wide awake. He sat beside her.

"Thank you," he said.

She looked at him. "For what?"

"Saving us back there. On the ship."

"I didn't just save you, I saved myself as well."

Jay stared at the ground, which appeared only a shade lighter than black. "I know, I know. But still, thanks."

She shot him a serious glance. "Don't think I'm part of your crew or anything. Men are savages. Ruthless savages. Even Thyran, who I grew to trust, proved to be nothing more than a vile animal. Once we get out of this mess, I expect you to fulfill your promise and let me go."

Her words stabbed through his chest, dragging his spirits even lower. "I will keep my word."

"Good." She rested her head against the jagged wall and shut her eyes, still gripping firmly onto *Amara*. "I'm going to get some rest now."

Troubled by her harsh words, Jay crawled inside the alcove with the rest of the crew and, wondering why Lyssa hated men so much, he drifted into a light sleep.

The sorceress's eyes sparkled blue, abnormally bright in the darkness of night. Without oars, Thyran's boats glided through the water towards the ashy beach of Storm Isle where the line the sorceress forged in the water led. Thyran smirked when he saw torn pieces of wood and other debris adorning the beach.

He noticed the sorceress biting her lower lip, suppressing her laughter. Then, a rather large wave brushed against the side of the boat where Kyros was sitting, and the water splashed him across the face. Kyros's face turned scarlet, but he confined his rage as the boat breezed forward. Thyran shook his head with disdain.

The sorceress's kitten sprung out of the water and landed in her lap. "Miuji!" she yelled, throwing her arms around her dark blue kitten and squeezing her against her chest. Her eyes fell shut as she rubbed her cheek against the kitten's striped fur. The current ceased, and, to Thyran's dismay, the boats slowed to a stop.

Thyran probably would not have said anything, for he detested speaking with her, but he noticed the black silhouette of a wounded man dragging himself out of the water onto the gray beach ahead. "Alcina!" he said sternly.

She jerked her head up from Miuji and scowled at Thyran, but her eyes again glowed blue and the boats gained speed. When Thyran's boat slid up the beach, he immediately leapt out of the boat, drew one of his scimitars, and trotted along the shoreline towards the fatigued man. "To your feet," he said coldly as the boats carrying his crew arrived on the beach.

Gripping a bloody gash in his arm, the man lifted his weary body but quickly collapsed back to his knees. His eyes darted frantically about. "Look out....it's coming for us!" The man spoke in a delirious voice.

The point of Thyran's scimitar pricked the man's cheek, guiding his eyes up to meet Thyran's. "Were you sailing with Jay Perry?"

"Little Blue!" the man shouted. "Is he okay? Where is he?"

Thyran heard Cyril barking orders to the men behind him. "And the locket, where is it?"

"The locket? Last I saw, Cain had—" the man stopped suddenly and looked at Thyran's crew pouring out of the boats by the dozens. "Wait...who are you?"

"My name is Thyran Vilkus," he said dismissively, his attention focused elsewhere. Cain...where had he heard the name before? Ahh yes, Cyril mentioned seeing him with Karen at the Wicker Pub, the man with the walking staff. In the sand, Thyran noticed a series of footprints traveling up the beach to the black ground farther inland. When he saw the print of Cain's staff in the ground, he smiled. Good, so they had the locket and made it to land safely. The locket was not lost beneath the sea. And even better, their ship was destroyed, so they had no chance of escape. He had them pinned.

"You...you're Little Blue's brother."

Thyran ignored him and instead turned to Cyril as he approached.

"Who's this?" Cyril asked in his usual gruff voice.

"A member of my stepbrother's crew. They made it safely, and they have the locket."

Cyril scanned the footprints. "I see. What are your orders, captain?"

"You're despicable!" the man yelled, spitting at Thyran's feet. "If I was well, I would kill—"

Thyran's boot smashed into the man's chest, and as he fell back, Thyran ran his scimitar through the man's heart. After Thyran slid his scimitar free, the man fell back into the sand, his head turned to the side, his eyes still open. Thyran dipped his bloody blade into the sea and rinsed it.

Bracing his double-headed ax over his broad, naked shoulders, Bruce waddled through the sand. "All ready, cap'n."

Thyran sheathed his dripping scimitar behind his back. "Good. Let's move out. No one rests until we gain possession of that locket. Kyros!" A few yards away, Kyros, who the sorceress and her petty kitten followed closely, looked at Thyran. "Light the torches."

Sparking a rock against the slab of flint on his necklace, Kyros lit several torches and distributed them to the pirates. The sorceress watched him with glossy eyes, her hands behind her back, her body swaying on her toes. The kitten rubbed its body against her legs, purring loudly.

Seizing his torch, Thyran walked to the edge of the beach and then lowered it to the ground, illuminating it with a bright, flickering orange. After a few waves of the torch, he spotted a trail of divots in the soil where a blade had punctured the surface. A grin spread across his lips. Perfect.

"This way," Thyran said as he followed the trail northwest.

A scraping noise snapped Jay out of his light sleep. When his pupils adjusted to the darkness, he made out a round figure moving down the valley through the night. Lifting himself to his feet, Jay quietly followed the figure. His feet moved swiftly to catch up. When he was close, the round figure spun around. "Lil' Blue? Is that you?"

"Aye," Jay said, recognizing Soleus's voice. "What are you doing up, Sol?"

Soleus shrugged his shoulders. "I can't sleep." He turned his back to Jay.

"Something bothering you?" Jay stepped next to him.

Soleus sauntered towards a round rock and plopped down. "I jus' feel bad is all. About Del. Ever since I tried to help her when she was havin' that dream o' hers, she's been avoidin' me."

Jay sat next to the rock. "She's probably just embarrassed about the whole scene. Wouldn't you be? I mean, the whole crew was there and saw her lose control."

"I know, I know." Soleus picked up a pebble and tossed it across the dry land. Its faint clatter echoed off the walls. "It's just...every time I try to get close to her, she always pushes me away. I try to get her to laugh and lighten up, but she always makes me feel like I'm annoying her."

"Hmm...." Jay had a feeling why, but now was not the time to mention anything.

"She's so pretty, so nice. But nothing I say or do ever seems to brighten her day. And it's not like I'm just trying to flirt with her because of her looks, ya know? There's something about her. Something...I dunno how to explain." He picked up another pebble and hurled it in the distance and out of sight. "Maybe I am annoying, or maybe she avoids me because of me size."

"Of course not," Jay said. "Soleus, she's not like that, and if you sulk about it and use your weight as an excuse, it will only hamper you."

Soleus threw another pebble and watched it skip across the ground. "I guess yer right." He hung his head between his round shoulders. "If she just looked at me one time with some respect in her eyes, some kindness. Not that harsh I-think-yer-an-idiot stare like always. It would make me so happy. That's why I try so hard to get her to laugh, to get her to notice me, to get her to smile."

"Well, do you think maybe the jokes you tell her may not strike her sense of humor?"

"Everyone else seems to find them funny though," Soleus mumbled to the ground.

"Yeah, but most of the crew are men. Females are different, Sol. What do you think of maybe offering a subtle compliment? Nothing too major or flattering, just something honest and sincere?"

"I do though. Every day, I tell her how beautiful she

looks. How much I'd love to kiss her. How much I'd love to have a drink and—"

Jay laughed. "No no. Don't you see the way she reacts whenever guys compliment her looks? She instantly turns away in disgust."

Soleus raised his head and looked at Jay. "Well, then what should I say?"

Jay lifted a pebble and threw it across the ground. Pale moonlight sprinkled down on them, and Jay saw his pebble land a few inches past Soleus's. "Well, she seems really reserved, which probably results from seeing her father murdered. What do you think about complimenting her on the way she holds her composure at times, especially after suffering such horrible nightmares? That would show you actually see something in her other than her appearance."

"But she never talks about her father's death." Soleus picked up another pebble and flipped it in the air.

"Exactly. She's probably holding it all inside. She's probably yearning for someone to just listen, but everyone she meets just flatters her all the time."

"So, ye think all I need to do is compliment her on her strength or somethin', and if she opens up, just listen? "

Jay nodded.

"Ye know what, Lil' Blue, that's the dumbest, craziest thing I've ever heard. But, out of all the people I know, yeh've been the best at readin' people. I'll give it a shot and see how it goes."

Jay smiled as Soleus perked up and no longer sounded gloomy. "Good. Just don't let yourself get down about it. You're a great person, and you've got to believe that."

Soleus brushed his hand against his cheek, maybe scratching an itch, maybe wiping a tear. Then, he swung his arm and flung the pebble through the dark air. It landed and bounced several yards beyond Jay's. "Haha, ye may have me when it comes to dealin' with people, but yeh'll never match me strength!"

Jay laughed and stood up, brushing his pant clean of dirt. "You got me there, mate."

"Hey, Lil' Blue. What do you think that is over there?"

Jay followed Soleus's finger and saw a large wall illuminated by moonlight. The wall rose to the height of the canyon, but it was different than the canyon walls. It was smooth, consisting of rocks plastered together. It did not look natural; it must have been made by humans. It was blocking off the other side of the canyon.

"I don't know. It seems kinda awkward. Maybe it's a dam or something."

Soleus scratched his chin. "Hmm...maybe."

Jay shrugged. "Well, come on, let's get some rest. We ought be leaving soon." Jay threw his arm around his friend, and the two returned to the rest of the crew to steal some more sleep before they pressed on.

Sometime later, Jay was not sure how long, but it was just as dark out, Hector nudged him gently. Wiping the sleep from his eyes, Jay saw the crew gathering outside the alcove. "Time to go," Hector said.

Jay wasted no time getting to his feet and walking after Hector and the others, who all followed Cain's lead. Feeble from lack of food and water, the crew scaled the canyon wall and again faced an endless vision of flat land. They traveled for some time before anyone spoke.

"This treasure better be worth it," Lynk said. "When this is all over, we better have enough money for mum."

"Yeah," Blynk agreed.

Jenkins wiped sweat from his brow. "How is she?""

Lynk swapped the rope he was carrying to his other shoulder. "The doctor still doesn't know what ails her, but they found a potion that seems to work well."

"What potion?" Karen asked.

"It's...umm...xanibreescate? Something like that."

"Xanabriskite," she corrected. "That's a blend of the sap of several rare trees and plants. Probably one of the most expensive potions."

"How do you know this?" Lyssa asked, sounding intrigued.

Ankin, who walked beside her, said, "She used to be a chemist. She knows more about chemicals and potions than anyone in Lassar."

"I see."

Jay's gaze stumbled upon the gorgrim-skin pouch tied to Cain's waist, and he suddenly remembered a question he had been meaning to ask. "Hey Karen, what did you make of that liquid Cain found in the Dryfus Mines?"

Karen glanced skyward for a second before answering. "Oh yes. That is nothing more than a basic solution. Very basic actually, by my test."

"Basic?" Soleus asked. "Like...very ordinary or something?"

Jay was unsure, but he thought he saw Karen roll her eyes. "No no. Basic as in having a very high pH." Seeing his dumbfounded expression, she added, "It acts similarly to an acid to the untrained eye."

"Oh." Soleus bowed his head, and Jay knew he felt dumb for asking. Fortunately, Delcato did not make any notion of disgust with the question. Her thoughts appeared to be wandering elsewhere, for she gazed off to the side as they walked.

"But anyways," Karen continued. "It's extremely strong, stronger than anything I've ever seen."

"I wonder what that was doing in the mines," Jay thought aloud. He recalled the engraving on the basin of a wizard holding that weapon and pointing to a cottage with an apple tree. Did that mean something? Was that a clue to the treasure?

They trudged onward through the dull atmosphere of Storm Isle for the better part of an hour. It was the steady rhythm of his feet that kept Jay moving forward. If he stopped now, he was sure he would not be able to continue. His head ached and stomach stung, but he allowed himself to be swept by the flow of the crew.

"Look!" Jenkins said, and they all jumped from the sudden breach of silence. "It's a small hill up ahead."

Jay's eyes followed Jenkins's finger, and sure enough, it pointed to a black hill up ahead. As they approached, the steep hill materialized out of its dark gray backdrop. It stretched nearly ten stories in the air. The top resembled the head of a bird; its beak stretched out a ways like half a bridge, its neck curved back down along the hill to the ground. Below the tip of the hill's beak, crystals of white moonlight danced over the ground. Excitement flooded through Jay's body when he realized the specks of white were moonlight reflecting off water.

The crew must have came to the same realization, for Soleus, Lynk, and Blynk charged with mad excitement, and the others hastened their step, eager to feel the rushing of water down their parched throats.

However, due to his lead, Cain was the first at the lake. But he did not drink; he stood still at the lake's fringe. When Soleus ran past, ready to dive into the lake, Cain struck him across the chest with his staff.

"Oompf!" Soleus moaned and stumbled back.

"Fool!" Cain said. "You're too rash."

"But I'm dying of thirst!" Soleus protested.

Cain kneeled to the ground and lifted a withered branch, about as thick as his staff, and tossed it in the lake. The water hissed as it dissolved the wood instantly.

"Ashlen was no fool," Cain said. "That would have been you. That lake would burn through your skin in a second."

Grumbling under his breath, Soleus kicked some dirt into the lake.

"There it is," Jenkins whispered.

A steep stone platform glazed with clear, crystallized glass poked out from the center of the lake. The curved, silver shaft of a glowing hatchet was firmly planted at the top of the glass platform. Gold patterns and varicolored gems glistened along the hatchet's arched blade. It appeared more like a decoration or war trophy than a weapon used in combat. And it had a mysterious glow about it, just like the inside of the locket.

Lynk revered the object. "Wow...is that really it?"

Cain flipped open the locket, and Jay noticed the emerald arrow pointing directly at the glass platform. "It appears so," Cain said.

"Well, how are we going to get there?" Soleus asked, still gloomy that his hope for water was shattered.

Jay looked around. Everything around them was flat, except for the hill.

The hill. The bridge-like structure that stuck out from the top hovered over the lake and ended almost directly above the hatchet.

"Up there," Jay said, directing their attention to the hilltop. "Lynk, can't we use your rope from up there and lift it?"

Lynk's eyes shifted from the rope around his shoulder to the cliff. "Yeah, I think that should work. Good thinking, Little Blue."

"Ughh..." Ankin slowly sat down with Karen's aid. "My arm's aching pretty badly. I think I'll wait here for you guys."

"Very well," Hector said with the air of just arriving at a verdict. "We'll go with Jay's plan. I'll stay here with Ankin in case anything happens. Ye all go up and try to get the treasure."

"Aye, cap'n," several members of the crew said.

"Let's go," Cain said.

And with that, they skirted around the lake towards the base of the birdlike hill.

Jay felt relieved the hill was not as steep as the canyon walls. The crew managed to ascend the hill without much difficulty, especially since no one needed any support. Not surprisingly, Lynk and Blynk were the first to the top. "It's so...sad," Lynk said, gazing out over the land at the top of the hill.

Jay soon realized what he meant. The land appeared even more dismal and barren from their vantage point. It was so lifeless.

"I hope we don't get stuck here, bro," Blynk said.

"Don't worry," Lynk assured. "Captain Hector is a smart man. He'll think of something."

There was the booming sound of thunder, and the clouds began to shed their tears in a light drizzle. They heard the lake sizzling down below as the rain battered its surface. By the time the entire crew reached the top of the hill, bolts of lightning stabbed the ground in the distance. Jay was amazed with how fast the storm appeared. Probably how the island got its name.

"Perfect," Cain mumbled. He was the last to the top due to his limp. He took a moment to examine the storm before leading the crew across the top of the cliff over the lake.

When they reached the edge, they peered down below. Splashes of water from the rain bubbled atop the lake; a thin veil of smoke rose from the lake's surface. Beneath them, the sparkling hatchet rested on the glass platform.

Cain backed away from the narrow edge. "Hurry up. Let's get out of here before the storm gets any worse."

Everyone stepped back by Cain to give Lynk and Blynk some room. Jay watched as they tied a noose at the end of the rope. Leaning on his stomach with his head over the edge of the cliff, Lynk lowered the noose.

"Think we'll have enough rope, bro?" Blynk asked as he held Lynk's feet.

"We should." Lynk's arms moved quickly to lower the rope.

The rest of the crew waited. The clouds grew more mournful, their tears fell harder. Fat raindrops lashed against the land, and the swords of lightning sliced through the sky, emitting a purple glow for that split second of their existence. The thunder roared louder and louder, a caged gorgrim struggling to break free of its binds. Gray clouds seized the sky, blotching out the stars. Jay had never witnessed such a fierce storm develop in a matter of seconds.

"You almost there?" Cain asked impatiently.

"Almost...."

"Have some patience," Jenkins said to Cain. "The treasure isn't going anywhere."

Cain ignored him.

"Okay, I just need to hook the loop around the blade...got it!" Lynk's arms shook as he tugged on the rope.

"Ugh...it's stuck in there good. Soleus, give me a hand here."

"Aye," Soleus waddled to the edge. Grabbing the rope, he helped Lynk pull, and then Soleus fell backward when they dislodged the hatchet from its base.

"Good!" Lynk said as he quickly lifted the hatchet. When it was close enough, he grabbed it and stood up. Twirling it between his hands, he admired the gold patterns scattered across the glowing hatchet. He rubbed his finger against some of the gems embedded in the blade. "This'll be worth a fortune!"

There was frightening crackle of thunder and flash of lightening. The mynx took off from Cain's shoulder and flew away to take cover. Cain stepped forward and extended his hand. "Let me see it, Lynk." His voice was unusually eager.

A strong gust of wind blew the rain so it pelted them horizontally. Lynk gave the hatchet to Cain.

"Well, ain't this cute?" Thyran sneered from behind. His cold words slithered through Jay's ears, causing him to spin around at once. The two men from the mines and dozens more of Thyran's crew stood behind him, all armed and grinning savagely. "That's twice you've led me to my treasure, Jay. Or is it Little Blue?"

Rage swirled inside Jay too strong from him to formulate words. He needed revenge. Rain pattering against his face, Jay whipped out his cutlass and charged across the wet hilltop. Lyssa grabbed his arms before he reached Thyran and tugged him back. "Not yet," she whispered.

A flash of purple lightning revealed that usual smirk on Thyran's face. Jay struggled to charge for him, but Lyssa held him back.

"Your current situation would warrant you giving in to my demands," Thyran said.

Jay scanned his surroundings. He counted at least

two dozen armed pirates behind Thyran. Jay and the others had nowhere to go—they were trapped at the edge of a cliff with a deathly lake waiting for them down below.

"What do you want?" Jay asked through clenched teeth.

Thyran laughed. "I think you know, my dear brother. The locket and the hatchet, nothing more. I desire not your deaths, just two items that rightfully belong to me."

"You can't have them." Cain said.

A man with black hair wrapped in a black bandana, the same man Jay remembered Karen talking to at the Wicker Pub, stepped forward, his long hair thrashing in the fierce winds. He carried a leather whip in his right hand. "Do not be a fool. You cannot defeat all of us."

Cain's eyes widened. "Cyril! I knew you were nothing but a bloodsucking fiend the moment I met you." He looked around his own crew and scowled. "Is Karen part of your crew too?"

For the first time, Jay realized Karen was not with them; she must have left them when they started climbing the hill.

Amid another flash of lightning, Cyril cracked his whip on the ground. "Your memory is impressive."

Thyran and his men advanced a few steps closer.

"Steady men," Cain said as they retreated close to the edge.

"I think I have a way of persuading you to come to your senses," Thyran said. "Alcina!"

Jay squinted to see a blue-haired woman squeezing between the pirates and settling beside the man with crimson spiked hair. She had a childish smile on her face as she regarded Jay. Chuckling, she approached him. "Is this the young one you spoke of?"

Jay held his weapon steady, pointed at her. But she paid no heed and simply walked beside it. "Back away," he warned as she ran her fingernails along his cheek.

"Hmm...you must be. So cute for a pirate." She bit her bottom lip and twirled back a few paces. Her eyes then flashed with glee when they settled on the shiny hatchet. "Mmm...so pretty. All those colorful gems.... Do you think you could make me a necklace, dear?" she glanced back at the crimson-haired man, batting her eyes.

"Alcina!" Thyran snapped. "Enough wasting time."

"Fine!" She stomped her foot, whirled back to Cain, and her pleasant voice suddenly transformed to a chilling, deep, raspy voice that caused a shudder to rush down Jay's spine. "Give me the hatchet."

Cain moved his hand over the side of the cliff and shook the hatchet. "Let us go, or I'll drop it into the lake."

Alcina screamed with a rage more ferocious than the most menacing roar of thunder. Her eyes flashed the brightest of blues. Flailing her hands angrily towards Jay, she curled her fingers back, and the falling rain began to spin around him and then surge into his mouth. Suddenly, he couldn't breathe. Choking on water, he dropped his cutlass. He tried to spit out the water, but it flew right back in as if by magic.

"Wha...What's goin on?" Lyssa stammered. Jay's lungs burned; he clawed at his throat, desperately struggling for air. He lost the strength to stand, and he fell to the ground.

Lyssa knelt beside him and lifted his head, searching for some way to allow him to breathe. The rain spun faster and slammed into Lyssa at high speeds. She screamed as the needlelike rain stabbed her body.

Delcato pointed her cutlass at Alcina. "Stop this magic! Stop it now or I'll stab this blade through your heart!"

Alcina laughed deviously and twisted her head towards Cain. "Your friend is dying."

Soleus and Jenkins rushed to Jay's aid. "Hold on Lil' Blue!" Soleus said. "We'll find a way to stop this."

"Eyah!" Delcato yelled as she charged for Alcina.

Alcina shifted one of her hands and aimed at Delcato. Like a cannon blast, a huge ball of water suddenly formed and slammed into Delcato, throwing her back near the edge of the cliff.

"Cain!" Lynk yelled. "What are you waiting for! Give them the hatchet! Jay won't last much longer."

Cain said something, but Jay could no longer hear. He was slipping away. His vision became blurred and quickly faded to black. Hands moved over his face trying to help, but to no avail. The roaring thunder diminished, sounding farther away, miles and miles away, like he was falling into an abyss.

Then he coughed, and the water gushed out of his mouth. Cool, fresh air rushed in his lungs and expanded his chest. He took many deep breaths before opening his eyes; he could see again.

"Jay..." he heard Lyssa say. He felt her hands rubbing his shoulders and back, trying to comfort him. "Are you alright?"

"Y-yeah...I'm—"

He stopped when he saw Thyran, with his usual grin, holding the hatchet firmly in his hand. "Good," he said to Cain, acting as if nothing happened to Jay, his own brother. "Now, one more thing: the locket."

"We don't have it," Cain said.

"Alcina," Thyran said, "I think they need more persuasion."

Alcina looked at Jay and again lifted her hand.

"Alright," Cain grumbled as he slid the locket out of his pocket. The glimmering green light morphed to a bright orange. Jay wondered what had changed inside the locket, but he was too weak to stand and too far to see.

Thyran stood still with his hand extended. "Hand it over."

Another sword of lightning lit the sky. Jay noticed Cain secretly untying his large, gorgrim-skin pouch full of the basic solution Karen had warned them about.

Cain moved fast. He lobbed the locket high in the air towards Thyran. While Thyran looked up to catch it, he lunged the opened pouch of deadly liquid from the Dryfus mines directly at Thyran's face, but before it reached him, Alcina blasted the pouch with a ball of water. Jay watched as it soared over the side of the cliff and fell into the lake.

Catching the locket with one hand, Thyran smirked at Cain. "It was a cunning move, I'll give you that. But alas, my friends, I must make my leave for the final piece of the puzzle. Don't worry, your lives will not be lost in vain. When we put the corrupt nations in their place, all of Lassar will know you played your part."

Recovering his breath, Jay stood up, leaning against Lyssa's shoulder. "So, you're going to kill us anyways?"

Thyran turned to Jay and walked towards him. Jay's heart raced and pounded inside his chest. He now stood face to face with Thyran. Their eyes met; caramel against dark green. Seconds passed before Thyran said softly, "Jay, don't take this so personally. Out of all the people on Lassar, I respect you the most."

"Then let us live," Jay pleaded.

Thyran smiled and braced Jay with a hug. Jay felt a surge of emotions bombard his body. Hate, sadness, sorrow, love, confusion. He didn't know what to think.

"I love you, brother," Thyran whispered in his ear. The words struck Jay's heart. He lost focus on everything but Thyran, his brother, hugging him, and despite his desire to avenge Captain Gaden's death, Jay was powerless to act in aggression.

He heard Lyssa's bow swing through the air towards Thyran, but Thyran effortlessly sidestepped it and grappled her neck. Glaring at her, he laughed a most scornful laugh, and before Jay could move to her aid, he threw her off the cliff.

"No!" Jay yelled. He could not believe his eyes. He rushed to the edge of the cliff and peered down. A lump of sadness swelled in his throat as he watched her fall and splash into the deadly lake. Her screams of agony rented his insides asunder.

"Ahh!" Jay screamed, grabbing his cutlass from the ground and jumping to his feet.

"Now!" Thyran said as he dashed back to his crew. The crimson-haired man tossed a small, sealed crate at Jay and the others. Despite the sheeting rain, the crate remained dry. Through the slits in the wood, Jay saw a spark traveling down a wick—fire sticks.

He made a charge for Thyran, but Alcina summoned a thick wall of water between Thyran and them that bounced him back, knocking him off his feet. They were trapped, trapped against the edge of the cliff with the box of fire sticks—

"Grab the box and toss it in the lake!" Jenkins shouted.

"There's no time!" Cain yelled. "Jump!"

Jay's body subconsciously obeyed Cain's final command, and, knowing the lake brought certain death, he ran for the edge of the cliff. As he jumped off the edge, the crate exploded, and the blast of heat engulfed Jay completely. He dropped down, faster and faster, through the pelting of rain, through the roaring of thunder, through the flashes of lightning, into the lake.

11

Web of Fire

It felt like fire ants swarmed his body, gnawing at every inch of his flesh, feasting on his blood. Everything stung—his feet, legs, neck, lips, nose: everything. Jay dared not open his eyes; instead, he thrashed in the lake, in the darkness, in the sea of fire—

Unsure how, he managed to resurface, and the sheeting rain cascaded down on his face, an elixir to his pain. He chanced opening his eyes. He was in the center of the lake, surrounded by the crew, who all struggled to swim ashore. Screams of agony filled the air; everyone suffered immensely, but they were not dead—

"Grrgg..." he heard Soleus gurgle as the lake swallowed him. Sol, his best friend, was drowning. Concern for Soleus blasted away his pain, and he dove back into the acidic lake for his friend. Blindly he swam, deeper and deeper in the direction he last saw Soleus—

Something brushed his shoulder, most likely Soleus flailing his arms, desperately trying to swim. Jay followed the movement, and then his hand met Soleus's. Suffocating from lack of air, he hooked his arms under Soleus's shoulders and kicked his feet to carry to plump pirate to the surface. But Soleus was too heavy, and the two of them started to sink—

Then he felt another hand help support Soleus, and they were rising, up and up, and in a few seconds, the chilling rain washed upon his face again. He could breathe.

Jay opened his eyes and saw Soleus had his arm around Lyssa's shoulders—Lyssa, she was alive. Jay's heart leapt, and despite the burns scarring her face and his own undying anguish, he was relieved. His faint light of hope shined brighter.

"Over there!" Lyssa flicked her head to the nearest bank. They, along with the rest of the crew, swam through the acid lake for land, struggling to be relieved of their pain and suffering.

They made it. Stripped of all energy, Jay and the others dragged themselves out of the lake and collapsed on the ground. Jay turned on his back and welcomed the falling rain. His chest heaved up and down as he gasped for air. Each breath seemed like a magical remedy that kept him alive; he had never appreciated clean air such as he did at that moment.

The lake had dissolved sections of his clothes. Blotches of his skin burned under the falling rain; he noticed the lake had eaten some of his flesh, leaving bright pink wounds and even gushing blood all over his body. He felt excruciating pain, enough to make a man go mad, but one thing kept him sane—he was alive.

How had they survived? The lake vaporized that wood instantly, so surely they would have survived just as long. Squinting, he stared up at the cliff. Smoke rose from the platform where the crate exploded. The burns from the explosion seared his back, and the ground he lay on felt like a needle bed stabbing into his skin.

He looked beside him; Lyssa collapsed on the ground and squirmed in pain, moaning her mother's name. "Amara...Amara...."

Jay's eyes watered when he realized she was missing her bow; *Amara* was lost in the lake. It was then Jay fully appreciated her love of that bow, of the potent sentimental value it held. He sympathized with her, taking her sorrow in within himself. Had he remembered his parents, he would have felt the same way.

"Thank you...for helping me with Sol," he said.

Jay thought he saw her nod in acceptance of his gratitude, but he heard her crying, whimpering her mother's name, clutching her chest with her hand as if preventing her heart from ripping apart.

He heard footsteps. Fearful it was Thyran, he turned his head, but saw, with relief, it was Ankin scurrying over to them. "You're alive!" he shouted. "We saw the explosion, and then watched you fall, and...and...I don't believe it!"

Ankin knelt next to Soleus, who writhed more violently than the rest. He went to help Soleus to his feet, but Soleus wriggled away, screaming in pain. "Ahh! Don't touch me!"

Ankin jumped back, clearly regretting touching Soleus's burns.

Jay saw another figure approach—Karen. "Remarkable!" she yelled.

Ankin turned to her and asked the question that was on Jay's lips. "How did they survive? The lake acted like acid and dissolved that wood—"

"Exactly!" she said, coming to a stop. "The lake is extremely acidic, or rather, was. But that pouch Cain had, that liquid, remember? I said it was the strongest base I had ever seen? It must have mixed with the acid and neutralized it." She regarded their blisters from the lake. "Well, at least somewhat, to the point they didn't die instantly. Normally, it takes a much larger volume to accomplish such an effect, but, as I said, that base was unusually strong, beyond anything I've seen."

Jay was amazed. She sounded more thrilled with the brilliant chemical phenomenon than concerned for her crew. But then he remembered Cyril, the black-haired man with the whip on top of the cliff. The same one she was talking with at the Wicker Pub. Why was she here if she was working with Thyran?

A hand swung around Karen's neck and gripped a dagger against her tender skin; the blade sunk in, blood trickled down her neck. Over her shoulder, Jay recognized Cain's sunken eyes glaring at her. Before she could speak in protest, Cain shouted in a raspy voice, "Treacherous fiend! I should slay you now—"

"What's going on?" Hector asked, running up to them. He was panting, lost for breath.

Karen struggled to break free of his grip. "He's trying to—"

"Shut up, wench!"

Hector drew his sword and pointed it threateningly at Cain. "I dunno what's in yer head. Let her go, now!"

Cain ignored the captain. Jay's eyes darted from Hector to Cain and Karen, his heart racing.

"How do you know Cyril?"

"Who? Uck!" she gasped for breath as Cain squeezed her throat tighter.

Hector moved closer. "Cain! Release her now!"

"Don't play dumb!" Cain said. "I saw him up there. He nearly killed us all! And where were you? Decided to leave us at the last minute, did you?"

"I don't know any—"

"You were with him at the Wicker Pub!"

"Ukk...oh him."

"Ahh yes, remember now?" Cain pushed the blade deeper into her skin. Blood began trickling down her neck.

Jay winced in pain seeing her suffer. He was not sure if he should say anything to her aid; everything Cain said was true.

"He just...showed...up there. I swear...." She grabbed his arms and tried to tug for air, but to no avail.

Soleus struggled to his feet and stumbled. "Cain, let 'er go!"

"This is me final warning, Cain," Hector said.

"Captain, she's a traitor. How do you think they found us here? She must have left some kind of trail for them to follow."

"Until we have proof, ye will release her."

"You're being weak, captain!"

Nearing the point of blacking out, Karen noticed a patch of skin missing on Cain's arm. She dug her nails into his wound. When he flinched, she elbowed his side and slid out from his grasp. Massaging her neck, she backed away, glowering at him with hatred.

Without the support of his staff, Cain fell to the ground. He dropped his head, soaking in the pain. "Your time will come," he said in a low voice. He seized his tarnished staff from the ground; the lake had chewed through his intricate carvings.

Hector brandished his sword at Cain. "Do not attack one of me crew again."

"Hmph. A crew needs a boat. So does a captain." Using his staff, Cain rose to his feet and began to walk past Hector when the captain grabbed his shoulder and spun him around. The two pirates glared at one another.

"You will follow my orders, sailor," Hector said.

"I will not compromise the *crew* for your weakness. When I find proof of her betrayal, I will behead her. With or without your permission, *captain*." Cain jerked his shoulder free and continued on ahead. Jay felt glad not to be the target of Cain's anger. Cain never forgave an offense without the stiffest of punishments.

"What happened up there?" Hector asked, sheathing his sword.

Jay choked on his own guilt. He had let them down. Cain relinquished the hatchet and locket to save *him*. Jay had insisted they listen to Lyssa and travel to the Dryfus Mines, which is just what Thyran had desired him to do. Now, the *Isabella* was destroyed, most of the crew dead, and the rest severely injured. And all for what?

Nothing.

They had lost everything now. His stepbrother outwitted him once again, and as he gazed at the crew, all cringing from pain, he had only himself to blame. His eyes burned with tears, and for a moment, he contemplated diving back in the lake and letting it take him to destroy his misery...and his life, the life of a fugitive, of a thief, of a pirate.

"I let my guard down." Jay said finally. "Thyran has the hatchet and the locket. We...have nothing. I'm sorry cap'n." He slammed his fist into the ground and welcomed the pain of rocks scraping against his burned flesh.

"Which way did he go?" Hector asked, scanning their surroundings.

"I dunno cap'n. It...it all happened so fast."

"Was he alone?"

Jay shook his head.

"There were about fifty pirates," Jenkins said. "And they had a woman with them. She was some sort of sorceress or something."

"A sorceress?"

"Aye. A bloody sorceress. She had this magical control over water. Nearly killed Little Blue. I've never seen anything like it."

Hector scratched his beard and peered out in the distance. "Well, we can only assume that's how they followed us here: some sort of magic. Let's hope their ship is by the beach we washed up on. Can ye all move? I fear our time is short."

The pirates who suffered the lake's wrath each, in turn, gathered enough strength to battle their tormenting pain and stand.

"Good." Hector drew his sword and stabbed it in the air. A flash of lightning. Purple light blared from the blade, giving it a brief mystical aura. "Let us go, then, and take revenge on Thyran and his crew! For Captain Gaden's death and all our suffering, I say we show Thyran the meaning of revenge!"

A wave of adrenaline and fervor washed over them; their strength flooded back.

"Aye, cap'n!" Soleus pounded his fists against his chest. "Let's get him!"

Delcato slid her blade out from its sheath. "I'm ready to catch those fiends and make them pay."

Lynk and Blynk jubilantly gave each other a high five. "Ready, bro?" Blynk asked.

"Let's make mum proud!"

Jay helped Lyssa to her feet. Her face was awash, but he blamed more than rain for that. "You okay?"

She nodded as a bolt of lightening struck the base of the hill and crashing thunder shook the ground. Hector gallantly flourished his blade in the air. "Let's move, mates! Let's bury those slimy scum beneath the high seas!"

The chase progressed through the raging storm. Wicked winds lashed the avalanching rain into the pirates as they dashed across the barren land. Flashes of lightning lit the scene, crackles of thunder rattled the air. Jay noticed a stampede of footprints in the now softened soil. Judging from their abundance, the eleven of them would be greatly outnumbered. Still, the pirates pressed onward.

While Thyran's men swept across the canyon, Kyros, as ordered, was fixing fire sticks in the massive stone wall stretching across the canyon floor, linking the two sides of the canyon together. Rubbing water out of his eyes, Kyros concentrated on securing the bundles of fire sticks so they would not budge. He extended the wicks by tying a frail rope to each tip of the fire sticks. The onslaught of rain battered against his head, its sound echoed between his ears.

"You know," he shouted above the thunder to Alcina, who was perched on a protruding rock beside him, stroking the midnight blue fur of Miuji in her lap. "You have a natural talent of using your powers in a most annoying fashion. But when they could actual serve a worthwhile purpose, you just sit there like a child."

Alcina laughed. Her sweet tone had replaced the harsh, raspy tone she used earlier. "Oh, is my dear upset at getting a lil' wet?"

Dear...she always called him dear. He cringed every time she said it, an effect of which she was rather fond. "Despicable..." he mumbled as he secured a knot between wick and rope. Zigzagging across the rocks, he let the threadlike rope slide through his fingers. He reached the tip of another dangling rope, which connected several bundles of fire sticks. He paused and bound the two ropes together.

Alcina was fast to follow. "Don't forget over there," she said, pointing to a wide area absent of fire sticks near the top of the wall.

"Quiet!" Confident the ropes were secure, Kyros starting climbing up the stone wall to the spot she indicated. He had to pause a couple times to reach in a pouch attached to his ribs full of white chalk so his hands could grip onto the slippery rocks. He glanced down and saw her peering up at him with a smirk, waiting for him to ask her assistance. He would rather fall to his death than indulge her with that honor.

And then he heard that childish, most annoying laugh of hers. A shield of water blasted against his side, which nearly caused him to lose his grip. He watched her soar passed him, up in the air, propelled by a rising platform of water gushing up along the wall. "See you at the top, dear!" she yelled back as she shot passed him.

He had to kill her. Every day she got worse and worse, somehow growing more fond of him despite his snide remarks and attempted insults. Clenching his teeth, he climbed up after her until he reached a small ledge. He removed the final bundle of fire sticks from his sack, secured it against the rock, and tied the tip of his rope to its black wick. With all the fire sticks in place, he scrambled to the canyon edge where Thyran and the rest waited.

"All set?" Thyran asked.

"Yes, captain."

Cyril stepped forward. "Captain, don't you think this is a waste of time? There's no way they could survive in that lake for longer than five seconds."

"That's your problem, Cyril," Thyran said. "You're too eager to complete a task. You overlook the small details. That could lead to your downfall. My cousin did not meet us as planned, so I am guessing not all of the crew was on the cliff. More must have survived. We must prevent anyone from following us." Thyran looked over to Bruce, who proudly held the tip of a thick rope soaked with oil. A mist surrounded the rope resulting from Alcina protecting it from the pouring rain. "Bruce, hand him the rope."

"Here ya go, bomber man!" Bruce swung his hand to Kyros.

Kyros grabbed the rope and held it against his flint necklace. He removed a rock from his pouch and struck it against the flint. Nothing. He tried again. Nothing. Snarling, he said, "Alcina...a little help, if you find it convenient."

Biting her bottom lip, she tip-toed to him, her kitten weaving between her legs. "What was that, my dear? I missed a word I think." She cupped her ear and leaned against him.

Damn her.

Kyros caught an impatient glance from Thyran, and then he gritted his teeth and closed his eyes with resentment. "Please, Miss Alcina." The words tasted like spoiled milk.

She chuckled and raised her hands in the air, her eyes flashed blue. Waves of water that rested inside the canyon blasted out, up the arching walls and into the sky as if a bomb exploded in the canyon's heart. The fresh rain drizzled alongside the canyon like it struck an invisible dome bending overhead. Water evaporated from Kyros's flint and rock, and he was protected from the torrential downpour. "All ready, dear," she said, smiling when he cringed at the word.

The fire-stick-filled wall shook relentlessly as if a giant monster was thrashing against its opposite side. A wide grin spread across Kyros's face as he sparked the rope.

Pride coursed through Kyros's veins. The dark canyon blossomed into vibrant colors of orange and red as the fire raced down the rope and split in a multitude of directions, creating a web of fire. The brilliant pattern of flaming paths covered the wall as the fire raced to its final destinations.

BOOM!

White light blinded them as the stone wall exploded. Chunks of rock soared through the air. Alcina's eyes flashed blue—raging water from behind the wall pounded through and poured into the canyon. Sloshing through the valley, the water shook the ground, sending towering waves crashing over the canyon walls.

Kyros clenched his fist in front of his chest and shook with triumph. His explosives completed their task with style—it was perfect.

Thyran grinned. "Well done, Kyros." He turned around and walked away from the canyon. "Let's move. The gem awaits."

Like a puppeteer, Alcina whirled her hands, intensifying the raging current through the canyon and creating miniature whirlpools. Catching Kyros's gaze, she cast him a wink. Tendrils of water flowed around her body as she slinked closer to him, staring at him through her glowing blue eyes.

"It's beautiful, isn't it?"

Speechless, he stood glorified with this magnificent fire show that brought down the canyon wall. She bobbed on the balls of her feet, bringing her head closer to his. His mind racing, replaying the explosion in his head, he turned to follow his captain, but her smooth hand grabbed the back of his neck, and before he could react, her lips pressed against his. Her lips were sweet, incredibly smooth, and sent a shockwave through his body, a tingling feeling, a feeling of pleasure. His eyes widened, but hers remained closed, clearly loving every second of the kiss.

When he snapped out of his dreamy state, he pushed her away. She glanced up at him, nibbling on her lip, and without giving him a chance to say anything, she skipped off in Thyran's wake, her kitten trailing close behind.

By the time Jay and the others reached the canyon, water raged through it, a current of immeasurable speed. Immediately, Jay noticed the wall Soleus pointed out the night before was missing—it really was a dam. They all stood dumbstruck.

"We need to cross," Cain said.

"Are ye crazy!" Soleus leaned over the edge of the canyon wall. The rushing water sounded like a cascading waterfall. "Ye be mad! I don't mean to be the grumpy one, but me body aches and me stomach is as empty as a dry mug. I can't swim across that now."

Cain's hooded eyes gazed down at Soleus. "Do you want them to get away?" He spoke loudly to overcome the din of the water rushing through the canyon.

Cupping rainwater in his hand, Jenkins slouched down and sluiced the cool water over one of his burns. "Soleus is right, captain. We haven't ate for two days and we're all in a great deal of pain. We'll drown if we cross it now with those kind of bloody currents."

"Yeah!" Lynk agreed full-heartedly. "No offense, Cain, but I think you would be no match for those currents."

"I agree," Hector said. He turned around, and after a flash of lightning, he pointed to a clump of leafless trees. "Come, we can rest over there."

Cain clicked his tongue and walked briskly past the captain. "I'll be back," he said, and set off into the storm.

Soleus shook his head. "What a grouch!"

The roaring sound of water rushing through the canyon subsided as they moved to the huddled trees.

"I dunno about the rest of ye, but I can barely move a

muscle." Soleus threw himself against a tree trunk.

"There there," Karen said, wiping her glasses free of water, only to be soaked instantly when she put them back on. "Just worry about getting some rest. The captain and I will go out and see if we can't find some food."

"Karen's right," Hector said. "There's got to be some life on this island. Wait here while we scout around."

Karen and Captain Hector traveled off as the rest of the crew tended to their wounds. As time passed, the rain mitigated to a gentle sprinkle.

Jay pounded his head against the tree as thoughts of Thyran churned in his head. How could he let Thyran get the best of him every time? Was there even a point of pursuing him at this point, only to fall in another one of his traps? Should he simply give up before more people got hurt?

"Jay, is sumthin' botherin' ye?" Soleus asked.

"It's nothing."

Lyssa brushed her damp, golden hair out of her eyes and looked at Jay. He knew she did not believe his lie.

"Come on, Blynk. Let's cheer him up." Lynk snatched a sickle-shaped rock the size of his palm from the ground, and the two brothers scooted over to Jay. "Just an ordinary rock, right?" He tossed it to Blynk.

"Yup, bro. Nothing fancy here." Blynk lobbed it back to his older brother.

"Now, watch carefully, Little Blue." Lynk waved the rock in front of Jay's eyes as he tossed it from hand to hand. But Jay was not in the mood for magic tricks. Not now. Without letting them finish their trick, he stood up and stormed off without a word. He heard the rock drop behind him and Lynk say, "Poor guy. I've never seen him this down."

Jay scampered across the gray plains to put as much distance between him and the crew as possible. He needed to be alone.

His weary legs gave out, and he dropped to the ground. The buildup of rage and sadness overpowered his defenses, and he began to sob. His body still burned from the lake, but the pain was minimal to the torment of Thyran's conniving grin blazing inside his head.

"I hate you!" he shouted into the storm. He clawed at the ground, scraping his fingers against the hard soil. He felt so childish, eighteen years old, crying to himself like a baby. But with tears came relief. His body forced out his feelings of anguish, guilt, and sorrow. He poured those emotions to the ground and swam with them, holding nothing back.

The cool wind blew against him, and he shivered, his ripped and partially dissolved shirt and pants stuck to his skin. He wrapped his arms around his chest and rubbed his shoulders.

Hearing footsteps, he leapt in the air, whipped out his cutlass, and pointed it at...Lyssa. Why did she follow him?

He sheathed his cutlass. "Get away! I need to be alone."

"Jay...."

"Leave!" He walked away a few paces before his legs gave out on him again. He dropped to the ground.

Silently, she strolled behind him and waited several seconds before sitting. His arms wrapped around his bent knees, Jay dug his nails into his arms as he bottled his emotions back inside.

"I know how you feel—"

"You have no clue how I feel. You have no idea what it's like to be haunted by someone you loved all your life. And no matter what you do, he finds a way to hurt those you love."

"You can't put the blame on yourself."

"Why not? Every time, I play right into his traps. Look where I am now? I just...I want him dead." The effect of those words resounded in his chest. "I want him dead," he repeated, amazed with his passion for killing another.

Lyssa gave him a minute or two to digest his thoughts before saying, "You know, my mother had a saying she used to always tell me. 'You never know how the flower will blossom.'"

Jay did not understand, nor did he care to understand.

"It means," she continued, "the question should never be *will* the flower blossom, the question should be *how* will the flower blossom. Good will triumph over evil, always. The only thing to be determined is how."

"Well, good doesn't seem to be triumphing over evil now."

"You're right. And you know what? It hasn't happened in my life either."

"Hmph, seems like a great phrase to live by." Jay knew he was being rude, perhaps even hurtful, but he didn't care.

"It gives us hope," she said. "It gives us hope something good may happen. A reason to keep moving forward."

"All I do is keep screwing things up!"

"Stop being so harsh on yourself!" She cast him a cold glance. "In the past few days, you've slain a giant sea monster and saved a friend from drowning. The last thing you should be feeling is guilt."

Jay ran his finger against the damp ground aimlessly. "I can never outsmart him. Every time, he's always one move ahead."

Neither of them spoke for several minutes. After what seemed like ages, the overcast sky permitted some evening sunlight to brighten the air. An azura flew overhead, flapping its magnificent blue wings rhythmically.

The brightly-colored bird settled on the ground not too far off. Its head twitched this way and that as it hopped around. Occasionally, it pointed its beak to the sky and warbled a perfect, relaxing melody. Jay watched the bird in peaceful silence, listening to the music ringing through the air. It soothed his pain.

Lyssa held out her hand, palm up, towards the animal and whistled. The bird craned its neck, looking towards her, and let out a friendly chirp. She whistled again, and the bird moved closer with successive tiny hops.

Jay watched with amazement. "How are you—"

"Shh..." she whispered. She continued trilling with the bird as it neared her. The bird pecked gently into her open palm, and then she lifted her hand and stroked its blue-feathered head. Humming sweetly, the bird pressed its head against her hand. "They are very friendly animals. They just need to be assured you mean no harm."

A feeling of joy washed over Jay. "I've always admired these birds, but I've never seen one this close."

She ran her finger over the bird's head. "Why don't you pet it?"

Jay leaned over and brought his hand near the bird's head. Startled, the bird hopped away. Lyssa chuckled. "No no...you scared the poor thing. Here, hold out her hand. Slowly, extend your arm. Good. Now, whistle."

Holding his hand aloft, he looked at her. "I don't know how to whistle."

"Here, bring your lips together like this." She scrunched her lips together, forming a small circle. "And blow."

He analyzed her form, studying her lips as she whistled. The bird warbled back. "Okay," she said. "Now it's your turn."

Mimicking her motion, he curled his lips into a circle and blew. The only thing radiating from his lips was air and spittle.

"No no. You're trying too hard. You just have to let it come naturally. Don't think about it. Just do it." She demonstrated again; the azura whistled back.

Jay closed his eyes and focused. He tried to relax his muscles and heed her advice. When he flicked open his eyes, he blew again. Unsatisfied, he blew harder, and harder, until even the bird seemed to laugh as his face burned red. Lyssa shook her head and laughed. "You're still trying to hard."

He abandoned his attempts to whistle and pounded his fist on the ground. "That's impossible."

"Come on now," she said, smiling. This was the first time Jay had seen her smile; he found the sight as peaceful and soothing as the azura's chirping. "You'll get it one day. It just takes practice."

The bird flapped its wings and took off from the ground to join its friends in the sky. Lyssa waved it farewell, and Jay watched her with a new fondness and admiration. "I don't know how people can eat those birds," she said. "They're so beautiful, aren't they?"

Jay watched the bird flutter away. "Yeah...."

Sighing, she glanced back at the ground. "It's too bad we can't be more like them. Peaceful rather than greedy."

"I know. We wouldn't be in this mess we are now."

"Yeah, I'd probably still be living with my parents."

He looked at her curiously. "Why aren't you?"

She stared wide-eyed in the distance before answering. "Things...weren't safe for my mom and I anymore."

"Why not?"

"I'd rather not talk about it."

She dusted off her black pants before standing up. Under the newfound sunlight, he saw burn marks all across her face and body from the acid lake. He tried not to blame himself for her agony, but he couldn't help it. He noticed something peculiar. "What's that?"

He pointed to a hole dissolved in her violet vest near her ribcage. There was a mark on her dark skin, a scar of some sort. "It's nothing," she said hastily, turning her body to conceal the mark. "Just a battle wound. We'd better get back to the camp before the others begin to worry." She extended her arm.

He hesitated a moment before grabbing her hand and rising to his feet. He knew she was lying, she was hiding something. But he owed it to her not to insist discussing something that made her uncomfortable. "Thanks, Lyssa. I feel better now," he said as they traveled back to the camp.

When they returned, Lynk and Blynk had just finished placing large rocks in a circle and were tossing piles of dry twigs in the center. "Ahh, Jay! Just in time. We went wandering to find old man grumpy, but we ran into a pile of wood safely stashed in a small cave. It's dry, so we can start a fire with this!"

"Stashed in a cave?" Jay repeated as he sat down with the others.

"Yeah." Lynk topped the pile off with logs as thick as his fist. He propped them up in a pyramidal structure. "Must have been left over from some other people who visited this wonderful paradise."

After plopping some tinder at the base of the pyramid, Lynk grabbed two stones from Blynk. Holding the hand stone in his left hand and the striker in his right, he brushed the stones together. After several strikes and a few flashes, Lynk finally hit the sweet spot and set a spark to the tinder. He cupped his hands over the tiny flame to ensure its survival against the wind. "Come on, show 'em what you got."

As the tinder burned, the brittle twigs caught flame. Satisfied the fire was strong enough, Lynk backed away and gave his brother a high five. "Alright!"

"Perfect bro!"

Huddling close to the fire for warmth, Soleus spread his pudgy fingers and held them near the flame. "Now all we need is some food."

Jenkins unfastened his sheath and set it on the ground. "The captain better come back with a bloody gorgrim. I'm starving."

Delcato slid closer to the fire next to Jenkins. "Are you feeling better, Jay?"

Jay nodded. "Yeah, thank you. I'm sorry for storming off like that. I just needed some time to think things through."

"Don't worry, Lil' Blue!" Soleus said. "We'll get that Thyrod sooner or later."

"His bloody name is Thyran," Jenkins said.

"Thyrod, Thyran. Whatever! I'm jes' sayin' not to fret. We'll get the brutal fiend."

Jay smiled. "Thanks, Sol."

Using his only hand, Ankin pointed off in the distance. "Here comes the cap'n."

As Captain Hector and Karen emerged in the distance, Jay saw the captain carrying something by its neck. When they neared the fire, Jay realized they had slain an azura. Hector tossed it on the ground by the circle of rocks.

"Sorry mates, that's all we could find."

Lyssa gasped, throwing her hand to her lips. "You killed an azura?"

"Would ye rather starve?" Hector held his cutlass in the air and prepared to behead it.

"They're such beautiful creatures!" She shook her head in disgust. "We'll get like three bites of food out of taking that life."

"I'm sorry, Lyssa," the captain said. She cringed as he swung his blade down, slicing off the bird's head. "I have to look out for me crew."

"This might be more appetizing."

The crew all turned to see Cain dragging a foxlike creature by its leg. When brought near the flame, its furry head lolled to one side, its jaw dangling open.

"Ahh, there he is!" Lynk said. "Glad you could join us. We've been starving over here trying to—" He stopped mid-sentence and gasped. "A vulpin! Where did you find that?"

Yellow, slanted eyes glistened from its feline face. Its body resembled that of a fox, only taller, thicker, and with hands resembling that of a human. Blood stained the fur around its neck where Cain had slit its throat.

Cain clutched a narrow spear in his hand along with his walking staff. "I snuck up on it while it was asleep." He stabbed the spear into the ground.

"Were there more?" Jenkins asked. "They usually travel in packs."

"It was alone."

"Sorry, cap'n." Soleus's mouth drooled with excitement. "That vulpin will do me stomach much more good than that bird."

"I agree with you there!" Lynk nudged Jenkins. "Why

don't you skin the beast while I get some stuff to cook with?"

Jenkins lifted his brown pant leg to expose a knife strapped to his leg. "Sounds good to me."

While Jenkins skinned and gutted the vulpin, Karen wrapped fresh gauze around Ankin's arm. Jay secretly attempted a few more times to whistle, careful not to let Lyssa catch him in the act. However, after numerous failed attempts, he gave up and watched Jenkins take his knife to the vulpin, slicing out chunks of meat.

When he was finished, the crew each grabbed a stick from the pile Lynk and Blynk found in the cave, stabbed a slab of meat, and held it over the glowing orange flames.

Jay muffled his laughter when he saw Soleus. His friend stared with hungry eyes like a starved panther, ready to pounce and devour the tender meat. Licking his lips, he prodded the meat with his fingers, sighed, and set it back over the fire.

"Easy boy," Lynk said. "The food isn't going anywhere."

But everyone was just as hungry as Soleus. They waited in silence, the only sound being the crackling of the fire, a sound Jay found particularly relaxing. By the time their food had finished cooking, the sun had set, leaving only the blazing fire to light the air. Under the flickering light, Jay noticed everyone except Hector, Ankin, and Karen had burn marks over their faces, and their clothes were ripped and torn. But their pain had seemed to subside, for no one complained or groaned.

As they ate, Lynk and Blynk monitored the fire and added more logs when needed. "Hopefully it won't rain again," Lynk said, securing a log at the base of the fire.

Soleus chomped into his meat, its juices spraying

down his pale cheeks. "Mm..yeah..I.mmm.don thin...mm.rain...because.."

Karen slapped her palm on the ground. "Soleus! Swallow your food before talking. You sound like a babbling fool!"

Delcato clicked her tongue in disgust as Soleus gobbled his meal.

Cain sat on a rock and took his knife to his staff to recarve the patterns dissolved by the lake. "So, captain. What do you plan to do now?"

Hector dislodged a scrap of meat from his teeth with his tongue. "Well, come dawn, the river should settle and we should have more strength. We should be able to forge across it. I say we head back to the beach."

Cain flicked a sliver of wood off his staff. "Thyran will be gone by then."

"Most likely. However, some debris from our ship have washed ashore. We can use that, as well as whatever we can rummage from this island, to build a raft and then sail to the nearest land. Then we can steal a ship and pursue them."

Cain looked up from his staff, his dark eyes glinting in the firelight. "But we have no idea which way he went."

Hector scratched his beard and looked up in thought. "True."

Jenkins twirled his white lock pick between his spiderlike fingers. "Let's worry about getting off this island alive."

"If we didn't have to rest all the time," Cain said, "we could be sailing away in Thyran's ship by now."

Lynk finished stretching some skin from the vulpin over a hole he carved in a giant piece of wood. "Cain, there's no way we could overpower nearly a hundred pirates. It would have been suicide!"

"Hmph...." Cain went back to his work, unwilling to discuss the matter any further.

Hector stood up and addressed the crew. "Listen. Ye all have been through a lot in the past few days. Get some rest tonight. Ye have earned it. Come dawn, we will go to the beach and see what we can do. Let us worry about it then. For now, just relax."

"Mmmm." Soleus wiped some juices from his lips. "Now yer speakin' me language, cap'n."

Relax...that was something Jay had not been able to do for four years.

"Aha, mates!" Lynk leapt to his feet with Blynk by his side. "Ladies and gentlemen. Luckily for you, my younger brother Blynk here managed to save his harmonica from the shipwreck. And I, Lynk Patrykus, have, for your listening pleasure, created a natural drum!" He flourished his wooden drum in the air: stretched vulpine skin covered a chopped, hollow tree trunk. Lynk slapped the drum, and then Blynk picked up his queue and blew into his harmonica.

"Bloody hell...." Jenkins rubbed his temples. "Not a minute of silence with you two."

"Oh come on, Jenky! You know you love it." Lynk pranced around the fire singing his self-invented song that complimented Blynk's tune.

Finishing their food, everyone sat around listening to the brothers' melody. The vulpin satisfied Jay's hunger; his stomach ceased aching. The heat of the fire, crackling of the embers, and peacefulness of the calm wind helped him relax and escape into the symphony the two brothers created.

You never know how the flower will blossom. He repeated her saying over and over in his head, and the more he thought about it, the more he saw his own flower shriveling in a pit of flames.

12

Left Behind

Jay had difficultly sleeping. He tried to piece it all together—the end his stepbrother was striving for, the dark history Lyssa concealed, Karen's potential involvement with Cyril. It was all blurry; none of it made any sense to him. What treasure has value beyond that of silver or gold? Some ancient power? Impossible. And yet, that sorceress on the cliff, she did things he would have previously deemed impossible. And the two artifacts—the locket and the hatchet—they both had a mysterious glow to them. There had to be something out there, something Thyran understood well and desperately sought, something he had to figure out.

A scraping sound, the sound of dried leaves digging their nails across stone, disturbed his thoughts. His eyelids parted a millimeter or two, just enough to see.

He thought the fox-like vulpins were figments of his imagination until one spoke in a raspy, chilling voice that compressed his muscles and prickled his face.

"Wiley!" the vulpin hissed. "Ssshh.... You're going to wake them up. One more sound like that and I'll ssslit your throat." He spoke each word in a slow, hushed, commanding voice. He was not abnormally large or muscular, but Jay noticed a powerful aura around him.

Frozen, Jay shifted his eyes across the scene. He counted nearly twenty, maybe even thirty, vulpins surrounding them. Instinctively, his hand coursed down his side, making its way for his cutlass. But before he reached it, he felt a furry paw smash his hand to the ground.

"Ssstupid move, young one," the vulpin hissed.

He had been caught.

"Wake up!" Jay yelled. He jerked his wrist free from he vulpin's grip and rolled to the side, rocks and twigs scraping his abdomen as he did so.

Several things happened at once. Captain Hector unsheathed his blade and leapt into the air. The captain swung his blade at the vulpin Jay assumed to be their leader, but it leaned back just enough to avoid decapitation—

Everyone was awake and struggling to their arms. Everyone but Delcato, who was held fast by a vuplin clutching her firmly with a spear pressed against her neck. Jay nearly rushed to her aid, but the vuplins were everywhere, all armed with spears. One move they did not approve of, and he would be speared instantly.

"Sssteady," the commanding vulpin said, pointing its spear at Hector.

The pack of vulpins closed in.

The vulpin holding Delcato spoke in a sly, feminine voice. "What are your orders, Okraku?"

The commanding vulpin slithered to Delcato, keeping his eyes fixed on the pirates. A smirk befell the vulpin's feline face, and Okraku's nail scraped down Delcato's cheek, leaving behind a trail of blood. She struggled, but to no avail. Jay noticed Soleus wince.

"Hmm...what do you think Lithia?" Okraku said to the female vulpin who strangled Delcato. "A life for a life...surely a fair trade, no?" He pressed his own spear against Delcato's neck.

"Waddya mean!" Soleus blurted, swinging his clenched fist in front of him. "We didn't harm any of yer kind. Let 'er go!"

Okraku's yellow eyes glistened in the predawn light. He pointed with his spear to the scraps of meat and bone on the ground from their previous night's meal. "No harm? I doubt Vennor willingly sacrificed his life to feed you ssscum."

Soleus shot Cain a harsh glance. Cain slipped a knife out from his black jacket and stood still with his mynx on his shoulder.

Hector stepped closer to Okraku. Delcato was trembling, still squirming to break free of Lithia's grip. "We will not hand over one of our own to be butchered," the captain said.

Okraku snickered, a sound echoed by the rest of the pack. "Of coursse you won't. Besides, one human death isn't enough to satisfy a whole pack of vulpinsss." He licked his white, jagged fangs. "But you...I think I'll save you for myself."

Okraku raised his spear above his head and let out a cry, a horrifying hissing sound soon reverberated by the rest of the pack. The crew huddled closer together as the vulpins rattled their spears in the air.

"Brothersss! Sistersss!" Okraku cried out. "Let us avenge Vennor's death!"

They all shouted in unison.

The ground trembled—a frightening roar pierced the sky, echoing off the distant walls of rock. Afraid to move, Jay rolled his eyes to the direction of the roaring, and outlined by the fiery orange of the sunrise, a huge beast raced towards them at an alarming rate.

"Gorgrim!" one of the vulpins shouted.

The gorgrim's arms and legs maneuvered in the motion of a gorilla to propel it forward. Its poisonous, barbed tail shook menacingly in the air. Under the predawn light, it appeared like a flaming shadow.

During that split second the vulpins took to glance at the gorgrim, Cain flung his dagger through the air, and Jay watched as it smashed into Lithia's skull—the vulpin dropped to the ground instantly, letting Delcato free. Delcato snatched the dead vulpin's spear from the ground and rushed over to the crew, nodding at Cain when she was clear of the vulpins. "Thanks, Cain."

Cain's eyes remained fixed on their leader, Okraku.

"Lithia!" Okraku cried when his attention shifted from the incoming gorgrim to Lithia, who lay facedown on the ground.

"What should we do?" Wiley asked nervously.

Shaking with fury, Okraku pointed his spear at the pirates. "Kill them! Kill them all!"

Spears soared through the air—the vulpins lunged at them like wolves.

"Take cover!" Hector shouted as he ducked to avoid an incoming spear.

Cain let loose another knife which dropped another vulpin. Amid the hissing and screaming of pirates, Jay heard the sound of muscle smashing against bone—looking up, he saw the gorgrim swinging its arm wildly through the air, crushing the vulpins in midair. The gorgrim's snakelike tail lashed a nearby vulpin, stabbing its gut. Standing two stories tall, the gorgrim roared and eyed Soleus, whose attention was focused on the attacking vulpins. Its poisonous tail shot at the oblivious pirate—

Delcato slammed her shoulder against Soleus. They both fell aside as the gorgrim's stinger penetrated the ground.

Threatened by the gorgrim, the vulpins diverted their attacks to the giant beast, leaping on its massive body, sinking their fangs and spears into its gray fur. Okraku, however, remained focused on Cain. He dove over the gorgrim's tail and sprinted on four legs for Cain with his spear in his mouth. Cain flung another dagger for the vulpin's head, but Okraku tilted his head to the side—the dagger whizzed by.

"Up!" Cain shouted, and the mynx obediently left his shoulder and took flight.

Before Jay could come to Cain's aid, Okraku collided into Cain and knocked him to the ground. Cain stumbled up and armed himself with another dagger from his coat. Okraku sliced his nails across Cain's hand; the dagger dropped to the ground—

The two glared at one another—Okraku's yellow shimmering eyes meeting Cain's deathly black pupils. Suddenly, faster than Jay could blink, the vulpin struck the butt of his spear against Cain's chest, knocking him to the ground. Okraku gave a raspy laugh, whirled his spear in the air, and swung it down to pierce Cain's throat—

The gorgrim's tail smashed into Okraku's side, sending him whirling through the air to be lost in the scrambling pack of vulpins.

Hector helped Cain to his feet. "Ye okay?" Cain nodded and stepped free from Hector's grip. "Good. Everyone! Move out, now!"

Jay took a final look at the fray. The gorgrim thrashed about with spears jabbing its skin and vulpins biting into its flesh. Sorrow crept inside Jay for the gorgrim, who was clearly losing ground. However, they had to leave now while the vulpins were occupied should they have a chance for survival.

When they reached the canyon, the river flowed calmly, its powerful current subsided. "Lynk, Blynk, help Ankin," Hector said. "The rest of ye, let's swim across the canyon before they catch up!"

By noontide, they had crossed the canyon and reached the ashy beach where they first entered the island. They were exhausted from the run, especially Cain and Ankin. But they made it, momentarily safe from the vulpins and the gorgrim.

Clumps of wood and other debris from their ship had drifted into the gray sand. The warm sunlight befell the beach and kissed their faces; sprinkles of water from the sea felt good against their acidic burns.

Soleus's plump form barreled across the beach and plopped down by the sea. Scooping up the chilly water, he sluiced his face. "Ahh...water...never thought meself would be this glad over water."

"Good man, Sol," Lynk agreed as he and his brother raced to the water and dove in.

The rest of the crew wasted no time joining. They lathered themselves with the water and splashed it over their faces like it was sweet honey. Jay cringed slightly as the salt water rushed into his wounds, but he welcomed the sensation.

"Men! Men!" Hector called. "Stop acting like a bunch of girls in the washroom and lend me yer ears for a moment!" When the commotion subsided, he continued. "We don't have a great deal of time, mates. Those vulpins, and perhaps even the gorgrim, could be hot on our tails. So, I need ye all to put aside yer pains and get to work. We need to make a raft to carry us off this island and bring us to land where we can steal a ship and continue our pursuit of Thyran."

Jenkins squeezed his brown sleeves to dry them. "How do we know where Thyran is going, and why are we bloody chasing him in the first place?"

There were a few murmurs of agreement. Jay could not blame them: they had lost their captain, the diamond locket, their ship, most of their comrades, and they nearly perished in the acid lake. And for what? None of them truly knew what Thyran was after, only that, according to Lyssa, he must be stopped before he obtains whatever he is chasing.

"He killed our captain!" Hector said. "Killed our captain and stole our treasure, that's why we chase him! And as far as where he be going, we'll deal with that when we get off this cursed island." The captain straightened his back, giving him a more commanding demeanor. "Our time is short. We must build that raft. Lynk, Blynk, you two scour the water for some seaweed we can use for twine. Karen, Lyssa, Delcato, wait here. When we come back with logs, you can help tie the crosspieces with the seaweed. The rest of ye," he bent down to pick up a hatchet and a small ax from the debris washed ashore, "come with me and help chop the logs."

They all broke into their designated groups. Jay and the others designated to cut logs each grabbed a tool—anything that drifted ashore from their shipwreck—for chopping and followed Hector inland. Hector stopped when they reached a group of withered trees. "Let's cut these down and bring 'em back to shore."

Soleus shouldered his hatchet and approached a thick tree trunk. "Watch this, Lil' Blue," Soleus said with a smirk. After flexing his muscles, he swung the hatchet into the tree. The thump reverberated through the air, and the hatchet wedged itself into the trunk.

Jay grinned and shook his head—the same depth would have taken him four or fives swings to reach. His eyes flowed up the tree. Its aged branches hung lifelessly over his head; dead bristles of pine rained down and coated the floor. He picked up a pile of the prickly needles and let them fall through his fingers like sand. "Looks like these trees used to be alive."

"Well yeah, how do you think they got here?" Soleus dislodged the blade and swung again, sinking it deeper into the tree.

"But everything is dead...I have yet to see a tree with living leaves. What do you think happened to everything?"

"Dunno Lil' Blue." He swung twice more. "Man! This tree is stronger than it looks."

Jay laughed and circled the tree, checking his progress. Although the tree did look aged and dying, its trunk was still very thick. "You know, I've never seen a vulpin before today. Well, last night I guess."

Soleus heaved the hatchet again, preparing for another swing. "Me eyes have seen one when I was young. It took several guards to put it down. Fast creatures they are. Faster than wind I'd say. It's kinda scary thinking they once ruled the planet and we were their slaves, isn't it?"

Jay remembered Thyran telling him the gruesome stories from books he read about the era when vulpins ruled over humans. The thought of being subservient to those foul creatures upset his stomach.

"She nearly died..." Soleus mumbled, continuing to hack away at the tree.

"Yeah," Jay said. "It amazes me how good an aim Cain has with those daggers."

Soleus nodded. "He may be the grumpiest and rudest pirate, but I'm damn glad he's on our side. Watch out!"

The tree leaned over and finally snapped. It smashed into the ground with a resounding thud. Soleus walked along the fallen tree to its tapered apex. As they walked, Jay noticed something curious on the ground. There were lines etched into the hard soil, like effects of a blade scraping against the ground. Peering up ahead in the direction of the mark, Jay made out a similar line, like a dotted trail. The lines pointed northwest, the direction they headed to get to the hatchet. Had Karen truly betrayed them?

Soleus's voice broke his strand of thought. "Alright, now let's chop up the tree into logs."

After chopping the tree trunks into smaller pieces, the crew each bore a handful of timber and walked back to the beach. Plopping them onto the firm ground just off the fringe of sand, they rolled them side by side as Karen, Delcato, and Lyssa gathered around.

Hector unsheathed his cutlass and dragged the tip across the logs near one end. "We need to carve notches into the logs so we can slide the crosspieces in place." He motioned to a pile of thinner logs. "Those need to be shaped to slide through the notches. We have plenty of knives you can use for carving. Also, we'll need to throw some brush over the base to keep our things dry. Del, gather some twigs or dried leaves or something."

Delcato nodded her head. "Aye, captain."

"I'll help her, cap'n," Soleus dropped a few more logs into the pile and moved closer to Delcato, but not his usual rush-to-impress style of movement. A more calm, relaxed movement. Jay smiled to himself.

Hector sheathed his cutlass. "No, I need you here to help carving."

"I'll fill in for him," said Jay.

The captain eyed Jay for a moment. Jay nodded his head slightly, trying to guide the captain to his decision. "Alright, fine." Hector's eyes shifted to Soleus, who wore a beaming smile. "Just hurry back."

Rolling her eyes, Delcato walked away from the beach with Soleus by her side. Jay watched them fade into the distance.

While the captain left to salvage any remaining supplies washed ashore, Jay and the others worked on carving dovetail notches into the logs. The sound of Blynk's harmonica swam through the air from where he sat on a dried piece of wood on the beach. The music gave them a rhythm to work, making them more productive. They had just finished smoothing out the final notch when Jenkins yelled,

"This bloody thing won't fit!"

Jay turned around to see Jenkins attempting to slide the trapezoidal crossbeam through the dovetail notches in the logs. Lynk, still wet from collecting seaweed, strode next to Jenkins. "Here, let me have a go, mate."

Surrendering his position, Jenkins walked to the water and rinsed his hands, chapped from carving notches in the logs. Lynk shared Jenkins's frustration with the log's inability to slide in. He grabbed a knife from the sand and chiseled away at the log's edges.

After sweeping across the beach in search for anything useful, the captain returned. "Lynk, did ye get the seaweed?"

"Aye, captain. Blynk?"

Playing his harmonica, Blynk motioned to the clump of seaweed next to the wood he sat on.

"Good. Let's hurry up and finish this."

They worked diligently for the better part of an hour. Lynk managed to fit the crossbeam through the dovetail notches, and Karen and Lyssa managed to secure the raft together with the seaweed. By the time Soleus and Delcato returned, the raft was complete.

Jay caught a sunny smile wiped over Soleus's face, a

smile of joy and wonderment. When Delcato turned to spread the brush over the raft, Soleus winked at him and nodded his head with appreciation. And after taking a doub-letake at Delcato, he noticed an unforced, completely natu-ral, smile. Wings of happiness fluttered in Jay's stomach. He felt elated for his friend.

"What happened?" Jay asked when Soleus ap-proached him.

"I did like you said," Soleus whispered. "Held back my jokes and basically just...listened. It actually worked. She opened up to me, and we...talked. She went on and on about her past and—"

"You listened though, right?"

"Of course!" Soleus, realizing he had just spoken too loudly, bent closer to Jay and lowered his voice. "I listened, and she thanked me, saying she felt relieved to get it off her chest."

Jay patted him on the back. "Good. I'm proud of you, Sol."

But Soleus was not listening; his mind was drifting on the clouds as if none of the tragedies in the past few days had ever taken place. Good for him. He deserves it.

"Hey, it's our spyglass!" Jenkins retrieved the cylin-drical object from the sand and wiped its lens on his velvet green shirt. Jay watched him gaze out through the corridor of towering rock walls that lined the water's path.

Jenkins leaned forward, still peering through the spyglass, and then shouted, "Incoming ship!"

Jay's body tingled. A ship? Whose ship?

Hector snatched the spyglass from Jenkins and gazed through it. "It be a merchant vessel with Eulian soldiers aboard. Heading this way."

The Eulian soldiers. They had caught up with them.

Jay suddenly grew dizzy, his legs felt weak.

"There's no bloody way they could have tracked us this far! You think they're here for the locket?"

The captain collapsed the spyglass and tossed it back to Jenkins rather forcefully. "What else would they be here for?"

"Can we use the rafts?" Soleus asked.

Cain whispered something to his mynx on his shoulder, and it extended its wings and flew up to the sky. "To what purpose?" Cain asked, limping closer to Jenkins. "Think they'll somehow miss us drifting on by in a damn raft?"

"Then what do ye suggest?" Soleus asked.

Cain peered through the spyglass; Jay's eyes scanned the towering cliffs lining the water. He massaged his sweaty palms with his thumbs. If the Eulian soldiers were lowering their boats, they had minutes until the soldiers would arrive on the beach. But this was their only way off the island. They had to do something.

Jay turned around to look inland, and then he glanced to the right where the towering cliff slanted down gradually to meet the parched flat ground of Storm Isle. An idea sparked in his head. He glanced over his shoulder once more to the water, the only thing separating them from the soldiers. It was their best shot.

"Faster!" McClevin's wide oar dipped in and out of the water as it propelled the boat forward. "Those pirates have to be stranded on this island somewhere. All that ship debris...they must have wrecked."

The princess brushed her snowy white hair from her face. Her eyes traveled up the tall landmasses surrounding the water. When the beach came into view, she gasped.

"This is awful. All the trees are dead, and the sand, it is like ash. Is there any life on this island?"

"Just those thieving pirates."

All was silent, save for the oars dipping in and out of the water. McClevin knew the pirates had to be on this island. Now was his chance to bring those criminals to justice and serve his king. He straightened his back as he paddled, envisioning the king holding a ceremony of celebration after their return. Yes, the gallant General McClevin saves Eulia from warfare and chaos. The honor. It would be bliss.

The boat came to a sudden stop as it crashed into the beach, snapping him back to reality, vanishing his daydream like a shadow in the sun.

"Alright men, off the boats." The soldiers leapt out and filed in formation on the beach awaiting further orders.

"Lord love a duck." McClevin's leather cuirass pressed against his chest as he waddled to a raft resting on the beach. "Looks like the fiends were trying to escape." He pinched a piece of seaweed used to bound the raft together. It was still damp; it must have been dragged out of the sea not too long ago. The pirates were near.

"Soldiers!" His soldiers all straightened their backs, slapped their hands by their sides, and lifted their chins. "Disperse in groups and search the surrounding area. They can't be too far."

The princess brushed some sand off a drum resting in the gray sand. She tapped it with her fingers—the sound was slightly off-beat. McClevin smiled, remembering when she would organize music groups to play for her father.

Then McClevin shook his head. He needed to focus on those pirates. Though they could be anywhere, and without a map of this island, he couldn't organize a valuable search operation. But maybe the red book may have a drawing of the island. Whoever wrote it knew enough to get them here. Maybe there was more.

"Winston. Where is that book? The red book?"

The short soldier pushed his helmet up above his eyes. "O-on board, sir. I didn't bring it."

McClevin's face boiled. He dug his nails into his hands. "On board? What use is it on board?"

The princess's voice helped him refrain from lashing out. "Relax, McClevin. Send one of your men to get it."

"That'll give the pirates more time to run away!"

"To where? They have no ship. Ten more minutes won't change a thing."

She was right. The time would be well spent acquiring a map of the island. "Very well, but I'll go back myself to make sure its done." He cast a cold glare at Winston. "Stay here. You're in charge until my return."

"I'll wait here with Winston," the princess said.

"As you wish." McClevin hopped in a nearby boat and drifted back towards the *Gemline*.

Marching in single file, the pirates skimmed the top of the cliff. Jay's heart echoed in his chest when he saw all the soldiers pouring onto the beach. If this plan didn't work, they would be captured without a doubt—the Eulian soldiers had them greatly outnumbered. Accused of Governor Almsy's murder and stealing the diamond locket, his fate would certainly be death. Wiping the sweat off his brow, he dismissed his concerns and followed the rest of the crew over the cliff.

After several minutes, Jenkins, who led the charge, stopped. "Good, we've cleared the ship."

"Alright, mates." Lynk unraveled the rope from his shoulder. "Time for a climb."

Fatigued, Ankin dropped to the ground. "I don't know if I have anything left in me. My arm is burning. I can barely move my feet."

"Enough of that nonsense," Hector said. "We aren't leaving anyone behind."

While Lynk secured the rope around a spiky rock, Jay anxiously waited. Lyssa stood beside him. "Just relax," she said. "If you think about it too much, you'll slip and fall."

He laughed feebly. "I know...it's happened before."

"Good to go." Lynk stood up proudly. He and his brother had fastened numerous ropes together so the length would roughly match the height of the cliff. "Come, Blynk. Let's help Ankin down first."

"Alright, bro!"

The two brothers and Ankin slithered down the rope along the cliff, and the rest soon followed. They were climbing far enough behind the ship to avoid detection, unless one of the soldiers happened to focus a spyglass in their direction. Despite this, Jay managed to calm his nerves enough to descend the rope rapidly, using protruding rocks as temporary braking points to regain his breath and wipe the sweat off his palms.

"Hang on, mate!" Jay heard Lynk say from below. He watched as Lynk, Blynk, and Ankin let go of the rope and splashed into the water. A few seconds later, the entire crew followed. They swam for the ship, careful to remain silent. Jay and Hector aided Soleus during their swim to the Eulian vessel.

Using their hatches, axes, and knives, they jabbed the wood of the ship and hoisted themselves out of the water. Jay's arms throbbed after the climb up the cliff and the descent down, but still, his fear-induced adrenaline carried him up the ship. To his side, he noticed Cain struggling up to the rail, his walking staff gripped between his teeth. He admired the old pirate, and inside, he felt proud Cain had accepted his idea without debate—it was like he gained some respect from a man he revered. That feeling of achievement trumped his feeling of anxiety.

As Jay suggested, the pirates waited just below the rail of the ship for everyone to reach their position. Within minutes, the pirates surrounded the ship, each waiting for the command. Confident everyone was ready, Jay nodded to Hector, who passed the signal along his crew, and they all scrambled over the rail and drew their weapons.

"Pirates!" one of the sailors shouted instantly, but before they could react, Jay and the others swarmed the deck and smartly disarmed the nearest sailors and shoved them overboard. The others sailors drew their daggers and swords then launched themselves at Jay and the crew.

Jay fought hard and fast, parrying incoming attacks, slaying his foes or tossing them overboard. He kept a watchful eye on Lyssa, who, after the loss of *Amara*, fought using a cutlass. She appeared expertly trained in wielding such a weapon; her moves appeared fluent and perfected.

After sidestepping a blow aimed for his head and whipping the sailor overboard, Jay noticed a soldier wearing a shiny leather cuirass emerge from the captain's cabin carrying a red book. This soldier wore a shining blue-crested helmet and had a long sword fastened to his hip. Jay recognized the man at once as the Eulian guard Captain Gaden had fought on the beach the night they stole the locket.

The soldier's eyes widened, his jaw dropped.

"All hands on deck!" he bellowed. He dropped the book and swung his sword in the air. A dozen guards stumbled up from below deck, all armed and ready for battle.

They charged at the pirates. Lyssa grappled her

sword firmly and stepped beside Jay, ready for the new on-slaught.

Swords banged against one another, Eulian shields slammed against the pirates, cries rang through the air, screams of falling soldiers echoed off the cliffs. When it became apparent the pirates were firmly holding their ground, the soldier with the leather cuirass called out,

"Sound the horn!"

Before Jay or the others could stop him, a Eulian soldier grabbed a yellow horn and blew into it, which sent out a reverberating sound that easily carried to the beach. The dozens of soldiers that had made it ashore would surely be heading their way now. They would be greatly outnumbered and would have no chance at victory.

Jay's eyes met those of the commanding Eulian soldier, causing the man to stop and stare wide-eyed back at him. "Jay!" his thunderous voice overpowered the clashing of steel around them. "I'll bring you to justice, Jay Perry!" The soldier squeezed his hands around his sword's hilt and rushed towards him. Jay swallowed and prepared for the attack.

The soldier's mighty blow caught him off-guard. He failed to maintain his grip on the cutlass as he blocked and watched in horror as it bounced across the deck. The soldier pointed his sword at him and snarled through clenched teeth. "Give me the locket, and I'll spare your pathetic life."

"Look out Jay!" Delcato swung her blade down at the soldier, but he caught the blade with his steel gauntlet, snatched her wrist, and twisted it forcefully. Her blade fell to the floor as the Eulian soldier threw her against the rail. The wood cracked from impact; she collapsed to the ground.

Lifting her by her hair, the soldier held his sword against her throat and locked his eyes on Jay. "The locket,

Jay. Give it to me now!"

Jay's muscles tightened as he watched the soldier strangling her. Thoughts bombarded his head—he needed to do something, and he had to act fast, for dozens of soldiers were on the way—

A disturbance caught the corner of Jay's eye. Soleus barreled through several soldiers in a mad sprint for the man choking Delcato. Before the soldier had time to react, Soleus crashed his immense shoulder into him—

The two fell to the side against the wooden rail, which snapped under the pressure, and the two toppled over the side of the ship and plummeted to the sea below.

"No!" Delcato screamed, throwing her hands out to catch Soleus before he fell.

She was too late.

Jay cried out as he watched his friend splash into the water. Struggling to stay afloat, Soleus clambered on the side of the ship, trying to climb.

"Come on!" Jay urged, but he knew it was useless.

The Eulian soldier grabbed Soleus's shoulders and yanked him back to the water. A horde of boats filled with Eulian soldiers from the beach drifted around the two. One of the soldiers dove off his boat, swam up behind Soleus, then clubbed him on the back of the head with the hilt of his sword, rending Soleus unconscious.

"Hurry!" Hector called from the center of the deck, oblivious to what just happened. Jay did not look back, but he no longer heard any battle sounds, so he assumed the Eulian soldiers had all been slain or tossed overboard. "Raise the anchor and turn the sails if ye want to escape this island alive! Ankin, man the bridge!"

"Captain!" Delcato said. "We can't leave. Soleus has gone overboard."

Sadness enveloped Jay's heart as night envelopes the sun. His brain was too cloudy to make out the captain's response, but Hector must have decided to act in the best interest of the crew, for he heard the rattling of the anchor being pulled up from the water and the sliding of rope altering the direction of the sails.

"No!" Delcato cried out, leaning over the rail beside Jay, who watched through teary eyes Soleus being hauled off by the soldiers back to their boats. Jay felt utterly useless as the ship began to skim away.

The pirates threw cannonballs, crates, shields, and any other heavy objects they could find to knock off the soldiers trying to climb aboard. Upon being hit, the soldiers plunged back into the glistening water. Jay heard their leader call off his men when the ship gained speed, then he saw him slap his blade madly in the water as Jay drifted away from him for the second time.

13

A Dark History

Drops of tears dripped from Jay's eyes, burning his retinas. They felt more like drops of blood pouring from his heart. His friend, his best friend, wrenched from him as the authorities broke into his home and wrenched his parents.

Indignation blazed through Jay's veins. Although he didn't quite understand everything, he knew that stopping Thyran from pursuing whatever he was would be doing good for Lassar. True, they were criminals, thieving pirates, worthy of receiving some of the harshest punishments, but one thing they were not—evil.

Jay, like many others in the crew, wanted to turn back, to pry Soleus back from the Eulian soldiers, for he was part of their family—the comic relief when tension was thick. But despite their pleas, Captain Hector ordered them onward. Even through his haze of sorrow, Jay could see the futility of a rescue operation—the Eulian soldiers greatly outnumbered them. Rescuing Soleus would be issuing a death sentence to the whole crew.

His stomach sunk into a black abyss when he replayed his fight with that Eulian soldier. He cursed himself for being so weak, for dropping his sword during combat, allowing the soldier to take hold of Delcato, which resulted in Soleus's act of bravery in sacrificing himself to save her. If only he would have maintained his grip on his blade, a mistake of which Thyran consistently chided him during their youth.

"You did all you could."

He whirled around to see Lyssa approaching him with a brown flask, her golden hair wavering like strands of silk in the wind. Apparently, he failed to conceal his emotions despite his attempts.

He felt both comforted by her approach but also angered—he didn't want her to see him like this, mournful, like a child who lost his toy.

"Leave me alone," he said, turning away from her and instead gazing at the water, which bathed under the afternoon sun.

She took his hand, his right hand, the hand that failed to grip his sword, the hand bruised from where his cutlass's hilt ripped out of its grasp, and turned his palm to the sky. He felt cool liquid pouring from the flask onto his bruise. It stung at first, but soon felt soothing.

"Thank you," he muttered.

"You're welcome." She ceased pouring, stepped up to the rail beside him, and leaned against it.

He paid her no attention. His mind still shuffled through all possible scenarios for Soleus's rescue, but none of his plans ended up with their escape even remotely possible.

A dolphin flew out of the water, leaping in an arc several feet high, and then plunged back with a splash into the sea. Several more silver dolphins followed its wake, and the herd galloped through the water. Like the azura, they were free.

"Beautiful, aren't they?"

She had a knack for reading his thoughts. Jay wasn't sure whether he admired that trait or resented it. He didn't ponder too long, for he found himself mesmerized by the beautiful dolphins. Tears built up in his eye, but with Lyssa by his side, he forced them back.

"You'll see Soleus again. McClevin won't kill him."

"McClevin?"

"Yes, he's the General of Eulia."

The soldier with the leather cuirass....

"How do you know his name?"

"Thyran told m—"

The mention of Thyran's name chilled Jay's bones like an arctic frost. He jerked his head to face Lyssa.

"What happened between you two?" he asked.

"Me and Thyran?"

He said nothing.

She closed her eyes, breathed very slowly. Jay sensed her brain whisking through her past, recalling all the memories with her and his stepbrother, and when she came across troublesome memories, her eyelids squeezed closer together, her lips caved into her mouth.

"He promised me something...something I would do anything for."

Promises. Thyran had made several of those to him as well, most of which he kept, one he didn't. "What was that?"

Her eyes opened but seemed focused to the side of Jay's head, where the white skyline met the blue water. "My father was very abusive. When I was younger, he would beat my mother whenever she disobeyed him. Such a despicable man. Money and power. That's all he cared for, all he longed for. He was actually the mayor of the town, and people actually *respected* him. My mother...she was too afraid to speak up against him, for everyone knew of her torment, but either they were too afraid of my father or they just didn't care."

She kicked a wedge of wood through the rail. It gave a faint splash in the sea. "When I was fifteen, I couldn't take it anymore. The abuse he gave my mom and me...was too much." She lifted her lavender jacket and red shirt to reveal a scar, slit sideways across her dark brown skin covering her ribs. The scar was thick, as if a blade sliced through her tender skin.

Jay felt sick. "What happened?"

She let her clothing fall back over her wound. "One night, I was sick and didn't finish my supper. We had steak, must have been expensive, for he didn't take too well to my loss of appetite. He took his knife...a steak knife." She struggled to keep her voice steady. Tears swelled in Jay's throat as he played the rest of the scene in his head.

"So, a week after that, I promised my mom, and all the other women in Craden, that I would come back for them. I promised I would liberate them from the abusive men that ran the village.

"I fled. At first I felt cowardly, but then I remembered my promise. I wanted to find others like me, women strong enough and willing to fight back, to stand up to abuse rather than submit to it. It was during my travels that I met Thyran, a handsome, intelligent, seemingly tender man." Her eyes narrowed, teeth bit down against one another.

"I overheard Thyran talking about his plan to forever change society. I was intrigued. I decided to sneak on board, thinking I could find out more about his plans, perhaps steal some of his treasure to afford my own ambitions should his differ. I overheard him discussing a lot about the legend of Dragons' End—"

Dragons' End...Thyran had mentioned that to him too. According to the legend, three hundred years ago, back when the world was ruled by vulpins, a group of slaves revolted and broke free. They then attacked the Castle of the Dragons, where Ashlen, the supposed creator of Lassar, had sealed his power, which the dragons guarded as sacred.

"Isn't that just a myth?" Jay asked.

"That's what I thought, and, thinking him for a fool, I decided to leave the ship when it next reached port. But...he caught me. He must have been impressed with my ability to remain hidden for so long, for he spared my life. When he asked me why I snuck on board, I couldn't lie. There was something about him. I thought if I lied, he would see right through me. So, I told him everything, about my past, about my father, about my desire to liberate the women of Craden. He seemed rather impressed and agreed to help me.

"After a while, he gained my trust and...I began to fall in love with him." She closed her eyes for a second, then her green eyes met Jay's. "I know this must be hard for you."

"No," Jay shook his head, although the word 'love' had made him want to vomit, or maybe stab himself with a dagger, something to inflict more pain than the thought of such an evil man romancing such a beautiful and gentle woman. He was angry at himself for feeling a hint of resentment towards her for falling for his stepbrother after all Thyran had done to him. But she couldn't have known. "I understand," he said finally.

She nodded, wiped a tear from her eye, and continued.

"When he told me his plan, at first I laughed, claiming the legend of Dragons' End was a myth. But he possessed extensive knowledge of the legend and the history of this world, stuff I had never heard of. And he had this map, which he claimed to have stolen. It was a map of the Dryfus Mines on the left side and a set of instructions on the right, outlining how to unlock whatever Ashlen kept sealed in the tower of the Dragons' Castle. It mentioned the three artifacts—the locket and the two keys it pointed to. But it didn't provide the location of anything, other than Ashlen's Tomb.

"After three years, he grew frustrated with his inability to find the missing pieces of the puzzle. I asked him numerous times what Ashlen kept sealed in the tower, but he refused to tell me—he just said that with it, he would make the world a better place, freeing it from warfare, liberating the women of Craden, and so on.

"Then one day, he stopped at Craden in search of clues. I beseeched him to use his crew to liberate the women there. Begged and pleaded for days. But he denied me, saying only after he found Ashlen's treasure.

"Despite his orders, I snuck my mom on the ship, planning to set her free at the next port, which was Eulia since Thyran learned that King Emory would bestow upon the winner of the Gorgrim Tournament a unique diamond locket, which fit the description of one of the artifacts in the legend perfectly. But, we never made it to the next port." Her eyes wandered off, directed at the dolphins but only seeing her past.

"What happened?" Jay asked after a minute of silence. Part of him didn't want her to answer, but part of him felt she wanted to give it, to release the burden of carrying this memory alone for so long.

"Thyran caught her." She swallowed. "I remember the look on her face as she sunk into the water, her hands bound behind her back, struggling to wriggle free, struggling to breathe, struggling to stay alive, struggling to get one final glimpse of me, standing horrorstruck on the ship. I was forced to watch her drown while Thyran laughed, laughed at my weakness, my childish thoughts that I could outsmart him."

She closed her eyes. Tears broke through.

"I...something came over me. I broke free of his grasp

and dove in after her, but I was too late. She was dead. I was alone in the ocean, watching as Thyran sailed away.

"That was the last I saw of Thyran until he ambushed us in the mines."

Jay felt his body rock as the ship swayed, its nose crashed through the rough waves ahead. Too many emotions swirled inside him to speak, so he stood in silence trying to understand how a man he once admired, loved, and trusted for so long could be so cruel...so evil.

He wanted to hug her, to tell her they would have their revenge, to tell her he would not rest until the women of Craden were free. But he couldn't. He had no idea where Thyran was, or how much longer they could evade capture, or how much time they had before Thyran obtained whatever Ashlen kept hidden.

To the side, he saw Karen rubbing Delcato's shoulder, probably comforting her, for she seemed the saddest of them all, weeping uncontrollably through the morning and afternoon. But, despite the overall sorrow shared by the crew, they pressed onward.

Onward to what? Where were they going? They had cleared the corridors of rocky cliffs and were sailing into the open sea, but their destination remained obscured.

"All hands, assemble on deck!" Hector called, descending the stairs from the bridge to the deck.

Jay looked back at Lyssa, who, like him, appeared to be fighting the urge to let her emotions run wild, to scream with fury.

He desperately wanted to say something. She had opened a terrible internal wound, and he felt obligated to help her close it. But again, she seemed to read his thoughts, and feebly smiled.

"Thanks," she said.

When the crew lined up on the deck, Hector paced in front of them, his hands clasped behind his back. They could hear the warbling from azura flying overhead and the whooshing as the ship sliced through the wind.

"Men, we all faced a grave loss earlier today," the captain said. "Please know that I acted in the best interest of me crew. If I thought there was the slightest chance of saving Soleus, ye all know I would have taken it. With the number of Eulian soldiers, they would have crushed us like bugs. We will do everything we can to help our dear friend, but for now, we must press on."

He let a moment of silence pass as everyone digested his words and silently prayed for Soleus's well-being.

"One pressing matter at hand is the issue of me first mate. It's taken me some time, but I've at last come to me decision." There was light murmuring among the crew, to which Hector responded by raising his voice. "After thought and consideration, I've decided to appoint to me first mate...."

Jay noticed Cain lift his head and watch Hector closely through his hooded eyes. Rightfully so, for every one on that ship knew he was the most practical choice.

The captain's next words stood out from the silence like a blaring trumpet. "Jay Perry."

The crew stood, stunned. Lynk was the first to make a sound. Leaping in the air, he threw his fist. "Hoorah for Little Blue!"

Jay blinked. It was a few seconds and several congratulations before it finally sunk in. Captain Hector had made him, Jay Perry, the pirate nicknamed Little Blue, his first mate. He stepped forward to shake the captain's hand. Amid all the excitement and commotion, no one but Jay noticed Cain slink away below deck.

When the murmur had died down, Ankin raised a question that Jay had been longing to ask. "Captain, what's our heading?"

"Keep her afloat and due north. Jay, come with me to my cabin." Jay followed Hector as he navigated his way through the bustling pirates and disappeared into his cabin.

Hector's cabin, formerly McClevin's, was decorated nicely, better than any pirate ship. Delicately painted glasses and plates were stacked in a metal cabinet along the wall, and a polished desk and wooden chairs in the center shined brightly, warmed by the sunlight pouring through the large, clear windows on both sides of the room.

As Jay neared a chair, he tasted the sweet scent of flowers in the air. To his left, he saw a round pot filled with black soil with bright yellow and purple flowers, full blossomed, bending towards the window, sipping the vibrant sunlight. Beside the flowers was a wardrobe, most likely for McClevin's uniforms.

Jay sat in front of the desk, which was empty except for a thick, red book in the center, probably the same book McClevin dropped earlier on the deck. "Thank you, captain," he began, but then an icy wind swept through his body; his muscles tightened at once—

That book. He had seen it before. In Ashlen's Tomb? No. In King Emory's bedroom? No.

He heard a sound, probably the captain responding to his words of gratitude, but he wasn't sure—his mind worked madly, flipping through the pages in his history.

Where...where had he seen it? Its bright red cover, he remembered it, standing out from the drab, darkened, dusty books beside it. It was nighttime, he was exhausted, his heart was pounding, he had just—

Then he remembered. That was the same book he saw

in Governor Almsy's bedroom, just before Thyran killed him.

"Something troubling ye, Lil' Blue?"

Jay's eyes remained transfixed on the crimson book. "That book. I've seen it before."

Hector raised an eyebrow. "Really? That's very interesting. I've heard only one copy exists." He spun the book around so Jay could read the cover. The title was emblazoned in bright blue amid its scarlet background:

Dragons' End

"Dragons' End," Jay read aloud, examining the cover. At the bottom, he noted the author's name: Laneth Kukorski. He had never heard of him.

"I have skimmed through it," Hector said. "This book was written three hundred years ago by a man who lived through Dragons' End. It seems this is how the Eulian soldiers tracked us down."

Jay ran his fingers over the letters of the title, feeling its smooth bumps. "What do you mean? How could this book lead them to us?"

Hector grabbed the book, flipped through it until he was close to the end, settled on a page, and turned it back towards Jay. "There's some sort of poem. Read it aloud."

Jay's eyes scanned down through the page before he began to read in a soft voice barely above a whisper.

Crystallize the head
Of the late wizard during his rest
If guided by a pure heart
The holy light brightens a path

Through raging storms
Find the burning lake of death
Which drowns the curved blade
Then shooting through the blue
Seize the pearl of vanishing crimson roses
Lost in a sea of emerald
And a sky of cerulean
In the basin the rock must rest
Disturbed only by the blade
Will the power unleash
His powers thou will absorb

As he read it, he matched parts of the poem to parts of their journey. *The late wizard during his rest*—Ashlen's Tomb, and then they placed the locket in his head, and the holy light activated the locket. *Through the raging storms*—they traveled to Storm Isle, where they found the lake, which surrounded the hatchet.

"This seems to have outlined our route," Hector said. "The Eulian soldiers must have somehow known this, and the fifth line probably clued them that we were sailing to Storm Isle."

Of course. This poem is a guide to the treasure Ashlen concealed in the tower of the Dragons' Castle. Apparently the treasure contains a great power, judging by the last two lines. Laneth must have learned about the location of the artifacts somewhere. But if he knew all this, why didn't he go after the treasure himself?

Jay cleared his thoughts and focused on the page. "*Shooting through the blue*," he repeated.

"Yes," Hector leaned over the book, reading it upside down. "I've made sense of everything up to that line, which appears to be where we're at now. Do ye have any idea what it means?"

Jay studied the poem. He thought of all the alternative meanings to the words, or even what *blue* meant in that context. He had a tendency to overcomplicate things—whenever a teacher gave a logic puzzle, he would be the one to overthink it while his classmates, who thought simply, solved it immediately. He drummed his fingers on the polished desk; the steady sound helped him think.

There was a pattern in the poem—step-by-step instructions to obtaining the artifacts. The first step, activating the compass. The second, traveling to Storm Isle. The third, acquiring the hatchet. Now, they were on the fourth, which, logically, should be an instruction specifying where to go. *Shooting through the blue.* He tried his best to think simply, to try and not look too deeply, and then he thought of something.

"Shooting through the blue.... Maybe that just means sailing across the ocean, meaning that whatever we seek next is not on Storm Isle?"

"Hmm." Hector inspected the page. "Maybe. So, what is this rose-covered pearl thing all about then?"

"I don't know." Jay began pacing the room.

Treading over the navy blue carpet, embroidered with golden designs, Jay again delved his thoughts. The description struck him as something vaguely familiar, but he could not pinpoint what it was. He knew he had once seen something peculiar that seemed to fit closely to that description.

He traveled through his memories. From his younger years dueling with Thyran in their parents' backyard to his years as a fugitive on the run, always ducking corners and hiding from authorities. He thought of the countless instances where he stole food from marketplaces for survival, but he had not recalled seeing any pearl with roses.

He remembered all the times training with Hector. He broke a smile thinking about it. The clever pirate always managed to outwit him, but he was a great mentor. Whenever Jay found himself in trouble, Hector was there to help. From saving him from capture in Delphina and welcoming him to the crew to protecting him from an overzealous necklace vendor in Eulia, Hector was there to—

"That's it!" he blurted out.

"Huh?" Hector eyed him curiously.

Jay vividly painted the scene in his head. "The necklace vendor in Eulia. He tried to sell me a necklace. I remember gazing into one of the necklaces. I was fascinated by it...it seemed mystical to me. It had tiny puffs of red that appeared and then vanished, like tiny explosions. And then the gem changed from green to blue, and then back again."

Hector reread the three lines aloud, pronouncing each word slowly.

"The vender in Eulia..." Hector said, scratching his shaggy brown beard. "Ye sure?"

Jay nodded.

"Hmm," Hector said. "I don't recall seeing anything like that, but yer a smart lad. Besides, that's the best hunch we've got. It's going to be quite dangerous, but we'll set sail for Eulia. I'm sure King Emory be searchin' every mountain and valley for us, so we'll have to be careful."

Jay scrunched his eyebrows. "One sec, cap'n. I don't think we should go to Eulia."

"But I thought you said—"

"Yes, I know." Jay concentrated on the red book as if it whispered clues to him. "When we were walking away, there was a little girl. She was with her mother it looked like. Her mother mentioned something. She spoke in a loud voice. Something about giving the necklace to her grandmother in...what was the name of the village...Selia! That's it." Jay's hands shook with excitement as he remembered the event perfectly. "She said the necklace would make her grandmother in Selia happy."

"Selia, eh?" The captain pondered a minute, looking outside the window. Then he nodded, arriving at a decision. "Sounds like the most sketchy idea I've heard in me life... something me brother would make up to watch me blunder through some fabricated quest of his. But alas, it's the best we got. We'll go with yer hunch, Lil' Blue." He stood erect, as he always did when delivering an order. "Notify the crew. Our heading is due north towards Selia. May fate be on our side."

"Aye, cap'n!" Jay said eagerly, satisfied to find at least some silver lining in the storm clouds, however bleak that lining may be.

McClevin was losing his temper. Standing a few feet in front of the captive pirate, whose hands were shackled behind his back as he sat on one of the rafts they made, McClevin felt beads of sweat dripping down his head resulting from a mixture of heat from the scorching sun and frustration from interrogating the pirate.

"Where's the locket?" he asked for the third time.

The pirate spat at him. Saliva splattered on McClevin's cuirass and slid down.

"I already told ye, ye stupid loaf!"

McClevin kicked some of the gray sand in the pirate's face. "Do you take me for a fool? I caught you and your sorry bunch in Eulia stealing the locket—"

"Actually, I don't believe ye ever caught us, if I remember correctly."

McClevin's temples throbbed. "Have you no respect

for His Highness and the kingdom of Eulia? Is all you care about the deepness of your own pockets? Tell me, where did Jay and the others go?"

"I dunno. Even if I did, I would never betray me friends."

This interrogation was proving hopeless. The pirate was either lying or truly didn't know anything. But this pirate was his only hope, the last withered thread that would guide him to the locket. Without the book, and without any more knowledge, he would undoubtedly fail his mission, and his people, his king, his family would suffer for it when King Cornelius discovered the locket missing.

He stepped closer to the captive pirate. "I don't have a great deal of time here. If I don't return that locket to Eulia soon, this world could be torn apart with war. You don't want that on your conscience, do you?"

The pirate glared up at him. "If ye would stop blabberin' and listen' to me, then yeh'd—"

The general cut his remark short with a punch across the face, knocking the plump pirate sideways off the raft. The pirate screamed in pain as blood flowed from his cheek where McClevin's gauntlet punctured his skin.

"Ugh! Ye...ye brutal hollow-headed sac o' seaweed!"

"What's the meaning of this?" Princess Catherine Alexandra stormed through the sand. "You cannot hit an unarmed prisoner!"

"Yeah!" the pirate agreed wholeheartedly.

McClevin squeezed his fists by his side. "We don't have time for his lies! Think of your people, princess. Don't you want them to live safely?"

"Remember your place, general," she spoke harshly.

His eyes widened instantly. His blood pressure rose. This was another reason he resented her tagging along; her heart was too soft. Sometimes, brutality was a necessity to keep the kingdom, her kingdom, safe. Some tactics of a soldier were beyond the comprehension of a princess.

Nevertheless, she was the princess, and her authority outranked his. Not wanting to dishonor himself, he dropped to a knee and bowed his head. "I apologize, princess."

"Leave us," she said, waving him away with the flick of her wrist.

"As you wish." McClevin swaggered off along the beach to consult with Winston, who was again pushing his helmet up above his eyes. "Any sign of Kileean?"

"No sir."

"Damn." McClevin had hoped Kileean would run into the pirates during their escape, but by now, the pirates would be clear of Storm Isle, and the odds of Kileean running into them would be slim.

He glanced back at the princess and the pirate. She had helped him off the sand and guided him to the raft. She was now cleaning the wound on his cheek. How could she be so kind to someone who threatened the very lives of her people? He regretted ever bringing her onboard for this voyage. Soon, the king would be worried sick over her absence, and the blame would fall on his shoulders.

It was his duty, above all else, to protect the royal family. For the next twenty minutes or so, he kept a constant watch on the princess, making sure the pirate would not find some way to harm her. When the sun began its hasty descent, he treaded back to them through the ashy sand.

"Come, princess. You should get some rest."

"Tell him!" the pirate beseeched.

"Tell me what?"

The pirate glanced at the princess, whose eyes were focused on the sand, lost in thought. The pirate said, "Jay is innocent. Thyran has the locket and is using it to—"

"Lord love a duck! Enough of this nonsense! I will not listen to any more lies. Winston! Take this man away. Station two men to guard him. Kileean should arrive sometime tomorrow morning." He cast the pirate a cold glare. "And tomorrow, the princess won't be around."

Winston had two men grab the kicking and cursing pirate, drag him across the beach, and set him against the towering cliff. Armed with swords, the two guards stood next to the pirate, ensuring he wouldn't escape.

Looking down at the princess, McClevin said, "I'm sorry princess. I know you don't like brutality. Please understand, it's for the best of your kingdom and your people."

Her eyes stared at the blue water rubbing against the sand. When she opened her lips, she spoke in a wishful, teary voice. "I hope so."

McClevin and his soldiers waited on the beach while the sun settled under the sea. Shadows shrouded the land, covering them in near blackness, save for the pallid moonlight drifting through the thin clouds. McClevin leaned against a rock next to the raft where the princess slept. His eyelids grew heavy. He struggled to stay awake. All he could think about was returning the locket to the king. He pictured the princess in tears of joy upon their return, the king and people cheering, knowing they were now safe from Cornelius's militant aggression.

He noticed a faint yellow twinkle atop the opposite cliff, several twinkles in fact, all of which came in pairs. He assumed it was his mind playing tricks on him, like when one sees multi-colored dots after squeezing one's eyes shut for a moment then flicking them open.

Shrugging, he gave into his sleepiness and drifted off into a deep slumber, dreaming of his heroic return to Eulia.

14

Sending Cornelius a Message

Thyran's deep red jacket billowed in the dawn wind, flapping furiously, trying to break free from its owner. Standing at the prow of the *Venator*, overlooking her progress as she blasted through the sea under the propulsion of the sorceress's induced current, Thyran welcomed the breeze.

In his right hand was the locket, flipped open, exposing its bright orange arrow, flickering against its diamond backdrop, pointing north. If the final artifact was in a town, it would no doubt be Selia. Thyran cringed at the thought of the name; he squeezed the locket.

"Captain?"

Thyran noticed the man's black, silk bandana thrashing about his thick black hair.

"Yes, Cyril, what is it?"

"Up ahead." Cyril tossed him a spyglass.

Through the spyglass, Thyran saw another ship, slightly bigger than his own. The bent, black sails contained the image of an almighty castle, complete with a watchtower and ramparts, with its base engulfed in crimson flames—the emblem of Valkadia. Thyran and his crew were in Valkadian territory without notification—Cornelius's men would view them as a threat.

The ship broadsided a large crested wave; cool water splashed over the rail and sprayed them.

"No doubt they have sighted us, captain. They will

attack us without a second thought. But we can probably outrun them with that sorceress's help."

Thyran considered Cyril's advice, but then an idea sparked in his head.

"No. We are not going to run with our tails between our legs like cowards. I have an idea much more fitting for those Valkadians. Have the men raise the Eulian flag and stay on course."

The *Venator's* canvas sails arced as they captured the vagrant winds. The image of a blue azura flying through a golden circle was embroidered in the Eulian flag Thyran stole several years ago, signifying his vessel as a Eulian ship.

Cyril left to deliver the orders. The crew hoisted the Eulian flag up along the main mast. The *Venator* proceeded forward, directly in the path of the Valkadians.

Thyran overlooked the crew, delivering commands and ensuring they were regimentally followed. Heaving an enormous, steel-plated shield, Bruce paced the deck, barking orders to those not moving quick enough to his liking.

And then, of course, there was the sorceress, Alcina Venclin, prancing on the deck with her kitten, her almond blue eyes flashing at Kyros with awe. Thrashing her arms wildly with excitement, she hopped on her feet alongside him, begging him for something, though Thyran could not hear what she desired. Whatever it was, Kyros promptly shook his head with the air of resisting the temptation to run his sword through her heart.

Kyros momentarily turned his back on her. Her eyes flickered sapphire, bright as jewels reflecting the sun. She gazed passed Thyran to the Valkadian ship. Thyran looked behind him; a huge ripple in the water beside the Valkadian ship morphed into a mound that rose from the sea like a giant standing from a hunched position. She was trying to capsize their ship, an act which would thwart his plan.

"Alcina!" he bellowed across the deck, but she appeared to not have heard, for she still focused intently on the Valkadian ship. "Kyros, stop her!"

Kyros whirled around and snatched her wrist from her rising hand, twisting it forcefully.

"Oww!" Thyran heard her whine, stomping her foot. Such a child. Afraid she would try again, he walked over to the two of them.

"I'll do whatever I please!" Alcina shouted back at Kyros.

"So will I," he said, twisting her wrist harder until she yelped in pain.

Then she tilted her head, her crystal blue hair dangling in front of her face, partly concealing her eyes. Nibbling on her bottom lip, she rose on her toes and ran her slender fingers up through his spiked, crimson hair. "You wouldn't harm me, my dear."

"Try me," Kyros said coldly.

Giggling, she ran her fingertip against her sleek lips and moved to kiss him, but he turned away, directing his attention to Thyran.

"There will be no more magic, Alcina," Thyran said, but her attention was still on Kyros—she seemed to be plotting her next kiss attempt. "Alcina!" he repeated in a scolding tone, which snatched her attention. "Did you hear me?"

She glowered at him. Thyran longed for the day when she would no longer prove useful. Out of all his crew, she was the most disobedient.

"Why not?" she complained childishly.

Thyran smiled. "I want to send Cornelius a message."

The ships drifted closer, nose to nose, neither exhibiting any signs of aggression. When Thyran saw the Valkadian vessel without the aid of a spyglass, he smiled. His plan was sheer brilliance. He could hardly wait for the wind to carry their ships together, at which time he would put the rest of his plan into action.

Cyril approached his side. Thyran said, "We should reach them in a few minutes. Are the men ready?"

Cyril nodded. "Everything is as you asked." He gave a questioning glance, which did not go unnoticed.

"What troubles you, Cyril?"

"Is this really necessary, captain? It seems rash and unwarranted."

Thyran snapped his locket shut and stuffed it in his pocket. "Do you have a doubt? A doubt against my abilities?"

"No captain, it's just—"

"Good. Because if you do, I can always find another first mate. Now, let us make sure Kyros is prepared."

Without waiting for Cyril to respond, Thyran left the railing and treaded across the deck towards Kyros, who was surrounded by a circle of small hand-sized crates. Through the slits of wood, Thyran saw the bundles of fire sticks, bound together inside the crates with their wicks hanging out along the side, ready to be lit.

Crouching next to one of the crates, Bruce picked it up and examined it. "Ye know, Kyros, I never did understan' this stuff. 'Tis too complex, if ye ask me. Personally," he set the crate down and lifted his massive ax from the floor, "somethin' like this appears much more deadly."

"Well," Kyros said, "when matched with a single stick of this," he waved a fire stick in the air, "I fear you would be at a slight disadvantage."

"Unless it happened to be raining," Alcina said with a

grin.

Kyros rolled his eyes and dragged an empty crate before him.

"How many more?" Thyran asked.

"This is the last one, captain."

Kyros rummaged through his drab bag of supplies and withdrew a bundle of spherical grenades; a thin fishing net bound them together. His eyes flashed with excitement as he set them in the crate.

"And against these beauties Bruce," Kyros said, tying the wicks together and threading them through a hole in the crate, "your ax would blow into miniscule, worthless pieces."

Bruce gazed dumfounded at the bundle of grenades. "What if yer fighting someone real close? Wouldn't this kill ye too?"

Kyros shook his head. "A true master of demolition would never present that opportunity."

The sorceress ran her sharp fingertips down the back of Kyros's neck, causing him to shudder. Thyran admired his ability to ignore her constant affections. Or did he actually welcome her advances?

"Don't worry," she said. "I won't let anyone do you harm, dear."

"Including yourself, right?"

She chuckled, nibbled on her bottom lip, and continued scratching the back of his head.

Kyros whacked some rusty nails with a stone mallet to fasten the lid on the final crate. "All set captain."

Thyran nodded. "Good."

Thyran heard the crack of Cyril's whip, a crewmate's agonizing scream. "That's right you dogs!" Cyril snapped. "We don't have time for breaks or rests. The next person I catch twiddling their thumbs will be going for a long swim!"

The vessels skimmed closer, each one bearing an emblem of an opposing kingdom. Thyran had ordered his men to slow down with the intent of coming to a light drift when the ships were side by side, close enough to shout from one to the other.

Thyran moved towards the rail closest to the other ship. Standing with Kyros, Cyril, Bruce, and the sorceress behind him, he anxiously waited as the ships grazed through the water at a slow rate. His fingers prickled with excitement.

When the ships began to cross, the man Thyran assumed to be the Valkadian captain shouted across the small gap between their ships. "My name is Kraus Bandekot, captain of this here Valkadian vessel. I see you are from Eulia. What brings you to these waters?"

Thyran simply stared at him with a smirk etched on his face. Kraus's patience soon vanished with his unwillingness to answer.

"These waters are part of the Kingdom of Valkadia, ruled by the great King Cornelius. We have a right to know the reason of your voyage. Failure to answer warrants the seizure of your vessel."

Thyran said nothing.

"Very well, you leave me no choice." The ships nearly lined up, Kraus turned to face his crew and shouted loud enough for Thyran to hear. "Men, this ship is in violation of our waters. By the law of King Cornelius, we must seize that vessel and imprison the crew."

Finally, Thyran spoke.

"There will be no need for that, Kraus Bandekot."

The Valkadian captain turned around. "Excuse me?"

Thyran drew one of scimitars and stabbed it into the overcast sky. Cyril cracked his whip on the deck, which triggered the crew to set ablaze the wicks of the fifteen crates—

Thyran watched the wooden crates his crew lobbed overboard soar through the air towards the Valkadian ship. Cannons blasted from below deck, which rattled the floorboards—

The sounds of cannon blasts and snapping wood filled the air. The impact of the cannons threw the Valkadian captain off his feet; his crew scrambled about the deck as the crates landed and exploded instantly, engulfing the Valkadian ship into a spectacle of orange and scarlet flames, fatally wounding most of the crew on deck.

To Thyran's surprise, he heard cannon fire, not from his ship, but from theirs, and he felt the *Venator* shake as the cannons blasted into her side.

Cyril glared at Thyran. "The *Venator's* taken damage! I told you your plan could go awry!"

Ignoring his first mate, Thyran barked orders at the crew. "Drop the sails, send another wave of cannon fire!" He dashed to Kyros, who watched with glory the flickering flames from his explosions burning through the Valkadian sails. "Kyros! Have Alcina summon a current to carry us out of range of their cannons!"

The *Venator* rocked again as both sides exchanged cannon fire. The heat from the blazing flames on the Valkadian ship seared Thyran's skin. The smell of burning wood sifted into his nose while black smoke stung his eyes, unleashing streams of tears down his cheeks. Still, he managed to see Kraus dive off the side of his own ship in a desperate struggle for survival.

The *Venator* gained speed, quickly skimming clear of the Valkadian cannons. The screams of the Valkadians echoed in the air as the mighty Valkadian warship crumbled under the cannon blasts and explosives that had decimated its upper structure. Several explosions cascaded from the inside of the ship as the powder magazine lit, blasting holes in its side, destroying the remnants of the ship.

The vast sea swallowed the ship, drowning most of the crew along with it. Though a few members of the crew, Kraus being one of them, struggled to stay afloat despite their burn wounds.

"I'll take care of them," the sorceress said, stepping closer to the rail, lifting her hands and curling her fingers, preparing to use her magic.

"No," Thyran said.

Frustrated, she dropped her hands to her sides. "Why not?"

Thyran sheathed his scimitar behind his back. "Because, Alcina, someone needs to tell King Cornelius who committed this horrendous crime."

15

Fallen Snow

Sometime during his victorious march through Eulia, terrorizing shouts and screams electrified the air, sending a jolt of fear through McClevin's body. Everything went hazy, like a mirage vanishing into nothingness, and then he was back at the beach in Storm Isle, awake.

"General," Winston whispered, in a mournful, quiet voice.

McClevin heard loud murmurings from the rest of the soldiers on the beach. They were clearly disturbed about something, but what? The prisoner, had he escaped?

Scrambling to his feet, McClevin shouted, "What is it? Don't tell me the prisoner—"

His eyes answered his question for him. Footprints, or rather, paw prints, in single file, trailed paths through the sand. The rafts were missing, all of them. But the most disturbing, nauseating thing he noticed were the dead bodies of his knights lying across the beach.

Unable to speak, McClevin blundered through the sand to his nearest fallen comrade—Danfor. The slender soldier appeared to have been conscious during the attack, for there were claw marks etched in his skin across his arms and legs. Dried blood painted his body and armor. His head lolled to the side, mouth agape, eyes open. A hole shot through his neck, which was no doubt the finishing blow.

McClevin glanced back—the pirate was still shackled, although his former guards had both been slain. But this was not the work of any human—something else had visited them during the night. He closed his eyes and remembered those faint yellow twinkles he saw before he drifted off to sleep.

Vulpins...it had to be. The yellow eyes, claw marks on Danfor's body, paw prints in the sand, an attack so silent he himself slept through it. Yes, they had to be vulpins. How many soldiers did they kill? How many—

The princess! He flicked open his eyes, whirled around, and looked down at Winston. "Where is she? Where's the princess?"

Winston seemed to be expecting the question. "She's fine, general. She's over there," Winston pointed across the beach where the princess huddled over a group of dead soldiers, resting on her folded knees, her hand on her chest, her head bowed reverently, her snowy hair hanging lifelessly from her head. "She's saying a prayer for them, general."

"Lord love a duck..." McClevin mumbled. His chest caved in when visions of the dead soldiers' families flashed through his head. He could only imagine the effect this had on the princess, the most loving and caring woman he knew. She would no doubt take up the charge of informing their families upon her return to Eulia, a task so grievous he would never bestow upon any of the Knights of Voorus.

McClevin's head felt like it doubled in weight. Allowing his head to dip down between his shoulders, he slowly made his way across the beach to the princess, stopping along the way to say a prayer of his own for each of his fallen men. He counted nearly two dozen lives, two dozen husbands who would never return home to their families, two dozen wives who would have to explain this tragedy to their children.

The princess's sobs gripped the hearts of those standing near. The pounding of McClevin's own heart faded, his breathing slowed. Behind the princess, he stood firm, like a commanding soldier should, brave and strong, proud and fearless.

"May you rest in peace," she said, closing the eyelids of the killed soldier. She rose to her feet, and when her glossy, round, emerald eyes met McClevin's, she collapsed into his arms, clawing at his leather cuirass, shaking with sorrow. "S-So many of them...."

McClevin allowed his right hand to rub her back, embracing her in a half-hug. He said nothing, for he could say nothing, nothing to ease her pain, nothing to bring back the dead.

The clanking of metal. McClevin recognized the sound as a pair of shackles. The pirate. He was approaching. Leaving his arm around the princess, McClevin twisted his head and shot the plump pirate a cold stare.

"I..." the pirate's eyes focused on the sand, apparently intimidated by McClevin's gaze, "am sorry for yer—"

"None of this would have happened if you and your plundering pirates would have stayed clear of Eulia."

The pirate nodded, but still did not look up. "We never intended—"

Overcome with rage, McClevin pushed the princess away, slashed out his sword from its sheath, and advanced towards the prisoner. Hatred flickered in his eyes. Vengeance clouded his mind.

"I ought to kill you where you stand, pirate!"

The pirate stumbled back, his empty hands displayed by his sides.

"Ye don't understand! They tried to kill—"

"Silence!" McClevin roared, pointing his blade at the pirate's chest. "You refused to cooperate, and now countless of my men have perished because of you and your crew. You have no right to live."

"I'm not refusing to cooperate! I'm telling you everything I—"

McClevin kicked the pirate in the stomach, sending him to the sand. He rested the tip of his sword on the back of the pirate's neck. One quick swipe of his blade, and the pirate would be no more—

"McClevin!" The princess clasped both hands around his arm and yanked back, causing McClevin to withdraw his sword. "What are you doing? You can't take this man's life!"

"He doesn't deserve to live. No pirate deserves to—"

"McClevin!" she berated. "That is not your decision to make."

The princess's narrow eyes, scolding face, harsh tone, it was enough to rattle some sense in him. His skin ceased tingling, his vision cleared, his blood pressure dropped.

"You're...you're right. Forgive me, princess. I was acting irrationally."

A crowd of soldiers had gathered around, and they all appeared relieved McClevin had returned to his senses.

"General," Winston said, stepping to his side. "Look to the sea. It's Kileean."

McClevin squinted under the sunlight and recognized the outline of the *Liberáte*. Kileean would arrive on the beach in a few minutes, and they could finally get off that foul island.

"We leave as soon as the boats arrive. Winston, secure the prisoner. Have Drexel begin the interrogation as soon as we get on board. We are running out of time. If we don't catch up with Jay Perry and his crew and recover that locket, all these men will have died in vain."

"What should we do with the dead?" one of the soldiers asked.

"Wrap them up and bring them aboard with us. They deserve a proper ceremony."

The Knights of Voorus scattered to obey McClevin's commands. When Kileean and his crew arrived in boats, they quickly loaded the dead and rowed them back to the ship. McClevin led the ceremony, honoring those soldiers who had fallen, and the princess gave a short prayer before the bodies, wrapped in blue silk embroidered with the emblem of Eulia, were dropped into the ocean, where they sank below the water for an eternal rest.

They sailed through the rocky corridors, clear from Storm Isle. Still unsure of a final destination, McClevin ordered the soldiers to let the *Liberáte* sail north, since there wasn't much land to the south. Throughout the day, McClevin remained in his cabin, studying maps, charts, books, anything he could get his hands on, anything that would clue them in where the pirates would go next. He tried to rehash the poem from the red book, but with no luck.

The blanket of night wrapped itself around the *Liberáte*. McClevin was consulting with Winston and Kileean in his cabin when a knock radiated from the door.

"Come in," McClevin said.

A tall man draped in a black hood entered the room.

"You asked for me?"

McClevin looked up.

"Yes, how is the interrogation coming?"

The muscular man removed his black hood, revealing his angry, tight face. His dirty brown hair was greasy and shabby from being cooped up in the hood. "Still no luck."

"Lord love a duck, you've been at it for hours!"

"I know, sir." Drexel's tone sounded irritated, as if he took McClevin's comment to be a direct insult to his abilities.

"He won't budge, but I'll get him eventually."

McClevin breathed deeply. More and more, that pirate seemed to be his only source to pry information regarding Jay's whereabouts. It seemed that the pirate could withstand any physical interrogations, but perhaps a mental interrogation would squeeze out the information. He would try that in the morning.

"Very well, Drexel. Send the prisoner back to the brig. I don't want to kill him. We'll continue interrogating in the morning."

"But sir, I think I can—"

"Not tonight. If he was going to break tonight, he would have done so a long time ago. At this point, the only thing we would be doing is torturing him. King Emory would not condone such cruelty."

Drexel sighed and bowed his head. "As you wish, general."

When Drexel left, McClevin looked over to Kileean, who was leaning over the wooden table, scribbling something onto a yellow-tainted parchment. "How's it coming?"

The dark-skinned, slender man peered up from his parchment. "I've rehashed some of it, but I can't recall the entire riddle."

"Well, what have you got so far?"

Kileean leaned forward, handing the general his parchment. "Have a look."

The night sky provided meager lighting through the windows, so McClevin held it beside a candle to read. Kileean had managed to rehash some of the poem, although the words, scribbled in black ink, clearly were not the same as in the book. The information could very well be hidden in the exact words used in the poem, making Kileean's writing useless. Sighing, McClevin dropped the paper back on the desk.

"This won't do. We need that damn book! I never should have left it behind."

Kileean snatched his parchment from the desk and skimmed over it.

"Do you think we should report back to the king?" Winston asked.

"With what?" McClevin asked loudly. "Two dozen dead soldiers and no locket? I'm sure he'll be real pleased with our return."

Winston bowed his head; his helmet slid down his forehead. "Sorry, I just thought that—"

"We need that locket, Winston. The Gorgrim Tournament will conclude in a few days. Cornelius is probably already asking for it and growing suspicious. I wouldn't be surprised if he's already preparing his cursed speech about our reneging on our agreement for our own economic gain. The crook will claim we can't be trusted to uphold our agreement for peace, and onward his armies will march." As he spoke, McClevin paced to the window, clenching his right fist by his waist, staring into the black sky strewn with white stars twinkling up above, reminding him of the yellow twinkles he saw the night before that he should have recognized immediately as danger. "Blast it!"

A breeze swept through the room and nipped at McClevin's skin—someone entered. He turned around, dropped to a knee instantly, and bowed his head.

"Princess Alexandra. We weren't expecting you." He heard shuffling as both Kileean and Winston took a knee.

"I had a difficult time sleeping." She quietly treaded across the floor to McClevin, who lifted his head but remained on his knee. "Did you manage any information out of Soleus?"

"Soleus?"

"The prisoner."

The prisoner? How did she know his—of course, on the beach: the princess had an aura about her that probably comforted the prisoner into divulging his name.

"No, not yet. He's unwilling to cooperate. I plan to personally continue the interrogation in the morning." He felt ashamed delivering such regrettable news.

"Hmm." Her emerald eyes searched the room. "Don't you think it's possible he could be telling the truth?"

"That he doesn't know about the locket? That some other pirate, Jay Perry's step cousin or whatever, stole it? That's ludicrous!" Recognizing the argumentative tone of his voice, which tasted as bitter as milkweed in his mouth, he lowered his tone.

"Princess, I know it's hard for you to see people suffer. Believe me, I take no pleasure in torturing prisoners. But I personally witnessed the prisoner—err, Soleus—that night in the act stealing the locket."

"And that he does admit to. But is it not possible another group of pirates may have attacked them and stolen the locket?"

"On this forsaken island? The chances are better of us finding the locket lost in the ocean than two bands of pirates meeting up here."

"But their ship is missing."

"You've heard the tales of Storm Isle. Numerous ships have went missing en route to this island." His blood pressure begged to rise the more he thought of their predicament, but he denied the pleas, concentrating, with difficulty, to remain calm. "Many of our men died last night. Slaughtered." She winced, and again he felt ashamed, ashamed of causing the princess grief. But it was necessary.

"They would still be alive were it not for Soleus and the others. Many more of your people will share the same fate if we don't get that locket."

She pondered.

"He's telling the truth. I sense it in his voice, read it in his eyes. I think we can make more headway by searching with him rather than searching in him. I...order you to release him."

McClevin's legs quivered. He had to bite the inside of his lower lip to refrain from letting his emotions take control, a battle from which he rarely walked away victorious. She was the princess. She outranked him when it came to politics, to running the kingdom, to almost anything.

Except this. As General, it was his duty to protect her nation at all costs. The king bestowed upon him the power to make militant decisions on behalf of the kingdom. The king trusted him and his ability to make the *right* decisions. Although he wished to agree with the princess more than his own safe return to Eulia, he did not. Reality slashed his chest, ripped his flesh, froze his lungs, making him speechless. But alas, it was his duty to announce his decision, to...contradict her, Princess Catherine Alexandra, daughter of King Emory. He placed his hand over his chest, covering his mental wound and warming his lungs, and then he could speak.

"I'm sorry, princess. We have discordant opinions. As General of the Knights of Voorus, I am entitled to overrule you should I see fit. I choose to enact that power presently. I hope, one day, you will view my decision as a prudent one."

He bowed his head to show respect despite his unwillingness to appease her wishes.

They remained still. No one spoke. Though he could not see, he heard the steady rush of water dripping from her eyes, felt her icy tears on his own cheeks, making the urge to break down himself potent. Then footsteps of rubber against wood, the creaking of rusted metal hinges, and the slamming of the cedar door. She left.

McClevin remained still a moment. He felt Kileean's and Winston's gaze; neither of them dared standing before he. When the time felt right, a moment or two later, he stood and addressed the two of them.

"I know I may have come across as rash, perhaps acting out of place, but it's for the best of our kingdom, for the safety of the people. Do you understand?"

They both nodded. "Yes, sir."

"Good."

Winston glanced at the parchment on the table. "Sir, do you have a heading yet? Or should we continue north until the prisoner gives us more information?"

McClevin's eyes focused on the flickering flame dancing atop the candle. He imagined that same flame scorching the beautiful kingdom he swore his life to protect. The people screaming, fields burning, smoke sweeping through the streets. He felt like he was drifting on a raft through raging rapids leading to a giant waterfall, moving too fast, too hazardously to stop.

"Men. We will set sail for Valkadia. If Soleus refuses to give us the information we need, we will hand him over to Cornelius and explain what happened. If luck is on our side, this will lift the blame from Eulia and hopefully divert Cornelius's fury elsewhere. I see this as our only hope."

"Yes, sir." The three soldiers saluted, and then Winston and Kileean left McClevin to himself.

As he blew out the candles from around the room, he mumbled to himself. "I'm sorry, Princess Alexandra. I promised to protect the locket at all costs, and I have failed. I know you do not approve of my methods now, but in time, I hope you see that I act only in the best interest of you, your father, and your people. I would never do anything to hurt any of that. My duty is my life. I will fulfill it until the day I die. That, I promise you."

The *Liberáte* sailed through the night waters, which were calm and serene. One could hardly tell the ship was in motion. McClevin had positioned the soldiers around the ship. He wanted a constant lookout in case Jay Perry and his crew came to rescue their friend. There would be no more surprises. This time, he would be ready.

Tendrils of smoke took the place of the once flickering candle flames in the room; the only lighting was the pallid moonlight pouring through the two windows along the eastern wall. McClevin stood before one of the windows and looked out, but not at the sea or the sky, but at his own faded reflection in the glass. Of all his features, his face reflected the clearest. His round head, indigo eyes appearing black against the window, bushy eyebrows...his entire face constricted into that of a soldier who just lost a best friend in battle.

Never before had he been so close to slipping off the edge of the trail to victory. Maybe if it was another army or group of assassins, he would not feel as ashamed. Angry, true, but not ashamed. But it was a blasted bunch of pirates that had thwarted him, not a force of specially trained soldiers. How could he have let this happen?

Agatha would be ecstatic, no doubt. This very well could lead Eulia into war, which seemed to be her favorite game. Orrin would be worried sick, probably lose sleep, perhaps even succumb to illness and perish. Marcus, like McClevin, would cast aside his sadness and do everything in his power to protect the kingdom. The queen, hanging on by a thread after that musket ball wound, probably would give into the grip of Death, allow herself to be dragged from this life into the next. The king...McClevin didn't even want to think about the king's reaction. Everything the king had worked for during his rule would crumble to the ground like the ramparts of an invaded fortress.

McClevin stayed by the window, staring into the eyes of his washed away reflection, pondering. He lost track of time, but at least an hour passed, maybe two, before he decided to retire from the window and get some rest, though he hardly deserved that privilege.

He turned around. The door was cracked open. Kileean and Winston must have failed to shut it.

He moved to the door. The floorboards creaked under his feet. When he grabbed the handle, he caught a glimpse of something outside. Two shadows glided across the floor, but swiftly, a rate too fast for soldiers on patrol. Due to the position of the moon and slant of the shadows, McClevin realized the two men were on the port side moving to the bow.

McClevin hurried back inside his cabin, rushed to his desk, withdrew his pistol, stuffed the barrel with gunpowder and a musket ball, and dashed back outside. Armed with his pistol in his hand and sword sheathed against his waist, he bolted along the port side of the ship.

They had to be pirates. Here on the ship to free Soleus, but they were heading *away* from the stairs leading below deck. Soleus must already be freed. So the two shadows must be Soleus and his rescuer.

His soldiers patrolled the middle of the deck, but with the dismal lighting and numerous crates of supplies scattered over the floor, they probably failed to notice the two pirates. Whoever was patrolling the port side was evidently taking a break, or the pirates killed him already. McClevin refrained from alerting the soldiers. If the two knew their furtiveness was compromised, they would act differently, and perhaps somehow thwart him and his soldiers. This way, he had the element of surprise.

Then he spotted them. They were up near the prow, against the rail, beside wooden arches that hung over the side of the ship with rope suspending a longboat in the air. One of them, tall, slender, draped in a hood and a drab brown cloak, stood next to the pulley mechanism, in position to lower the boat. The other, much shorter and rounder than his companion, stood before the rail, ready to hop in the rowboat. McClevin knew he had little time.

Soleus looked up at the hooded man with awe. The man motioned with his finger for Soleus to jump in the boat. Soleus gripped the rail, placing his foot on the lower rung—

"Stop right there, Soleus!"

Soleus's foot slipped off the rail, and he stared white-faced at McClevin. The hooded man did not move.

McClevin's pistol aimed right for Soleus's chest. He was close enough to ensure he would not miss his target. Soleus apparently recognized this too, for he did not move, save for his trembling.

"We don't have the locket!" Soleus shouted, no longer concerned of being clandestine. "I'm tryin' to help ye and yer kingdom get it back afore Thyran and his gang use it."

"Quiet!" McClevin snapped. One squeeze of the trigger, and Soleus would die.

"Are ye mad?" Soleus swung his fists in the air. "Ye interrogated me all day when ye know I'm tellin' the truth! Yer a filthy criminal, no better than any pirate!"

The words scorched a nerve—it blazed with fury. McClevin spoke in a deep, threatening voice. "Both of you, step away from the boat. On your knees, hands behind your heads. You have no where to go."

Neither person moved. Were they scheming something? Luck allowed him a glimpse of the secret gesture of the hooded man's hand urging Soleus to hop in the boat. But Soleus remained still, frozen with fear. McClevin was running out of time. "You have three seconds before I blow a hole in your chest. One...two...."

Swift as a fox, the hooded man lunged for Soleus, blocking the path between McClevin's pistol and the escapee. The hooded man grabbed a hold of Soleus's shoulders and began forcing him over the rail—

Now was the time. McClevin had to act. They could *not* escape.

He steadied the pistol.

Squeezed the trigger.

The blast roared through the night like a vicious thunderclap.

The hooded man staggered. He stretched his hands to the sky as if trying to grab the moon, snatch any strands of life from its pale glow. Silk threads of moonlight slipped through the man's slender fingers, and then the he collapsed backwards to the ground.

The man's hood fell back, but it wasn't a man. The pale moonlight illuminated Princess Alexandra's snowy hair as she stared wide-eyed into the sky, struggling to breathe. Her emerald eyes sparkled under the moonlight like jewels.

McClevin's heart stopped.

"Princess!" McClevin rushed to her side and knelt to the ground. Her face was paler than the moon, her tears colder than ice. Blood, dark under the night sky, soaked the cloth around her chest.

"P-please...McClevin..." she said, gasping for breath. She squeezed her eyes shut, trying to withstand the excruciating pain. She raised her delicate hand in the air, which McClevin grabbed instantly, putting her flesh to his cheek. "Please...my people...." Her mouth and eyes still open, her head dropped lifelessly to the side.

"No!" Streams of tears gushed from McClevin's eyes as he pressed his face against her smooth, icy hand. His whole body trembled with sorrow. Tears flooded his throat, making breathing difficult. He felt the sharp claws of guilt ripping at his chest, tearing his body apart. The sorrow was too much to bear. He contemplated putting another musket ball to his head.

Numerous soldiers, led by Kileean and Winston, flooded the scene, their eyes flickering from Soleus to McClevin, who was hunched over the dead princess. "We heard gunshots and..." Winston began. "Is that the princess?"

McClevin clenched his teeth so hard he thought they would shatter. His eyes flashed open. He leapt to his feet with fury splashed across his body. He pointed at Soleus, who remained motionless beside the boat, his face whiter than before.

"The pirate murdered her as he tried to escape." A new rage McClevin had never before felt consumed his voice. A commanding rage, the rage of a dark lord mandating the unwarranted doom upon thousands of innocent people. "Kill him!"

The group of soldiers charged for the pirate, each drawing their swords. The pirate's mind regained control of his body, and he moved, faster than ever, up along the rail, away from the pursuing soldiers.

"After him!" McClevin cried.

When the pirate cleared the long boat and saw he would soon be cornered at the front of the ship, he clambered up the rail, and before McClevin's soldiers reached him, he leapt off, plunging into the midnight sea.

16

Alcina's Secret

The cannon fire from the Valkadians gouged numerous holes alongside the bottom of the *Venator*, allowing seawater to rush inside with too strong a force for the sorceress to repel for long. They tried plugging the holes with spare canvas, but even that failed to impede the influx of water. Thyran had ordered them to sail to the nearest land, and, when they reached the closest beach, with the sorceress's aid, the ship's keel plowed up through the sand and out of the water. With the *Venator* resting on her side up on the beach, the crew chopped down trees, sliced slabs of timber, and bandaged the holes. By midnoon, the preparations were nearly complete.

Thyran and Cyril stood on the beach, overlooking the crew.

Despite this rather undesired delay, Thyran had enjoyed the battle. With the explosions rattling the deck and cannons blasting away their ship, Thyran had not expected much resistance. A battle with no opposing resistance is a boring battle indeed. He thrived on the vehemence of the battle, the sheer brilliance of outmaneuvering a formidable opponent, and sailing away victorious. Due to his superior swordsmanship, it was the first challenge he faced in quite some time, albeit not a substantial challenge, but a challenge nevertheless.

"A wise choice attacking their ship, wasn't it?" Cyril said.

Normally, Thyran would punish him for making such a disparaging remark, but today, he was more cheerful than usual. Thyran continued watching his men patch the *Venator*.

"Sounds to me like you're not having any fun, Cyril."

"We can have all the fun we want when the time is right. For now, I think we should stay focused on our task."

"What exactly is our task? Sometimes I fear you forget our goal...our purpose."

"But captain, right now, we are vulnerable and—"

"Vulnerable! We destroyed a Valkadian warship with no casualties, slew a captain of a pirate ship before his very crew, blew up a building in Eulia, murdered a governor, and *still*, no one suspects us, no one has come close to stopping us. You worry too much, Cyril. A trait of the weak."

Thyran saw Kyros walking closer, a brown sack of explosives flung over his shoulder, and, of course, the sorceress trailing close behind. She had seemed unusually placid that day. Her blue eyes roamed the sand rather than Kyros's spiked hair, her step lost its childish bounce, her lips remained closed more than a minute.

Kyros allowed the sack to plop into the lush sand, which appeared golden after the gray sand in Storm Isle. "We should be ready to set sail in an hour, maybe two."

Thyran nodded. "Good. We will leave as soon as the ship is ready."

"We will need more wood," Kyros said.

Thyran pointed behind him to the tropical forest rich with deep green trees and vivid blossoming flowers of red and blue. "Bruce and a few others should be back soon with more wood."

"Ahh okay." Kyros watched the men work on the ship for a minute. "How close are we?"

Thyran dug his hand into a deep pocket of his velvet jacket and removed the diamond locket. He flipped it open. Its flowing orange arrow glowed brightly against the sun.

"The arrow points directly to Selia. If it's not in the village itself, it's probably close by. We're about a day's travel south of the village." He collapsed the locket shut and stuffed it back in his pocket. They were so close...so very close. "Cyril, let's have the crew pick up the pace. I want no man resting until she's in the water."

Cyril let his leather whip uncoil in his hand and allowed its tip to drop to the sand. "Yes captain." He treaded off to the ship, and Thyran smiled when the crew, catching a glimpse of Cyril approaching, instantly hastened their pace.

When Cyril left, Thyran noticed only two shadows in the sand—one of him and one of Kyros. He had not seen the sorceress leave. He loathed letting her out of his sight since her wild nature could not easily be controlled.

"Where's the sorceress?" he asked Kyros, who, judging from his confused expression, had not noticed her leave either.

"Over there," Kyros said after searching for a few seconds.

Thyran looked where Kyros pointed; the sorceress was traveling into the tropical forest.

"What is she doing?" Thyran asked.

"I'm...not sure."

"Keep an eye on her. I don't trust her by herself."

"Yes, captain." Leaving his bag of explosives in the sand, Kyros, for the first time, followed the sorceress.

Unsure why, Kyros felt the need to keep himself concealed from her. He was intrigued to see why she would leave so suddenly. Maybe he would find out why she had been solemn all morning, not that he had any complaints with the resulting peacefulness. But he was curious.

When he entered the forest, he saw her sapphire hair up ahead. She was several yards in the distance, navigating her way through the trees. Her head looked this way and that like an animal searching for prey. He kept his distance, careful not to step on anything such as a twig or dried leaves that would give away his presence.

The forest was cool, much cooler than the beach. The arching branches several stories high created a thick canopy that shrouded the sun. The air felt misty, like he was moving through a rain cloud. Looking at the ground, he realized he could walk freely—it was carpeted with wet leaves and patches of bright flowers, none of which make any crumbling or cracking noises under the weight of a foot.

He wondered what kind of wildlife inhabited such a lush rainforest, perhaps vulpins, panthers, tigers. Well, anything that came across, Alcina could no doubt—

No, he scolded himself. He was ashamed he, even for a second, put his faith in Alcina, the sorceress, the woman who had been nagging him for the past fifteen days. He longed for the day to be rid of her, to sit in peace and imagine the most glorious demolition spectacle and then craft it. Thyran could have whatever power he sought; Kyros cared not for domination or control. He longed for, in a word, *freedom.*

Alcina suddenly jerked her head to the right and paused, for a second, then pursued a new path. Kyros ducked undercover of the trunk of a fallen tree. Above its hair of moss, he watched her travel off to the right, and when he was confident she would not catch glimpse of him from the corner of her eye, he stood up and continued his pursuit.

The more he thought about it, the more he wondered if she would ever leave. Where did she live? Did she have a family? She just fell in his lap that day in Eulia and allowed herself to be carried off by the crew. Were there any other descendents of Ashlen roaming Lassar?

She was wild. Extremely wild. A trait which, though he hated to say it, attracted him. Her energy reminded him of when he was ten and had discovered his first explosive. His father used explosives for mining purposes, but he found that rather dull. While his father saw explosives as a means to an end of finding hidden diamonds underground, he saw explosives as a means to an end of a spectacular explosion...the beautiful blossoming of red and orange and black and white, the vivid wave of heat, the resounding *boom* through the air...it excited him more than a first date with the prettiest girl in school. He craved every aspect of a brilliant explosion; it was to him like flies to a spider, a necessity of life. Whenever he witnessed an explosion, he felt free.

So lost in thought, Kyros failed to notice he was no longer under any cover. He had just stepped into a small glade in the forest, a clearing of trees with only grass and small plants covering the ground. Alcina was up ahead in the same clearing walking away from him. Quickly but carefully, he retreated back a few paces and took cover behind a tree trunk twice as thick as he. Confident he had not been seen, he peered out from the side of the trunk.

Kyros noticed another figure at the opposite side of the glade. It was a man. A pirate. Kyros knew the man was part of the crew (probably one of the members chosen to go with Bruce to fetch more wood), but he did not recognize who. Kyros wondered why the pirate was so fascinated with the tree, but then he realized the man was relieving himself.

Alcina bent over and picked up a thick stick, a small

branch that had fallen from one of the massive trees. A snake stalking its prey, she treaded towards the pirate through blotches of sunlight penetrating through the canopy, her stick held ready to strike.

Kyros's eyes saw clearly what was happening, but in the few seconds he could have shouted out in warning, he instead tried to understand her thinking. By the time he abandoned that task, it was too late—she clubbed the pirate across the head.

The pirate spun around and collapsed to his hands and knees on the ground of purple flowers. Kyros still failed to make out his face. The pirate grabbed his head and cursed in pain.

"Ugh...you dirty little—"

Kyros stepped out from the tree, ready to come to the man's aid, but then something happened that froze him in place.

From behind the pirate, Alcina's lips parted into a vicious smile. Her jaws separated, her cuspids elongated, growing sharper and longer. A black, milky liquid filled her eyes, giving her a frightening, ghostly appearance. She dropped the stick to the ground and walked up along the pirate's side.

She kneeled down, and as the pirate tried to turn around, she grabbed at his hair and shoulder, yanked his hair to expose his neck, and sunk her fangs deep into the man's throat.

Kyros stood. Water filled his eyes from sheer shock. He was not afraid, not tempted to run. He was paralyzed.

Her blue hair dangled from her head, blocking her mouth from view. She bit into the man's neck, kept her fangs buried into his throat. No blood dropped to the ground. Was she sucking it? Like a vampire storytellers describe during their horror tales?

The pirate's eyes floated upward as she sucked the life from him. His feeble struggles to free himself proved useless against her firm grip. At last, his torment ended, and she dropped him to the ground. Blood, dead blood, continued pouring from his neck.

Alcina's head hung low, her hair still blocking her lips and eyes from view, which was a blessing, for the same hair prevented her from seeing him. Her kitten toddled out from a nearby flower patch. Kyros had not noticed before, but realized now that it was the kitten who had altered her course earlier, as if notifying her the whereabouts of the pirate.

Alcina reached out a hand and stroked the kitten, tracing the kitten's light blue stripes with her fingers. The kitten nudged herself closer to Alcina, who remained hunched over on her knees, the dead pirate lying on his stomach beside her.

Kyros was unsure how to feel. He was not sad or afraid, but more confused, maybe even mystified. He knew what he saw was impossible, but then again, so was her ability to control water. It must be real then. But why? Was this the explanation for her odd behavior that morning?

Kyros wanted to know the answer, but now did not seem the time to find out. Wild and daring he was, but not stupid. He would find a way to trick her into revealing her secret, but if she knew he watched her kill that man, she may feel threatened.

Satisfied with his decision, he slid his right foot back but forgot about the tree. His foot rubbed against the bark, chipping off a small piece. He winced, praying she would not hear, but when he looked back at her, he gazed no longer into her blue hair but into her black eyes.

He shuddered. Blood dripped from her scarlet teeth,

her dark black eyes glared into his like a savage beast staring down its next victim. Her kitten scurried off to the side, giving her room to attack. She rose to her feet and strutted towards him, swaggering her hips as she walked. She cleaned her bloody teeth with her tongue. Her lips curled into a smirk.

"What's wrong, my dear? You look frightened." Her voice was raspy and deep, like when she spoke on the cliff in Storm Isle, only not threatening, but rather, playful.

He stepped back, but to his dismay, his heels thudded against the round tree trunk. Alcina continued her approach, but he stayed there, either unwilling or unable to move, he wasn't sure. Soon, his back pressed flat against the tree.

Cackling softly, she ran a finger down his chest. Then she wrapped her arms around his waist and flung her head close to his. Her lips grazed his, but they were not sweet and sugary as when she kissed him before; they smelled and tasted of blood. And they were cold, very cold. He cringed when she brought her lips to his ear. He wanted to push her aside, to run back to the beach, but some part of him wanted to stay.

"Do not fear, my dear," she whispered.

His vision blurred as her pointed fangs scraped across his neck. Trembling with his back against the tree, he looked at the pirate across the glade, whose blood still trickled from his neck.

"What did you do to him?" he managed to ask.

Her teeth still scraping his neck, she whispered, "I did it for us, love. So we can be together."

Her vague response angered him, which gave him the strength to shove her off him. She fell back to the ground, landing on her hands. Screeching with indignation, she instantly leapt back to her feet and pinned him against the tree before he could make another move.

"Careful, my love." She hissed in his face, baring her white fangs, cleansing them with her red tongue. Her body pressed against his. When her hand gripped his head and turned it to the side, he was powerless to stop her. She licked his exposed neck. "You taste good, my love. It would be a shame if I had to sever such a pretty neck."

His eyes squeezed together as he envisioned her sinking her teeth into his flesh. "Why did you do it?"

She bent her fingers and dug her nails into his chest, but not in a motion of rage, but that of passion. "To live, my love."

"What do you mean?"

She leaned her head back and batted her eyes, which had returned to their normal cerulean color. She flattened her palms against his chest and leaned against him. Her voice dropped back to her usual girly pitch.

"How old do you think I am?"

"What?"

"How old?!" she cried fiercely.

Kyros jumped due to her surprisingly loud voice. "I don't know...twenty, twenty-five?"

"Ha!" She released him and twirled around in the red and purple flowers, her loose blue pants and long sapphire hair fluttering in the air. "In two months, I will be celebrating my one thousand thirtieth birthday!"

Kyros gave her an incredulous look. Impossible...just like controlling water.

"It's a technique a man once taught me. Every Aquarius has that ability."

"Aquarius? What's an Aquarius? And who's your father?"

She blinked. "I already told you."

"No you—" but then he remembered their first conversation in Eulia. "You said Ashlen, but that's impossible because he died about..." his voice trailed off.

"About a thousand years ago," she said.

So that explains why she has no family. Her parents have been dead for ten centuries, nearly the age of the planet.

"The year is 1020," Kyros said. "If you are as old as you claimed, you must have existed before Lassar."

She smiled at him, clearly loving him taking such interest in her.

"Where were you before here?"

"My home."

"And where's that?"

"I only vaguely remember it." She nibbled on her lower lip, still red from the blood. "But none of that matters any more. I'm here with you now, my love."

"But where—"

She stifled his speech by pressing her moist lips against his and kissing him. His brain was running faster than a vulpin chasing its prey, leaving him too preoccupied to push her away. He could taste the bitterness of blood on the edge of her lips, but he hardly paid any attention. She squeezed her arms around his waist and pulled him closer. Her fingernails scraped down along his back. And though he loathed his emotions, he found himself more attracted than repulsed by her touch.

When she finally parted from him, she snatched his hand and whistled for her kitten. "Come, my love. Let's not keep your captain waiting." With her kitten following close behind, she pranced ahead in the woods, dragging Kyros along with her, singing a wordless song.

His head aching from his myriad thoughts, Kyros followed.

When they emerged from the trees, he squinted under the sun's intense rays. The air felt quite hot, much hotter than the forest, but at least a gentle breeze drifted over the sand. Alcina skipped ahead across the sand with Miuji and dove into the water, splashing around and laughing with glee while her kitten watched from the shore.

"Ye alright, mate?" Bruce asked walking up to him.

"Yeah..." Kyros said, still dazed by what happened in the forest. "I'm fine."

"Ye sure?"

Before Kyros could respond, the captain walked up and stopped in front of him. Kyros looked at Thyran; his reddish-brown hair seemed more fiery than usual, which Kyros accounted to his eyes still adjusting to the intensity of the sun.

"What was the sorceress doing in the woods?" Thyran asked.

Kyros shrugged. "Went for a walk I guess. She seems chipper now." He nodded his head in the direction of the ocean, where Alcina continued to splash in the water.

The captain shook his head. "Like a ten year old...."

Kyros laughed.

"Make sure she's ready to go. We leave shortly."

"Yes, captain."

The captain and Bruce headed back to the ship, where the crew finished patching the holes. Shaking his head with his lips still curved in a smile, Kyros walked to the ocean where Alcina was swimming.

Once ashore, she turned her back to him, folded her legs under her body, and appeared to be meditating. When Kyros reached her, he saw her eyes tightly shut. He almost said something, but refrained, and instead looked out to the horizon.

He envisioned a dynamic explosion in the distance, one of his own creation. Then he saw the Valkadian ship and recreated in his mind the explosions that consumed its upper deck the day before. And then he saw Alcina by his side, her sparkling cerulean eyes, warping the water, protecting them from enemy fire. The two of them, man and sorceress, fire and water, an unstoppable pair.

Miuji brushed against his ankle. He crouched down and lifted his hand. The kitten rubbed against his knee and suspended hand, purring noisily. The kitten's fur was soft and brushed. Not a single knot of hair. Petting the kitten, listening to the crashing of waves, he closed his eyes as happiness spread through his body, filling all his bones and veins with a powerful surge.

A few minutes later, the captain's voice woke him up from his sedative state. He opened his eyes and saw Alcina kneeling before him facing the ocean. Her sapphire hair blew to the right, undulating as water undulates to form waves.

The kitten had fallen asleep beside him and began stretching when he stood up. He glanced back to the ship where the crew stood waiting.

"Come, we must leave."

She lifted her left hand beside her head. "Help me up, dear."

He had a snide comment ready, but thought better of it. Locking his fingers around her slender hand, he began to lift her up, but when she was halfway up and depending on his support, he released his hand from hers and let her plummet back to the sand. Her face scarlet, she threw her hair back and stormed to her feet. She glowered at him, baring her teeth, which had returned to their normal size.

"Do that again, and I'll drown you in your sleep!"

Kyros laughed and walked through the sand back to the ship, which still lay on its side in the sand. Kyros admired how the light brown paint faded darker and darker down the side of the ship until it was nearly black at the ship's keel. The underside of the ship was no longer wet as it had been when they brought it ashore. Still, it was an interesting sight, the underside of a ship. A sight few people ever saw.

"We're ready," Thyran said to Alcina.

She glanced at him a moment before turning to the ship and raising her hands. Her eyes flashed; a huge tide of water rushed up along the sand, grabbed hold of the ship, and dragged it down a few inches. She repeated this again and again; each time, the ship moved a greater distance into the sea. Finally, one monstrous rush of water swallowed the ship's keel and dragged it completely off the beach. The ship rocked back and forth as it steadied itself in the water.

"To the boats," Thyran said. The crew scampered to the boats, which were lined up on the beach.

Alcina and Kyros approached the same boat. When Kyros sat down on a wooden plank stretched sideways across the boat, he felt cold water absorb into his pants. Standing up, he saw that he had sat in a puddle of water. He glared at Alcina, who sat on another plank, biting her bottom lip and batting her eyes innocently.

"Something wrong, dear?" she asked.

He opened his mouth to say something, but he flew back to his seat when the boat, powered by Alcina's magic, rocketed off the beach and towards the ship. When he secured himself on his seat, he looked at Alcina, who closed her eyes, soaking in the liberating feeling of happiness. He understood, for he felt the same way whenever his explosives went off in a spectacular performance. The feeling of tranquility, of absolute bliss.

Kyros watched her with a new admiration. He realized that despite the attempts to convince himself that he resented her, he had developed a fondness for her, a fondness stronger than he had felt for anyone in his life. For whenever he was with her, he was free.

17

Alexia Avalon

None of the nights since their departure from Storm Isle did Jay sleep peacefully. Each night, black nightmares shrouded his dreams, causing him to wake numerous times. Most of the nightmares were not of Thyran murdering the governor, which had plagued his sleep for years, nor the death of Captain Gaden, but rather, his nightmares consisted of Soleus and the cruel fate to which he had voluntarily succumbed for their safety. Jay wanted to abandon the pursuit of Thyran in favor of rescuing Soleus, but harsh reality prevented such action—they had no idea of Soleus's whereabouts or even if he was alive.

Jay lay wide awake, staring at the ceiling from his bunk bed. It was eerily silent without Soleus's snoring from the bed below, a sound Jay actually longed for.

The reflecting sunlight brightly shimmered on the ceiling. It was no longer morning: probably early afternoon. The merchant vessel had come to a full stop, indicating they arrived at their destination. Jay was ready. Ready to go ashore. Ready to get that necklace and stop Thyran. Ready to move on.

But Thyran had left a day prior to them from Storm Isle. And with a sorceress who controlled water, they would no doubt be far ahead of him. Thyran had most likely already come and gone, making their visit here pointless. He had thought of this earlier and considered suggesting changing course for the Dragons' Castle to intercede at the finish, but with an army of only ten, one of whom was missing a hand, against all of Thyran's crew, the odds of success would be miniscule at best.

Jay heard Captain Hector's voice rebounding through the hallway calling a meeting up on deck. It was time.

He followed the rest of the crew up to the deck where they fell in line and stood at attention as Captain Hector addressed them. The day was warm and sunny, a few scattered white clouds painted against light blue, the third beautiful day in a row.

"Keep a sharp eye, mates," the captain said. "We may very well meet up with Thyran and his crew here if the gem be in this village. Again, Jay remembered seeing a little girl with curly hair buying the necklace for her grandmother. The gem be decorated with magical vanishing red spots, so it should be easy to identify." He turned to Karen. "Karen, when we go ashore, get some herbs and medical treatments so you can dress Ankin's arm. Everyone else, we'll split into groups, although no one goes alone. The moment we retrieve the necklace, we will set sail. Any questions?" Silence. "Very well. To the boats!"

The pirates piled in, four to one boat, five to another, with Ankin remaining on board to await Karen's return. Quite a distance away, a thin beach stretched across the land. A verdant forest of tall, tropical trees guarded the beach's rear. From the boat, Jay did not see any trace of the village, but according to the map, Selia was not far off the ocean.

When they reached the shore, Jay hopped out of the boat. His feet sank an inch or two in the fluffy sand as it molded around his foot, giving it a soft, therapeutic feel, much more welcoming than the stubborn ash-sand in Storm Isle.

They dragged their boats ashore, hid them under some green shrubbery in case any unwelcome guests should arrive. Though the odds of that were slim because, by Cain's suggestion, they had anchored a mile south of the Selian docks, meaning they had to trudge through a pathless jungle to get to the village. This way, they would keep Jay's identity secret (since the village was occupied by Valkadian soldiers who wanted Jay's head as much as the Eulians for killing Governor Almsy, a Valkadian noble). And, if by some miracle they beat Thyran here, this would prevent Thyran from finding them, at least initially.

They set off through the jungle, which was misty and cool. Little critters—squirrels, mice, monkeys, turtles, numerous other rodents and small animals—came out of hiding to watch the crew pass. Jay admired their audacity to present themselves seemingly without fear of pain or torture. In school, he had learned the people of Selia had an unusually close relationship to the woodland creatures, but he had not expected the animals to take such a warm welcome to them that quickly. He considered breaking from the rest for a moment to see if he could pet the monkey splashed with red and blue who swayed back and forth on a log about twenty yards away. But now was not the time for that. If Jay came out of this whole mess alive, he would definitely return to this jungle.

Captain Hector emerged first from the forest. Jay squinted under the sudden surge of orange sunlight. He saw the outlines of small houses and roaming people, which appeared as black silhouettes until his eyes adjusted to the sun.

There was no wall or gate or fence to protect the village from the forest. All the houses were made of wood and stone with round roofs, and as they walked closer, Jay realized that not all the black he saw was a trickery of his eyes.

The outsides of the houses were blackened, as if they caught fire, a fire put out before its flames could engulf the entire building.

Many houses were partially destroyed. Sections of their walls or roofs were completely blown away. Some roofs caved in to the living space, making residency nearly impossible. Jay noticed vases with wilted flowers drooping on the side spread across the porches of those houses he assumed to be deserted.

Lyssa pointed to a house with bugs and rodents gnawing at the rotting wood. "The village is still recovering from the *Night of Endless Screams*."

"The vulpins did all this?" Jay asked.

"Yes. In a single night. They stormed in the village, killing most and enslaving the fortunate survivors. It was months before Valkadia and Eulia agreed to send soldiers to liberate the village."

"Why did they wait so long?"

Jenkins stepped beside them. "Couldn't spare the soldiers. They were too bloody concerned over their own defenses should the other attack. They chose to look the other way."

"And they call us pirates criminals!" Lynk said.

Women and men, wearing plain, drab clothing, carried baskets of fruit, pales of water, and other essential items around the village. Captain Hector led them to the dirt path that navigated through the houses and stores.

"Any sight of her, Lil' Blue?" Hector asked.

Jay had been too absorbed into the crippled buildings and the overall sorrow that lived in the village to be on the lookout for the young girl with curly hair. He glanced around, eyeing each of the numerous people bustling about.

"I don't see her yet."

"Are you sure she's in Selia?" Cain asked, limping a few paces ahead.

"I remember her mother saying the necklace was for her grandmother in Selia." As Jay spoke, he wondered if only the grandmother lived in Selia, in which case they had no chance finding the girl with curly hair; then their only chance would be if the grandmother was walking about and he caught glimpse of the necklace as she passed by. Or the woman could be dead, in which case the necklace would be buried in some cemetery under a woman's grave of whom they did not know the name. Either scenario appeared grim.

"And the gem is in a necklace?" Cain asked.

"Yes."

Cain turned his head right, and his mynx crawled down his arm and perched up on his wrist. Cain looked at his pet, eye to eye, and though he said nothing, Jay sensed they were communicating somehow. Whatever Cain said, the mynx apparently understood, for it took flight and glided down the path, its head flicking from one side to the other as if scouring the village for the girl.

"Alright," Hector said. "Let's split up into groups of two. Be quick, we only have an hour or two until nightfall. We'll regroup after the sun sets at the inn." He pointed to a square building standing three stories high in the center of the village. Its stone was painted tan along the base with mottled green near the top, resembling a tree. It was the tallest building in the village.

The pirates separated into five groups: Lynk and Blynk were together as usual; Hector was with Cain; Jenkins with Delcato; Jay with Lyssa; and Karen was by herself. With swords sheathed to their waists, and Lyssa with her spear propped over her shoulder, the groups ventured in different directions.

Up ahead, the dirt path forked. The left path led to the inn and was clearly longer and fuller than the right; Jay and Lyssa chose to veer right, though they saw it end rather abruptly after a hundred yards or so.

Walking alongside Lyssa, Jay watched a group of young children bouncing a huge, lightweight ball back and forth in a yard. Despite the children's happiness, Jay felt something odd. He didn't notice any parents nearby. Perhaps they were some of the unfortunate victims slaughtered by the vulpins.

"How many people were killed during the *Night of Endless Screams*?"

"Over half the village," Lyssa said. "That was four years ago, and look at the village now. Still recovering from the carnage. I bet most of those children are in an orphanage."

Jay scanned their faces; no one resembled the girl he remembered in Eulia. Jay shifted his focus to those passing. Nearly everyone was walking the opposite direction with grim faces and, in some cases, wet cheeks due to recent tears.

Jay remembered his promise to Lyssa. "You don't need to help us," he said. "We promised to release you when we landed ashore."

She tilted her head up at the sky and away from him. The orange sunlight gave her golden hair a warming glow.

"I know. But the whole reason I got caught up in this mess in the first place was to stop Thyran, which is what we're doing here. Once I'm confident that tyrant will never complete his mission, we'll go our separate ways."

Jay's eyes dropped when she finished her last sentence. He admired her very much and hoped she would reconsider her departure altogether. A stupid thought though it was, it had been on his mind for a while.

But he made her a promise.

As they walked, Valkadian soldiers, armed with jagged scimitars, wearing red uniforms with a burning castle embroidered on the front and backs outlined in black, patrolled the streets.

Jay turned the other way when passing the soldiers in case one would recognize his face from the sketches of his appearance distributed all over Lassar. He had seen some of such drawings and was amazed how close a resemblance they had.

"Look..." Lyssa said, pointing to the end of the path.

The brown, dirt path dissolved into a grassy hill with light gray stones poking out from the ground. A graveyard. Jay understood why those walking past looked so grim.

At the end of the path, to the left, a wooden sign stabbed up from the ground angled to the right. They approached it. Black letters were painted over its rectangular head. Jay read the words aloud:

"Here lay the victims of the *Night of Endless Screams*."

Jay and Lyssa gazed over the vast field littered with gravestones. Lyssa brought her hand to her face, touched her finger to her eye. "It's so...horrible," she said. "If only those men in power weren't such greedy savage pigs, these people would be alive."

A leaden weight of sorrow hung from Jay's chest as he saw groups of people, all with plaintive expressions on their faces, gathered around some of the gravestones with flowers or other gifts that held sentimental value to the deceased. "These were just farmers and peasants, not soldiers. They must have been defenseless against the vulpins."

Lyssa nodded, apparently too consumed with grief for words. A minute passed before either spoke.

"Well, there doesn't seem to be anything here," Lyssa

said. "We'd best turn back."

"Wait," Jay said before she turned. Though he shamed himself for the thought, he realized that there was a slim chance that the girl could be here, perhaps laying flowers for her family or friends she lost, or even her grandmother. Though it would be cruel to interrupt someone during such an intimate and dreadful time, if it would stop his stepbrother, it would be worth it.

"She might...be here," he said.

Lyssa breathed deeply and nodded. "Alright. Let's check it out."

As they walked through the cemetery, Lyssa used the butt of her spear to sweep away fallen leaves and brush piling around the gravestones.

Most of the groups of people consisted of many children with one or two adults. A gagging sensation swelled in Jay's throat: so many children's parents—dead. Although his parents were arrested in front of him when he was five, at least he still held on to the hope that they were alive...somewhere.

"Jay?"

He glanced at Lyssa.

"Any sign of her?"

"No."

Lyssa pointed up ahead to the right. "Come, let's check over that hill."

They weaved through the gravestones and up the knoll, approaching the neighboring hill Lyssa identified. Huge weeping willows guarded the land with their massive branches and dense leaves. Occasionally swaying with a crisp breeze, their green stringy hair drooped low to the ground. The crimson rays from the sun gave the mighty guardians a flaming outline, making them an awesome appearance.

Jay rubbed his hands against his arms; goosebumps engulfed his skin due to the chilly evening air. Leaves and twigs crunched under their feet as they moved through the graveyard. After a few minutes, he nearly bumped into Lyssa when she stopped so suddenly.

"What is it?"

Her eyes were fixed on a gravestone in front of her feet. Crouching down and brushing her smooth hair behind her head, she ran her thin fingers over the name etched in the stone. "Alexia Avalon."

"Did you know her?"

She scooped up some dry dirt in front of the stone and let it fall through her fingers. "No. I never met her." She hung her head, her long hair fell beside her face. "Alexia...she used to live in Morad until her mother met an explorer, fell in love with him, and moved with him to Selia. Alexia's father had died several years prior."

Jay thought back to his childhood, though he didn't recall anyone by that name living in Morad. "How do you know all this?"

"Alexia...she was Thyran's girlfriend."

Jay gasped. "His girlfriend was among those murdered?"

"Yes."

He closed his eyes, and a wind, far icier than the breeze outside, ripped through his skin, exploded through his veins, chilled the marrow in his bones. A shudder raced down his spine, realization stung his entire body.

Ashlen waits for me. Her death will not go unnoticed. That night, in Morad, just after he murdered the governor, Thyran spoke those words to him. Thyran had kept his relationship with Alexia secret, so none of it made any sense to him at the time. But now it was clear as glass. In the Dryfus Mines, Thyran said he killed the governor because he played a role in *her* death. *Alexia's* death. Eulia and Valkadia failed to send soldiers to protect the village despite their knowledge of the approaching vulpins. They were too consumed with one another. And Governor Almsy, Jay had known he was a nobleman of the Valkadian council. He was just as guilty as the two kingdoms, which is why Thyran put him to his death.

Now, Thyran was rushing to get this hidden artifact, this hidden power Ashlen himself supposedly concealed atop the tower in the Dragons' Castle, to punish the two kingdoms...to bring them crumbling to the ground and establishing himself, Thyran Vilkus, the one and only ruler of Lassar.

Revenge. Revenge and a sick, twisted sense of justice. That was the foundation of it all. In part, Jay actually sympathized with his stepbrother. Weeks before the murder, Thyran was very solemn, not his usual self. He had not known it then, but Alexia's death scarred his heart. He had been her guardian, her protector, and as such, he must now avenge her death, hunt down those responsible and make them suffer.

But Thyran's rage burned too intensely. By bringing down the only kingdoms in Lassar, he was, in a sense, destroying *everyone's* lives, not just the nobility. But he did not see it that way; he was blinded by the flickering flames of rage.

"Jay, are you okay?"

Jay opened his eyes, which were watery from him clenching them so tightly.

"My brother...he's gone mad."

Lyssa probably gave him a confused look, but his vision was too blurry to notice.

"He...was so good to me...protected me from bullies...taught me how to fight. I have tormented myself the past four years asking why, asking how someone so nice and genuine could commit such acts of cruelty. But it's all just...rage."

He noticed Lyssa's blurry form nod, her attention return to the grave.

"I'm sorry, Jay."

But he wasn't listening. He was still too absorbed in his own revelation. "And now...I must use those skills he taught me against him. I must fight him." The words caught in his throat, making it difficult to breathe. "I must fight him. Kill him."

He had not seen Lyssa get up, but she now stood beside him, rubbing his shoulder. "There's no use getting upset about it now. Worry about it when the time comes."

Jay stared at the ground. "I can't beat him...no one can. He's too strong. I've never met anyone as good a fighter as him."

"Come on," she urged him, tugging on his shoulders, pulling him away from the grave. "If we find the gem first, then no one has to fight him."

Jay closed his eyes again. Even then, he knew fighting him would be a necessity. For Thyran had the locket, and no matter where Jay and the others took the gem, the compass would point straight and true to its location. But Jay recognized her attempt to pacify him, and he appreciated it. Besides, as she said, there was no use worrying about it now.

"Okay. Let's head back and continue searching the village."

"Hold on a second." She grinned and plucked the tallest piece of grass she could find and handed it to him.

Jay eyed the blade of grass. "What am I suppose to do with this?"

Grabbing another piece of grass, she turned to him, held it in front of her smooth lips, and blew. The blade of grass shook and emitted a high-pitched whistling sound. Smiling, she brought the grass away from her lips. "You try."

"I told you, I can't whistle." He held his hand out to her, offering back the grass.

She pushed his hand back. "This is easier than whistling. Trust me."

Although he never told her, Jay felt embarrassed every time he tried to whistle and failed miserably. This was just another opportunity to make a fool of himself. Reluctantly, he placed the grass like she demonstrated in front of his lips and blew. At first, all he heard was the usual painful sound of wind, but just before he gave up, the grass vibrated and gave off a low whistle. In the dark cave of his internal grief and frustration and fear, a tiny candle, a tiny flame of joy flickered dimly. That flame prevented him from suppressing his smile.

Jay and Lyssa left the cemetery and began searching the houses. They would knock on a door, and if the person answering was not a young girl with curly hair or an elder lady with a mystical necklace around her neck, they would claim to be at the wrong house. Of course, they took intermittent breaks to avoid suspicion, and they strived to blend in whenever a Valkadian soldier strolled by. House after house they searched, but to no avail.

"It's starting to get late," Lyssa said, looking up at the sky. "Most people are probably sleeping."

The people in the streets quickly vanished, leaving them vacant. The chirruping of crickets from the dense forest outlining the village echoed in the air. Jay shivered and rubbed his arms for warmth. To his right, he noticed one more house with light glimmering out of the square, curtained window.

"Let's check that house first, then we'll regroup at the inn and see if anyone else had any luck."

The two-story sandstone house looked the same as the rest of them. A few dark blemishes from fires spotted its tan exterior and a few holes, patched with several boards, decorated the curved roof. Arriving at the house, Lyssa rested her spear against the wall next to the door. After three knocks on the wooden door, Jay and Lyssa waited.

Footsteps. Unlatching of the door. Then it creaked open.

Jay sighed. The lady who answered was not young, but rather in maybe her early thirties, nor did she have short curly hair, but rather long, straight, auburn hair. She wore a plain, dark green apron.

"Good evening," she said in a slightly disturbed voice, which Jay attributed to the late hour. "Hmm...I don't think I've seen you two around here."

"We don't live here," Jay said.

"Oh, I see." She peered out the door and glanced at the star-strewn night sky. "Well, it's getting kind of late. What can I help you with?"

"Well, we were looking for a—"

"Who is it mama?" a girl called from the hallway.

"Be with you in a moment dear," the lady said without looking back.

Jay heard thumping coming from the dark hallway beyond the door, and a young girl stopped by her mother's side. She was young. She had short curly hair. Her light blue dress, the same Jay had seen in Eulia, convinced him that she was indeed the same girl.

He nudged Lyssa with his elbow.

The girl slid around her mother's waist and waved. "Hello!"

"Claudia, go back to your room," her mother scolded.

"Aww, come on mama! I just wanted to say hi."

Her mother looked down at her. "What did I say about talking to strangers?"

"But I—"

"Back to your room. I'll be there in a minute."

Claudia stomped on the ground and began retreating back to the house. Jay had to say something. Anything he said would raise suspicion, but now was the best chance he would get. "Hold on a minute, Claudia."

Claudia's mother cast him a cold, suspicious glare. "How do you know my daughter?"

Jay contemplated how to describe their predicament without sounding insane. "I know this is going to sound crazy, but she has something we need."

"I do?" Claudia asked excitedly. She was back by her mother's side in an instant.

"What could she possibly have that you want?"

"It's nothing major," Lyssa said. "But we have reason to believe that some very bad people are trying to steal something your daughter purchased in Eulia. These people will harm whoever is in their path. We were sent here from Eulia to find this item and lay a trap so we can catch these villains. We need to borrow it for a few days, then we'll give it back."

The lady wrapped her arms around her daughter and pulled her closer. "Get out of my sight, the both of you, or

I'll call for the guards!"

Jay's hands turned clammy. His face prickled. If the Valkadians arrested him, they would discover his identity. He would be killed.

"Please," Lyssa said kindly. "We are not here to threaten or harm you."

"What do you want?" Claudia's mother snapped.

"A necklace. A necklace your daughter bought in Eulia."

"Grandma's necklace?" Claudia asked, staring wide-eyed at Jay.

"Yes," Jay said. "The one that magically changes colors inside."

Claudia stomped her foot on the floor. "No! That's grandma's. You can't have it!" She broke free from her mother's grasp and ran down the hall.

Her mother glowered at the two. "Please, her grandma is very ill and probably won't live more than another day or two. This is a very rough time for us."

"I'm so sorry to hear that," Lyssa said. Her tone was sincere.

The woman sniffled and wiped her nose with her white handkerchief she held in her left hand. "Come back in a few days. My mother loves that necklace dearly...she needs its comfort right now."

Jay's chest contracted. He was surprised Thyran had not arrived here already, but he would, without a doubt, arrive in the next few days. But how could he deprive a dying woman of something she treasured?

The lady began to close the door but stopped as Claudia sprinted down the hall carrying a necklace in her hand. "Here!" She tossed the necklace to Jay.

Jay caught the necklace and exmined it. The ovular

gem centered on the fine necklace had a sea of green with spots of red dotted around its surface. Jay's heart raced faster as he waited, but the gem did not change colors nor did the red spots go away. He shook his head to Lyssa, indicating it was not the gem they needed.

Before Lyssa or Jay could say anything, the lady bid them goodnight and slammed the door. Jay stood, staring at the wooden door.

"What do you think we should do?"

"I don't know," Lyssa said, sounding more saddened than disappointed.

Jay hung his head and nodded. He shared her grief. The thick air of the village depressed him more than anything. So much sadness. He longed to hop back on the merchant vessel and sail away. But he knew he couldn't, for then no one would be there to stop his stepbrother.

"Let's meet up with the captain and see what he thinks," Jay suggested.

Lyssa snatched her spear from the wall. "Alright."

Sighing, Jay slid the necklace Claudia gave him in his pocket and walked with Lyssa to the towering square building near the center of the village. Jay's depression thickened when he saw that the giant tree painted on the front of the inn had been conquered by darkness.

The moon was high in the cloudless sky when Thyran Vilkus walked into the village of Selia. Followed by Cyril, Kyros, Bruce, the sorceress, and eighteen others he personally chose from his crew, he slithered silently on the fringe of the jungle behind the small houses, following the orange arrow on the locket. A short while later, he stopped outside a two-story house to which the arrow pointed.

"Captain?" Kyros asked. "Why are we stopping?"

There, in that house, the final artifact he needed. Thyran's body urged him to plunge forward and claim the gem for himself, but he had trained himself against acting rashly.

Valkadian soldiers still patrolled the streets, even at such a late hour. Though the operation could go smoothly, he refused to rely on luck. Someone could wake, see him lurking in the darkness, and it would only take one shrill scream and a nearby soldier to alert the entire village of his presence.

Thyran pressed against his velvet coat around his waist. Through the smooth fabric, he felt the outline of the seashells, and when he pinched his fingers together, he felt her hair. He desired to do something here in Selia and had originally anticipated doing it after securing the gem, but if the soldiers were made aware of his presence, he would need to make a quick getaway.

Ten minutes could cause no harm. With his stepbrother dead, Eulia and Valkadia enthralled by their own well-being and riches, no one would even consider breaking into this house this late and steal a random necklace. Only he knew its true value.

There could be no harm indulging himself, just for a moment.

"Wait here," he said.

Cyril stepped in front of Thyran before he moved. "We don't have time for this," he said between gritted teeth.

"Out of my way, Cyril."

Cyril's eyes narrowed over his hooked nose. His greasy black hair shielded his face from both sides. "What would you have us do?"

"Wait here," Thyran repeated. "The gem is in this house, so watch over it. Keep your presence here a secret. If anyone walks out of that house with the gem, kill him and meet me by the boats."

Cyril breathed twice, then stepped aside. "Be quick."

Thyran did not intend to be long.

Alone, Thyran snuck to the graveyard and strolled through the gravestones in a determined path. His icy blood chilled his veins, making the coolness of night feel warming to his skin. He had not felt this solemn in a while.

Then he reached her grave. He stood a moment and read her name several times. He remembered her beauty, her gentle touch. He felt so alone without her.

He drew both scimitars from behind his back, knelt down on his right knee, and stabbed the curved blades into the cold ground with one motion. Reaching inside his black coat, he lifted out the seashell-heart Alexia made him.

"Alexia," he said plaintively. "Please forgive me for taking so long. Shortly, the entire planet will mourn your death, and the two kingdoms will perish for being so blinded by their own greed. Everything will be as I promised."

Thyran refused to allow himself to cry, though he felt pressure building behind his eyes. Soon, when this was over, he would grant himself the privilege of crying, of properly mourning her death, because by then, he would have earned that honor. Until then, he denied himself any bodily desires—only after he avenged her death.

He pressed the seashell-heart against his chest and squeezed tightly. He closed his eyes, imagined he was hugging her. Her sweet smile and flowery perfume haunted his senses. He clenched the seashell-heart harder, loving its texture, the smooth shells, her silky hair tying them together, its beautiful shape. It was the most precious thing he owned.

His eyes snapped open with fury when a man's voice interrupted his thoughts. "You, what are you doing out so late? It's not safe alone around here this close to the jungle."

Two Valkadian soldiers armed with scimitars in their right hands and shields in their left stood to the side. "You should be getting back inside," one advised.

Damn them for interrupting his time with her, which, thanks to their king, had been drastically reduced. Thyran slowly relaxed his grip around the seashells and gently placed them back in the inner-pocket of his velvet jacket.

Thyran got to his feet, grabbing his scimitars as he did so and thrusting them out of the ground. His blades by his side, he slowly advanced towards the soldiers. Their eyes widened, and Thyran realized he must make a rather fearsome appearance. The moonlight blackened his body and outlined it in a sharp midnight blue. The pale light glistened off his two blades by his waist and reflected onto his menacing face.

When he was close enough, before either of the soldiers could move in defense, Thyran stabbed his glimmering blade through the night, piercing into the heart of one of the soldiers, killing him instantly.

The other soldier gasped. "Are you mad?" he yelled, raising his blade. He swung at Thyran, who effortlessly side-stepped to the left, evading the strike. With the shield in his left hand, the soldier had exposed his right lower ribs. Thyran stabbed his left scimitar into the man's ribs, and when the soldier leaned back in agony, Thyran swung his right scimitar and decapitated the man. His head, and then his body, landed on the ground with a thud.

After scraping the blood off his blades against a neighboring gravestone, he sheathed his scimitars, returned to Alexia's grave, and knelt down. Some blood had splattered on her grave. He wiped off the few spots of blood with his hand and then pressed his lips against Alexia's grave and kissed the cold stone.

"I love you, Alexia."

18

Thief in the Night

Jay, Lyssa, and the rest of the crew, save for Ankin, who rested on the ship, gathered in one of the small rooms on the third floor of the inn. Other than the dim moonlight flowing in from the single rectangular window, the only lighting in the room was that from flicking candelabra on the two nightstands beside the bed.

Jay leaned against the wall adjacent to the window and gazed out it longingly, thinking of any solutions that did *not* involve prying a necklace away from a dying woman.

"Alright," Hector said after pacing back and forth a few times, the floorboards creaking with his every step. The crew shifted their eyes to him. "Unfortunately, we don't have the time to wait until her grandmother passes. We need to steal it tonight."

Jay kicked off the wall in protest. "But the necklace holds sentimental—"

"If we do nothing and Thyran slaughters them all and steals the necklace for himself, then how would ye feel?"

"But captain, can't we wait and guard—"

"It's not that simple, Jay." Karen removed her glasses, started wiping them with her shirt. "No matter what decision we make, people will get hurt. The only question is how much."

Lynk nodded his head. "She's right, Little Blue."

"Well what if we get caught tonight?" Delcato, who was sitting on the mattress, asked. "Then who will be there to stop Thyran? I say we wait until tomorrow and try asking for it again."

"Get caught?" Jenkins repeated. "We broke into the Eulian castle, snuck into the bloody king's bedroom, and escaped unharmed with the kingdom's most precious treasure."

"I wouldn't necessarily say unharmed," Lyssa said.

Jenkins ignored her. "What makes you think we'll get caught?"

The crew argued for a few minutes trying to arrive at a verdict but stopped instantly when Cain rapped his staff against the wall he was leaning against. He regarded the room through his hooded eyes. Jay wondered where his mynx was.

"Unfortunately," Cain said. "We don't have time for you kids to fight all night. May I suggest that we get this over with before Thyran's arrival?"

"Cain's right," Jenkins agreed.

"That's the spirit!" Lynk said, clasping his hands together. "Let's get going."

"Hold on a second," Hector said, extending his arm, blocking Lynk's path to the door. "If all of us go, the soldiers will be suspicious. Two should be all it takes: one to sneak inside, the other to stand watch."

"I'll go," Cain said.

Hector shook his head. "No...me and Jay will go."

Jay, who had withdrawn back to the wall, felt a thunderclap of anxiety resounding through his body. "No, I think Cain should go in my stead."

"Jay," Captain Hector said, "Yer the only one who's actually seen this gem. I wouldn't trust anyone, even meself, to properly identify it."

"But Captain—"

Hector silenced Jay with his hand. "This is not up for debate. Come, we must leave now. The rest of ye, stay here and wait for our return."

Jay's stomach churned at the thought of stealing the necklace from the dying woman. His eyes met Lyssa's, whose green eyes shared the same internal conflict as his. She nodded her head, a nod of encouragement, a nod of endorsement. Jay reflected the nod in his mind, and, eyes focused on the ground, he followed the captain out of the room.

The night felt overbearing, weighing down on him as if he walked across the ocean floor. Its darkness and freezing temperature probably even matched that of the bottom of the ocean. Everything appeared to move in slow motion as they journeyed through the night ocean to Claudia's house. The scratching of leaves blowing over the dirt, the eeriness of moon shadows elongating with the rising moon, the suddenness of crickets skipping across the ground, every sound and movement seemed magnified as the carnivorous sharks of fear and guilt taunted Jay's body.

Thankfully, they reached Claudia's house with no event. The two skirted around the house to the back where they would be concealed from passing soldiers. As they swung around the back corner, Jay heard a shuffling, a crunching of pine and dried leaves, from the forest twenty yards behind Claudia's house. Alert as a deer, Jay jerked his head in the direction of the noise, but under the meager lighting, saw nothing but darkened leaves and shadows.

"Did you hear that?" he whispered.

The captain paused for a moment, then shrugged. "Probably just woodland creatures. But, if it's any comfort, the only creatures we would have to worry about would be vulpins, and if *they* were lurking in the forest, we wouldn't be able to hear 'em."

Hector's words weren't exactly comforting, but Jay realized he was being overly paranoid, especially now, in the heat of the mission. Jay's fear of the forest subsided, and he turned to the back of the house.

There was a round hole in the wall with a beige curtain draped over it on the inside. The rest of the wall—bare, solid rock. The window proved their only method of entry.

Hector approached the window and crouched down beside it. "Okay, ye go in through here," he whispered. "They should all be asleep by now. I'll stay out in back and warn ye if anyone is coming."

Jay rubbed his palms with his thumbs. His legs trembled. Hector seemed aware of his uneasiness, for he said, "You can do this, alright Lil' Blue?"

Breathing in heavily through his nose, Jay moved to the window.

I can do this. It's for the good of Lassar. If they knew, if they only knew of the circumstances, they would understand and approve.

"Wait here," Jay said. "I'll be back in a minute."

Jay peeled the curtain aside, slightly at first, making sure no one was in view, and then, noting the vacant hallway, he slipped into the house.

When the curtain swooped back over the window after his entry, darkness invaded the house. He was in a hallway, the same hallway Claudia had sprinted across earlier that day. Thin dashes of pallid light lined the hallway—moonlight creeping under the doors. But the light from the doors quickly surrendered to the empowering blackness, thus providing little illumination for navigation.

The silence dragged him down. Outside, the leaves rustled, the crickets chirped, the wind whistled. But in here, nothing: the stone walls blocked out the leaves, crickets, and wind. Any sound he made, any cough or sneeze or breath, would sound magnified, a signal of alarm to anyone fortunate enough to be awake. Standing there, still by the window, he blended with the silence.

But he had to move.

Slowly drawing in a deep breath that would spare him a few seconds of breathing, Jay took his first step. Fortunately, the floor was padded with thick rugs, which cushioned his footfalls enough to prevent any creaking of the floorboards underneath. Probably set in place to prevent disturbing Claudia's grandmother's sleep.

Jay sidled down the right side of the hall; he felt too exposed moving down the center. He reached the first door. Grabbing the round, wooden handle with his sweaty palm, he cracked the door open just enough to peer inside. Through the slit in the door, he saw only half a bed. The shaft of moonlight from the window revealed the back of a head snug against the fluffy pillow. Long, curly hair. Not Claudia's grandmother. He closed the door slowly then continued down the hallway.

Running his fingertips along the wall, he progressed to the next door. Again, he squeezed the knob and creaked the door open. Its hinges gave a tiny squeak, which sounded like fire sticks exploding in the silent atmosphere. Closing his eyes, praying no one heard, he pushed open the door a little farther. The view was nearly identical—half a bed with a shaft of moonlight splashing on the blankets. This person faced the doorway. Much older. Older than Claudia's mom. He squinted, hoping to see the necklace around her neck, but darkness obscured his view. He needed to move closer. Squeezing his eyes tightly, as if hoping that would block out any sound he made, he slid in the room, leaving the door slightly cracked behind him.

Tip-toeing through the room, Jay approached the sleeping woman. He feared that the relentless pounding of his heart against his breastbone would waken her, for his ears vibrated with every pulse.

His eyes fixed on her neck, so he didn't even notice the nightstand beside her bed. His hip smashed into the wood, and with little resistance, the nightstand toppled over to the bed. A vase of flowers landed on the edge of the mattress and began rolling off the bed. Jay lunged forward, snatched the vase in mid-fall. Frozen, he chanced a glance at her eyes.

They were closed.

She appeared to still be asleep. He gripped the circular nightstand, pulled it back to its standing position, and set the vase back on top. Then he stood still, listening, ears perked up as a rabbit listens for predators. A minute went by. Then two. Nothing. No sound from the hallway. Everyone seemed to be asleep. Or perhaps they were waiting outside the door with a group of Valkadian soldiers waiting for him to slip out so they could arrest him.

He needed to focus. He looked back at the sleeping woman. She lay on her side, her shoulder propped up, blocking the moonlight from her neck. Jay wiped his fingers on his cotton pants, cleansing them of sweat, and then placed his shaky hands around the top of the mattress cover and peeled it back until the moonlight painted her neck.

There it was—the necklace. Resting on the mattress was the gem. Under the moonlight, he watched the fiery red spots explode and vanish, the emerald sea swirling to blue and then back to emerald. He recognized it immediately as the necklace the vendor had tried to sell him back in Eulia. If he only would have made that purchase.

Holding his breath, he moved his unsteady hands to the thin silver strand wrapped around her neck.

Guilt clamped down on his chest. Leaning forward, he felt a lump form in his throat, making it difficult to breathe. Fighting back the urge to quit, to retreat back to the safety of the inn, he unfastened the locking mechanism by the nape of her neck. He gripped the gem and slid the necklace off the dying woman.

"I'm sorry," he whispered, though too quiet for her to hear even if she was awake. He dropped the necklace into his pocket and crept back to the door, which still stood ajar.

He peered into the hall; no soldiers waiting to ambush him.

Back in the hallway, he closed the door behind him. Confident there was no furniture obstructing his path and the padded rugs would muffle his steps, he slinked faster than before to the window.

The door up to his left glided open, allowing a surge of pale light to illuminate the hallway, annihilating the army of darkness that kept Jay concealed. Still as a tree, he planted himself against the wall to his left.

Yawning, clutching a blanket by her chest, Claudia stumbled out of her room and shuffled down the hallway towards Jay. Her head was down, eyes staring at the floor. If she looked up, she would see him.

The hallway began to spin. Pressure built up inside his head. His temples throbbed.

Without looking up, she moved across the hall to his right and entered a room, closing the door behind her. Jay released his held breath and continued down the hall.

Jay raced across the rugs on the balls of his feet, down the hallway, back to the curtained window. He flung the curtain aside, felt the icy rush of wind on his sweat-covered face, clambered up to the round hole, balanced on his knees, poked his head out into the night—

An elbow smashed into his face.

He lost his balance, fell forward, headfirst to the grass, scraping his knees against the window ledge as he fell. He flicked his eyes open. A crowd of people gathered around, encircling him against the wall as did the Eulian soldiers during their escape in Eulia.

Pain flared in his nostrils. Blood dripped down. He looked up to see his attacker. The moonlight revealed loose hair with a reddish tint. Dark green, ravenous eyes. A conniving grin.

Thyran.

Jay's pain swirled into rage, a rage that sprung him to his feet. Clenching his hands into fists, he swung his right fist at Thyran's face—

Thyran caught his fist, twisted it fiercely to the side, and just when Jay thought his wrist might snap, Thyran's foot stabbed his gut, just below his ribs—

Out of breath, Jay threw himself at Thyran, swinging his fists, kicking with all his might, jabbing with his elbows. Rage blinded him, making his actions uncalculated and foolish, a vice about which Thyran had warned him when they were younger. But he didn't care. He wanted so badly to feel the connection of his fist with Thyran's face, his foot with Thyran's kneecap, his elbow with his stomach—*something*, something to cause him pain. Thyran had destroyed his life and received no punishment, no suffering.

In cool, calculated movements, Thyran blocked or evaded Jay's attacks and countered with such ferocity that pain and blood blinded Jay. He could barely breathe, but he continued fighting, continued trying to harm the man he hated—

Biting down on his teeth to wash away the pain attacking his every limb and joint, Jay lifted his right foot, faking a front kick to Thyran's groin, and just before he kicked, he pivoted on his left, morphed the kick into a roundhouse aimed to crush Thyran's ribs, snapped his right leg—

But Thyran was ready. Thyran caught his foot in midair, swept Jay's left leg, and with nothing on which to balance himself, Jay fell, his back smashed hard against the ground.

A flash of pain blinded Jay with its bright white light. Blood and tears washed over his face. Squeezing his eyes, hoping to block out the pain, he gripped his stomach and attempted to get to his feet, but the pain was too great. Hunched over his folded legs, he dropped back to the ground at Thyran's feet.

"I'm not sure," Thyran said, delivering another kick to Jay's side, knocking him over, "if I should be annoyed or thankful. No matter how many times I leave you for dead," Jay cried out as Thyran kicked him again, "you always come back; however, you always save me the trouble of stealing the treasure myself."

Jay's side burned; it felt like a sword ripped through his side and up across his chest. His body stung with such intensity that it blurred his vision. Where was Hector? Had Thyran killed him already?

"My patience is growing thin with you, Jay. Now, give me the gem." Thyran held out his hand, palm up, for Jay to surrender the necklace. Glancing past Thyran, Jay recognized the sorceress, the spiky crimson-haired pirate, the muscular, bald, shirtless pirate, and Cyril with his thick, greasy black hair swathed with a black bandana. Those four pirates stood closer to Thyran than the others who lingered in the distance.

Jay's ribs dug into his insides as he lifted himself up to Thyran's hand. "Ahh!" Jay yelled, throwing his fist at Thyran, trying to at least inflict some pain.

But Thyran didn't even have to move to evade it, for Jay, nearing the point of unconsciousness, did not have the energy to complete his swing and instead fell back to the ground.

"I feared you would be reluctant to comply," Thyran said solemnly. Thyran dropped to a knee and planted his elbow into Jay's back. The sting dropped Jay flat on his stomach. "Do not make me search your dead body, brother."

His spirit shattered, Jay dug his aching fingers into the soil and dragged himself a few inches away from his stepbrother. His eyes scanned the area in search for the only person who could help him: Hector.

Thyran shook his head with disdain. "You disappoint me, Jay. Damn you for making me do this." Jay heard the chiming of steel sliding against metal. Then footsteps. He saw the shadow of Thyran's head on the ground in front of him.

Jay set his left hand against the grass after moving a few more inches away, and then screeched in agony when Thyran's foot stomped down on his wrist, breaking it instantly. He struggled to slide his broken wrist free, but it was no use. Jay's eyes widened when he saw the shadow of Thyran's curved scimitar in the air, above his head, ready to strike, and then the shadow swung down across the grass—

Jay had never before felt such pain. Thyran's scimitar stabbed through the center of his left hand, effortlessly ripping through his flesh. A bundle of tiny needles exploded in his hand and ripped through his flesh and bone. He buried his head in the grass, biting his tongue to suppress his scream—he would not give Thyran the honor of hearing him wail in agony. Thrashing his feet, Jay suffocated himself into the grass, hoping to black out from lack of air and free himself from the pain.

"I can do your other hand as well," Thyran said. "A fitting sentence for a thief."

Unable to bare the thought of more, Jay lifted his head from the ground. "W-wait...."

Thyran released his foot from Jay's broken wrist and crouched down beside his head. "Yes?"

Quivering with the flaming pain burning inside his body, Jay dragged his unwounded hand across the moist grass to his pocket. He reached his fingers inside, gripped the braided chain, and withdrew the necklace. His hand dropped to the ground, too fatigued to hand it to his stepbrother.

Thyran bent over Jay's back and grabbed the necklace. He inspected it for a moment before saying, "Cyril, give me the locket. I need to make sure this is the real gem."

Jay heard Thyran catch the locket and snap it open. Jay waited, unable to see anything but grass. A few seconds passed before Thyran spoke to his crew.

"Excellent. Men, this is the one." Thyran's crew breathed in awe, shuffling to get a better view. "We now have everything we need."

The crew gave a hushed, yet enthusiastic yell. Amid their celebrating, Jay heard a woman's voice—the sorceress—whisper to someone, "Soon, love, the world will be our playground."

Then came Thyran's voice. "Thank you, Jay."

Footsteps. A massive hand, too large to be Thyran's, grabbed his hair and waist, pulled him up from the ground, and slammed his back against Claudia's stone house. The back of Jay's head thudded against the stone; he was temporarily deaf, except for the high-pitched ringing in his ears. He opened his eyes and saw the bald-headed pirate in front of him, grappling his neck.

Thyran stepped closer, touched the tip of his sword against Jay's chest. Thyran's smirk set loose birds of fury in Jay's heart. They flapped around insistently, trying to break free of their cage and take wrath upon their prey. But Jay was too weak, too near unconsciousness to set them free.

"I had rather hoped to avoid killing you myself," Thyran said, his cruel eyes gazing into Jay's.

Panting, Jay thrashed every limb he could, but the bald pirate's massive muscles restrained him in place.

"Good-bye, brother." Thyran took his stance, ready to plunge the blade through Jay's heart—

"What's going on here?"

To the side, three Valkadian soldiers scurried over with a large mob of reinforcements quickly advancing from behind. Moonlight glistened off their scarlet shields. A dozen, maybe two, it was hard to tell. Jay's screaming must have alerted them.

Jay noticed Thyran's crew silently fade into the dark forest before the soldiers caught sight of them.

"Release him," Thyran whispered to the bald pirate. The pirate complied; Jay collapsed to his knees.

The three soldiers stopped a few feet away. "What are you doing outside Myria's house this late?" one of them asked.

Thyran pointed to Jay with his scimitar. "We found him trespassing. This is Jay Perry, the man wanted for the murder of Governor Almsy of Morad."

"No..." Jay moaned, clutching his side, but he knew the Valkadians couldn't hear him.

One of the Valkadian soldiers approached him,

crouched down, and peered up into his face, studying him for several seconds, comparing his image to that of the wanted posters. "So it is!" The other two soldiers stepped closer. The reinforcements were not far off. "By the will of the honorable King Cornelius, Jay Perry, I place you under arrest."

Overcome with indignation, overcome with fear, overcome with anger, Jay's adrenaline kicked in; he mustered the strength to scramble to his feet and bolt off into the trees before the soldiers could grab him. Thyran's crew, hidden in the woods, did not stop him as the stampede of soldiers closely followed—

Blood dripping from his hand and face, his every muscle throbbing with pain, Jay forced himself onward. Bumping into trees and stumbling through bushes, he darted through the forest. The angry yells of soldiers behind him only fueled his adrenaline, enabling him to block away his impeding pain and continue forward—

He desperately wanted to stop, to tell the Valkadians how the governor really died, to watch Thyran be arrested and taken away to finally suffer the consequences of his actions, but he knew the Valkadians would not believe him. Even if they did, Thyran was too cunning. He would slip away, somehow.

Jay made out the thin shards of moonlight gliding on the water ahead. If he could just reach the sea, he may escape. Though once his adrenaline died out, he doubted he would have the energy to swim. Nevertheless, clinging onto his implausible dream, he continued forward, each step snipping away a chunk of his energy and injecting him with a larger dose of fatigue—

He heard the yells and stomping of countless soldiers running after him. His salty sweat stung his eyes, thin branches whipped across his face. He prayed Hector would magically appear to rescue him, but he knew even the entire crew would not be able to fend off so many soldiers.

Jay sensed his body would collapse any minute—he couldn't keep running for much longer. If he had a little more distance between him and the soldiers, he may be able to dive to the side and take cover, but the guards would surely notice due to their close proximity.

"Stop at once!" one of them yelled.

Pale eyes illuminated by moonlight flecked the black forest. Animals. Jay wished they would understand his predicament and leap out to ward off his chasers. If only he could somehow communicate with them.

His heart lifted as the dense forest thinned, indicating he was near the end. Arching forward, he exerted himself even harder and raced to the treeline—

Then he was out of the jungle. Up ahead was the beach, and then the ocean.

Freedom.

He took three steps before the mighty shield of a Valkadian soldier pounded against the front of his skull. His brain jumbled, Jay toppled to the sand. He struggled to stand, but the Valkadian soldiers from behind caught up and snatched his arms, gripping them tightly. Despite his struggling, they shackled his hands behind his back.

"I did not murder the governor!" Jay screamed. Tears poured from his eyes, swelled in the back of his mouth. "Thyran did it! You must arrest him! You must—"

One of the soldiers clobbered the side of Jay's head with the hilt of his sword.

Blackness.

19

The Kingdom of Valkadia

Five days after their departure from Storm Isle, McClevin and his men arrived in Valkadia. In his cabin, McClevin fastened his silver-plated armor over his body and sheathed his blade in its shining metal scabbard fixed to his waist. He stared at his reflection in the mirror: his stern face, scruffy brown hair, silver armor: noble and honorable. No one would suspect that he, of all people, took the life of Princess Catherine Alexandra. His indigo eyes narrowed at himself, scowling at his own image. He envisioned the hood slipping from the princess's face, her red lips, her sparkling emerald eyes, her final words. "Yes," he said to himself, dropping to a knee and bowing his head before the mirror. "Yes Princess. I will do everything in my power to protect your people. Jay, Soleus, and all the others will pay for the harm they've caused you and your kingdom."

His insides felt blended by the sharp blades of guilt as he knelt before the mirror. Squeezing that trigger destroyed everything he spent his life working for. How could he go back to Eulia the proud, noble general he once was? Every day, every minute, every second, he would forever carry the burden of the most gruesome crime a man could commit. Nevertheless, he swore to himself that no matter how ugly the future became, he would, until the day he died, commit his heart and soul to the good of his kingdom. He owed it to her.

Grabbing his blue-crested silver helmet from the

floor, he stood up and secured it over his head. Approving his appearance in the mirror, he nodded to himself and exited his cabin, stepping out into the warm, sunkissed afternoon. His silver armor glistened brilliantly under the bright rays from the sun. Looking out over the rail, McClevin saw Valkadia, the kingdom's capital city.

They had arrived at the city's rear. The port consisted of narrow wooden docks jetting out from the vast sandy beach. The water near the beach was too shallow for ships, so they anchored out a ways into the ocean and would row ashore on smaller boats.

The beach stretched for miles across the shore and a hundred yards inland where it met the massive stone wall that circled the capital city. Beyond the wall, McClevin saw plumes of black smoke and tips of buildings stretching for the sky. Rather than Eulia's agrarian culture, Valkadia was more industrialized; the city consisted of numerous towering buildings squished together with little room for farmland. Flat stones, pushed into the ground, served as roads that coursed through the vast city.

To the left, centered between the city's entrances, King Cornelius's elegant castle glimmered, standing taller than any other building. The castle's rear was barricaded by mountains, some of which vanished up in the sky behind a cloudy mist.

On deck, Winston and Kileean stood ready, awaiting McClevin's command. "Kileean, I want you to stay here on the ship. She'll be under your charge. Winston, come with me. We must see King Cornelius at once."

"Yes, sir!" They both saluted their general and took their positions: Kileean strode to address the crew, Winston followed McClevin to the boat. After he grabbed a slender pole with the Eulian flag—blue with the Eulian emblem embroidered in the center—, McClevin and Winston hopped in the boat and waited for the men to lower them to the water.

"Sir," Winston said after rowing a short distance, "shouldn't we send a messenger back to Eulia to inform the king of his daughter's death?"

Gritting his teeth, McClevin stopped paddling and stared up at the sky where he saw her dying face resembled in the clouds. "The king is troubled enough already. We'll inform him upon our return."

"Don't you think he ought to know immediately?"

"I know her death is tragic, but, harsh as it may sound, we have more pressing matters to attend. Once we deal with Cornelius and those pirates, then we shall inform the king. Right now, I need all the men I have with me should trouble arise."

Winston sighed, clearly not satisfied with McClevin's response, but yet unwilling to press the matter any further. "Very well, general."

"I know it's hard," McClevin said. "But our duty remains to protect Eulia. You understand, don't you?"

"Yes, sir. I do."

"Good. Now, let's press on. We're almost there."

When they reached one of the wooden docks, a burly Valkadian soldier assisted with tying the boat to the post. When McClevin and Winston exited the boat, the soldier eyed McClevin's flag and said,

"Eulia.... What business do you have here in Valkadia?"

"I seek an audience with the king," McClevin said.

"What news demands such a request?"

"I must speak with him personally."

The soldier eyed them for a second then stepped aside. "Very well." He turned to his comrade. "Axle, take them to the entrance."

Axle nodded, then silently turned on his heel and began leading them inland. McClevin grumbled under his breath, furious to be on Valkadian soil.

They trudged through the hot sand to the metal threshold planted in the gray, mottled ramparts. McClevin heard the bustle of people inside the city and could now smell smoke rising from just inside the wall. The blacksmith.

The gate featured a relief of a castle engulfed in flames. Glancing up to the parapet, McClevin saw two guards, clad in red uniforms bearing the Valkadian emblem, stationed on the wall with quivers of arrows strapped to their backs. King Cornelius refused to allow his men to wield firearms, claiming it was a sign of weakness to rely on mechanical devices such as that. Besides, the time it required to reload such an instrument was valuable, and if his soldiers relied too much on firearms, their combative skills would decline. Still, even without guns, McClevin had to admit the Valkadians were highly trained, just as deadly with bows and arrows as anyone with a gun.

"Identify yourself," one of the guards said.

McClevin raised the pole in the air and swung it from side to side, revealing the Eulian symbol. "We come from Eulia!"

"What are your names?" the other asked.

"Ever friendly..." McClevin mumbled to Winston.

"Your names!" the guard repeated.

McClevin stabbed the pole into the ground. "I am the Eulian General, Arthur McClevin, and this is Winston Kefkan, a soldier of Eulia."

"What business do you have here?"

"We request an audience with King Cornelius. We have an urgent message from King Emory."

"What message?"

"I was ordered to deliver it personally to the king."

The guards discussed with one another, then one said, "Axle, watch these soldiers carefully. Escort them directly to the king's castle." Axle nodded. "Now stand back while we open the gate!"

McClevin heard the clunking opposite the gate as soldiers removed the metal beam locking it shut. With three soldiers pushing on each of the doors, the metal threshold screeched open, revealing the city of Valkadia. After lifting the flagpole from the sand, McClevin, followed by Winston, stepped through the gate and into the city.

Passing by the blacksmith to their right, McClevin smelled the charcoaled smoke and heard the clanking of metal inside. Winston stared around in wonder.

"So this is Valkadia...."

"Yeah," McClevin grumbled. "Not nearly as beautiful as Eulia, is it?"

The sight of the city sickened McClevin. The flowers blossoming in gardens found in Eulia were replaced with towering wooden and stone buildings; young kids frolicking through the vibrant fields, with young soldiers training for war in the narrow streets; lush trees decorating the landscape, with beggars sifting the crowds rattling their money jars.

The two navigated their way across the city to Cornelius's castle. Spectators swarmed the streets, anxious to witness the final rounds of the Gorgrim Tournament. Valkadia's coliseum was centered in the heart of the city, its cylindrical walls rising tall, embellished with vulpins clashing with their spears, gorgrim ripping apart their opponents, and other militant images.

Skirting around the massive coliseum, they heard the

roaring and cheering from inside as gorgrim were locked in combat. "Look at all these people..." McClevin thought aloud. "Cornelius must be making a fortune."

Winston focused on a grotesque image carved in the stadium wall of a soldier striking a sword through his fallen opponent. "Do you think Cornelius will be upset that we still haven't delivered the locket? I'm sure his kingdom has benefited more than the locket is worth."

"It won't matter to him. He's so wealthy, another treasure will do little for him. He's just greedy. A slimy tyrant who will never be satisfied."

Winston pushed his helmet up above his eyes and looked at McClevin. "What are you going to say to him?"

McClevin pondered Winston's question. He knew he had to keep Cornelius calm and prevent him from taking vengeance on Eulia. "I'm...not sure. There's got to be something that will pacify the filthy swine. Maybe a mallet upside his thick skull will do the trick." The two laughed, keeping their eyes averted from Axle, and weaved through the crowds to Cornelius's castle.

Strolling through the silver gates into the grassy courtyard in front of the castle, McClevin and Winston examined the castle's magnificence. On the ornate castle walls, the polished stones glimmered in the sunlight and spiraled up the castle's four towers. Tall, diamond-paned windows segmented the front wall; sunlight illuminated their varicolored faces, sending a cascade of colors splashing onto the grassy courtyard. Water trickled from three stone fountains in the courtyard, a sound McClevin found soothing as he treaded through the grass to the castle's threshold, where two soldiers stood guard.

"We're here to see King Cornelius. We have an urgent message from King Emory," McClevin said before the soldiers interrogated him.

They glanced at the flag, back to McClevin, then to Axle, who nodded. The guards stepped aside, opened the door, and ushered the two inside. "They're here to see the king," one of the soldiers said to a guard in the castle.

"I'll show them the way," the guard responded. He waved his hand for McClevin and Winston to follow.

Silently, they walked behind the guard through the labyrinth of wide hallways. Their footsteps echoed off the tall walls as their feet treaded across the stone-tiled floor. Luxury and wealth thrived in every decoration in the castle: the mirrors with gold trim along their edge, former kings illustrated in portraits with diamond-strewn borders, massive chandeliers with strands of silver and gold woven into its metal, all very majestic.

After climbing three flights of stairs, the guard stopped in front of an arched doorway with two sentries stationed in front. "Inform the king of two Eulian soldiers who request to speak with him," their escort said to the sentries. One of the sentries slipped inside the doorway.

"The king's throne is in this room," their escort said. "Before you enter, I'll need your weapons."

McClevin and Winston both drew their swords and surrendered them, along with the flagpole, to the guard. "Don't damage them," McClevin said.

Their escort took their weapons and waited until the sentry returned from inside the chamber.

"The king is ready to see them," he said. He held the door open and allowed them to enter King Cornelius's throne room.

McClevin and Winston both removed their helmets and held them by their sides before walking down the stretch of red carpet guiding to the throne. Crystallized statues of great warriors and kings lined the red carpet on either side, all glaring with a look of intimidation to the Eulian soldiers as they approached the king. When they reached the steps leading up to Cornelius's elevated throne, they both bowed with respect and waited for the king to speak.

"Rise, knights of Eulia." Standing to his feet, McClevin saw the king clearly in the well-lit chamber. His thick red cloak draped over his square shoulders as he sat in his cushioned throne. Black hair, slicked back with oil, dangled from behind his head past his shoulders. His massive arms rested on the armrests of his throne.

"What business do you have in my kingdom? Have you finally arrived to deliver the locket your king promised?"

The king's scornful tone tasted sour in McClevin's mouth. He clenched his fists by his sides, struggling to remain calm.

"King Cornelius, we are here to inform you of—"

"The locket, brave knight." The king's myriad necklaces of precious stones rattled as he leaned forward. "Do you have it or not?"

McClevin inhaled a deep breath, trying to control his temper. "Please, Your Highness, listen for a moment. Two weeks ago, some—"

King Cornelius slammed his fist on the wooden armrest of his throne. "Thievery! That's what you and your king committed! That locket is rightfully mine."

"With all due respect, Your Highness, I will not stand here silently while you insult my king. He is not a thief."

"Then tell me what you call it when one reneges on an agreement and withholds treasure that is rightfully someone else's. We had a deal, your king and I. I let Emory house all the wealthy merchants from around the world for the economic benefit of his kingdom in exchange for a small gift...a certain diamond locket to be offered to the victor. And now your king has kept the locket for himself. The greedy—"

"He does not have the locket!" McClevin growled.

King Cornelius scrunched his dark, bushy eyebrows. "Then who does?"

"It was stolen."

"Hmph." Cornelius threw his back against the throne. Fixing his golden crown upon his sleek, black hair, he said, "By whom?"

"Pirates, Your Highness."

Cornelius scoffed at McClevin. "Ha! You're telling me a crew of measly pirates infiltrated your castle through all your kingdom's defenses and stole the most valuable possession you owned right under your eyes? Tell me, knight of Eulia, do you take me for a fool?"

Winston stepped back a few steps, intimidated of the king's venomous voice. McClevin, however, firmly held his ground. "No, Your Highness. But these weren't just ordinary pirates. They were led by—"

"I don't care! Excuses mean nothing to me, knight." He lifted his hand and pointed in the distance. "Do you see that?"

Enraged and insulted, McClevin's eyes followed the king's finger, which pointed to an open, empty chest resting on a stone pedestal. "See what?"

"Do you see what is in the chest?"

McClevin squinted, but the chest still appeared empty. "Nothing."

"Exactly my point!" The king leaned forward, his militant, calloused face entering a column of sunlight pouring through the window. "Now, tell me, knight, how would I appear handing that to the victor of the most prestigious tournament of the year?"

"Your Highness—"

"I'd look like a fool!"

"Please, listen to me—"

"I want that locket!"

"But Your Highness, we can't—"

"I don't want to hear what you can't do! Your kingdom has less than a day to deliver the locket, or I'll view this as a violation of trust. And without my trust, Eulia cannot be my ally. I will view our treaty as void."

McClevin was unable hold in his rage any longer. His face burning with indignation, he stomped his foot on the stone floor. "You're being ridiculous! Pirates stole the locket, and we are doing everything in our power to bring it back. How dare you threaten us with war!"

"Watch your tongue, knight."

"I will not allow you to drag my people through another war."

"Then you'd serve yourself best by giving me that diamond locket."

McClevin threw his hands in the air. "We're doing all we can to retrieve it! We just need—"

"Good, then there is no point in further discussing this issue. The final round of the tournament is tomorrow. You have twenty-four hours to deliver it, or I will view this is as a violation of our agreement."

"But Your Highness, we—"

"This discussion is over."

"You're a fool!"

King Cornelius shot daggers through his eyes at McClevin. "What did you say?"

Emotions boiled in McClevin's blood; he was in a

state of madness. "You're acting like a ruthless tyrant, not a king!"

The enraged king stood up from his throne and thundered down the steps. Cornelius's red cloak dragged along the floor as he approached McClevin. "What is your name, knight?"

McClevin puffed out his chest and raised his wide chin. He would not allow himself to be intimidated by this man, even if he was the king. "My name is Arthur McClevin."

"You would be wise, Arthur McClevin, to watch your tongue," Cornelius snarled.

The door to the king's chambers cracked open. A soldier peaked his narrow head through the crack. "Your Highness."

"What is it?" the king asked, his eyes fixed on McClevin.

"Ralfor and the others have just arrived. They are carrying a prisoner and request your presence in the dungeons."

"Who is it?"

"I'm not sure, Your Highness. Ralfor said you would be very pleased to see who we captured. That is all I know."

"Very well." The king dismissed him with the flick of his hand. "Our conversation has come to an end, McClevin. Since I'm feeling generous, I'll forget your insults." He turned around and walked back to his throne. "Guards! Please escort him out of the castle."

The two sentries entered the room and hastily walked toward him. "Your Highness..." McClevin began.

King Cornelius spun around. His narrow eyes focused on McClevin. "You have one day to bring me the locket, McClevin. If not, I see difficult times ahead for you and your kingdom."

Jay eyed the flat stones in the ground as the Valkadian soldiers led him through Valkadia. Two burly guards
gripped his elbows. Steel shackles bound his wrists and ankles. His body still ached from his fight with Thyran. He
supported his broken wrist, which felt like it shattered every
time it brushed against the tight metal shackle imprisoning
it. A deep purple scab scarred his left hand where Thyran
stabbed him. Every time he caught sight of the mark, his
stomach twisted.

He wondered if Thyran had escaped, or if the Valkadians even attempted to arrest him. Probably not. They were
too intent on chasing him. And now, after hunting him for
four years, they had finally captured him.

He thought of how Soleus must have felt, struggling
in the water, watching his crew sail away while the Eulians
held him captive.

Jay wondered what Cain and the others had done
when he did not return as planned. Maybe they were caught
as well. Maybe they ran into Thyran and were captured, or
killed. He desperately wished to see them...Cain, Hector, Karen, Jenkins, Lynk, Blynk, Ankin, Soleus, Delcato, Lyssa...they were his family. And for all he knew, they could
very well be dead, a fate to which he would soon succumb.

Unaware of his surroundings, Jay shuffled forward,
wincing in pain with every step. Were they leading him to
the dungeons, or would they execute him right away? There
wouldn't be any trial, he knew that much.

They entered a courtyard with water trickling from
the fountains. He glanced up at an azura circling overhead,
trilling a sweet melody. Now, more than ever, he envied the
peaceful animals. He drifted into another daydream, pre-

tending to be an azura—

"No stopping," a guard scolded, shoving his back. Jay stumbled forward, but the guards' firm grips on his elbows prevented him from falling. After snapping back to reality, he saw two Eulian soldiers, one with silver armor, exiting the castle. He recognized him instantly, the one he had fought on the ship, the one who had taken Soleus captive—McClevin.

Their eyes met.

The two stared at one another in silence as they approached. They slowed their pace, glowering at one another like carnivorous animals. Then McClevin lunged at him. He leapt back. The surprised Valkadian guards snatched McClevin in midair and shoved him back. "Stay back! We're transporting a prisoner!"

"Jay!" McClevin shouted, his veins pulsing in his forehead. "Give me the locket!"

"Where's Soleus? What did you do to him?"

"I killed him! Just like I'll kill you if...."

But Jay didn't hear the rest of McClevin's sentence. Shards of sadness ripped into Jay's chest, puncturing his heart and lungs. His legs grew wobbly. "You...killed him...?"

"Give me the locket!"

Tears flowing down his face, Jay catapulted himself at McClevin, but the Valkadian guards caught him and jerked him back, sending another wave of pain through his hand and wrist. As the Valkadians dragged him in the castle, he shouted, "How could you kill him? He was a prisoner, an unarmed prisoner! Let go of me!" Flailing his arms and legs, sobbing uncontrollably, Jay watched the castle doors slam shut, trapping him inside.

The guards led Jay down a spiraling staircase with flaming torches hanging from the walls. When they reached the bottom, the guards dragged him down a dark hallway with small cells on both sides. Jay coughed as the thick scent of mold and rodent dung flowed into his nostrils.

Then the guards stopped at a vacant cell. One fiddled with a brass hoop of keys, found the right one, unlocked the cell, tossed Jay inside without removing his shackles, and slammed the barred door shut, locking it in place. All the guards left, except for two, who stood watch.

The cell was bare. No bed. Nothing. Just a damp, cement floor and walls of rock. Jay crawled across the solid floor, too weak to stand, and huddled against one of the back corners, as far away from his captors as possible.

His eyes stung from crying. He felt weak, embarrassed. But Soleus, his best friend, was now dead. The world suddenly felt darker. Colder. He felt more alone than ever.

Though tears still threatened his eyes, he could not shed any more. The damp, bleak, dreary dungeon drained his remaining strength and life from him, leaving him more depressed than ever. Too depressed to cry.

He heard footsteps in the distance. A flickering yellow light sprayed over the concrete floor in the hallway. Someone was approaching.

First, he saw a man wearing silver and black, with a short sword sheathed at his waist. The man had a narrow face and long, silver hair. Behind him was a much larger man with a red robe, sleek black hair, and numerous necklaces around his neck. He wore a golden crown lined with jewels.

The skinnier man straightened his back and flourished his hand towards Jay. "King Cornelius, I present to you the most wanted man in Lassar, Jay Perry."

Jay looked away; he did not want the king to see him

in such a pitiful state.

He heard the king step closer. "You're sure this is him, Ralfor?"

"Yes my king. His face matches the sketch perfectly, and like a fool, he fled upon hearing mention of his name."

"Hmm," the king said. "Well, in that case Jay, it's a pleasure having you as a guest in Valkadia."

Jay's body quivered. His eyes felt like weak dams blocking a raging river.

Jay jumped when a sharp clanging sound reverberated off his cell walls. They had hit the bars of his cell with metal.

"Look at the king when he addresses you!" Ralfor said.

For a moment, the only sound was the dripping of water from the walls; no one moved. The flickering torchlight from the hall invaded Jay's cell. He felt the warmth of the flame.

"I must admit," the king said. "You've been on the run a long time, Jay. For four years, you haven't left a single trace of existence except that once in Delphina. You or your brother. How is he, by the way? Did you kill him too?"

Jay's eyes snapped open. He stared at the wall, orange by torchlight. The Valkadians probably didn't even recognize Thyran in Selia. It was too dark, and their focus was on Jay, not Thyran. Part of him wanted to leap up and explain the situation and beg to be released. But a greater part of him was overcome with sorrow for Soleus and hatefulness towards society. Wrongly accused, beaten until near death, Jay sat in his cell without a word, his thoughts jetting out in a multitude of directions.

"Hmm...you must have. It's amazing the horrendous crimes one can commit at such a young age, isn't it?"

Jay sensed Ralfor grinning in agreement.

"It is, Your Highness. What shall we do with him? Shall I torture him? Make him pay for killing Almsy?"

A shudder ran down Jay's spine hearing the word *torture*. He could not fathom his body withstanding any more pain. He felt on the brink of death.

"No," the king said. "Look at him. His body won't survive any more beatings." A pause. "How much longer until the last round of the tournament today?"

"About two hours," said Ralfor.

"I see." The king cleared his throat. "Jay Perry. I, as well as the Kingdom of Valkadia, find you guilty for the murder of Governor Almsy and your stepbrother, Thyran Vilkus. Your penalty is death. Your public execution will be in two hours."

Ralfor snickered. "Enjoy the last two hours of your life." Then Jay heard footsteps, the torchlight withdrew from his cell, and the two were gone.

The last two hours of your life. Those words reverberated inside Jay's head like the screech of a siren. He needed to escape.

His eyes darted around the cell. Two guards armed with scimitars and shields hovered around the entrance, the only exit, which was lined with sturdy steel bars. He looked up. No window. He searched his cell, but he could not even locate a sharp piece of rock. There was nothing. No way out.

Sighing, he closed his eyes and slammed his head against the wall. Thyran had finally done it; Thyran had got the best of him. Despite all his efforts, he could not stop his stepbrother. Down here, in the depths of the Valkadian dungeon, there was no melody of the azura, no warmth in the air. He felt so alone, like a lost child in the forest, his candle flame killed by a crisp breeze. How could Jenkins survive eight years in such a dismal place? But he had escaped, somehow. Though if it took Jenkins eight years, it would take Jay eighty. All he could do now is wait, wait as time rolled by, bringing him to his death.

The first hour nearly drove him mad. Alone in a dark cell with no company save for two sentries outside, he felt insanity creeping into his mind. He dragged his nails through the solid wall, hoping to inflict enough pain to keep his mind preoccupied.

Whenever thoughts of Soleus flashed in his head, he wept and dug his fingernails into his chest. The pain seared his heart, burned any sensations to physical touch. Over and over, he replayed McClevin's words in his mind, hoping somehow to alter them and bring his best friend back from the dead.

Thoughts of Soleus eventually numbed his mind, and he drifted into a state of delirium.

A while later, his delirium rendering him incapable of shedding any more tears, he remembered the challenge Lyssa offered him. Satisfied to have found something to keep his mind busy, he sat upright and licked his lips. Parting them in the center as Lyssa had taught him, he blew.

No luck.

He tried again. Still no luck.

You're blowing too hard, he remembered her saying. Dampening his lips, he gave it another shot, this time blowing peacefully, not forcing it as much. A faint whistle parted from his lips, though it sounded to him like he produced a melody as sweet as that of an azura. Despite his dismal circumstance, despite knowing death waited for him less than an hour away, his heart leapt. He smiled.

As the minutes rolled by, he improved upon his whistling abilities. They became crisper and louder. Despite the constant complaints and threats from the guards, he continued practicing the art of whistling; it was the only thing keeping him from falling off the cliff of insanity.

He was still whistling when the rattling of keys disturbed the silence in the hallway. Leading a herd of guards, Ralfor stopped at Jay's cell and pointed to the lock. "This one," he said to the guards. Jay noticed a scar slashed across the right half of Ralfor's mouth and cheek. The scar was thick, and it appeared that at one point, the right half of Ralfor's mouth had been completely ripped open.

"Jay Perry," he said in a formal tone. "Your time is up. I am here to deliver you to the Gorgrim Ring where you will be executed."

20

Kreios, King of the Gorgrim

Four guards, their immense shoulders bulging up against their blood red uniforms, entered Jay's cell, gripped him by the shoulders, and forced him into the hallway where Ralfor waited, clad in black and silver, a torch in his right hand spewing light around the dungeon.

The guards held Jay with his face inches away from Ralfor's. Jay averted his eyes from the man, staring at the ground instead. Ralfor stood a minute, probably snickering to himself, proud to be the soldier who would finally bring Jay Perry to his death.

"Let's move," Ralfor said, and the guards, led by Ralfor, escorted Jay out of the dungeon and castle, back into the grassy courtyard with fountains trickling in the distance and azura singing in the sky.

The streets were calm; the majority of the people were gathered in the Gorgrim Ring. Even around the castle walls, the roaring of the beasts entangled in combat shook the air.

Another group of armed guards awaited at the gate of the courtyard, and when Jay passed, they followed, ensuring he would not escape. Head down, spirits low, Jay walked down the pebbled path to the Gorgrim Ring.

"Can you hear it, Jay?" Ralfor taunted. "The cheering of the crowd, the clashing of the beasts? In a few minutes, the crowds will be cheering as justice is finally served. Your death will remind all of Lassar that no one gets away with such heinous crimes."

Jay knew there was no point in arguing. Anything he said would be branded as lies. Sighing, he looked up to the sky and watched the thin veil of white clouds brush over the sun. A cooling breeze tickled his skin. Rays of sunlight warmed his body. Closing his eyes, he imagined himself walking across the deck of his ship. Up ahead, he saw Lyssa leaning against the rail, her long golden hair swaying rhythmically as she peered over the water. He strutted up to her, licked his lips, and startled her with his perfected whistling. Overcome with joy, she wrapped her arms around him in a warming hug. So proud of his new ability, so glad of his safe return. And then, unsure why, that dim candle in the cave of darkness lit, and he felt a hint of bliss engulfing his body. He smiled, licked his lips, whistled—then felt a sharp jab to his side. He fell to his knees.

Squinting into the sunlight, he saw Ralfor's scarred face glaring down at him. Ralfor brandished the torch in his face. "One more peep out of you, and you'll be begging me for your death. Now get up!"

Suffering another blow to the side from the tip of the torch, Jay stumbled to his feet. His wrist and ribs burned; his injured left hand pulsed. However, his pain soon subsided when the massive Gorgrim Ring came into view, and Jay's body succumbed to the deathly claws of fear.

Shuffling through the crowd in the Gorgrim Ring, McClevin and Winston made their way to the king, who sat in a shaded platform.

Inside the coliseum, thousands of wild fans filled the seats and watched the two gorgrim battle. The creatures battled in an arena of sand encircled by a moat of water wide enough to prevent the gorgrim from leaping across. Since gorgrim couldn't swim, the moat confined them to the sandy arena.

Their venomous tails striking, immense arms swinging, fearsome mouths roaring, the two vicious animals charged at one another. The taller and bulkier gorgrim used its tail to keep the other one at a distance. The smaller, lighter-colored gorgrim bellowed and thrashed sand in the air, trying to blind its opponent.

When the larger gorgrim withdrew its tail, the smaller gorgrim bowed down, exposing its deadly horn atop its head, and charged forward using its arms like a gorilla. At the last second, the mightier creature slashed its claws through the air and pounded its adversary's side, sending the unfortunate gorgrim soaring across the sand.

At once, all the roused fans leapt up and let out a joyous cheer. They began chanting the dominating gorgrim's name. "Kre-ios! Kre-ios! Kre-ios!"

Fueled by their chant, Kreios pounded his mighty chest, bared his lethal white fangs, and growled at the other gorgrim. His opponent recovered its footing and glared at Kreios, who repeatedly slammed his fists into the sand menacingly. This further roused the crowd, and the din of yelling intensified.

McClevin found himself mesmerized by the animal's ferocity.

Raising its venomous tail in the air, the smaller gorgrim again charged for Kreios. When his opponent was close, Kreios extended both claws, one grabbing the other's head, the other snatching its tail. Despite the gorgrim's attempt to break free, Kreios's massive strength kept it confined. With a swift movement, Kreios whipped his tail around and sunk his stinger into the back of his opponent's neck. The gorgrim dropped to the ground, lifeless.

Amid the uproar of cheering, McClevin noticed a man

cloaked in a deep purple cape walk through the gates and into the arena. It was Lasheer—master gorgrim trainer. Behind him, several Valkadian soldiers ran into the stadium. Some carried a net that they used to drag out the dead gorgrim, and the rest had rakes to comb the sand and prepare it for the next battle.

Lasheer held his hands high, welcoming the thunderous applause. Kreios strode over to him and bowed his head to his master. Flourishing his hand to Kreios, Lasheer shouted to the crowd. "Kreios! King of the Gorgrim!" The fanatic crowd stomped their feet and roared even louder as Lasheer took a bow.

Seated on his royal platform shaded with a red and gold canvas, King Cornelius stood up and clapped his hands, smirking down at Lasheer, who smiled back at the powerful king.

"Your Highness!" McClevin shouted over the din of cheers when he reached the platform.

Without moving his head, Cornelius said, "I dismissed you, general. You are overstaying your welcome."

"But Your Highness, the prisoner you have is Jay Perry."

"Yes, I know. Look," the king pointed to the metal gate at the threshold of the arena where a group of soldiers and a mysterious man with silver hair led Jay into the arena. "You are just in time for his execution."

Even from such a high distance, McClevin clearly recognized Jay's face. He clenched his fists and raised his voice. "Your Highness, *he* has the locket."

King Cornelius shot him a harsh glance. "He has nothing. My soldiers searched him at the time of his arrest."

"Then his crew has it, and only he knows where they are. Please, Your Highness, let me have a moment alone with him before you execute him."

The king waved his coarse hand to the crowds of people. "Look at them, general. I have promised them a public execution. I am not a man to go back on my word, unlike your king."

McClevin gritted his teeth and removed his silver helmet. Gripping his helmet with one hand, he pointed it at the king. "Do not insult King Emory again, Your Highness. I'm telling you, that man you are about to execute knows where the locket is. Let me find out—"

"I have made my decision. Feel free to stay and watch, but I will not delay his execution."

"But Your Highness!"

Ignoring McClevin, the king raised his hands, letting his red cloak fall behind his back, and stepped out from the shade of his platform. A hush swept over the crowd, and everyone gazed at the king. King Cornelius spoke in a booming voice so the entire stadium could hear.

"That is the final round for today's portion of the tournament. This annual's Gorgrim Tournament will conclude tomorrow." A few moans radiated from the crowd, but it soon fell silent. "However, as promised, I have a special treat for you." He directed their attention to the center of the arena where the Valkadians circled the shackled prisoner. "Jay Perry, the man wanted for the murder of Governor Almsy."

Allowing the crowd to bash the prisoner with threats, the king leaned to McClevin. "Hopefully, the murderer won't go for the water."

McClevin tilted his head. "Why?"

"Unfortunately, that's how most gladiators die in the arena. The water is filled with vicious serpents such as snakes and flesh-eating fish. If he dies in there, the display won't be nearly as fulfilling."

McClevin looked down at Jay. In a way, he felt sorry for the pirate. Despite his desire to bring him justice, McClevin felt King Cornelius was just as villainous. In Eulia, Jay would only be hung rather than slaughtered as a public spectacle. He searched for something to say that would persuade Cornelius to postpone the execution, but the king spoke before he had a chance to say anything.

"Lasheer. Please accept this gift to Kreios, a token of our gratitude for his entertainment."

Lasheer nodded and backed away from Kreios. "The King of the Gorgrim appreciates your kindness, my king."

"Unshackle the prisoner," Cornelius ordered. The man with silver hair released Jay from his bondage and led his guards back to the entrance of the arena. Lasheer backed away from Kreios and followed guards out.

The metal gate slammed shut.

The angry cries and jeers from the crowd sunk Jay's spirit. Looking around, he saw thousands of people who all despised him and longed to see his execution.

When the gate slammed shut, Jay stood alone in the arena, surrounded by thousands of angry men and women. He stared at Kreios, standing two stories tall, the most powerful and vicious gorgrim in Lassar. Kreios's black eyes flickered under the sun. His dark gray fur shook as he pounded his arms into the sand. His tail whipped back and forth, occasionally stabbing the air in front of him. Growling, Kreios bent his head, presenting his hooked horn illuminated by sunlight. The crowd laughed as Jay stepped back in fear.

Up until now, Jay had accepted his fate—he was willing to die. The world was cruel and unjust, destroying the lives of the good while protecting those of the evil. He could not survive in such a place. But when he saw Lyssa during his trip from the dungeons to the ring, he remembered something. Her nod. Back in the Selian inn, she gave him that nod of approval, that nod of encouragement. She *knew* he was strong enough to complete his task. She had faith in him. How would she feel if she knew that he stood here, in the Gorgrim Ring in Valkadia, bathing in a tub of self-pity?

She would not approve.

For her and her abused mother, for Soleus and his untimely death, for Delcato and her assassinated father, for Lynk and Blynk and their dying mother, for Ankin who lost his hand saving Lyssa, for Gideon who lost his life to the sea monster, for Captain Gaden who perished protecting his crew, Jay must be strong.

He would not grant himself a moment of weakness. For all his family who had suffered with and for him, he had to be strong.

Straightening his back, he faced the gorgrim, not with fear, but with anticipation. Death was inevitable—unarmed, he would never be able to defeat such an immense monster. But he would hang onto that last thread of life until the gorgrim pried it from his fingers.

When the crowd's jeering subsided, the king addressed the stadium once more. "Jay Perry. We, the Kingdom of Valkadia, hereby find you guilty for taking the life of Thyran Vilkus and Dorian Almsy. Your penalty is death. The time of your execution is now." The crowd held their breath and bottled their excitement when King Cornelius lifted a mallet in the air. "Gentlemen and ladies, I present to you the execution of Jay Perry!"

The king swung the mallet into a golden gong to his side, and at that instance, Kreios shot off like a musket ball.

The whole arena shook as the massive gorgrim charged towards him. Adrenaline pumping through his veins, Jay dashed across the sand away from Kreios. His eyes darted around in search for a weapon, but the only thing in the arena was sand and the surrounding moat. A steep wall dropped into the moat opposite the sand where the crowd watched. The wall was too steep to climb. Jay looked to the entrance, but the metal gate bit firmly into the ground.

No weapons. No way out.

He ran out of time to think; Kreios was only a few yards away. Running with all his energy, Jay neared the moat. He turned around and saw Kreios's mighty arm already in full swing. Out of options, he dove into the water.

Underwater, he heard the gorgrim's mighty blow in the sand where he had stood a second prior. His eyes open, he swam through the murky green water around the arena. He saw the wall on the other side of the moat that led to the stands. He guessed it was about fifty yards away. Thinking quickly, he decided to swim for the wall and try to climb it despite its steepness.

Something sharp bit into his bare foot. Flicking his head over his shoulder, he let out a gasp. Through a fog of blood, a snake's slanted yellow eyes glared back at him, its teeth digging into his skin. Shaking his leg, he noticed another snake the size of a small tree trunk swimming towards him. Hearing the gorgrim stomping in the arena, he swam deeper in the water and frantically swam away from the approaching snake. With his free leg, he kicked the snake's head attached to his foot, causing it to release its grip and slither away.

His lungs burning, he swam through the dangerous waters. He caught a glimpse of shiny armor glimmering at the bottom of the moat. Inside was a man's skeleton.

The trailing snake caught up to him and sunk its fangs into his outer-thigh. He squirmed in pain and began growing dizzy from lack of oxygen—he needed air. The snake shook its body left and right, trying to rip his leg out of its socket. Jay curled around and smashed his fist into the snake's head, hard enough to temporarily daze it, allowing him to pry it off his leg and swim up towards the surface.

Out of the corner of his eye, he saw three, four other snakes racing for him. He would not be able to fend them off or sustain too many more injuries before the pain would overwhelm him. Exerting himself harder, he kicked with all his strength, and then his head broke the surface of the water.

Wheezing from exhaustion and lack of oxygen, he dragged himself out of the water back onto the sandy arena. He winced in agony as sand invaded his open wounds. Blood trickled out of the teeth marks in his right foot and thigh, but fortunately, it wasn't gushing.

In the distance, Kreios stared in the water, stabbing his venomous tail in and out of the moat. The gorgrim hadn't noticed his presence. Keeping quiet, Jay rose to his feet and began limping to the gate.

In an uproar, the crowd pointed at Jay. "Kreios! Kreios!"

Jay glanced back. Alerted by the crowd, the mighty gorgrim peered over his shoulder and snarled when his eyes set on him. Pounding his chest and delivering a massive roar, Kreios slammed his fists into the ground and charged for him, using his arms for propulsion like a gorilla. Feeling the ground shake, Jay faced Kreios, who hurled himself across the arena, his tail stuck high in the air like a scorpion's.

Jay crouched in a deep stance and gathered his

breath. The beast's growling rattled his bones as it neared. The crowd all stood to their feet, waiting for Kreios to serve the final blow. Jay felt dizzy from pain and exhaustion, but he remained steady, his feet firmly planted in the soft sand. Looking up, he saw Kreios's dark eyes and massive gray chest, which appeared strong enough to withstand a musket ball.

Kreios's shadow blanketed Jay. Still charging at full speed, Kreios opened his claws and lunged for him. Quick as a vulpin, Jay dove to the side, evading the gorgrim's claw and falling to his back. Sliding past him, the grogrim aimed his tail for Jay's head and struck—

Jay rolled across the sand as Kreios's stinger punctured the ground an inch from his head.

Digging his feet into the sand, Kreios stopped himself and whirled around. Jay leapt to his feet, sweat poured down his forehead. He pressed his right hand against the snakebite in his thigh to stop the bleeding. A headache tore through his head, blurring his vision and deafening his hearing. He could no longer think straight; he had to rely on instinct.

Bowing his head and kicking up sand with his feet, Kreios bolted at Jay, his sharp horn aimed for his chest. Jay twisted sideways and leapt back. He barely dodged the horn but flew off his feet when Kreios's head plowed into him. He soared through the air, and as he fell to the ground, he instinctively threw out his hands to break his fall. The sand was molten lava against his broken wrist. Streams of fire shot up along the veins in his arm—the pain was so excruciating Jay thought his arm would shatter and sever from his body.

"The young pirate is putting on quite a show," Cornelius said.

Furious, McClevin pointed at Jay. "He's almost dead! I'm telling you, call this off. He's the only one who can help us get back the locket."

King Cornelius lifted his crown to scratch his black hair. Looking at McClevin, he said, "I will not call this off. This man knows nothing. You would be best searching elsewhere, general."

The crowd cheered when Kreios began another assault on Jay. "If you kill him, you'll never get the locket. You'll be—"

Cornelius turned away from McClevin. "Look! Kreios is about to deliver the finishing blow."

Jay ducked under Kreios's swooping claw and dashed to the side. His speed barely surpassed that of a brisk walk due to his wounded leg and foot. Skirting the edge of the arena alongside the moat, he ran with all his energy away from Kreios. He saw the gorgrim's shadow in front of him and noticed it leaping off the ground in a dive. Realizing he could not outrun the attack, he leapt back into the predator-infested moat.

Through the dusty green water, he saw an enormous elongated fish with numerous layers of teeth swimming for him. There was a glimmer of armor on the ground. Jay decided to pursue it.

He swam downward. Every stroke with his broken wrist shot a bolt of lightning through his body, but his determination carried him to the armor. Beside the armor was a hilt, then the glimmer of a blade. A sword. He stretched out his hand, clasped his fingers around the handle, whipped around, and swung the dead man's sword through the murky water, slicing into the fish's mouth. He injured the fish enough for it to cease its pursuit and scurry away.

On the other side of the armored skeleton was a shield. Jay went to grab it, but a school of other predatory fish and giant snakes came into view. Taking stock of the situation, he abandoned the shield and swam for the surface. Twice he had to swing his blade to fend off an approaching sea creature, but he made it to the surface with no further injuries.

Splashing out of the water, he flung his sword onto the sand, freeing both hands so he could drag himself out of the water. The serpents of the moat thrashed about wildly, creating bubbling white foam on the edge of the moat. The splashing from the sea creatures alerted Kreios. The gorgrim spun around and faced Jay, who choked from swallowing too much water.

"Finish him, Kreios!" King Cornelius shouted. The crowd cheered with enthusiasm.

Spitting out a final gulp of water, Jay at last caught his breath. Still sprawled on the ground, he looked at Kreios, who stood fifty yards away. Arching his head low, Kreios watched him wobble to his feet. The gorgrim planted his feet in the sand. Waiting.

Jay snatched the rusty blade from the sand and held it steady. The crowd snickered—even he knew the blade stood no chance at piercing Kreios's thick skin. But it was all he had. He stood ready.

Kreios rocketed forward, dashing to Jay with his horn aimed to kill.

Struggling to keep his head steady, Jay waited for Kreios's attack. The pain and loss of blood were taking their toll as his adrenaline began to wane. His vision blurred; his consciousness was slipping away. Simply standing proved challenging. His bones felt like brittle twigs that would soon snap under his own weight.

Mustering his final ounce of strength, his last bit of hope, he pointed the sword at Kreios. Just before they collided, Jay sidestepped the gorgrim's deadly horn—

A splash of cool liquid sprayed Jay's face when the point of his rusty sword pierced Kreios's left eye. The collision sent Jay soaring through the air once again. He fell hard on the sand a few yards away, this time tucking his hands in his stomach for protection.

Kreios screamed in agony and pounded the sand with his arms, thrashed the air with his tail. The sword dropped from his eye, and Kreios launched it through the air to the aghast crowd.

Partially blinded, the gorgrim growled at Jay and dashed towards him. Jay stumbled to his feet but was unable to react quickly enough—

Kreios's tail sideswiped him, slamming into his ribs and blasting him across the arena. Jay landed with a thud just off the edge of the moat. He began sinking into a world of blackness. All his energy struggled to keep him conscious. He could barely breathe or move. He lay there helpless.

"Finish him!" he heard King Cornelius bellow.

The crowd started chanting with increasing intensity. "Kre-ios! Kre-ios! Kre-ios!"

The beat of Kreios's feet thundering against the sand shook the stadium. Faster than ever, the gorgrim dashed across the arena. The crowd stomped their feet with wild fervor.

Eyeing the crowd, Jay was amazed at the people's excitement to watch him die. What pleasure did they receive out of witnessing such things? He would not let them have that pleasure. Amid the immense din of noise, Jay rose to his knees, for he was too weak to get to his feet.

The two foes glared at one another. Jay faced death—but he was not afraid. He had been strong to the last second.

When Kreios was close enough to strike, Jay rolled off the arena back into the water, presenting his defenseless body for the fish to rip apart. At least now, the crowd would not have the satisfaction of witnessing the gorgrim renting him to pieces.

He opened his eyes and saw the serpents closing in on him—

Kreios's injured eye must have prevented him from seeing the danger until too late, for the massive gorgrim stumbled over the edge of the arena and crashed into the water. Jay watched with amazement as the massive creature plunged into the water only feet in front of him.

Seeing the extremely large prey dropping into their domain, the fish and snakes ignored Jay and swarmed Kreios. Unable to swim, Kreios thrashed his arms madly as he sunk into the depths of the moat, his body feasted on by the vicious sea creatures.

On the brink of unconsciousness, Jay raised his arms before he sank too deeply, gripped the edge of the arena, and lifted himself ashore. The crowd was silent. Flipping on his back, Jay collapsed on the sand and welcomed the warming sun basking his face. Unable to move, he lay still.

"Arghh!" Cornelius screamed with rage. "Guards! Drag him to the center!"

The gate creaked open. Though Jay could not see them, he heard numerous guards rushing over to him. They grabbed his arms, he felt a jolt of pain along his left, but he was too weak to cry out. The Valkadian soldiers dragged him across the sand to the center of the arena.

Jay squinted at the king. Beside him stood McClevin,

who thrashed his arms madly at the king as if protesting something.

The guards backed away and left the arena, closing the gate behind them.

"Archers!" the king called out. Through his blurry vision, Jay saw a circle of Valkadian soldiers from the highest points in the stadium stand tall, equipped with bows and quivers strapped to their backs. Jay remembered hearing about the deadliness of Valkadian archers: deadlier than any sharpshooter, they never missed.

Simultaneously, like an army of assassins, they strung their arrows, stretched the strings of their bows, and awaited the command to fire.

"Jay Perry's sentence must be carried out!" the king roared.

The crowd remained still, watching Jay, barely conscious, lying in the middle of the vast arena with nowhere to hide, with nothing to defend himself. His injuries racked his body so viciously that when King Cornelius gave the command to fire and the archers launched their weapons, Jay welcomed the dark cloud of arrows raining down upon him.

21

Granting a Death Wish

A blast.

The ground shook. An explosion rang through the air. A blanket of blue water swept over ten feet above Jay's face. Unsure if he was alive or spiraling into the land of the dead, he admired the beautiful streams flowing mellifluously through the air. The water thickened, raced faster, hurrying towards its destination. The horde of arrows pummeled the water, but the powerful current swept them aside.

His body quivering with pain, Jay allowed his head to fall to the left. Two figures approached. A man, slender with spiked crimson hair, and a woman, smaller with flowing sapphire hair and eyes that glowed bright blue.

Alcina held her hand aloft as she reinforced the dome of water encompassing the three of them, shielding them from the archers' arrows. The crimson-haired man followed behind, continuously glancing at the relentless downpour of arrows above them.

The sorceress giggled. "Relax, my dear, my shield will protect you. So long as you behave." She smirked at him.

A group of Valkadian soldiers rushed through the entrance and poured into the arena, pointing their scimitars or bows at the man and sorceress. The water dome deflected the arrows from the archers; jets of water shot out from the shield and pummeled the melee soldiers.

Inside the protective water dome, Jay watched the pair approach. "What do you want?" He gave a rasp cough and grabbed his aching side. Blood dripped to the sand from his wounded foot and thigh. The scab on his left hand had ripped open during the fray with Kreios; warm blood oozed onto his skin.

The spiky-haired man knelt down beside him and spoke in a calm voice. "I think you know, Jay."

The sorceress whirled around in the sand, firing streams of water off in different directions, knocking the surrounding soldiers off their feet. She laughed as they frantically held up their shields defensively and retreated away from the dome. Thin tendrils of water surrounded her beautiful body, spinning faster and faster around her blue dress and dark skin.

"I don't know what you're...ahh!" Jay's ribs cut into his side; it felt like they punctured his stomach.

The man watched him shake in agony. "Thyran has ordered me to kill you if you don't cooperate."

"Then kill me!" Jay shouted, tears breaking through the dams in his eyes. "Kill me already! He's already destroyed everything in my life!"

"Give me the gem," the man said, extending his hand.

Jay turned on his side, his back facing the man. Reaching inside his pocket with his right hand, his fingers brushed against the necklace, the real necklace, not the fake one Claudia had given him that he surrendered to Thyran. Stuffed deep in the corner of his pocket near his inner-thigh, the necklace had remained concealed when the soldiers patted him down after his arrest. The gem was small, not much larger than a dragone, which helped it avoid detection.

After all he and the crew had been through, he could not allow Thyran to have the necklace. Furtively, he slipped the necklace out of his pocket. The edge of the shielding water dome wasn't far off; maybe he could toss it through to the Valkadian soldiers. Better them than Thyran.

Winding his arm back, he moved to throw it, but the man was too quick. He snatched the necklace from Jay's hand and ripped it free from his grasp.

"No!" Jay swung his arms trying to grab the necklace, but the man had stepped out of reach.

Eying the gem, the man watched as the specks of red came and went while the background changed from green to blue. At once, he realized this was the true gem. "Alcina, let's go."

Laughing hysterically, Alcina shot a ball of water at one of the archers atop the stadium, sending him flying over the stadium wall. Turning to the man, she hopped on her feet with excitement. "Such a pretty necklace! Let me see it." She went to take the necklace, but the man evaded her.

"No, we must take this to Thyran at once."

"Eyah!" she shouted and sent a block of water soaring into the man's stomach, knocking him off his feet. Before he could get up, jets of water swirled around his hand, seized the necklace, and carried it to Alcina. She grinned as she placed the precious gem around her neck. "Thank you, my dear."

She offered a hand to help him up, but he swatted it away and rose to his feet. "Do not lose it," he warned.

Biting her bottom lip, Alcina swung her arm around his elbow and pulled herself closer to him. "Watch this, my love." She threw her free hand in the air, her eyes flashed even brighter, and she watched with glee as the dome exploded, sending arrows of water soaring in all directions, blasting people off their feet.

Alcina summoned another dome, this one protecting only herself and the man, and the two vanished into the frantic crowd of people outside fleeing the Gorgrim Ring.

"What is this?" King Cornelius shouted.

McClevin stood just as dumbfounded as the king. "I...don't know."

The sound of people frantically trying to escape the stadium prevented King Cornelius from issuing orders to his soldiers, who appeared just as baffled as the public. A short soldier rushed up to the king and took a knee.

"Your Majesty," he said.

"What is it?" Cornelius snapped.

"It's Kraus Bandekot. He just arrived on a merchant vessel. He needs to speak with you at once."

"I don't have time for—"

"Your Majesty, his ship was attacked and sunk."

"What? By whom?"

"I do not know Your Majesty. But he wishes to speak with you at once. He says it's urgent."

McClevin noticed the king clenching his fist, and even he dared not say anything that would upset the king any further.

"McClevin!" the king said. "Go with my men and get down there immediately to secure Jay Perry before he escapes. I'll have my other soldiers secure a perimeter around the city so the other two don't escape. Go!"

Without a word, McClevin and Winston raced across the stands, charging for the arena down below.

Most of the guards that had surrounded Jay had fled, fearful of the sorceress. Only three soldiers remained, but more had to be on their way. When the soldiers recovered from water explosion, they immediately charged for Jay.

"Little Blue!" The sound of Lynk's voice carried over the din of yells and screams from the crowd.

Lifting his head, Jay saw Lynk, followed by the rest of the crew, enter the arena and sprint towards him. The sight of his friends rejuvenated him—Delcato with her usual look of determination, Lynk and Blynk with their wild excitement, Hector with his gallant stride, Cain with his dark jacket and wooden staff, Lyssa with her golden hair. His fellow pirates killed off the Valkadian soldiers and then rushed over to him.

"Come on Little Blue!" Lynk said, motioning for Jay to stand.

Jay struggled to stand, but collapsed back down. Lyssa knelt in the sand beside him and placed her hand on his shoulder. Jay smiled, savoring her touch...the warm sensations of happiness and hope flowed from her fingertips into his shoulder and engulfed his body.

"I need some help!" Lyssa said.

Hector sheathed his sword and bent down beside Jay. Next to Hector's scruffy brown beard, Jay noticed a mark, a cut from a dagger, across his left cheek. "C-captain...."

"Quiet, Lil' Blue. Yer in no shape to be talkin'." Captain Hector scooped him up and sprinted back to the threshold of the arena. "Back to the ship!"

Lyssa, Delcato, Cain, Lynk, and Blynk led the way, fending off any soldiers who approached. A mob of frantic people fleeing the coliseum filled the streets. Jay spotted Valkadian soldiers searching for them in the crowd.

Amid the chaos, Hector and his crew zigzagged through the masses of people, making it difficult for the soldiers to find or follow them. Jay closed his eyes; Hector's fingers dug into his sore muscles. Every footstep sparked a jolt of pain through his body. But he clung onto his consciousness as the wind whipped across his face during their race for freedom.

Alcina screamed with excitement as her summoned ball of water blasted open the metal door guarding the back entrance of Valkadia. Shuffling through the dense trees, she and Kyros made their way through the beach.

"Ha!" Kyros said. "Did you see that? The explosion...beautiful! It was perfect!"

Alcina smirked. "A waste of time is what that was. We would already be back on the ship if you would have listened to me."

"Water alone could not have broken into the arena!"

She clicked her tongue. "Water can do more than your petty little explosives."

"Even so, nothing compares to the grand spectacle of my explosives. The gratifying bang, the glorious fire, the majestic smoke...I'd like to see your water do that."

She bit her bottom lip and glanced at him. "It was rather impressive, my love."

"I know."

They raced down the dock. Hooks of water sprang up from the sea and knocked the Valkadian soldiers off the docks. The two hopped in their boat; Kyros drew his dagger and sliced the rope binding the boat to the dock. Then he dipped both oars into the water and began paddling, eager to put greater distance between them and the Valkadian soldiers.

Alcina grinned. "My dear, what are you doing?"

"We need to get back to the ship. If you would quit gawking around and help me, we may actually—whoa!"

Kyros fell back in the boat as it rocketed forward. Screaming wildly, Alcina held out her hands, summoning a swift current that blasted them through the water like a cannonball. Kyros struggled to regain his seat due to the high speed of the boat and its frequent crashing up and down on the waves. "S-slow down...you're going to toss me overboard!"

But Alcina appeared too absorbed into the heat of the moment to pay him any heed. The wind ripped past them, water splashed over them. Faster and faster they raced through the water to the *Venator*.

"Here they come, captain," Cyril said, pointing over the rail to Alcina and Kyros barreling through the water.

The *Venator* rested in a cove surrounded by tall mountains, secluded from the rest of the sea so no one would notice them. Thyran squeezed the necklace Jay had given him, angry at his own stupidity. He would have ventured in Valkadia himself to retrieve the real necklace, but he was concerned the Valkadians would recognize him, in which case they may, just may, believe his stepbrother's tale and pursue him instead. Not that he feared they would succeed in arresting him, but nevertheless, it was a complication he desired to avoid.

"They'd better have it."

Thyran stepped to the rail to watch the boat pull in. The sorceress halted the boat so fast it launched Kyros over the edge and into the water. She laughed wildly as he clambered back on the boat completely drenched. Standing to his feet, he glared at her. "If you ever—"

He fell back in the boat as she formed a column out of the water that raised the boat in the air, up to the rail where Thyran awaited. Before Kyros regained his footing, she leapt out of the boat and onto the ship, where her kitten rushed to her feet, begging for attention. Pirates rushed to secure the boat so it would remain hoisted when the column of water sank back to its home.

Kyros climbed aboard then ran his hand through his matted hair. He glowered at the sorceress.

"Where is it?" Thyran asked, his gaze shifting from Kyros to the sorceress.

Dripping with water, Kyros pointed to the sorceress, who now wore a necklace.

There, on her chest, the gem glowed, emerald at first, then blue. Mystical red dots puffed into view and then vanished just as quickly. It was magical. It *had* to be the right one. But Thyran refused to take any chances.

"Give it to me."

The sorceress's smirk faded to a frown. She hesitated a moment, then surrendered the necklace to him. She sauntered over to Kyros and began drying him with her powers.

Thyran dug his hand into his jacket pocket, seized the locket, whose arrow had returned to its orange glow. The arrow pointed at the necklace Alcina gave him. Once again, the arrow morphed into a bright cyan color and pointed southeast to the Dragons' Castle.

Thyran's heartbeat returned to normal. "Well done."

Thyran caught a glimpse Cyril's hooked nose from the corner of his eye. "Captain," he said, "how can you be so sure? The arrow changed last time, and that gem was a fake."

"Because, Cyril, the other night, I had the hatchet fixed to my waist, and Jay must have had the real gem in his pocket. The locket responded because both artifacts were in such close proximity. That's why it returned to orange when we were far enough away from my brother."

"I see." Cyril examined the arrow. "So, shall we set sail for the castle?"

Thyran nodded. "Yes, right away."

While Cyril gave the crew the command to set sail,

Thyran examined the necklace Jay had given him. Despite having to deal with this detour, he was impressed with his stepbrother. Combat is always more thrilling when the other party has a brain.

"Nice move, Jay," he said quietly. He tossed the fake necklace overboard and watched it sink into the sea. "Kyros."

Kyros jerked his arm loose from Alcina's grip and walked to Thyran. "Yes, captain?"

Thyran stared at the sun-specked water. "How's my younger brother?"

"We left him near death. My guess is the Valkadians captured or killed him."

"Near death? You let him live?"

"Yes. We got the gem as you asked. He was in no condition to put up a fight, so we took the necklace and left."

Thyran smiled. "Ahh I see." He stepped closer to Kyros and punched him in the stomach, knocking him to the ground. The sorceress dashed towards him and beckoned a jet of water from the sea, but before she could strike him, Thyran drew one of his silver scimitars and flicked it against her neck. Her eyes faded to their normal color, the water plopped back to the ocean. She glared at him, though seemed afraid to move. Her kitten stood by her side, hissing viciously at him.

His blade pressed against the sorceress's neck, Thyran looked at Kyros, who was catching his breath. "I will not tolerate weakness aboard my ship."

Kyros glanced up, his arm by his side. "The objective was to obtain the gem, which we did."

"The objective was to obtain the gem and eliminate any threats. We needed my stepbrother to unlock the locket in Ashlen's Tomb, but since then, he has done nothing but impede our progress. You had a perfect opportunity to kill him, but you were soft."

Kyros breathed heavily, looking at his captain unblinkingly. "Forgive me, captain."

"You're one of my best, Kyros. Don't let weakness become a habit. And you," he regarded the sorceress, "if you ever threaten to harm me again, I'll slice your neck and make your precious sea your grave."

Thyran withdrew his blade and left the two to themselves. He wrapped the silver chain around the gem and secured it in his jacket pocket along with the locket.

The *Venator* started moving. Her canvas sails bent with the wind, bringing her near the mouth of the cove.

Thyran resented having to discipline Kyros. Kyros was one of his best men, and he had respect for him. But he would not tolerate stupidity. Oversights like that lead to disaster. It takes great strength to do the right thing. Valkadia and Eulia, they were being weak when they refused to send soldiers to save Selia...too concerned with themselves rather than others. When this was all over, if Kyros proved himself worthy, he may even replace Cyril with him.

Cyril...the man grew too suspicious of his actions. One day, Thyran would have to silence him.

The *Venator* drifted out of the cove into the open sea. "Captain!" Bruce shouted, pointing to the starboard side. "Ship approaching!"

Seeing an incoming ship, a merchant vessel, Thyran hopped up the stairs to the bridge and grabbed the spyglass from the pirate manning the wheel. Peering through the spyglass, Thyran read the ship's name, the *Gemline*, painted across its side. Shifting the spyglass up, he recognized Hector and his crew on deck preparing for battle. To the right, he saw his stepbrother, his arm around a woman with golden hair for support, walking across the deck. "Ever persistent, aren't you?" Thyran said softly.

Cyril stepped beside him and uncoiled his whip. "Your command, captain?"

Thyran collapsed the spyglass and tossed it back to the pirate manning the wheel. "My brother has a death wish. I suggest we grant it."

Hector's ship nosed through the water towards Thyran. Most of the crew rushed below deck to prepare the few cannons aboard the *Gemline*. Jay winced as Lyssa set him down on a barrel on deck. "You okay?" she asked.

He nodded. "Thank you." Despite his pain and the upcoming battle with his stepbrother, he wished he had the strength to whistle for her. Perhaps that childish desire would keep him strong enough to survive a bit longer.

Lyssa left to assist the rest in preparing while Ankin knelt in front of him and set his bag of surgical implements on the deck. "I'm going to apply some salve to your wounds here. It's going to sting a bit."

But when Ankin applied the medicine, Jay felt nothing. After Thyran beat him, Valkadian soldiers starved him, sea serpents bit him, and the King of the Gorgrim nearly killed him, the slight burning sensation from Ankin's salve felt like a dream. Jay even managed to release a weak laugh.

While Ankin dressed his wounds, Jay stared ahead at Thyran's ship. The ship was too far away for him to identify faces, but he knew Thyran was somewhere on deck. Jay scanned the deck of their own ship and saw everyone bustling around, making preparations for battle. He had seen everyone since his rescue, everyone except Karen.

"Where's Karen?" Jay asked.

Ankin's eyes fell to the floor. "She tried to kill Hector

the night you were captured."

Jay's eyes widened. "That's why he wasn't there...."

"Huh?"

Jay coughed. His throat burned. "He was supposed to be guarding the house while I got the necklace. When I came out, he wasn't there. It was just...Thyran."

"Ahh...." Ankin concentrated on cleaning Jay's wounds.

"Is that how he got the mark on his face?"

Ankin nodded. "She pulled a knife on him."

"Where is she now?"

"Down in the brig. Hector nearly killed her when Jenkins interfered, arguing she may be working for Thyran and is more useful to us alive."

Ankin finished wrapping the gray gauze over the bite marks in Jay's right foot and thigh and then stood up. "It's best you take it easy. Your body needs rest."

"Thank you, Ankin."

Jay watched him travel below deck. The wind died down. The sun took refuge behind a blanket of gray clouds. Jay gazed up ahead as they quickly approached Thyran's ship. The *Gemline* was small compared to the *Venator*. But since they could not outrun Thyran, fighting was their only chance.

Hector walked in front of him and was about to speak when Cain approached from behind and said,

"The cannons are ready, captain."

Hector looked off at Thyran's ship. "Good. We're nearly in range. Have the crew turn the *Gemline* to the starboard side and prepare to fire the cannons on my command."

Cain nodded. "Aye, captain." He limped off to the crew to deliver the orders.

"How are ye feeling?" Hector asked Jay.

"Alright." But Jay's mind wasn't focused on his pain. They were closing in on Thyran, who Jay knew was preparing some sort of surprise.

Jay motioned to the spyglass in Hector's hand. "Mind if I have a look?"

"Sure." Hector handed him the spyglass.

Jay peered through the device and saw Thyran's crew gathered along the rail. Standing firm. Not adjusting the sails, not preparing the cannons, not moving at all. Just...standing—standing and watching.

He moved the spyglass back and forth and stopped when he located Thyran, standing proud, with that devious grin on his face. He seemed just as unnerved as the rest of the crew, standing with his scimitars sheathed behind his back, his deep red jacket hanging still in the windless air, his hand resting on the rail.

Something was wrong.

"What are they doing?"

"Hmm?" Hector asked.

"They're just...standing there."

"Here, let me see."

Jay relinquished the spyglass.

What was Thyran scheming? Jay looked around. No other ships were positioned for an ambush. On the mountains, he didn't see any men preparing the launch catapults. And all around them, the water was calm.

The water.

Jay suddenly knew what Thyran was planning. His mind raced to think of a defense. Without him realizing it, the *Gemline* had already turned almost completely sideways, ready to fire. Only a few seconds more.

Cain called from the deck. "Captain, they're in

range."

Hector, still peering into the spyglass, shouted, "Fire!"

Boom!

The ship rocked to the side as the cannons fired. A surge of water shot up in front of Thyran's ship with such ferocity that a rampant wind swept the *Gemline* back, rocking it even further. The shield of water dropped down and pounded the cannonballs into the sea like a giant's mighty fist. Then another wall of water rose for the sky, spraying down upon Jay and the others.

All the crew stood mesmerized by the magical barrier. But Jay knew what was next.

"Grab on to something!" he cried. "It's coming right for us!"

The giant wall charged forward, spraying needles of water at the crew that stung like hail. They could do nothing but hold on and watch as the surging water collided with the *Gemline*, lashing violently at her wood and sails. And then came another wave, rocking her further on her side. And another. The force of the water was too much for Jay to hold onto the mast any longer. His fingers slipped, his body flew off the deck. His eyes were shut for protection from the lashing water, but he heard the creaking and snapping of wood as the *Gemline* buckled. Then all was silent as he collided with the sea and at last his consciousness slipped away.

22

Isis Canal

Everything was silent. No crashing of waves, no snapping of wood, no screaming of pirates. Silence. Jay moved his right leg; a sting of pain in the teeth marks in his thigh notified him that he survived.

He chanced opening his eyes, just a crack. Though everything was blurred as his vision adjusted, he realized he was lying on wood. Polished wood. It felt smooth and warm against his skin.

And then his ears slowly regained their ability to hear. He heard footsteps, some shouting. He recognized the voice—McClevin.

Jay coughed, spat out a mouthful of water. The inrush of cool air felt soothing inside his throat.

"He's awake!" Jay heard someone say.

"Lord love a duck, so he is."

Hands gripped around Jay's shoulders and waist and lifted him to his knees. The blurriness in his vision subsided; his temples pulsed with rage when he saw McClevin standing before him.

"I have captured you and your crew," he said. Jay glanced around and saw his crew, all awash, unarmed, on their knees, encircled by Eulian soldiers with long-barreled muskets.

Jay clenched his fists. McClevin had killed his best friend and now held his crew—his family—hostage.

"What do you want?" Jay said between clenched

teeth.

The man laughed. "What do I want...I don't think any man on this planet could give me that."

"You killed my best friend."

"He was a pirate."

"A good man."

"A thief."

"Soleus?" Delcato lunged forward, her black hair thrashing alongside her horrorstruck face. "You killed him?"

"Yes," Jay answered.

"Back on your knees!" McClevin ordered her. When the armed soldiers advanced, she reluctantly complied.

Jay glared at him. "Who are you?"

The man straightened his back. "Arthur McClevin, General of the Knights of Voorus."

Jay repeated his name and rank mentally. "I'll expose you for killing an unarmed prisoner."

McClevin rushed over to him, leaned down, gripped his shirt, twisted it before his neck, and dragged him up off his knees.

"You are in no position to make any threats, pirate!"

Jay spat in his face.

McClevin threw him to the ground and landed a kick in his side. Jay lost his breath.

"Stop this!" Lyssa screamed after McClevin kicked him again.

"Yeah, this isn't right!" Lynk said.

"Quiet or you'll be next," McClevin snapped.

Jay hacked, struggling to regain his breath. Gripping his side, he returned to his knees. He had to be strong. For Soleus.

McClevin stepped in front of Jay, his hand extended, palm up. "Give me the locket."

The locket. Jay cringed at the thought.

"Now!"

"I don't have it."

"Lies!"

"Weren't you watching back in the coliseum?"

"Give me the locket, now!"

"Are you that thick?"

The next blow made Jay fearful his jaw may have snapped—McClevin's fist rounded the side of his face, connecting with his lower jaw, sending him once again crashing to the wooden floor.

"Stop!" Lyssa screeched.

McClevin thundered away from him, and when Jay peered up, McClevin gripped Lyssa by her golden hair. Jay's insides tightened when McClevin kicked the back of her legs, causing them to buckle and bring her to her knees. McClevin drew his sword from his waist and held it firmly against her throat. Jay's crewmates snarled, some took a step forward to her aide, but the encircling guards closed in menacingly, holding their pistols steady.

"Don't touch her," Jay said.

"Then give me the locket."

"I told you! I don't have it!" Jay's rage started consuming his pain.

"Then so be it."

McClevin yanked back her hair, completely exposing her tender neck. He whipped his hand across her neck so the edge of the sword's hilt rubbed against her skin. One swipe, and the blade would cut through her neck, and she would suffocate until death.

Jay lunged forward, but, due to his fatigue, he moved little more than a foot before crashing back to his knees.

"Stop! I'm telling you the truth!"

"I'm no fool."

"This is murder!"

McClevin turned his back to Jay, planted his feet on the ground, preparing to strike. The blade quivered, resulting of McClevin's fury coursing through his hands. Lyssa was not crying, nor did she close her eyes. Her glossy green eyes gazed at Jay, but they were also eyes of strength, of courage. She was not afraid.

Jay held his breath. He was too weak to help, and anything he said, McClevin wouldn't believe anyways.

Then McClevin growled, swung his sword up, and stabbed it into the wooden floorboards. Fists clenched by his sides, McClevin approached Jay, but did not kick or punch him. Rather, he stepped by Jay's side and stopped. Jay felt the man's fury radiating from his body, but he did not care: Lyssa was alive.

"I did not kill Soleus," McClevin whispered, quiet enough so only Jay could hear.

Jay looked up at him, though he had to squint due to the sunlight.

"He escaped. Jumped off the ship and swam away. We never caught up with him."

Soleus is alive. Jay's eyes watered, his heart pounded faster.

"Why did you lie to me?"

"I was..." McClevin dropped his head, his eyes stared at the floor. His voice was no longer mean and threatening, but more gentle, like a soldier who had exhausted all his energy and strength and just longed for the battle to cease. "Your escapade in Eulia had many far-reaching consequences. Your actions have caused my king and his kingdom more grief than you can imagine."

Jay opened his mouth to defend himself, but his

throat swelled with guilt, making it difficult to speak. True, society was to blame for persecuting him for the murder of Governor Almsy. True, society was to blame for branding him an outcast. But he, and only he, was to blame for all his acts of thievery, especially the one in Eulia.

Jay closed his eyes, mentally flashing back to the day before the heist, when Captain Gaden offered him a chance to back out. Part of him had wanted to, but a larger part wanted to be accepted by the crew, be accepted as one of the family. Strong and courageous, not weak or cowardly. Acceptance. That's all he wanted. That's all he ever wanted...acceptance by his parents, acceptance by his stepbrother, Thyran, acceptance by a crew of pirates. For all his life, society had never accepted him, and that day, just before the Eulian mission, he was willing to sacrifice his innocence for that acceptance.

Only now did Jay realize truly how stupid he was. If one must prove oneself to his friends in order to be accepted, then they are not true friends to begin with. People get accepted by who they are inside, not by acting brave or courageous or giving into peer pressure. Because, if one sacrifices his morals and values for acceptance, then what does he have left?

"I..." Jay swallowed, delving for the right words, but then he realized he was again acting, trying to excuse his acts. Speaking from the heart is the very essence of living, of being who one truly is inside. No longer would he act, put on the mask of someone he longed to be. He would, for the first time in his life, be himself.

"I stole the diamond locket from your king that night. It was a heinous crime, and I deserve to be punished. I am deeply sorry for whatever grief I have forced upon you and your king, and I do not ask for forgiveness, for I know I am undeserving of that.

"More than anything, I wish to give back the diamond locket, to give back to your king what is rightfully his. But I do not have it, and I beg you to believe me. My stepbrother, Thyran Vilkus, stole it from us in the Dryfus Mines, and we have been pursuing him ever since."

"Thyran Vilkus?" McClevin repeated. "I thought you killed him?"

"I never killed Thyran or the governor. Thyran is alive, and he and his crew of pirates are sailing for the Dragons' Castle to obtain an artifact Ashlen hid there."

"The book..." McClevin mumbled.

"We must stop him before he reaches that tower. I don't know what Ashlen has hidden, or how powerful that artifact is, but with such power, he plans on destroying Valkadia and Eulia and claiming Lassar under his own rule. Please, McClevin, help me stop my stepbrother. Then you can take back the locket, and I will surrender myself to you."

Everyone seemed to be holding their breath, for there was not a sound, save for the creaking of wood as the ship rocked. Jay peered out in the distance for the first time since he awakened. The *Gemline* had sunk; splinters of wood floated where she made her last stand. The *Venator* was out of sight, already gaining distance on them towards the Dragons' Castle.

"Winston," McClevin said. "Fetch me some bandages."

Jay looked back at McClevin, who was focused on Jay's foot. The gauze Ankin secured over his wounds had been washed away, and blood now trickled out.

"Yes, sir!" Winston hurried below deck.

McClevin knelt down in front of Jay.

"You're sure of this?"

Jay nodded. "I swear it."

"Very well." McClevin rose to his feet and signaled to one of his soldiers with short, curly black hair. "Kileean. Set sail for the Dragons' Castle. We'll take the Icis Canal, so we should gain some time on Thyran and his crew." He looked at Jay. "Thank you for your honesty. I accept your offer. Though, from here on out, you and your crew are my prisoners. You will remained unarmed until we get to the Dragons' Castle. Any signs of aggression or escaping—"

"I understand," Jay said.

"Good. Then men, secure their weapons and lock their weapons below deck. I want soldiers stationed at all times to guard that room. It will take us seven days to reach the castle, so take that time to eat well and get some rest, for when we arrive, I don't think it'll be too long until we engage Thyran and his crew, if Jay's tale is even true."

The next few days proved relatively uneventful, a change Jay welcomed. Twice a day, he met with Ankin, who cleansed and dressed his wounds. Ankin prescribed so much steaming herbal tea that Jay thought the liquid was starting to burn through the tissue in his throat. But still, he couldn't argue that Ankin's medications were helping. His muscles weren't as sore, the wound in his hand was no longer yellow and filled with puss. His body still ached, but he could finally move around without stopping every few steps to let his pain subside.

Every night, Lynk and Blynk blessed the crew with their symphonies of the harmonica and drum or accordion—whichever Lynk was feeling up to at the time. Jenkins was ever prudent at challenging everyone, even the Eulian soldiers, to games of Elementum. He still remained undefeated, except to Cain.

Delcato had a bit more spring to her step since hearing the news of Soleus. Though still quiet, she smiled and laughed more than ever.

Jay had not seen Karen anywhere. He attributed her absence to her drowning as the ship sunk outside Valkadia. Though she nearly had him killed, he wanted to speak with her, to understand why she betrayed them.

Lyssa spent most nights by herself, leaning against the rail, staring at the moon-specked sea. Jay figured she must be thinking of her late mother, eager to finally avenge her death.

And Cain...was Cain. Quiet, secretive, grumpy, angered at the confiscation of his knives: he no longer had the tools necessary to finish the carvings on his staff. His mynx still had not returned since its departure in Selia.

On the fifth day since sailing from Valkadia, they approached a land mass, which Kileean had mentioned was the mouth of the Icis Canal. Under the bright, yellow sun, Jay saw mountainous land stretching endlessly across the horizon with a wide canal guiding through its heart. Two gray cylindrical towers stretched up from both sides of the canal's mouth; azura embroidered into the giant blue flags poking up from the towers fluttered in the breeze, marking the canal as Eulian territory.

Most of the soldiers and pirates gathered along the prow of the ship to watch. The ship nosed through the calm water, inching its way closer to the canal. McClevin, standing at the port side of the ship, hoisted a Eulian flag in the air and waved it slowly back and forth. When the ship was close to land, Jay saw cannons lining the rocky edge of the canal; a pair of Eulian soldiers accompanied each of the cannons.

One of the soldiers at the base of one of the towers

waved. "Good day, General McClevin! Beautiful day, isn't it?"

"Indeed it is, Alex," McClevin shouted back. "Has another ship passed through recently?"

Alex shook his head. "No, no vessel has passed through the canal in over a week. Just the longboats of the Agapo tribes."

"Very well. Keep a sharp eye on the horizon. We are tracking some pirates and suspect they may pass through here."

Alex raised his sword nobly. "Fear not, general! No pirate shall pass this post alive."

McClevin nodded to Alex. As the ship entered the canal, Jay stared in awe at the numerous cannons scattered across the lands with soldiers ardently patrolling the area. "Are there guards all along this canal?" he asked McClevin.

McClevin rolled up his flag. "Yes, though the rest are hidden. In case an enemy is strong enough to breach the entrance, the other soldiers will catch them by surprise."

"Then shouldn't we bring some of them with us?" Jay asked. "Thyran has many pirates under his command."

McClevin shook his head. "I need them to stay here. My king made a promise to protect the Agapo tribes. I am not about to break that promise."

"A promise?"

"The Icis Canal," Ankin said, stepping up beside Jay and resting his single hand on the upper rail, "was built by the will of King Emory's father, Albus, to protect the Agapo tribes."

Jay raised an eyebrow. "I thought they were all killed off."

"No," McClevin said. "That scum King Cornelius took all their land and tried to enslave them, viewing them as an inferior race. However, King Albus had an affinity for the primitive tribes and created a haven for them in the southern peninsula of the Yeru continent. He then built a canal the tribes could use for water and irrigation. He promised the Agapos he would protect them against any aggressions from Valkadia."

Jay noted all the cannons and soldiers mounted throughout the rocky terrain. Even with the sorceress controlling water, Thyran would have a difficult time immobilizing the Eulian soldiers. Rocks jetted out in strategic angles to guard the soldiers from cannonfire from passing ships and the stone towers were built out of the sides of steep hills, so they could not easily be knocked down.

"Why is it called the Icis Canal?" Jay asked.

"It leads right across the narrow strip of land to the sea just north of Island Gorsid," Ankin said.

"Which is where the Dragons' Castle is, right?"

Ankin nodded. "So, King Albus named it after the Queen of the Dragons, Icis."

McClevin regarded Ankin, clearly respecting the man's knowledge of his kingdom's history.

The *Liberáte* skimmed through the wide canal, past the final ranks of cannons. The rocky terrain gave way to grassy fields scattered with trees and ponds. The trees were magnificent. They had strong, burly branches that clawed through the air. Their leaves were splashed with vibrant colors of red, orange, and green, colors that glistened under the sun, giving them a mystic glow.

Women and children clad in simple, plain, cotton shorts and shirts and straw hats gathered on the grassy shore of the canal; they held wide shallow baskets filled with fruits and plants.

"Are those the Agapos?" Jay asked.

"Yes," McClevin said.

The Agapos took a break from their laboring to wipe their brows and look up at the passing ship. Smiling, they all waved. "Look! Look!" one of the kids shouted. "It's the Eulian soldiers!"

Soon, all the Agapos joined in waving and smiling at the passing ship, grateful for the protection the Eulian soldiers offered. Jay found it beautiful, the peaceful, powerful relationship the Agapos shared with Eulia. Such potent love, like that of the flocks of azura laughing together in the sky. Understanding the immense generosity of the Eulians, Jay wondered how he could have ever stolen the diamond locket from such an altruistic kingdom.

Jay waved back at them and returned their smiles. "Are there many of them still alive?"

McClevin turned to Jay, his leather cuirass stretching as he did so. "Agapos? Lord love a duck! There are more of them than Eulian citizens. They're so peaceful ...wouldn't harm a fish without good reason. And the land, they love the land. I can only imagine what they would think if they saw Valkadia. Ha! The only sign of plantlife there is outside that maggot's castle."

Jay lost himself in admiration of the Agapos. He saw a group of males armed with wooden spears in the distance. Probably hunting for food.

"It should take us a day and a half to get through the Icis Canal, then we should be less than a day away from Island Gorsid," McClevin said, backing away from the rail.

Jay nodded and continued watching the Agapos. They were so peaceful with the way they handled the land. The very sight of them relaxed Jay. So soothing. Even more so than Ankin's herbal tea.

"Hey look," Ankin said, pointing to the sky. "It's

Cain's mynx."

Jay looked up and saw the mynx, silhouetted by the sun, swooping down towards them. A single azura flew overhead, which Jay found odd; they typically flew in groups. The mynx flew directly for Cain and landed on his shoulder. It grappled the edge of Cain's tapered black beard and tugged playfully.

"It was gone for a while," Jay said.

"Yeah," Ankin said. "The longest it's ever been away from him. Well," he pushed off the rail, "I'm going to head down below for a nap. I'll see you tonight for another treatment?"

Jay nodded.

Ankin smiled. "Alright. Take care, Jay."

"You too."

As Ankin left, Jay noticed Lyssa at the bow of the ship, kneeling down with her back to him, her golden hair falling past her shoulders. She was working on something, but as to what, Jay did not know. Curious, he treaded across the deck to her.

When he was a few paces away, he saw her tying a small rock to a strange weapon: two curved, crimson-painted scimitars connected at their hilts, their arcing blades bending through the air in the shape of an 'S.'

"What's that?" Jay asked.

She yanked on the string to ensure the rock was secure around the hilt, then she grabbed the fused center of the scimitars and rose to her feet.

"Isn't it beautiful? This weapon...deadly as an ax, swift as a knife." She twirled it through the air as she used to twirl her bow.

The weapon did indeed look magnificent—webs of fine black lines coursed along the blades creating intricate patterns whose illustrations were up to the viewers' imagination. He himself could never wield such a weapon—its wide curves and long form would prove difficult to handle.

"Where did you find it?"

"Below deck in one of the rooms. I saw a guard stow it away."

Jay glanced over his shoulder, making sure no soldiers were nearby. McClevin had mandated they not bear weapons until they reached the Dragons' Castle. Confident no one was near, he turned back to her.

Sunlight poured over her dark purple corset, making it appear bright compared to her black pants. She wore a shallow grin as her green eyes admired her weapon.

"What's that?" Jay asked, pointing to the stone she tied to the weapon.

"It's a fossil, one my mother gave me when I was young." She ran her finger across its surface. "I collected them as a child. I would spend days digging in the ground, searching the beach for the most unique fossils. My mom found this fossil one day when planting in her garden. Look." She held it up for Jay to examine. "Two worms, petrified together. It looks like they died cuddling up against one another."

Jay made out the sharp image of two worms curled together like a woman cuddling her child. "That's so...detailed," he said. "Do you have many more?"

Lyssa shook her head. "I've lost most of them over time. This is all I have left. One day, I'll rebuild my collection." Her eyes shifted from the fossil to him. "What about you? Collect anything as a child?"

Jay watched the blur of red and black whip through the air in front of him; it was amazing at how fast she could spin those blades. "Well, I used to read a lot of books."

"Books? What kind?"

"All kinds. Though, my favorite were books on fighting and psychology."

"Fighting and psychology? Those are two very different subjects."

"Not necessarily. Sometimes, understanding your opponent proves invaluable in combat." Jay lowered his eyes. "I found psychology books fascinating because they helped me understand people and how they think. And for the fighting books...well, Thyran was flawless in combat. Every time we dueled, he won. He even beat most adults in combat.

"I wanted to outdo him. It was a personal goal of mine. So, I read books on fighting, trying to find some secret move or ability to beat him."

"Did you find anything?"

"No, nothing. He's too brilliant. Since I've known him, he's always outwitted anyone who steps in his way. I'm not so sure even McClevin and his soldiers can stop him...." His voice trailed off, and he felt himself sinking back into that black pit of despair with that flickering candle of hope nearly expired.

Sensing his anxiety, Lyssa smiled and shook her head. "Hey now, don't get yourself down about it. You never know how the flower will blossom."

Jay smiled and looked up. "Heh, yeah, I guess you're right. Especially with that new weapon of yours, he'll be in for a surprise or two."

"Ha! You got that right." Another blur of red and black, and Lyssa struck down her invisible foe.

Jay's legs felt weary, still sore from Valkadia. He stepped to the rail and sat down, leaning his back against the wooden bars. A small flock of azura flew overhead. The

warm sun baking his skin and the sound of the azura singing in the distance, he closed his eyes and tilted back his
head, soaking in the tranquility.

Staring at the orange glow on the inside of his eyelids,
Jay remembered his dream in Valkadia. He moistened his
lips, inhaled a slow, steady breath, scrunched his lips to
form a tiny hole, and gently blew.

A tingling sensation exploded through his body as a
sweet whistle drifted out of his mouth and fluttered in the
air to join the singing of the azura in the sky. Even with his
eyes closed, he felt her gaze upon him. His heart echoing in
his ears, he blew slightly harder, just a tad, but enough to
enlarge the wings of his sweet, fluttering whistle.

Amid his whistling, Lyssa said, "Well well...I'm impressed, Little Blue."

He opened his eyes and saw her seating herself beside
him, smiling with approval. "Well, I didn't have much else
to do locked up in Valkadia. They don't provide much in the
form of entertainment."

She chuckled and shook her head. "Yeah, I can imagine."

The next several hours passed by like minutes. Jay
was so absorbed in conversation with Lyssa that he hardly
noticed the sun beginning to set. He listened to stories of her
youth, told some of his own, laughed at their less-than-
brilliant acts in the past, and simply relaxed. Once, some
guards approached and tried to confiscate Lyssa's weapon,
but after she demonstrated its power and swiftness, they
soon reconsidered.

Under the dark purple afterglow when the sun had
set, the two were engaged in a vicious game of thumb war.

"You can't bend your wrist like that!" Lyssa shouted.
"You need to keep it straight!"

Feeling her nails dig into his palm, Jay straightened his wrist. Both on their knees, she remained calm and still, but he decided to play much more aggressively. He swung his thumb around hers—he caught the edge of her thumb and pinned it down.

"One...two...three...."

She plowed her shoulder into his chest and knocked him to the ground. Pinning his arm and wrist down with her knee, she wrapped her thumb around his and slapped it down. Four seconds later, she was the victor.

"Aha!" she laughed, throwing her fist in the air victoriously.

"Ugh..." Jay rubbed his wrist. "I'm not so sure that fell within the rules."

"Haha, whatever," Lyssa said. "So, you have any other games?"

"Hmm..." Jay shook his wrist in the air, hoping to resume the circulation of blood to his fingers. "Well, Soleus and I used to skip rocks over the water and see whose went the farthest. Nothing too original, but—"

"I used to do that too! My mother taught me when I was younger." Her eyes darted across the deck. "Those will do."

Jay watched her stand up and walk over to a wooden crate which had three ceramic plates from when some soldiers took a few minutes reprieve. She returned to the rail and tilted the plates over so the crumbs dropped down to the sea for the fish.

Lyssa jerked her head to fling her hair back behind her shoulders. "Alright, you go first."

"Plates? I'm not sure how well those will skip."

"Oh, quit complaining!"

"Alright, alright." Jay backed away from the rail and

gripped a plate with his right hand. He took a breath, focused on the water, and prepared to charge forward when she stepped in his way.

"Whoa, easy there Little Blue!" she said, stifling her laughter.

Jay looked at her, confused.

"Let's spice it up. I'm going to spin you around first."

Jay rolled his eyes and allowed her to spin him around, once, twice, thrice, up to ten times. The purple clouds, wooden rail, and dark sea swirled in his head, causing him to wobble.

"Alright, now throw it."

Jay's run felt more like a stumble to the rail, but he made it and lofted the plate through the air. It bounced once in the water before settling a few feet farther. It quickly vanished under the shadows of night.

"Your turn," Jay said, stepping away from the rail.

When she was in position, Jay whirled her around ten times and then stepped back and leaned against the rail. "Whenever you're ready."

Lightly giggling, she stumbled this way and that, trying to catch her balance. Then she straightened her back, lifted the plate, charged for the rail, and thwacked Jay in the head with the plate as she tried to throw it.

The blow temporarily dazed him; all he saw were bright, varicolored spots. Moaning, he massaged his head where the plate had struck.

"Oh, I'm so sorry!" Lyssa threw her hands over her mouth. Probably to hold back her laughter. "Are you okay?"

His brain still rattled around in his head. "Geeze," he said, grinning. "First you smash my wrist in the thumb war, and now you smack me upside the head with a plate. You're beginning to turn into your father."

Even in his giddy mood, Jay realized he was out of line. Lyssa's smile at once vanished into a frown, her eyes fell to the floor. He even felt her haunting memories bombarding her from all sides, forcing her to envision her abusive father.

"I-I'm sorry. That was out of line."

Her green eyes turned glossy; a tear departed from the left. She picked up her weapon that leaned against the rail, looked at him for a moment, then hurried away without a word.

Jay didn't blame her—he knew her past haunted her. Her cruel father had scarred her so deeply that any mention of him would inflict internal pain. What was he thinking bringing that up? Stupid. Stupid stupid.

Cursing himself, Jay walked back towards mid-deck. Lynk and Blynk were playing the accordion and harmonica, Jenkins was playing a game of Elementum against Delcato, and the rest were gathered around, talking. Jay had promised to meet up with Ankin that night, but he was not in the mood.

A few steps from the door leading below deck, Jay heard Cain's voice.

"Jay."

He turned around. Cain was limping towards him, his mynx on his shoulder.

"Yes?"

"Where are you going?"

"I'm heading down to sleep."

"Very well. Get some rest. We should be there soon."

Odd. Jay looked into Cain's hooded eyes curiously a moment, but his mind was too preoccupied to try and understand him. "Thanks," he said and departed below deck.

The only lighting in the room was the purple glow

from the horizon shining through the window he locked before tucking himself in. The thin cotton sheets didn't offer much in terms of warmth or comfort, similar to his bed in Morad. But his mind was elsewhere to pay much attention to physical comfort. *You're beginning to turn into your father.* Over and over, he repeated that line in his mind, wishing he could jump back in time and change it. Never again would he say such a stupid thing. Never again....

White light. A flash of pain. Jay flung himself up in a sitting position gripping his forehead, which burned like hot iron embedded into his flesh. His vision blurred due to his quick awakening. He had been asleep, but he was unsure how long. Pallid moonlight had replaced the purple glow in his room.

He heard a noise. A creaking noise. The blurriness subsided slightly, and he made a shadow stepping outside his room and slamming the door shut.

Someone had been in his room.

He removed his right hand from his burning forehead, expecting to support himself on the bed so he could roll off, but his fingers did not feel the cotton sheets. He felt smooth feathers. His eyes adjusted further, and he gasped when he saw an azura perched on the edge of his bed, its black, beady eyes gazing at him.

The bird was calm, not fearful of his presence. How had the bird gotten in? The window was locked, but someone had entered his room. Did he bring in the bird? Why was it so tame? It was just...sitting there, gazing at him. He had never before been so close to an azura. He was delighted and suspicious at the same time.

There was a scream. From across the hall. A woman's scream.

Lyssa.

Jay leapt off his bed. The bird fluttered up, struggling to gain altitude, but the low ceiling impeded it. Withoug thinking, Jay unlocked the window and flung it open. The azura took off, soaring free into the black sky.

Jay hurried to the door. His forehead still burning, his head still pounding, he swung the door open and rushed into the narrow hallway.

Jenkins, Lynk, and Blynk were gathered outside Lyssa's room. His heart hammering inside his chest, Jay pushed his way through them and peered inside.

He first saw Delcato, her face white as a ghost, trembling in her bed. Lyssa was beside her, running her hand through her black hair. "Shh..." she said. "You're alright. It was just a dream."

"The tattoo!" Delcato screamed. "My father—where is he?—I saw it—the tattoo—I know—Soleus, where are you?"

"Shh..." Lyssa repeated. She wrapped her arms around the delirious Delcato. "You're going to be alright. Just breathe."

Delcato's black hair stuck to her moist face. Her head shifted frantically around the room as if she suspected her father's killer to be lurking in the shadows. "He killed him. Shot him right in front of me."

"What's going on down here?" McClevin's voice boomed through the hallway. The pirates stepped aside when McClevin, wearing his white cotton sleeping attire, reached the door. "What happened?"

"She had a nightmare," Jay said.

"A nightmare?" McClevin asked doubtingly.

"Yes," Jenkins said. "Her father was killed right in front of her when she was young. She frequently has nightmares of his death."

"Who killed him?"

"We don't know," said Lynk. "She remembers her father's assassin wearing a Valkadian uniform and a tattoo on his shoulder, but that's it."

"Is she going to be alright?" McClevin asked.

"She'll be fine," Lynk said. "Lyssa's doing a good job calming her down."

McClevin nodded. "Alright." Then, without another word, he walked down the hall to the stairs and retired to his room.

"I feel bad for her," Lynk said when McClevin left. "Those nightmares appear to be getting worse and worse."

"Yeah," Jay said. "She needs some closure or those nightmares will drive her mad."

"Hopefully we'll find that bloody assassin," Jenkins said through clenched teeth. "I'd love to introduce that man to my blade."

"Is there anything we can do?" Blynk asked Lyssa.

She shook her head. "No, she just needs to calm down. You all should get back to bed. She'll be fine."

"Alright bro, let's head back to our room," Lynk said. "Let us know if you need anything."

"I will," Lyssa said. "Thanks."

Jenkins, Lynk, and Blynk all retreated to their rooms, leaving Jay by himself. He watched the two of them. Two women, both who've had such a rough childhood. Both tormented by the past. Both so strong, taking each day at a time, not letting their past interfere with the present. Perhaps he should do the same.

Come noontide two days later, Jay took his usual position on the ship—his hands wrapped around the rail, his eyes admiring the sea, his hair blowing in the breeze. His forehead had finally ceased burning after two days of replaying that night repeatedly in his mind: the intruder in his room, the strange azura, Delcato's screaming....

But though his head was drowning in those thoughts of confusion, only one thing shined brightly in his mind at that moment—Thyran.

Any time now, they would arrive at Island Gorsid, where they would soon clash with Thyran and his crew. Jay was ready, ready to encounter his stepbrother at last, to confront him after running for four years.

"I'm ready, brother," Jay said.

He closed his eyes and rested his forehead on the smooth wooden rail. He cleared his mind and concentrated on his surroundings: the whistling of the wind, the smell of fresh seawater in the air, the sweet taste of pineapple in his mouth, the polished wood against his forehead, the vision of his stepbrother emblazoned on the backs of his eyelids. Thyran taught him to clear his mind before every battle, to focus on his surroundings. Every movement, every sound, every sight, every feeling was important in battle. Jay absorbed the nature around him and sunk into a sedated state until he heard the calling of a Eulian soldier,

"Straight ahead, it's in sight! The Dragons' Castle!"

23

A Cloudless Rain

Jay's eyes opened.

A wide stretch of land in the distance with thick mountains poking up to the cloudless sky. Flocks of birds circling the tall, massive trees guarding the mountain bases. Further into the land, just visible between the mountain peaks, the massive black walls of the Dragons' Castle. They had reached their destination.

"Bring her closer to land and then we'll lower the boats!" McClevin's voice boomed across the deck. "Everyone, secure your arms and grab the ladders."

Ladders? Why did they need ladders?

"Me crew be needing weapons as well," Hector said to McClevin.

"Don't forget, you are still my prisoners."

"How do ye expect us to defeat Thyran and his crew without weapons?"

McClevin rolled his eyes. "Lord love a duck. Winston!"

Winston, the short, stout soldier, stumbled over to the general, pushing his silver helmet above his eyes. "Y-Yes general?"

"See to it that these pirates get some weapons." McClevin stepped closer to Hector. "Any attempts to harm me or any of my soldiers, and I'll put a musket ball through your heart. Understood?"

"Don't worry, general. One enemy at a time."

Winston led Jay and the crew below deck to return their confiscated weapons. Once armed, everyone boarded the boats and rowed ashore. The landscape reminded Jay of Storm Isle: barren, dead, robbed of all color. When they landed ashore, they trudged through the damp soil and weaved between the mountains.

After clearing the mountains, Jay heard something crunch beneath his foot. He gasped when he realized he had stepped on a human skull. He looked around. Strewn across the flat terrain of dark soil were small specks of white—bones protruding from the ground. Spearheads, swords, and other rusty weapons also littered the soil—remnants of a battle fought long ago.

The scenery dampened their moods; no one spoke as they approached the side of the Dragons' Castle.

The black castle spread over nearly two hundred acres of land with its backside protected by the jagged mountains. Jay's eyes traveled up its mighty stone walls that stretched nearly ten stories high. Atop the walls were enormous, round parapets. Much larger than necessary for any human.

"What's that?" Jay asked, pointing to two mountain-tops off in the distance. Fixed at the apex of each mountain were four giant iron rings in front of a single small one making a total of ten rings with three hundred yards between the two groups of five.

"I'm not sure," Ankin said. "It looks like a game of some sort."

"Who would be playing games on the top of two bloody mountains?"

"Dragons," Cain said to Jenkins, though he had not even glanced up at the rings.

"Here's the entrance," McClevin said.

They skirted around the edge of the castle wall to the front, where a portion of the wall was blown away, leaving a gaping V-shaped crevice they could walk through.

"Where's the castle door?" Jay asked.

"This castle used to be the home of the dragons," Ankin said. "Why would they need doors to enter their castle?"

"Then what created the rift?"

"War, mate," Hector said, stepping past the two of them, closer to the threshold.

Jay stole a moment to examine the castle. Staring at the castle's intimidating black walls, he felt apprehensive about setting foot inside it. Off to the right, he noticed a small, blue lake. The surrounding land was calm and quiet. Nothing moved. No sign of any life other than the occasional trees. It felt eerie.

Lynk clasped his hands and nudged his brother. "Well bro, I dunno about you, but I'm sick of standing here."

"Let's do it." Blynk said.

Lynk and Blynk climbed through the threshold into the castle. After absorbing one final glimpse of the environment, Jay followed them.

Inside, the vast walls surrounded an open yard of fertilized dirt and dried leaves blown inside the castle. An inner and outer wall connected with a flat wall top lined the perimeter. The inner wall had wide arching thresholds, large enough for even the largest gorgrim to fit through. The thresholds led to a shady area underneath the wall top. Around the arches, green vines crawled along the walls from top to bottom like scrambled spider webs.

Straight ahead at the back of the castle, a single round tower poked up into the sky several stories above its neighboring walls. The outside of the tower was bare stone, save for some wide, glassless windows lining its zenith. On both sides of the tower, along the back wall, Jay counted ten giant alcoves of stone protruding from near the top of the wall, but there were no stairs nor ladders leading up to them.

"What are those?" Jay asked.

"Those?" Ankin pointed to the alcoves. "Those were the chambers of the ten Dragon Lords. Those two large ones in the center were for the Emperor and Empress: Snowball and Icis."

Jay examined the chambers. They were huge. Dragons had been extinct for three hundred years, so he had never seen one. He wondered if they were beautiful and majestic like azura, or fearsome and cruel like gorgrim.

When they were halfway through the open yard, McClevin spun around and halted, waiting for everyone to fall in line. Yellow sunlight glistened off his silver breastplates and blue-crested helmet; his pistol and sword rested at his waist. When everyone gathered in front of him, he unsheathed his sword and stabbed it into the moist ground.

McClevin looked at Jay. "Where is it?"

Jay thought, but then Lyssa spoke. "Up there, in the tower."

McClevin regarded the tower a minute, then he looked at his soldiers.

"Alright men. We must defend this castle against Thyran and his pirates. Their target," he pointed to a window atop the black tower, "is in that room. Jay, you will accompany me and some of my men to verify that that is indeed Thyran's target. The rest of you, raise the ladders and assemble our fortifications. We must keep a lookout during all hours of the day. And you pirates, you're under the command of Kileean and Winston. I expect your full cooperation in this operation."

Kileean and Winston stepped beside McClevin and turned to face the pirates and soldiers.

McClevin straightened his back. "Men, keep a weather eye. If Thyran took the route I think he did, he should be here in less than a day. Now, let's move!"

All the soldiers raised their right hand to their hearts and gave a quick shout from their guts—a shout of allegiance, of eagerness to defend their kingdom.

McClevin parted for the tower. Following the Eulian general, Jay glanced back at Lyssa, who, with her double-bladed crimson scimitars in her right hand, followed the soldiers to the far wall.

"You're sure this is where your brother is heading?" McClevin asked.

Jay nodded and looked on ahead. "He believes in the legend, believes Ashlen has some artifact in the top of that tower."

"I've never set eyes on it," McClevin said. "A man in Morad explained the legend of Dragons' End to me, but he did not know exactly what was up there."

Jay looked up at him. "Why were you in Morad?"

"Tracking you down."

The words wrenched Jay's stomach, making him queasy. "Oh."

When they reached the tower, McClevin signaled the soldiers to lay the ladders together on the ground. "We'll need three ladders bound together," he said. "Fetch some of those vines off the wall. We can use them as rope."

The soldiers dashed to the wall, chopped off long segments of vine, and dragged them back to the ladders. Using their blades, they carved holes into the wooden ladder tops and bottoms and threaded the green vines through. Fastening sturdy knots around each loop, they bound the three ladders together.

"Are you sure the vines will hold?" Jay asked.

Snatching a piece of vine from the ground, McClevin yanked on the ends trying to sever it, but the strong plant remained whole. "It'll be fine. Raise the ladder!"

A group of the blue-uniformed soldiers gathered around the wooden ladders and, all in unison, lifted the heavy structure in the air and propped it against the tower; the tips of the ladder pressed against the stone a few feet above one of the windows.

McClevin approached the ladder. "Stay close behind."

The ladder wobbled as they ascended up the tower. The soldiers down below firmly held the base of the ladder to prevent it from sliding. Midway up, Jay decided he liked this far better than scaling walls by rope as he did in Eulia.

Jay hopped through the windowsill into the room atop the tower. The thud from his feet greeting the ground echoed throughout the circular room. Jay's eyes quickly focused to the only object in the room—a basin in the center resting on a curved stone pedestal. An aura of green light glimmered from the large basin. Transfixed on the light, Jay treaded across the stone floor.

Carvings of the ten dragons and the great wizard Ashlen, his cloak billowing behind him, his staff raised in the air, decorated the outside of the stone basin. A tiny sliver of transparent crystal spread atop the basin. When he reached the basin, he gazed inside. Beneath the crystal, bright, yellow-green liquid swirled around like a funnel cloud. Jay pressed his slender fingers on the smooth crystal; he felt a strange sensation. He sensed a mystical power raging inside the basin: his fingertips felt hot and cold at the same time—they throbbed with pain yet the feeling was soothing. Running his fingertips over the crystal, he touched a raised relief in the center. He mentally recited the end of the riddle:

> *In the basin the rock must rest*
> *Disturbed only by the blade*
> *Will the power unleash*
> *His powers thou will absorb*

Suddenly, Jay realized the purpose of the raised ovular structure: its shape perfectly matched that of the gem in the necklace he stole from Claudia's grandmother. The blade...Ashlen's Hatchet, from Storm Isle. The hatchet would shatter the crystal. And the yellow-green swirling liquid inside....

Jay swallowed. His fingers trembled. There was no artifact waiting here. Ashlen had never created any powerful device. He had sealed his own magical power in this basin and guarded it with the Dragon Lords so it would remain forever sealed. Someone, whoever wrote *Dragons' End*, somehow knew the only way to unleash it, and Thyran, due to his avid reading, had stumbled across that information.

Thyran would not possess any powerful artifact. *He himself would absorb the power of Ashlen, the great wizard who created the planet.* An icy current washed through Jay's face; he felt himself turn pale.

"Well?" McClevin said, his round eyes on Jay.

Running his fingers inside the ovular crevice in the crystal, Jay said, "Yes, he's coming for this."

"Excellent." McClevin turned away from the basin to a group of his soldiers who stood at attention. "Men, we must defend this room at all costs."

Jay's eyes left the basin and examined the room. Due

to the room's inadequate lighting, blackness covered the edges where the wall met the floor. Three arched windows lined the wall; they had climbed through the middle one. He walked to the window on the far left. Peering through it, he saw a vast stretch of land in the distance, mostly flat with scattered clumps of massive trees. Beside the castle, he recognized the small lake. A few birds circled the blue sky as the sun began its descent. The soldiers down below flung their ladders, bound with green vines, against the wall top; soldiers and pirates ascended the ladders to take watch behind the round parapets lining the castle. Two stories beneath him, a wall top led straight into the side of the tower. Jay stood a moment and pondered.

"Jay?" McClevin asked from the center of the room. "Something wrong?"

Finishing his thought, Jay turned back to the soldiers. "I have an idea."

The sun had set, leaving that familiar purple glow in the horizon. Some soldiers and pirates stood watch on the ramparts while the others rested in the courtyard. Jay, Jenkins, and Delcato wandered through the dark corridors underneath the wall tops between the inner and outer walls. Their faces faded in and out of the purple glow as they passed through the arching thresholds segmented throughout the inner wall.

"Here's one." Delcato knelt down and lifted a fossil from the soil. Holding it under the light, she said, "It looks like a scorpion."

Jay stood beside her and examined the fossil. "Yeah, that's a good one." He turned to Jenkins. "Jenkins, here's another."

"Hold on a bloody moment, I'm trying to finish this

one." Kneeling on the ground, Jenkins finished carving a tiny hole in another fossil they had collected previously. "Alright, let me see it." Delcato tossed the flat fossil to Jenkins, who immediately began prodding at it with his sharp knife. His white lock pick necklace dangled from his neck as he leaned over, concentrating on his work.

"How many is that?" Delcato asked.

Jay counted on his wounded left hand, which no longer pained him, but Ankin still recommended he keep it wrapped in gauze. "Seven. Let's find three more."

While Jenkins carved a hole in the top of the scorpion fossil, Jay and Delcato delved the soil. After a few minutes of searching, Delcato asked, "Do you think he's okay?"

"I'm sure he is, Del. Soleus is strongest man I know. He's probably in some tavern stuffing his face with chicken or fresh gorgrim and downing a few tots of rum."

They both giggled as they envisioned the gluttonous pirate feasting on his food with juices dripping down his round cheeks.

"I feel bad," Delcato said. "I haven't exactly been the nicest person to him, but he has always went out of his way for me. I just hope we see him again."

Jay discovered another rock in the soil and examined it. "Of course we will. When all this is over, I'm sure Captain Hector will begin the search for Soleus. Everyone in the crew misses him. He always managed to lift everyone's mood."

"Heh," she grinned. "What about you? Are you really going to turn yourself in when this is over?"

The rock was indeed a fossil, one appearing to be the jaw of a small fish. Jay pocketed it. "I need to. I can't go on running all my life."

Delcato scooped up a small, flat rock, but after examination, tossed it to the side. She brushed her black hair behind her ear and looked at Jay. "Know that no matter what, we'll protect you, Little Blue. We all know you didn't kill Governor Almsy, and we'll make sure the rest of the world knows that as well."

Jay smiled. The thought of turning himself in wasn't as troubling to him as he expected; he almost longed for it, to finally stop running.

"Thanks Del. I appreciate it."

"Any more fossils, or can I finally take my nap?" Jenkins asked from a few yards away.

Jay lobbed his fossil over to Jenkins. "We need two more."

Jay and Delcato continued talking as they discovered two more fossils partly buried in the ground, one of a winged insect and the other of a pointed tooth of some creature, maybe a dragon. "That's all," Jay said, handing them to Jenkins.

"Now we need some kind of string," Delcato said, glancing around.

Jay pointed to a thin piece of vine coursing up the wall. "We can probably strip a small sliver off that. You think that'll work Jenkins?"

"How am I suppose to know? Bring some over here, and we'll find out."

Walking to the vine, Delcato whispered to Jay, "Is it just me, or does he seem a bit grumpy?"

Jay looked at Jenkins over his shoulder. The man's knee trembled, his slender fingers frantically twirled his white lock pick. "He's probably nervous. He does better with covert operations than direct combat."

"Yeah, it's probably just nerves." Delcato grabbed a green vine fastened to the black castle wall while Jay used his cutlass to peel off thin strips from the thick stalk. The atmosphere dimmed as the horizon's purple glow began to wither.

The strips of vine fell to the soil and curled up like a snake. Jay picked up three strips he thought were thick enough to hold the fossils together. "How are you holding up?" he asked Delcato. "I know you had another nightmare on the ship a couple nights ago."

When Jay looked back at Delcato, her eyes stared at the ground. "I'm fine," she said. "I had a dream that both my father and Soleus were killed, and it seemed so real. Lyssa helped me through the night though." Her eyes shifted up. "I'm better now."

"That's good," Jay said softly. "If you ever need anyone to talk to, I'm here."

She smiled and nodded. "I know. Thanks Jay."

By the time they reached Jenkins, he had finished carving small holes in the final two fossils. Jay handed him the three strips of vine. "These will do," he said, curling and licking the tips of the green vines and threading them through the ten fossils. After trimming off the excess length, he tied a tight knot and presented the finished product to Jay. "All set."

Lined with ten unique fossils, all different shapes and sizes, yet all with smooth undersides, the bracelet appeared just big enough to fit around a wrist. A wide smile spread across Jay's lips. "This'll be perfect. Thank you."

"All in a day's work," Jenkins said twirling his knife in the air before stowing it in his leg strap above his ankle. "But, I'm going to take a bloody nap before my sentry duty."

"Yeah, me too," Delcato agreed.

"Aye, I should as well."

Jay tucked the fossil bracelet in his pocket and joined the other two for a few hours of sleep.

He never managed to fall into a deep sleep. Visions of Thyran and his crew marching towards the castle made the night seem all the more chilly and dreary. He tossed and turned over the cold ground, trying to find a comfortable position, but it was useless. He finally gave up the struggle and lay on his back staring at the vault created by the arch in the inner castle wall.

Jay lost track of how long he had been resting, though he knew dawn had to be approaching soon. He heard footsteps and turned his head to see Lynk wearily walking towards him, fatigued from lack of sleep.

"Lil' Blue, you're up."

Jay's eyes stung with sleepiness, but he nevertheless stumbled to his feet.

"Where were you stationed?"

"Over there, by the lake." Lynk pointed to the eastern wall.

"Alright, thanks. Get some rest."

Lynk collapsed on the ground and was asleep before Jay exited the shady area beneath the wall top.

A damp breeze swept over his skin. Up ahead, Kileean was delivering orders to three soldiers. Jay walked away from him, towards the ladder leading up to the eastern wall.

Before he reached the ladder, he glanced left to the tower. Due to the darkness, a faint glimmer of greenish-yellow light was visible from the tower windows. In the night, that tower served as a beacon to guide Thyran directly to the castle.

When he reached the ladder, Hector jogged up beside him. "Lil' Blue, I know you didn't sleep well last night and must be tired. Why don't ye go over to the front wall, then yeh'll have Cain for company to keep you up. I'll take yer watch here."

Jay looked up. The wall was empty. Since the only thing opposite the wall were mountains and a lake, McClevin must not have deemed it necessary to station many guards there. The front wall was much more populated. Jay recognized Cain at once due to his third leg.

"Alright," Jay said. "Thanks cap'n."

Smiling, Hector patted him on the back. "Anything for me crew."

Jay strolled through the courtyard to the front wall and climbed the ladder up to the round parapet where Cain stood watch. As usual, he was not sure what to say at first; it was always awkward starting a conversation with Cain.

Leaning against one of the round elevations on the wall top, Cain propped his wooden staff beside him and breathed deeply. "You look tired."

Jay stepped between two round elevations to view the moonlit land. "I didn't sleep well."

"Anxious?" A crisp breeze caused Cain's black jacket to flap back against the wall. "You should learn how to manage your fears. Never let them get the best of you."

"I'm not afraid," Jay said. "At least, I don't think I am. It's just...now that I know I finally have to confront my brother, everything feels like it's moving so fast, like the world is rushing by me."

"Your mind is playing tricks on you."

"Maybe, but I'm still concerned. I feel like this is all just another one of Thyran's traps, like he expected us to be here, like this was part of his plan."

"Perhaps."

"Doesn't that concern you?"

"There's not much I can do about it, is there?"

Jay pondered Cain's response. "Well, I guess not."

Cain regarded him for a moment. "You are very wise for such a young age. You have no need to fear."

Cain's praise warmed Jay's skin. "Thanks. I feel more comfortable knowing you're fighting on our side."

Cain stroked his mynx on his shoulder. "Jay, you need more confidence in your own abilities. You can't go through life depending on others. Live strong. If your life is constantly plagued with regrets or doubts or insecurities, then you're not living. You'll never beat Thyran until you gain a strong sense of confidence."

Cain's words further increased Jay's admiration for him. The man was right: he needed to be confident. Courageous. Just as he had been when fighting Kreios. Had he been weak and full of self-pity, the gorgrim would have ripped him to shreds. He needed to utilize that strength now.

As Jay thought, a light spray of cooling rain splattered on his forehead. Seconds later, the rain came down faster, harder.

"Wow, that rain came quick," Jay said, holding out his hand, watching the water drops burst on his skin.

"Yeah," Cain said, peering up to the sky. "Odd...there aren't any clouds."

Jay glanced up. The newfound dawn light lit the sky. There were no clouds.

Goosebumps enveloped Jay's skin. His eyes watered with realization.

Not a single cloud in sight. Just the faint, scarlet tint of dawn illuminating the dark sky. Yet, the rain pelted down harder and harder. Sheets of water lashed the ground and castle walls, making it difficult to see.

Alcina. They were here.

"McClevin!" Jay shouted over the din of rain. "Prepare your men! Thyran is here!"

Sentries nearby heard Jay's cry and immediately relayed the message to their companions. Soldiers scurried across the walls, shouting at the men in the courtyard, waking all those who were asleep.

Dozens of soldiers scrambled through the muddy courtyard and climbed the ladders to the parapets for reinforcements. The lashing rain impaired Jay's vision, his thundering heart impaired his hearing. Shielding his eyes from the rain, he gazed out in the distance. All he saw was rain slamming into the ground; the torrential downpour grayed out the land in the distance.

"Do you see them?" McClevin's voice boomed over the slapping of rain against stone.

"No!" Jay called back to the general, who was standing in the courtyard.

Lyssa rushed along the wall top to Jay. "Here!" she said, tossing him a collapsed spyglass. He expanded it and eyed the land. After a few seconds, she asked, "Anything?"

"No, all I see is—"

And then he saw him. Even through the intense rainstorm, Jay recognized his stepbrother, Thyran Vilkus, with a loose, deep red jacket draped over his shoulders, the two hilts of his scimitars poking up from behind his back, an army of bloodthirsty pirates at his rear. A shudder slashed through Jay's body as he saw Thyran's ravenous eyes. How did Thyran know they were there? He must have sent scouts under cover of the rain and spotted them over the wall.

"Do you see anything?" Lyssa repeated.

Jay opened his mouth, but something clogged his throat. Frozen in place, water beating down on his head, he watched Thyran draw both his curved scimitars from his back and thrust them in the air; all at once, Thyran and his army of pirates brandished their weapons and charged for the Dragons' Castle.

24

Pirates of Ashlen

"Here they come!" Jay shouted down to McClevin, collapsing the spyglass and tossing it back to Lyssa. He raced for the ladder and scrambled down.

He heard McClevin bellowing commands to his soldiers below. "Men! Take your positions! Kileean, take the men to the wall and arm them with muskets. Winston, position the soldiers on the ground to guard that crevice! Knights of Voorus, prepare for battle!"

Jay's feet hit the ground; mud splashed up over his pants. He watched as the crew gathered around him.

"Where's the bloody captain?" Jenkins asked.

Jay peered over to the eastern wall, but the rain cast down a foggy gray curtain that prevented him from locating the captain. "He should be up on the wall top guarding the east side by the lake."

Their feet sloshing through the mud, the crew formed a semicircle in front of Jay and drew their weapons. "What are your orders?" Lynk asked.

"Me?" Jay asked.

"You're the first mate, Jay," Delcato said. "Since the captain is elsewhere, you're in charge."

She was right. Jay wanted to turn to Cain, to relinquish command to him, but one look into Cain's hooded eyes reminded him of Cain's advice. He had to be strong.

Jay glanced up into the sheeting rain. Dozens of Eulian soldiers bustled up the ladders and filed along the front wall, each armed with muskets and shields, and either a sword or spear strapped to their backs. A few more dozen soldiers gathered around the V-shaped crevice in the front wall. Thyran would have a difficult time penetrating such a small opening with the countless soldiers surrounding it. The castle appeared well fortified.

Jay felt the gaze of the crew. A few hundred yards away, Thyran led his villainous army towards the castle. They did not have much time. Shifting his eyesight to the ground, he watched the fat raindrops plop into the puddles, sending splashes of water across the soil.

"I..." he paused for a second. "For years, we've been stealing for our own benefit. But since Eulia, we've been doing something different. For the past couple of weeks, we have been fighting a battle, not for ourselves, but for all of Lassar." Jay lifted his head and faced the crew. "We are and always will be pirates. But for today, we fight not for treasure, but for life...the lives of everyone of Lassar. Ashlen desired his ancient powers be sealed and protected for peace on this world, and I say we defend this castle in the name of Ashlen!"

Lynk stabbed his blade in the air where scarlet streams of sunlight shot through the dawn sky like chain lightning. "Aye! We're the Pirates of Ashlen!"

"Pirates of Ashlen!" the rest repeated, each raising their weapons with fervor and giving a triumphant yell.

"Alright men," Jay shouted, "everyone to the—"

Bang!

The ground trembled. Chunks of rock from the eastern wall blasted through the air. Jay struggled to maintain balance. He stared to the east, but a veil of rising smoke and dust obscured his vision. When the veil thinned, he gasped at the giant hole blown through the wall.

"What the—?" one of the soldiers yelled but was cut off when a giant serpent shot through the opening and soared through the air to the wall top. The serpent was huge—larger than the one that attacked their ship outside Storm Isle. The leviathan consisted solely of water.

The water serpent charged across the wall top. Soldiers screamed as the serpent slammed into them, knocking them off the wall for a ten-story plunge to the ground. Jay and the others stared in awe as the serpent slithered through the sky like a wingless dragon. The leviathan purged the entire front wall of soldiers then dove for the courtyard.

Suddenly, the rain ceased and the water serpent exploded, drenching all the soldiers and pirates on the ground and knocking them off their feet.

Wiping his eyes clear of water, Jay heard McClevin yell,

"Incoming!"

Jay opened his eyes and saw, in front of the lake, which was now completely dry, Alcina and the man with crimson, spiked hair leading an army of pirates through the newly-formed hole. Like a flood, they poured into the courtyard and gave a thunderous battle cry. Alcina's cerulean hair wavered in the air as streams of water jetted out from the damp soil towards the nearby soldiers and swept their muskets away.

"To the East Wall!" McClevin drew his sword and darted across the muddy soil to the pirates swarming into the castle. A few soldiers managed to hold onto their muskets. They fired a couple shots, dropping a few pirates as they entered, but, with no time to reload, they soon abandoned their guns and charged into battle with their spears or swords.

Jay watched as a cyclone of water surrounded Alcina,

knocking down anyone who got close. Right beside her, the red-haired man pushed through the soldiers, swiftly swinging his sword, blocking incoming strikes and slicing through his enemies. He and Alcina then diverged from the rest of the battle and made way for the front wall where Jay and his crew waited.

"Here they come!" Jay said to his crew. He glanced to Lyssa out of the corner of his eye. A resolute expression on her face, she nodded to him and raised her crimson synthesized scimitars in the air.

"Ankin, wait for me up top as planned," Jay said. "The rest of you, charge!"

The pain from his injuries, fear from his stepbrother, concern of his fate after the battle, they all fled from Jay as he bolted through the moist dawn air towards the enemy.

Jay swung his blade at the red-haired man, who blocked the attack and jabbed his sword at Jay's exposed side—

Jay side-stepped the attack and slammed his sword into the man's, steel against steel. Jay elbowed the man in the side, causing him to stumble back and lower his guard. Jay went for the finishing blow, but a sphere of water blasted into him and knocked him off his feet—

When Jay looked up, another pirate was hovering over him preparing to strike—

"Eyah!" Lyssa yelled, bringing a blur of red down upon the pirate. Jay exhaled in relief. Grabbing his sword, which had half-sunk into a puddle of muddy water, he regained his footing and took stock of the battle.

Lynk and Blynk fought in front of Cain, shielding him while he flung his daggers at the enemy. Jenkins and Delcato battled alongside Lyssa, the three each covering each other's backs.

His eyes darted hither and thither, scanning for the red-haired man and the sorceress. Then he spotted them. The man hunched over by the crevice in the front wall while the sorceress shielded him with her cyclone of water. What were they doing?

Then he saw something.

Explosives.

Blood rushing through his veins, Jay held his sword by his side and darted for the entrance. The tiny sliver in the front wall served as a filter for Thyran's forces. If they blew a bigger hole, Thyran's men would pour in unobstructed and greatly outnumber McClevin's soldiers. He had to stop them.

The cyclone collapsed to form a tight sphere surrounding the two. The thick layer of water swirled around them faster and faster, and before Jay reached them, a ball of fire engulfed them as another explosion shook the ground. The sound shattered the air and black rocks from the front wall sprayed into the courtyard.

When the dust from the explosion settled, the hairs on the nape of Jay's neck prickled. His two curved, silver scimitars by his side, Thyran Vilkus leapt over a stone from the expanded threshold and landed in the courtyard of the Dragons' Castle. Wave after wave of pirates flooded in behind him. When Thyran's gaze passed over Jay, he stopped and smirked.

Less than fifty yards away, Jay stared at his stepbrother for a moment; the noise from the rest of the battle faded. Jay noticed Ashlen's Hatchet, decorated with its colorful gems, fastened to Thyran's waist.

Thyran's gaze averted from Jay and instead focused on the tower at the back of the castle. He raised his hand and pointed one of his scimitars to the top of the tower where the glowing green light poured out of the windows.

"To the tower!"

The sphere of water around the sorceress and the man burst; the force sent Jay and several of his crew sprawling on the ground. While they retrieved their weapons and regained their footing, Thyran and his men charged for the tower.

When Jay recovered his footing, he looked behind him towards the tower. Thyran and his men had clashed against McClevin and his soldiers. Amid the clanking of steel against steel, the yelling of triumph and agony, and the bustling of armies splashing through the mud, Jay noticed McClevin struggling to maintain order. By blowing a hole in the entrance of the castle, Thyran had caught him off-guard.

For a moment, Jay stood frozen, watching his step-brother in combat. Thyran was swift, using both scimitars offensively. Ducking and leaning to evade the Eulian soldiers' attacks, he effortlessly sliced his blades through the air and killed his enemies in single blows. Jay had never seen one move with such speed and accuracy.

Jay heard a stampede of feet splashing in the mud behind him. More of Thyran's men were entering the castle.

Wiping the mud off his brow, Jay tightened his grip around his cutlass and shouted, "Pirates of Ashlennnnnn!" He and the rest of the Pirates of Ashlen dashed forward to attack the incoming wave of Thyran's pirates.

Training with Hector paid off; during combat, Jay's instincts kicked in, and without thinking, he defended himself expertly and brought down his opponents. The soaked ground made movement difficult, something he was not used to. Nevertheless, he moved quickly enough to evade enemy strikes and timed his attacks perfectly to strike his enemies in their exposed areas.

He heard Lyssa scream.

Jay twisted his head to see a pirate who had swept her feet and shoved her to the ground. The pirate's blade stabbed through the air, aimed at her chest, but Jay lunged forward, parried the pirate's attack, and smashed the pirate's head with the hilt of his cutlass. The pirate dropped to the ground, unconscious.

"T-thanks," Lyssa said, spitting out mud.

Jay extended his hand for Lyssa to grab. "No pro—"

Thwack!

Something crashed into Jay's skull, causing him to stumble back, dazed.

"No!" Lyssa yelled, leaping to her feet and swirling her scimitars in the air.

Through his semi-blurred vision, Jay recognized the man as the bulky, bald, shirtless man that pinned him against the house in Selia. He wielded a massive ax with both hands.

"No one defeats Bruce!" the man growled in a deep voice. "Time fer yer death!"

Raising his muscular arms, Bruce swung the ax up and then sliced it down, aimed for Lyssa's head—

Lyssa raised her crimson scimitars and blocked the attack, but the unexpected force behind his blow knocked her weapon from her hands. With her unarmed, Bruce swung the ax again. She ducked and dove for the ground.

Jay's head still pounding, he struggled to regain his senses.

"Argg!" Bruce yelled, bringing down the ax to the ground, but Lyssa rolled to the side. The blade of the ax sunk deep into the soil; before he could bring it up, she snatched her weapon, twirled it through the air, and sliced through the wooden shaft of the ax.

Bruce stepped back and puffed his chest. "Ye broke me weapon!" he roared.

"Eyah!" Completely to her feet, she whipped the edge of her fused scimitars at his chest, but he stretched out his hand and grabbed the blade. Blood trickled down his arm as the scimitar dug into his flesh. Apparently unnerved by the pain, Bruce swung his massive fist upside her head, and she fell to the ground.

Jay's head ceased pounding; he lunged at Bruce, blade in the air. Bruce dropped the scimitars and aimed a punch for Jay's face. Not expecting Bruce to react so quickly, Jay jerked his head to the side, sacrificing his attack and falling off-balance to the ground—

He was up in a flash and whirled around to face Bruce, who had already thrown his next punch. Relying on pure instinct, Jay dropped to his knees to duck the punch and stabbed his cutlass through Bruce's right foot.

"Argg!" Bruce yelled. The massive pirate swooped his hand down for Jay's throat. Jay's weight was too heavily placed on his knees for him to dodge Bruce's hand—

Bruce's fingers wrapped tightly around Jay's neck and lifted him in the air. Struggling to breathe, Jay thrashed his arms and legs.

"Now you pay for hurting Bruce!"

Bruce raised his other hand, preparing to crush Jay's skull. Jay squinted and leaned his head back, anticipating the pain of this next blow—

Bruce's eyes widened, his mouth lolled. The grip around Jay's neck loosened enough for Jay to squirm free and drop back to his feet. Bruce staggered back and forth a few times before falling lifelessly to his side, his head splashing in a puddle of mud. There was a wound on his back behind his heart where Lyssa had stabbed him.

Panting, Lyssa stood a few paces in front of Jay. Blood dripped from the tip of one of her scimitars. "Are you okay?"

Jay nodded, rubbing his neck, inhaling deep breaths, welcoming the inrush of cool air against his throat.

"Jay!" Jenkins shouted from behind. "We need some help over here!"

Exhausted from their battle with Bruce, Jay and Lyssa rushed back to the castle entrance where Jenkins and the others defended against the constant stampede of pirates coursing through the enlarged threshold.

"Aha!" Kyros shouted as one of his grenades created yet another magnificent explosion. "What's wrong Alcina? You looked famished."

Alcina, who had been ever cheerful and wild since their glorious entrance in the castle, had lost the bounce to her step. She glared at him, clearly taking offense to his comment. "Well if I didn't have to protect your petty little grenade toys from water every five seconds, I wouldn't be so tired. My powers have their limits, you know. I need to rest soon."

Kyros laughed, though inside, he felt somewhat concerned for her, a feeling he was reluctant to show.

"Well, I should probably be saving some of my grenades as it is. This battle is pretty much ours. And besides, wouldn't want to force you to use your magic if it's too much for you to handle."

"Hmph," she snorted, looking away from him.

They were chasing after Thyran, who had battled his way through the Eulian soldiers and was now advancing for the tower. Cyril stayed back to lead their crew in the battle, shielding Thyran against any incoming soldiers.

"Alcina!" Thyran shouted when he reached the black tower.

She hesitated. Kyros felt the urge to do something to assist, though he knew he couldn't. He watched her carefully, ready to intervene should she show any signs of fainting.

Alcina bowed her head and raised her hands. Her eyes flashed blue. Water droplets from all over the courtyard leapt in the air and swirled into two streams of water that flowed along the castle walls. The streams snatched three wooden ladders and plopped them against the tower; she maintained a geyser of water that held the ladders upright and steady.

"I'm going up alone," Thyran said. "I'll meet you back down here shortly. Our glory is near. This is our dawn of victory!"

Kyros noticed Alcina's arms and legs quivering, her face turning pale. He stepped closer to her, allowing her to clutch onto him if she lost her footing.

Thyran sheathed his scimitars behind his back and ascended the ladders to the top of the tower.

Darkness spread inside the tower, even with the faint, scarlet dawn light crawling through the windows. When Thyran entered the tower, his eyes transfixed at once onto the glowing green basin in the center.

Finally.

As he moved towards the basin, the battle cries from the courtyard subsided; the only sound he heard was his own footsteps across the dry stone floor. His skin tingled with excitement; his fingertips ran down his side to feel the blade of Ashlen's Hatchet on his left and the gem in his right pocket.

Step after step, he neared the basin that held

the most awesome power in Lassar. Ever since he murdered Governor Almsy, Thyran had waited for this moment. From aiding his stepbrother in stealing the locket in Eulia to acquiring Ashlen's Hatchet above the deadly lake in Storm Isle to stealing the gem from his stepbrother in Valkadia, it had been a long journey. But it ended now.

"Don't move!" someone shouted.

At once, fifteen soldiers clad in blue uniforms leapt out from the shadows surrounding the room, all pointing their muskets at him. Then another soldier in a darker shade of blue, a sign of a higher rank, stepped out from the back of the room into the glimmering green light. His silver helmet was pushed back to keep out of his eyes. The short soldier stepped closer to Thyran, keeping his musket aimed at his chest.

"My name is Winston Kefkan, a Eulian Lieutenant, one of the Knights of Voorus. I am placing you, Thyran Vilkus, under arrest. Drop your weapons."

Thyran wondered how he had not noticed them before. Looking around, he recognized the deep blackness that engulfed the edges of the room where the wall met the floor; the darkness was thick enough to conceal anything in its grasp.

Clever.

Curling his lips, Thyran turned his head to mark the positions of all the soldiers. Even at his speed, he knew if he moved, he would be shot and killed. Gritting his teeth, he reached behind his back, drew his scimitars, and let the silver weapons fall to the ground.

The soldier calling himself Winston coughed to clear his throat—he was nervous. Good, he should be.

"Alright men, keep your guns on him." Together, all the soldiers advanced towards him. "Keep your distance,"

Winston warned, and the soldiers stopped several feet from Thyran.

This man was not so stupid after all. This should be interesting.

Winston lowered his weapon to get a better look at him. "Your brother laid this trap for you."

Jay...impressive. Jay knew he would come alone, not willing to chance one of his crew absorbing any of the power. And Jay knew that if *he* had been missing from the battlefield rather than this Winston character, his stepbrother would be suspicious and anticipate a trap. Clever little boy.

Thyran closed his eyes and breathed slowly. "Did he now?"

"Was it really you?" Winston asked, his voice barely above a squeak. "Are you really the one who murdered Governor Almsy?"

"Aye," Thyran said softly, keeping his eyes closed. "I put that fool in his place."

"So Jay was telling the truth all along...."

"It's funny," Thyran shot his eyes open, "when a murderer with such clout is killed, the entire planet is flowing with sorrow, but when a village of innocent children is annihilated, no one bats an eye."

"The governor was not a murderer! He was a respectable man."

"A selfish man interested only in his personal wealth, that was all Almsy was. No different from your king."

"You're mad!"

Thyran clenched his fists. "Almsy and Emory had the power to stop that slaughter, but they did nothing. As a result, hundreds of people lost their lives. I cannot let this tyranny go on any longer. It ends now!"

"Enough of this nonsense. Charles, Axley, slap some

irons on him!"

Thyran remained still as two burly guards in blue uniforms hesitantly stepped closer. All fifteen soldiers kept their muskets aimed at Thyran; the serious expressions on their faces revealed their readiness to slay him at any sign of aggression.

"Hands behind your back," one of the soldiers said in a deep voice.

One of the two soldiers aimed his gun at Thyran's chest while the other rounded his back. Closing his eyes and tilting his head back, Thyran slid his hands behind has back and rubbed his wrists together. He listened to the clanking as the soldier fumbled with the iron shackles. He felt the stillness in the air. He smelled the metal of the musket barrel inches from his chest. He envisioned the scene in his mind. He tasted their anxiety.

When the damp iron brushed against his skin, fast as a mynx, Thyran swung his foot through the air in a crescent kick to force the man's musket to the side. Lunging forward, he slammed into the man's chest and ripped the gun from his fingers. In a flash, he pointed the gun at the closest soldier with a musket and blew a hole through his chest. The gunshot echoing off the walls, Thyran kicked up one of his scimitars with his feet, snatched it in the air, and, grasping the nearest man for cover, sprinted towards the line of soldiers. Surprised by the sudden move, the soldiers hesitated a fraction of a second before blasting their weapons. Shielded on the one side by his hostage, Thyran moved quickly and efficiently—

He slithered behind one of the soldiers, stabbing his blade through the man's back. Musket balls punctured the soldier's chest but did not penetrate enough to harm Thyran—

Thyran counted twelve gunshots, but several soldiers fired simultaneously, so he could have easily miscounted. The sound of the frantic soldiers reloading their weapons filled the air. He released his hostage and bolted after the nearest soldiers. Still unready to fire, they were defenseless as he slashed through them.

"Reload!" Winston yelled. Some soldiers frantically grabbed their musket balls and gunpowder and began preparing their weapons for another offensive while others abandoned their guns and unsheathed their swords.

One by one, Thyran battled through the soldiers, killing most of them before their weapons were ready for fire. Two soldiers had managed to get a shot off, but they were trembling too much to aim properly.

The final soldier screamed, a sound quickly silenced by Thyran's blade. Only Winston remained.

When Winston realized Thyran killed off all his comrades, he dropped his musket; trembling, he drew his sword and held it to Thyran. Sweat beaded down his brow.

Thyran found the man's nervousness amusing. Taking his time, Thyran scooped up his other scimitar from the ground and whirled both blades through the air, intimidating the Eulian Lieutenant.

"You'll need more than that to stop me."

"S-stay away!" Winston stammered, fearful for his life. Tears broke the seals in his eyes; he struggled to breathe steadily. Gasping for air, he backed away as Thyran advanced. Then, noticing he was nearing the wall, Winston swung his blade forward—

Thyran crossed his blades to form an X and trapped Winston's blade between the his. Using his advantage, Thyran pushed Winston back, closer and closer to the wall. When Winston's ankle brushed against the back wall, his eyes widened with horror, and he pushed forward against Thyran, exactly what Thyran was waiting for.

Thyran released his blades from Winston's and side-stepped. With his forward momentum, Winston stumbled ahead a few steps. His blade dropped. Thyran immediately stabbed both his scimitars forward. One sliced through Winston's chest; the other, through his throat.

When, seconds later, Winston breathed his final breath, Thyran withdrew his blades, allowing the man to collapse to the floor.

"Good plan, Jay. I'll give you that. Made the finale all the more interesting."

Thyran sheathed his scimitars and headed for the glowing basin.

When Jenkins pointed out Thyran ascending the ladder for the tower, Jay ran for the nearest ladder and scurried up to the wall top. Once he reached the parapet, he darted across the stone ground along the eastern wall. Still no sign of Hector, but he didn't have time to worry about that now.

The clashing of weapons and screaming of wounded men down below increased his sense of urgency. The flaming sun rays thickened over the castle, illuminating the battle scene in the courtyard as a dense layer of fog condensed down below. Up ahead, he saw Ankin waiting for him by the base of the wooden ladder propped against the black tower to the window Jay had gazed out of the previous evening.

"You ready?" Ankin asked, stepping away from the ladder.

Jay took several breaths to ease his pounding heart. His throat throbbed with anxiety. "Yes, are you?"

Ankin lifted his musket with an unusual long barrel

for deadly accuracy. "I'll give you a few minutes to distract him, and then I'll shoot."

"You sure you can hold it with one hand?"

"I'll be fine."

Jay massaged his palms with his thumbs—they were bright red and calloused from all the fighting. "Hopefully, Winston and his men have already got him."

"In any case, you better hurry. We don't have much time."

Running his hand through his damp hair, Jay nodded. "Right. I'll see you soon, Ankin."

"Be well, Jay." The two embraced in a hug before Jay quickly ascended the ladder two stories and disappeared into the tower.

Jay's feet landed softly on the solid ground in the tower. He struggled to fight back crying out when he saw all the Eulian soldiers dead on the ground, their muskets lying beside them. His eyed watered at the sight of so many lives lost.

Then up ahead he saw the back of Thyran's dark jacket, his reddish-brown hair dangling just below his shoulders. His scimitars were crossed behind his back. He walked to the basin, his left hand held outright with the necklace dangling from his fingers. Silently, Jay drew his weapon and crept over the stone floor. Thyran seemed unaware of his presence.

Thyran stopped in front of the basin. He brought the necklace above the crystal film and lowered the gem until it fit snug inside the crystal cradle.

A screech of whistling wind escaped the basin when Thyran secured the gem in place; the glimmering green light shined brighter. Judging from the lighting on the ceiling, the liquid inside the basin swirled more violently.

Thyran stared for a moment down at the swirling liquid in the basin. His left hand reached for the hatchet by his waist. He lifted it and held it in front of his chest. Jay continued his advance, careful not to make a sound.

"Alexia..." Thyran said, his head bowed.

Jay jumped when suddenly Thyran's head jerked up and he raised the hatchet in the air, ready to shatter the crystal captivating Ashlen's power.

"No!" Jay yelled, lunging forward with his cutlass lofted in front of him. Thyran spun around and braced the hatchet for defense against Jay's strike. Jay's cutlass wedged itself between the hatchet's blade and shaft. Jay flicked his wrist, prying the hatchet free from Thyran's grip and sending it crashing to the floor several yards away. Thyran leaped away and instantly whipped out both his scimitars. Panting, Jay kept his distance and stared into his stepbrother's ravenous eyes.

"Most impressive," Thyran said with his typical devious grin. "You have managed to put up quite a fight, I must admit. More than I anticipated."

Keeping a watchful eye on Thyran, Jay sidled over so he was standing between Thyran and Ashlen's Hatchet.

"What are your plans after this? Hmm?" Thyran stepped away from the pedestal supporting the basin. "Kill me and then turn yourself in to be executed or spend the rest of your days rotting in a five-foot dungeon cell?"

"All that matters is now. What happens after is insubstantial."

Thyran moved closer to him. Jay backed up, step by step, closer to the hatchet.

"Why stop me, Jay?" Thyran asked. "Can't you see I'm trying to better the world?"

"One man cannot rule an entire planet. Your greed

would destroy everything."

"Greed? Brother, I'm hurt you would accuse me of such a feeling."

"You've left me for dead numerous times for nothing more than your own selfish desires. You're no better than Cornelius or any of the other people you blame for Alexia's death."

Thyran's eyes narrowed; Jay had clearly struck a nerve.

"Careful with your words, brother," he snarled. "I could have had killed you many times in the past."

Goosebumps popped over Jay's skin as he listened to his stepbrother's cold, threatening voice. Watching Thyran move closer made his palms sweaty. Thyran's dark, reddish brown hair covered the sides of his narrow face, appearing contorted with evil under the flickering green light. His loose, dark red jacket swung just above the ground while he walked. The echoes of Jay's pounding heart seemed as loud as gun blasts echoing off the walls.

Stop, he chided himself. Be strong, like Cain advised.

He halted in place, not willing to take another step in retreat.

Surprisingly, Thyran stopped as well. "You have made me proud," he said. "When we were young, you were an amazing student. I taught you everything I knew about fighting, and you picked it up flawlessly." He blinked. "I love you, Jay. I'm honored to have you as a brother, but I will not hold back in this fight. I will do whatever it takes to kill you; I expect you to do the same. Don't be weak."

Thyran's friendly tone reminded Jay of when they were younger, training in the fields outside Mr. and Mrs. Vilkus's house. But then Thyran's admonition stabbed Jay in the heart, and a raging fire burned away his peaceful visions of his youth.

"Calm yourself," Thyran said. "Remember what I taught you. Don't let your emotions cloud your mind during battle. Focus only on you and your opponent."

Jay inhaled long, steady breaths. He absorbed his surroundings, honing his senses to the environment. His heart rate returned to a normal, steady beat, his brain ceased pounding against his skull, he could see clearly.

"Good," Thyran said. "Now, let's begin."

Time stopped. Standing ten feet away, the two stared at one another. Jay kept his cutlass aloft in front of him. The only sound Jay heard was the pounding of his own heart. Jay bent his knees and brought his cutlass back in his battle stance. All was still—no movement, no sound, no aggression, nothing.

Then Jay sprung forward. He stabbed his blade at Thyran, who slapped it aside with his left scimitar and swung with his right—

Jay jerked his head away, avoiding Thyran's blade. He whirled around, crouching and bringing his blade to Thyran's knee—

Thyran lifted his foot, catching the blade with the sole of his thick black boot. Jay withdrew his blade and rolled away, avoiding Thyran's incoming strike.

Leaping to his feet, Jay spun around to face Thyran, who was already charging forward. Thyran launched an offensive. Jay had to be quick to block and evade Thyran's strikes—his stepbrother moved with such agility, Jay's only option was to fight defensively. Instinct guided his hands to the proper positions to block and his body with the proper movements to evade.

Then Thyran swung with both blades diagonally, making a block with Jay's single cutlass impossible. Jay

leaned back so far he nearly lost his balance, but determination kept him on his feet as Thyran's blades swept past.
When Jay straightened his back, Thyran's blades were still
off to the side, finishing the strike. His stepbrother was
slightly off-balance. Jay went to stab Thyran's chest, but
Thyran leaned over his own blades and side-kicked Jay beneath his ribs, knocking him windless.

Jay stumbled back to catch his breath. Thyran was
still regaining his balance; he needed to strike now—

Jay shot forward, aiming his blade down for Thyran's
skull, but Thyran regained his balance too soon and trapped
Jay's blade with his scimitars crossed in an X—

With Thyran pressing him forward, Jay backed up,
step after step. His heart hammered inside his chest, sweat
poured from his brow and stung his eyes. He was satisfied
to see that Thyran too appeared to be sweating and breathing heavily.

Jay was nearing a wall. He needed to act. He halted
his retreat and pushed forward—

Thyran's blades dropped at once, causing Jay to
stumble forward. Remembering this maneuver from his
youth, Jay anticipated the next strike and jerked his body
away from Thyran's incoming blades. He stepped fast to regain his balance, and again stared eye to eye with Thyran.

"Impressive," Thyran said. "Just as I had hoped."

Panting, Jay took a moment to gather his breath.

Thyran leapt forward, launching another offensive.

McClevin sloshed through the mud, swinging his
mighty blade at his opponents, using his powerful shield to
stymie their attacks. The pirates had finally ceased pouring
through the threshold, and he had managed to reestablish
order among his ranks. Jay's pirates fought alongside them

in the center of the courtyard as they battled against Thyran's crew.

McClevin had been wounded twice: stabbed in his left shoulder and cut in his left knee. Still, he raged on, battling with more ferocity than ever in his life. This battle was for the king, for the land, for the people, for the princess. He would not lose.

"Kileean!" he shouted, noticing a herd of pirates racing for a group of wounded soldiers. "Take a squad to the western wall!"

From the corner of his eye, McClevin saw the glimmer of a blade swooping down. He raised his shield to deflect it and then ran his sword through the pirate's stomach. When the pirate fell, McClevin looked to the eastern wall top to see if Jay had ascended yet.

The single-handed pirate waited by the base of the ladder with his musket as planned. Jay was nowhere in sight, probably already up in the tower. But someone was advancing to the waiting pirate. Squinting, McClevin recognized him as the pirate captain they called Hector.

Hector reached the waiting pirate, then the two engaged in some conversation.

Another of Thyran's pirates moved to attack him. McClevin parried the attack with his sword, slammed his shield against the pirate, and finished him off on the ground.

McClevin looked up and gasped.

Hector drew his sword and promptly ran it through the single-handed pirate. After stealing the man's musket, Hector tossed him off the side of the wall, where he plunged to his death.

Another of Thyran's spies! McClevin knew there had to be more than just the girl.

He had to warn Jay.

Just as he began to dash for the ladder leading to the wall top, a group of Thyran's pirates surrounded him, leaving him no chance of escape.

Jay's arms throbbed after the repeated blows of Thyran's scimitars against his cutlass. As he dueled, his breaths were short and quick, his reactions were instantaneous, he let his instincts take over to defend himself from Thyran's deadly swings.

"Ahh!" Thyran yelled, blasting both his scimitars together through the air into Jay's cutlass.

His fingers weak from gripping his sword throughout the battle, Jay failed to maintain his grip; his weapon slipped from his hand and banged against the ground. Unarmed, Jay backed away from Thyran.

"It's over," Thyran said, readying his silver blades for the final blow.

Unwilling to succumb to defeat, Jay moved to pick up his cutlass, but Thyran delivered a powerful kick to his chest and slammed the hilt of one of his scimitars into Jay's face. Jay stumbled back, raising his fists to defend himself. The room swirled around him, making it difficult to focus. Feebly, he threw a punch for Thyran, but his stepbrother effortlessly slapped his hand away and kicked him fiercely in the chest, nearly cracking his sternum. Jay stumbled back, tripped over a dead soldier, and fell to the ground.

Twirling one of his scimitars through the air, Thyran stepped beside him.

"Good-bye, brother."

Jay grabbed the only thing he could: a musket of the fallen soldier beside him. He snatched the musket, aimed it at Thyran.

Bang!

Jay flinched as the gunshot echoed off the walls, the clang of the musket ball ricocheting off Thyran's scimitar. The force behind the shot ripped the blade from Thyran's right hand, leaving him armed with a single scimitar. After he recovered from the gun blast, Thyran swung his remaining scimitar for Jay—

Jay rolled to the side, grabbed another musket, and pointed it at Thyran. Anticipating the attack, Thyran threw himself to the side, narrowly avoiding the musket ball as it shot by.

Something sharp brushed his leg. Feeling around with his hand, he realized it was Ashlen's Hatchet. With ten feet between him and his stepbrother, he picked up the hatchet, struggled to his feet, and limped for the middle window.

"Stop!"

A few feet from the window, Jay turned his head to see Thyran, armed with a musket pointed at his chest, slowly stepping closer. His lungs burning, Jay held the hatchet closer to the window. "You'll kill me anyways. I can't let you have it."

"Throw the hatchet out the window, and I will torture you, brother! You'll drown in a sea of pain so wicked you'll go mad. Do not make me do that to you. Give me the hatchet."

"I would gladly suffer in the stead of the rest of Lassar!"

"Damn you Jay!"

His musket aimed for Jay's chest, Thyran squeezed the trigger—

There was a click, but no gun blast. The musket was not loaded. Snarling, Thyran threw the weapon to the floor.

"You're finished, Thyran," came a voice from the side

window.

Jay turned his head to see Hector, who had just climbed up the ladder, standing a few feet away from the window with Ankin's musket aimed at Thyran.

"Captain!" Jay yelled, relieved. "Where's Ankin?"

"He be waiting for us down below. I didn't want to put another member of me crew at risk. Is that Ashlen's Hatchet?"

Jay squeezed his fingers around the base of the hatchet and held it over the edge of the window. "Yes. I'm getting rid of it so Thyran can't unlock the seal."

"Give it to me, Lil' Blue. I'll toss it back down to Ankin. If ye drop it there, one of Thyran's mates may recover it."

Thyran's eyes flicked from Hector to Jay. "Jay, I'll give you one more chance. Give it to me unless you want you and your friends to suffer a slow and agonizing death."

"Don't listen to him," Hector said. "Jay, give me the hatchet so we can end this."

Jay looked at the two. Hector's voice sounded more demanding than usual—not nearly as friendly.

Thyran made a dash for Jay. Startled, Jay tossed Ashlen's Hatchet to Hector and backed up against the window to prepare for Thyran's assault.

Thyran stopped.

Jay watched as Thyran bowed his head, shaking it plaintively from side to side.

"I told you..." Thyran said softly before looking up. "*I told you.* You disappoint me."

Jay stared at him, confused.

Thyran turned around, walking slowly back to the basin. "Back in Morad, the night of the governor's murder, remember?"

Jay delved through his memories, trying to recall everything Thyran had said that night, but pain and fatigue clouded his thoughts.

"I told you my cousin would be watching after you," Thyran said. "Though you never met him, I thought you would have figured it out by now."

Halfway between the window and the basin, Thyran spun around. "When you escaped that night in Morad, you evaded not only the guards, but also my cousin as well. Two years he spent searching for you. By that time, I no longer wished you dead, since I came to realize only one with a pure heart could unlock the hidden compass in the locket. A heart of *good*, whatever that may be. Despite my noble intentions, I realized I would not be considered one of a 'pure heart.' Nor anyone in my crew.

"So who better, I asked myself, than my own stepbrother? When my cousin located you among the slums of Delphina, I had him join Gaden's crew and help them take you in. Ever wonder how convenient it was when he picked you up after you were caught stealing from that marketplace? Of course, I needed to make sure your fighting skills remained up to par should the need arise, so I had him take you under his wing.

"But, what surprises me the most, is that after Hector stayed back when you entered the Dryfus Mines, refrained from joining you during your ascent up the hill in Storm Isle, and abandoned you in Selia, you never once doubted him. Instead, you all blamed that woman Karen, who actually sneaked out that night in Selia to protect you, but instead was captured by my cousin. Funny how the world works, isn't it?"

Thyran bent down, picked up his scimitars, and sheathed them behind his back. Jay's eyes watered; he didn't know what to think. Betrayed. Betrayed by one of his closest friends, the man he looked to as a father.

No...not Hector. Hector saved him and the crew more than once. Thyran had to be lying. This was just another one of his mind games.

"And now," Thyran said, holding his arms out in front of him. "This story deserves an ending! Cousin!"

Jay gasped as Hector lobbed the hatchet to Thyran, who caught it and immediately dashed for the basin—

"NO!" Jay yelled. His lungs on fire, his body aching from combat, his head and heart pounding relentlessly, he raced after his stepbrother. If Thyran reached the basin first, it was over—Thyran would win.

Bypassing his cutlass on the ground to save time, Jay sprinted with all his might after his stepbrother. Tears streamed down his face and whipped across his cheeks. His vision clouded his surroundings—all he saw was Thyran and the glimmering green light from the basin. Closer and closer he ran.

But it was too late.

Thyran reached the basin, and, with a mighty swing, he slammed the blade of Ashlen's Hatchet down on the gem centered over the crystal.

Bright green light. An explosive sound. It all happened instantaneously.

Forceful winds threw Jay across the room and back against the stone wall. Pain seared his back. When he forced his eyes open, the bright green light from the basin swirled high in the air before funneling down into Thyran, whose body shook as it absorbed the energy from the great wizard Ashlen.

Then Jay saw something else. Floating above the basin and in front of a blue vortex in the air was a deformed man with dark gray, nearly black, skin; streaks of long black and silver hair fell down his head to his waist. His numerous loose layers of ripped black cloth floated around him majestically like smoke. He ran his long, skeletal fingers through the air and admired them as if he had just awaken from a deep slumber.

"Ahh..." Thyran groaned as the last of the green streams of light entered his body.

The floating man's dark red eyes focused on Thyran. Simply watching the man's movement frightened Jay—it was like he had just been tortured near the brink of death and was now drifting through the air—half dead, half alive.

Thyran's eyes flashed a vibrant crimson color, a fireball shot out from his hands to the wall, slamming a hole through it with incredible force. His eyes then flashed white, a strong sea of wind spun around the room, blowing the muskets and armor from the dead soldiers over the stone.

"Ahh!" Thyran screamed, gripping his head and snapping his eyes shut; the winds instantly vanished.

"Relax," the floating man said in a raspy, chilling voice. "You have absorbed a colossal amount of power today. You must learn to control it."

Digging his fingernails into the side of his head, yanking on his reddish-brown hair, Thyran said, "W-who are you?"

The man flicked his slender fingers through the air, leaving behind black trails of smoke. "You may call me Mystro."

Jay rubbed the back of his head. Blood seeped out from his wound where his head banged against the wall. His mind rattled, a deafening screech rang in his ears. He was unable to move.

"What is this I feel?" Thyran asked, closing his eyes,

hunched over on his hands and knees.

"You have absorbed the power of Ashlen Venclin, a great wizard. Your body is unable to control it as of yet. But, come with me, my brave knight. Let me teach you how to control your powers."

Mystro's chilling words triggered some hidden energy inside Jay. Gripping onto the wall for support, he lifted himself to his feet and moved forward. "Brother..." he managed to spurt out as he staggered towards the basin. This time, he picked up his cutlass on the way and raised it in the air.

Jay caught a glimpse of Lyssa, followed by the rest of the Pirates of Ashlen, climbing through the window and dropping into the room. Lyssa's eyes shifted from Hector to Jay to Thyran to Mystro.

"Hmm...." Mystro tilted his head back, revealing his snakelike neck. Curling his long fingers to the ceiling, his eyes flashed bright cyan. Rocks from the ceiling violently shook and then dropped down, but a forceful wind swept them up and slammed them together, merging all the rocks into one large mass of stone with a tapered, pointed end facing Jay. With a flick of Mystro's fingers, a blazing fire blanketed the stone and it shot off through the air with an icy powder drifting to the ground in its wake.

Jay had no time to evade the deadly projectile. The tapered end of the fiery rock plunged into Jay's solar plexus—

The momentum carried him back against the wall; he dropped to the ground. Lyssa screamed. Dropping her weapon, she dashed across the stone to Jay's side.

The flames burned Jay's insides. The pain was too great to bear. He struggled to scream, but no sound escaped his lips.

Then the flames died down, but the large rock still pierced through Jay's body, sucking his life away by the second. Placing her hands on the rock, Lyssa yanked on it, trying to wrench it free. But it remained stuck.

"Ahh!" Jay screamed, pain searing his body. "S-stop...." Tears streamed down his cheeks.

Lyssa grabbed the back of Jay's neck and pulled him up.

"Jay? Jay! Can you hear me?"

Realizing his time was short, Jay mustered his strength, his remaining energy, and slid his hand down in his pocket and retrieved the fossil bracelet he and Jenkins and Delcato made the previous night. He lifted his hand to her.

"H-here. W-we...made this, for you."

Though he couldn't see her expression due to his tear-filled eyes, Jay felt her take the bracelet from his hand. He sensed her appreciation. He sensed her love.

Then he died.

A light weight of sorrow hung from Thyran's chest when he saw Jay's head hang lifelessly to the side. He truly did love his stepbrother; it pained him to see Jay so still and helpless. He watched the golden-haired woman weeping, her head buried in his dead stepbrother's chest.

"Come, my knight." Mystro unfolded the blackened fingers of his right hand for Thyran to grab. "We will return soon and finally finish what I started before Ashlen intervened."

Hector's men gathered around the window, staring in horror at their dead crewmate. Thyran looked at his cousin, who appeared just as mystified as the rest.

Thyran's head started pounding, a raging headache

he had never before felt. His insides felt alit. The feeling did not cause him pain, yet he felt ready to explode from all the energy. He dug his nails into his palms to refrain from screaming.

"Come on!" one of Hector's crewmates shouted. "Let's get those bloody bastards. For Jay!"

They all shouted in agreement, except for his cousin, who remained in place. Waving their weapons in the air, the pirates charged for him and Mystro.

Thyran closed his eyes for a moment out of respect for his younger stepbrother. "Good-bye, Jay," he whispered.

Turning around, he grabbed Mystro's open hand and felt his feet leave the ground as Mystro's powers lifted him in the air.

Mystro's red eyes scanned the room; from behind his silver and black hair, his dark face smirked at the incoming pirates. "We will see you all soon...very soon. Enjoy the serenity while it lasts."

Turning around, Mystro levitated Thyran in the air. The two of them drifted into the circular, swirling blue vortex. Cool wind whipped across Thyran's face, a sprinkle of something similar to water splashed over his skin, and then he was absorbed into the bright cerulean light.

Epilogue

Gray clouds and a crisp breeze rolled over Eulia. Up in his bedroom, King Emory bent over his dying wife, who laid in her bed, still and silent, her white eyelids covering her eyes and her grayed hair sprawled on her pillow. The heavy clouds shrouded the sunlight and darkened the room. Emory's large hands clasped his wife's cold fingers and rubbed them to provide warmth.

"It's been three days," he said, tears flooding his lungs, "since you looked at me. Three days since I saw your beautiful blue eyes. Please...Elizabeth...don't be in pain." He bowed his head and pressed his wide forehead against her icy fingers. "I love you so much...." A tear coursed down his cheek.

Footsteps thundered in the hallway outside his room, but he kept his head buried in his wife's hands. He heard a knock on the door. He raised his head and moved his lips above his wife's face. Her faint breath blew against his cheeks, the shallow feeling racking his insides, burning his nose, dampening his eyes.

"King Emory!" Marcus shouted from outside the door. "I need to speak with you. It's urgent."

Ignoring Marcus, Emory bent down and kissed his wife's soft, cold lips. "I—I love you, Elizabeth. You mean the world to me. P-Please...fight a little longer. Our daughter Catherine should be back from Delphina any day now. I know she'll want to see you as soon as she returns."

"Your Highness," Orrin's aged voice sounded from opposite the door, "Are you there?"

Dropping his wife's hand back to her side, Emory steadied his shaky breathing then walked across the floor and opened the door. "What is it?"

Orrin, Marcus, and Agatha crowded the doorway. Clad in his crisp blue Eulian uniform, Marcus held up a yellow-tainted peace of parchment with black ink written over one side. "It's from King Cornelius," Marcus said, handing the paper to him.

Emory's calloused fingers secured the parchment. He lowered his hooded eyes to read it as raindrops began pattering against the glass of his window. The air thickened. Breathing became difficult. Before he could finish reading, the paper slipped through his fingers.

He fell back against the wall, his glossy eyes watching the parchment fall.

"Cornelius is accusing us of sinking one of his vessels," Orrin said softly.

"But we don't have any ship that would be crossing those waters, except for maybe McClevin's" Marcus said.

"McClevin would never commit such a monstrous crime!" said Orrin.

"I know." Marcus shifted his eyes to the king. "Any word from him?"

Emory shook his head, his eyes never leaving the ground. "We won't have time to wait for his return. Cornelius wants us to surrender over the Agapo land within a week, or he'll declare war against us."

"Ridiculous!" Marcus said, stomping his foot on the ground.

Agatha brushed her silver-lined black hair out of her eyes. "I told you we could not trust him. It was unwise to bank on him being merciful. We could have had our armies in position to strike if you would have listened to me."

"Watch your tongue!" Orrin snapped.

Emory's eyes rose from the ground. "She's right." He took a deep, shaky breath. "I should have foreseen this."

"But you can't blame yourself for—" Marcus began before Emory raised his hand, demanding silence.

"Cornelius has backed us into a corner, but we will not give into his demands. My father swore to protect the Agapos, and I fully intend to honor his promise. Agatha?"

She flicked her dark eyes at the king. "Yes?"

"Due to McClevin's absence, you are in charge of the army. Prepare the men for immediate mobilization."

"My king," Marcus said. "With all due respect, are you sure you can trust her? You and I both know how militant she—"

"That'll be enough, Marcus," Emory said. "Agatha's military brilliance has won us numerous battles in the past. I have no reason to suspect any of her actions will bring illness to my kingdom."

Agatha tilted her narrow head. "Thank you," she whispered.

"Orrin and Marcus, prepare the rest of my council of advisors. In thirty minutes, we'll discuss our military strategy. And also, prepare an emissary to deliver a message of our refusal to King Cornelius."

"But my king," Marcus said, "perhaps it is not wise to inform him of our decision. Now is the opportune time to catch him off-guard."

"I will not compromise my kingdom's integrity," Emory said harshly. "We will maintain our kingdom's honor. Now, you three are dismissed."

The three of them bowed as the king turned around

and retreated back further inside his bedroom to the window. He overlooked his kingdom under the raining sky. Children were running along the streets, relishing the fresh water falling from the sky, playing ball in the streets, swimming in the ocean off the sandy beach. He closed his eyes, savoring that vision of unyielding happiness over his kingdom, that happiness so many died to protect.

He heard footsteps behind him.

"What is it, Orrin?"

Orrin stepped beside him. "There is one other thing. Yesterday, a sailboat arrived at our port. The captain claimed to have sighted several longboats drifting ashore on a beach west of the Agapo lands. The boats were filled with vulpins. It is not typical for vulpins to invade human territory like that."

The king rotated his diamond ring around his finger. Vulpins on the move, another terror he loathed to deal with. The vulpins knew the Agapos would easily repel any attacks, unless the vulpins coordinated with their other packs to create an army to rise up against the humans. A two-fronted war.... Something was not right.

"This is more than a petty dispute over a locket or ship attack. Someone or something is playing us. Maybe it is Cornelius himself, or maybe the vulpins seeking revenge, or maybe something else. It's too coincidental for this all to be happening at once."

"Your Highness?" Orrin asked in a tone seeking clarity. But despair imprisoned Emory's heart, lifting it in his throat. Probably what scared him the most was not knowing. Not knowing why a group of pirates would steal such an important treasure from Eulia when Lassar was littered with riches just as valuable, why a ship posing as a Eulian vessel would attack a Valkadian ship, or why the vulpins were invading human territory. Sleep would evade him until he figured that out, that key link binding them all together. Without knowing that, he was but a mere pawn to whomever was orchestrating the scene.

Emory closed his eyes.

"Do you sense it?" Emory asked. "The unforgiving breeze, the bleak clouds, the unspoken cries of fear, the threatening sea. A great war is coming, Orrin. One that will shatter the foundation of both our kingdoms."

Then the sound of a trumpet blared from one of the towers of his castle. Emory opened his eyes and watched the men down below react immediately, leaving their wives and children and rushing to the castle to prepare for war. Women held their children close. Emory could feel their pain as his own. Their silent sobs echoed inside his head and burdened his chest.

He turned to Orrin and said, "It has begun."

LaVergne, TN USA
02 June 2010
184631LV00003B/5/P